THREE MEN IN A BOAT

✦ THE BARNES & NOBLE LIBRARY OF ESSENTIAL READING ✦

THREE MEN IN A BOAT
(To Say Nothing of the Dog!)

JEROME K. JEROME

ILLUSTRATIONS BY A. FREDERICS

INTRODUCTION BY ADAM ROVNER

BARNES & NOBLE
NEW YORK

THE BARNES & NOBLE
LIBRARY OF ESSENTIAL READING

Introduction and Suggested Reading
© 2004 by Barnes & Noble, Inc.

Originally published in 1889

This 2004 edition published by Barnes & Noble, Inc.

Barnes & Noble, Inc.
122 Fifth Avenue
New York, NY 10011

ISBN: 978-0-7607-5756-7

Printed and bound in Canada

11 13 15 17 19 20 18 16 14 12 10

◆ THE BARNES & NOBLE LIBRARY OF ESSENTIAL READING ◆

THREE MEN IN A BOAT
(To Say Nothing of the Dog!)

JEROME K. JEROME

ILLUSTRATIONS BY A. FREDERICS

INTRODUCTION BY ADAM ROVNER

BARNES & NOBLE
NEW YORK

THE BARNES & NOBLE
LIBRARY OF ESSENTIAL READING

Introduction and Suggested Reading
© 2004 by Barnes & Noble, Inc.

Originally published in 1889

This 2004 edition published by Barnes & Noble, Inc.

Barnes & Noble, Inc.
122 Fifth Avenue
New York, NY 10011

ISBN: 978-0-7607-5756-7

Printed and bound in Canada

11 13 15 17 19 20 18 16 14 12 10

CONTENTS

INTRODUCTION

CRITICS TRIED TO SINK JEROME K. JEROME'S COMIC CLASSIC, *THREE Men in a Boat (To Say Nothing of the Dog!)*, when it appeared in 1889. The late-Victorian-era reading public, however, made the lighthearted depiction of a Thames River journey into a bestseller and launched Jerome on a long and successful career as author, playwright, and editor. *Three Men in a Boat* remains one of the most widely read and beloved works of British fiction. The novel's global popularity has proven unsinkable. *Three Men in a Boat* has never fallen out of print, and its style has influenced generations of British writers, from P.G. Wodehouse to Douglas Adams. The book has been translated into many languages, including Japanese, Swedish, and Russian, and its colloquial tone has been used to teach English worldwide. Radio, film, and stage adaptations of Jerome's timeless story have appeared with regularity since the 1920s, including a 1975 teleplay by Tom Stoppard. Jerome, a self-proclaimed "idler," would surely be surprised by the busy post-publication lives led by his famous trio and their dog.

Despite his literary evocations of leisure, Jerome's own life was marked by labor and deprivation from an early age. He was born into a deeply religious family of Nonconformists (Protestants who did not join the Anglican church) in Walsall, Staffordshire, in 1859. His preacher father, also named Jerome, gave his youngest child the unusual middle name Klapka in honor of a Hungarian general, George Klapka, who once lived with the Jeromes and became a family friend. It is tempting to suspect that growing up in a household of Jerome Jeromes and Hungarian expatriates encouraged the author's nascent talent for bemused observations of everyday life. After the Reverend Jerome embarked on a series of failed business schemes, the newly impoverished family moved to cramped quarters in London's crime-ridden East End. At the age of ten, Jerome began his formal education at a school located a great distance from his home, which necessitated a lonely and tiring daily commute. He recalled in his autobiographical novel, *Paul Kelver* (1902), that it was on one such cross-town journey that he met Charles Dickens and expressed to the great author his own intention of becoming a writer. Whether the story is true or not, Dickens would likely have appreciated a chance meeting with an intelligent young boy of reduced circumstances set on pursuing the literary life. What is certain is that Jerome's childhood came to an abrupt and fittingly Dickensian end when he was orphaned at the age of fourteen following the untimely deaths of his father and mother. The hardworking youth left school to take up a series of unhappy clerkships. He eventually turned to eking out a living as an actor in a traveling stage company.

Three years treading the boards in provincial theaters exhausted Jerome, who returned to London destitute and demoralized. But the would-be actor soon turned his abortive stage career into the first of his many published triumphs. After several painful rejections, Jerome's humorous essays on the theater finally caught the attention of a small periodical, *The Play*. The initial interest in his personal, backstage reminiscences led to the publication and modest success of his first collection, *On the Stage—And Off* (1885). A year later a second volume of essays appeared, *The Idle Thoughts of an Idle Fellow*. Jerome's figure of an idler is akin to a Victorian "slacker," one who shirks work in order to better comment on the recline and sprawl of the British Empire. With typical insouciance, Jerome affectionately dedicated his book of comic philosophizing to a "very dear and well-beloved friend"—his pipe. The publication of his "idle thoughts" demonstrated that Jerome had been very busy refining the garrulous style of genial wit and wisdom that became his trademark.

The contradiction between Jerome's professed idleness and his actual industry was only one of the internal tensions that came to define his later work. He quickly became associated with the "new humour," originally a term of derision meted out by London's notoriously venomous critics. His longtime friend, writer and ideologue Israel Zangwill, explained that the "new humourists" created characters and stories that "stand for comedy as well as for tragedy." Given the deprivations Jerome faced as a child and the hardships he endured as a young adult, it is not surprising that his humor was occasionally infused with underlying sorrow. What is striking, however, is that the once homeless and desperate Jerome went on to epitomize the aspirations and increasing confidence of the *fin de siècle* British middle class.

Jerome never envisioned the enduring popularity of *Three Men in a Boat* when he began publishing installments in the periodical *Home Chimes* in 1888. In fact, Jerome had not planned to write a comic work at all. Originally intending to write a travelogue recording the history of the Thames River, Jerome found that the episodic nature of a lazy journey accommodated the sort of humorous digressions and witty reflections that had first made his name. As he revised his book, he shifted the emphasis from landscape to the narrative stylings of J., a thinly veiled stand-in for Jerome himself. An idler who exhibits a "general disinclination to work of any kind," J. also holds a jaundiced view of society, which leaves him "yearn[ing] for the good old days, when you could go about and tell people what you thought of them with a hatchet and a bow and arrows."

Two other members of the boating party, George and Harris, also have their real-life counterparts. The fictional George, who "goes to sleep at a bank from ten to four each day, except Saturdays, when they wake him up and put him outside at two," was based on Jerome's fellow theater-goer and old friend from his dosshouse days, George Wingrave, who had become a bank manager. Their companion, Harris, appears as an inveterate drinker who even in Paradise would likely find "a nice place round the corner here, where you can get some really first-class nectar." Jerome's depiction of a bibulous Harris is an inside joke. The real Harris, a theater enthusiast named Carl Hentschel, was not fond of alcohol. Montmorency, a small fox terrier who steals several scenes in the novel, appears to be "born with about four times as much original sin in [him] as other dogs are."

Montmorency gets into scraps with cats and stray curs, loses a battle with a kettle, howls at George's banjo recital, donates a water rat to the trio's Irish stew, and generally makes a nuisance of himself. As vivid a canine as ever appeared in literature, Montmorency was in fact wholly conjured to life by Jerome's imagination.

The cheeky preface to *Three Men in a Boat* states that the book purports to "form the record of events that really happened. All that has been done is to colour them; and, for this, no extra charge has been made." Indeed, the real-life triumvirate of Jerome, Wingrave, and Hentschel did set out on a trip up the Thames in the spring of 1889, though they had made several river excursions before. Boating was the latest recreational craze at the time, and Jerome sought to capitalize on the novelty with his travelogue. Jerome's resulting chronicle of the trip retains some elements of his intended "story of the Thames," notably his rambling comments on riverside towns and their attractions. But the soul of the book remains the vernacular style of the narrator. Many of Jerome's amusing anecdotes and recollections of the young friends' foibles are undoubtedly based on real events and are embellished with a skill reminiscent of the great American yarn-spinners Mark Twain and Josh Billings.

Hallmarks of Jerome's digressive style include the use of understatement, the matter-of-fact invocation of absurd logic, the piling up of exaggerations, and the attribution of emotion to the inanimate. George's profuse cursing is euphemistically down-played as "express[ing] wishes and desires concerning Harris' fate in this world and the next that would have made a thoughtful man shudder." When lost at night, the friends consider "assaulting a policeman" in order to have "a night's lodging in the stationhouse," but they reject the proposition, fearful that he would hit them back without locking them up! A dispute over whether to pack cheese for the trip devolves into a ridiculous tale of cheeses so ripe that they could not even be buried without the coroner raising a "fearful fuss . . . [saying] it was a plot to deprive him of his living by waking up the corpses." Several hilarious episodes detail the threesome's tussles with malicious objects such as tents, tow lines, tea kettles, and a particularly contrary tin of pineapple: "We beat it out flat; we beat it back square;

we battered it into every form known to geometry—but we could not make a hole in it. [. . .] There was one great dent across the top that had the appearance of a mocking grin, and it drove us furious."

The many mishaps unfold in brief chapters headed by diary-like encapsulations. This technique, combined with the first-person narration and its highly colloquial language, bolsters the sense that Jerome's tale is faithful to the human comedy of real men seeking to escape the pressures of an industrialized society. In *Three Men in a Boat*, Jerome crafted an idyll of idleness whose humor derived from the misadventures of the late-Victorian Everyman. Literary scholar Donald Gray has commented that Victorian laughter functioned "to furnish a holiday from taking things and ideas seriously." Jerome dramatizes the unimportance of being earnest when his narrator flippantly remarks, "I like work; it fascinates me. I can sit and look at it for hours." His rambling accounts of his characters' circuitous progress, their plunges into the river, and their hopelessly misguided navigations of Hampton Court's famed hedge maze provided Jerome's contemporaries with a much-needed vacation from solemnity.

At a time when critics and educators still demanded that literature present some elevating moral, Jerome merely paid lip-service to "the lesson that the story teaches." He drifted instead from commentary on "the natural cussedness of things in general" upon arising too early on vacation, to the "natural obstinacy of all things in this world," when a boat fails to obey its captains. Readers were not accustomed to descriptions of their own frustrations in a vernacular that comically deflated the significance of their grievances. The novelty of Jerome's prose and the fresh depiction of middle-class mores helped make *Three Men in a Boat* a fabulous success and the author a wealthy man. As usual, the critics were less kind, lambasting Jerome for lowbrow sentimentality, vulgarity, his use of slang, and the "poverty of the life [the book] only too faithfully reflects." For readers who were flattered to see their own human failings described in print, such "faithful reflection" was exactly the point. The reviews stung Jerome, who never completely abandoned the pieties of his youth. He was baffled by critics responding to his book's popularity as if "the British Empire was in danger."

Writing nearly seventy years after *Three Men in a Boat* was published, critic V. S. Pritchett praised Jerome for seeing "that one of the funniest things a human being has is his conscience." Indeed, Jerome's characters' hypocrisies, their pettiness, and their ironic observations throw into comic relief fundamental truths of human nature. J. bemoans uncharitable holiday-makers: "I don't know why it should be, but everybody is always so exceptionally irritable on the river." He then undercuts his musings with the revelation that: "When another boat gets in my way, I feel I want to take an oar and kill all the people in it." Here, a lack of self-awareness reveals an essential selfishness common to everyone. Perhaps such revelations are responsible for the long-standing appeal of Jerome's work across the globe.

Although Jerome produced literary works well into the twentieth century, he was never able to escape the notoriety of *Three Men in a Boat*. A sequel set during a cycling trip in Germany, *Three Men on the Bummel* (1900), reunited the characters and achieved considerable success. Jerome lectured and traveled widely, and even enlisted in the French army during World War I at the age of fifty-seven as an ambulance driver. He penned an entertaining account of his early struggles and later triumphs in *My Life and Times* (1926). For most of his professional life, he lived with his wife, Georgina, and daughter in London and socialized with a cadre of famous, forward-thinking intellectuals, including Arthur Conan Doyle and H. G. Wells. Jerome continued to write popular books, well-received plays, such as *The Passing of the Third Floor Back* (1907), and edit publications, most notably *The Idler*, until his death from a stroke in 1927. His own verdict on his future legacy has proven accurate: "I may come to be quite a swell dead author." While American literature rhapsodizes over epic journeys on the road or down the mighty Mississippi, the British canon celebrates Jerome's more modest, but equally captivating narrative of a voyage undertaken by three men in a boat—To Say Nothing of the Dog—one spring over a hundred years ago.

Adam Rovner holds a Ph.D. in Comparative Literature from Indiana University. He has lectured and published articles on comic literature and humor theory for both popular and academic audiences.

Publisher's Advertisement

It may not, perhaps, be out of place in this new edition of *Three Men in a Boat* to place before its readers the enormous hold it has upon the reading public in Great Britain and her colonies. Originally published in August, 1889, it has been year after year reprinted, until there has been produced the large number of 202,000 copies. Adding to this the 5,000 of the present edition, a total is reached of 207,000 copies. It is remarkable that during this period there has been only one edition, and this published at the price of 3^s. 6^d.; the publisher ventures to believe this is unprecedented. It is not as though, as is too often the case with an ordinary novel, an enormous sale took place during a few months and then ceased, inasmuch as in the present case there has been, and still is, a constant and steady sale year after year. The present opportunity has been taken to reset in new type the letterpress, and to re-engrave (from the originals) the whole of the drawings. The publisher trusts that *Three Men in a Boat*, appealing as it does so much to human nature both in its pathos and its humour will still continue its pleasant voyage, and find new friends in every home in the land which gave it birth.

Bristol, March, 1909

Author's Advertisement

My Publisher suggests my adding a few lines to his. To refuse to do so, under the circumstances, might appear surly. The world has been very kind to this book. Mr. Arrowsmith speaks only of its sales in Great Britain. In Chicago, I was assured by an enterprising pirate now retired, that the sales throughout the United States had exceeded a million; and although, in consequence of its having been published before the Copyright Convention, this has brought me no material advantage, the fame and popularity it has won for me among the American public is an asset not to be despised. It has been translated into, I think, every European language except Arabian, also into some of those of Asia. It has brought me many thousands of letters from young folk, from old folk; from well folk, from sick folk; from merry folk, from sad folk. They have come to me from all parts of the world, from men and women of all countries. Had these letters been the only result I should feel glad and proud that I had written the book. I retain a few blackened pages of one copy sent me by a young colonial officer from South Africa. They were taken from the knapsack of a dead comrade found on Spion Kop. So much for testimonials. It remains only to explain the merits justifying such an extraordinary success. I am quite unable to do so. I have written books that have appeared to me more clever, books that have appeared to me more humorous. But it is as the author of *Three Men in a Boat (To Say Nothing of the Dog)* that the public persists in remembering me. Certain writers used to suggest that it was the vulgarity of the book, its entire absence of humour, that accounted for its success with the people; but one feels by this time that such suggestion does not solve the riddle. Bad art may succeed for a time and with a limited public; it does not go on extending its circle throughout twenty years. I have come to the conclusion that, be the explanation what it may, I can take credit to myself for having written this book. That is, if I did write it. For really I hardly remember doing so. I remember only feeling very young and absurdly pleased with myself for reasons that concern only myself. It was summer time, and London is so beautiful in summer. It lay beneath my window a fairy city veiled in golden mist, for I worked in a room high up above the chimney-pots; and at night the lights shone far beneath me, so that I looked down as into an Aladdin's cave of jewels. It was during those summer months I wrote this book; it seemed the only thing to do.

PREFACE

THE CHIEF BEAUTY OF THIS BOOK LIES NOT SO MUCH IN ITS LITERARY STYLE, or in the extent and usefulness of the information it conveys, as in its simple truthfulness. Its pages form the record of events that really happened. All that has been done is to colour them; and, for this, no extra charge has been made. George and Harris and Montmorency are not poetic ideals, but things of flesh and blood—especially George, who weighs about twelve stone. Other works may excel this in depth of thought and knowledge of human nature: other books may rival it in originality and size; but, for hopeless and incurable veracity, nothing yet discovered can surpass it. This, more than all its other charms, will, it is felt, make the volume precious in the eye of the earnest reader; and will lend additional weight to the lesson that the story teaches.

LONDON, August, 1889

THREE MEN IN A BOAT

CHAPTER I

Three invalids • Sufferings of George and Harris • A victim to one
hundred and seven fatal maladies • Useful prescriptions • Cure
for liver complaint in children • We agree that we are overworked,
and need rest • A week on the rolling deep? • George suggests the
River • Montmorency lodges an objection • Original motion
carried by majority of three to one

THERE WERE FOUR OF US—GEORGE, AND WILLIAM SAMUEL
Harris, and myself, and Montmorency. We were sitting in my room,
smoking, and talking about how bad we were—bad from a medical
point of view I mean, of course.

We were all feeling seedy, and we were getting quite nervous about
it. Harris said he felt such extraordinary fits of giddiness come over him
at times, that he hardly knew what he was doing; and then George said
that *he* had fits of giddiness too, and hardly knew what *he* was doing.
With me, it was my liver that was out of order. I knew it was my liver
that was out of order, because I had just been reading a patent liver-pill
circular, in which were detailed the various symptoms by which a man
could tell when his liver was out of order. I had them all.

It is a most extraordinary thing, but I never read a patent medicine
advertisement without impelled to the conclusion that I am suffering
from the particular disease therein dealt with in its most virulent
form. The diagnosis seems in every case to correspond exactly with
all the sensations that I have ever felt.

I remember going to the British Museum one day to read up the treatment for some slight ailment of which I had a touch—hay fever, I fancy it was. I got down the book, and read all I came to read; and then, in an unthinking moment, I idly turned the leaves, and began to indolently study diseases, generally. I forget which was the first distemper I plunged into—some fearful, devastating scourge, I know—and, before I had glanced half down the list of "premonitory symptoms," it was borne in upon me that I had fairly got it.

I sat for a while frozen with horror; and then, in the listlessness of despair, I again turned over the pages. I came to typhoid fever—read the symptoms—discovered that I had typhoid fever, must have had it for months without knowing it—wondered what else I had got; turned up St. Vitus' Dance—found, as I expected, that I had that too—began to get interested in my case, and determined to sift it to the bottom, and so started alphabetically—read up ague, and learnt that I was sickening for it, and that the acute stage would commence in about another fortnight. Bright's disease, I was relieved to find, I had only in a modified form, and, so far as that was concerned, I might live for years. Cholera I had, with severe complications; and diphtheria I seemed to have been born with. I plodded conscientiously through the twenty-six letters, and the only malady I could conclude I had not got was housemaid's knee.

I felt rather hurt about this at first; it seemed somehow to be a sort of slight. Why hadn't I got housemaid's knee? Why this invidious reservation? After a while, however, less grasping feelings prevailed. I reflected that I had every other known malady in the pharmacology, and I grew less selfish, and determined to do without housemaid's knee. Gout, in its most malignant stage, it would appear, had seized me without my being aware of it; and zymosis I had evidently been suffering with from boyhood. There were no more diseases after zymosis, so I concluded there was nothing else the matter with me.

I sat and pondered. I thought what an interesting case I must be from a medical point of view, what an acquisition I should be to a class! Students would have no need to "walk the hospitals," if they had me. I was a hospital in myself. All they need do would be to walk round me, and, after that, take their diploma.

Then I wondered how long I had to live. I tried to examine myself. I felt my pulse. I could not at first feel any pulse at all. Then, all of a sudden, it seemed to start off. I pulled out my watch and timed it. I made it a hundred and forty-seven to the minute. I tried to feel my heart. I could not feel my heart. It had stopped beating. I have since been induced to come to the opinion that it must have been there all the time, and must have been beating, but I cannot account for it. I patted myself all over my front, from what I call my waist up to my head, and I went a bit round each side, and a little way up the back. But I could not feel or hear anything. I tried to look at my tongue. I stuck it out as far as ever it would go, and I shut one eye, and tried to examine it with the other. I could only see the tip, and the only thing that I could gain from that was to feel more certain than before that I had scarlet fever.

I had walked into that reading-room a happy, healthy man. I crawled out a decrepit wreck.

I went to my medical man. He is an old chum of mine, and feels my pulse, and looks at my tongue, and talks about the weather, all for nothing, when I fancy I'm ill; so I thought I would do him a good turn by going to him now. "What a doctor wants," I said, "is practice. He shall have me. He will get more practice out of me than out of seventeen hundred of your ordinary, commonplace patients, with only one or two diseases each." So I went straight up and saw him, and he said:

"Well, what's the matter with you?"

I said:

"I will not take up your time, dear boy, with telling you what is the matter with me. Life is brief, and you might pass away before I had finished. But I will tell you what is *not* the matter with me. I have not got housemaid's knee. Why I have not got housemaid's knee, I cannot tell you; but the fact remains that I have not got it. Everything else, however, I *have* got."

And I told him how I came to discover it all.

Then he opened me and looked down me, and clutched hold of my wrist, and then he hit me over the chest when I wasn't expecting it—a cowardly thing to do, I call it—and immediately afterwards butted me with the side of his head. After that, he sat down and wrote out a prescription, and folded it up and gave it me, and I put it in my pocket and went out.

I did not open it. I took it to the nearest chemist's, and handed it in. The man read it, and then handed it back.

He said he didn't keep it.

I said:

"You are a chemist?"

He said:

"I am a chemist. If I was a cooperative stores and family hotel combined, I might be able to oblige you. Being only a chemist hampers me."

I read the prescription. It ran:

1 lb. beefsteak, with
1 pt. bitter beer every 6 hours.
1 ten-mile walk every morning.
1 bed at 11 sharp every night.
And don't stuff up your head with things you don't understand.

I followed the directions, with the happy result—speaking for myself—that my life was preserved, and is still going on.

In the present instance, going back to the liver-pill circular, I had the symptoms, beyond all mistake, the chief among them being "a general disinclination to work of any kind."

What I suffer in that way no tongue can tell. From my earliest infancy I have been a martyr to it. As a boy, the disease hardly ever left me for a day. They did not know, then, that it was my liver. Medical science was in a far less advanced state than now, and they used to put it down to laziness.

"Why, you skulking little devil, you," they would say, "get up and do something for your living, can't you?" not knowing, of course, that I was ill.

And they didn't give me pills; they gave me clumps on the side of the head. And, strange as it may appear, those clumps on the head often cured me—for the time being. I have known one clump on the head have more effect upon my liver, and make me feel more anxious to go straight away then and there, and do what was wanted to be done, without further loss of time, than a whole box of pills does now.

You know, it often is so—those simple, old-fashioned remedies are sometimes more efficacious than all the dispensary stuff.

We sat there for half-an-hour, describing to each other our maladies. I explained to George and William Harris how I felt when I got up in the morning, and William Harris told us how he felt when he went to bed; and George stood on the hearth-rug, and gave us a clever and powerful piece of acting, illustrative of how he felt in the night.

George *fancies* he is ill; but there's never anything really the matter with him, you know.

At this point, Mrs. Poppets knocked at the door to know if we were ready for supper. We smiled sadly at one another, and said we supposed we had better try to swallow a bit. Harris said a little something in one's stomach often kept the disease in check; and Mrs. Poppets brought the tray in, and we drew up to the table, and toyed with a little steak and onions, and some rhubarb tart.

I must have been very weak at the time; because I know, after the first half-hour or so, I seemed to take no interest whatever in my food—an unusual thing for me—and I didn't want any cheese.

This duty done, we refilled our glasses, lit our pipes, and resumed the discussion upon our state of health. What it was that was actually the matter with us, we none of us could be sure of; but the unanimous opinion was that it—whatever it was—had been brought on by overwork.

"What we want is rest," said Harris.

"Rest and a complete change," said George. "The overstrain upon our brains has produced a general depression throughout the system. Change of scene, and absence of the necessity for thought, will restore the mental equilibrium."

George has a cousin, who is usually described in the charge-sheet as a medical student, so that he naturally has a somewhat family-physicianary way of putting things.

I agreed with George, and suggested that we should seek out some retired and old-world spot, far from the madding crowd, and dream away a sunny week among its drowsy lanes—some half-forgotten nook, hidden away by the fairies, out of reach of the noisy world—some quaint-perched eyrie on the cliffs of Time, from whence the surging waves of the nineteenth century would sound far-off and faint.

Harris said he thought it would be humpy. He said he knew the sort of place I meant; where everybody went to bed at eight o'clock, and you couldn't get a *Referee* for love or money, and had to walk ten miles to get your baccy.

"No," said Harris, "if you want rest and change, you can't beat a sea trip."

I objected to the sea trip strongly. A sea trip does you good when you are going to have a couple of months of it, but, for a week, it is wicked.

You start on Monday with the idea implanted in your bosom that you are going to enjoy yourself. You wave an airy adieu to the boys on shore, light your biggest pipe, and swagger about the deck as it you were Captain Cook, Sir Francis Drake, and Christopher Columbus all rolled into one. On Tuesday, you wish you hadn't come. On Wednesday, Thursday and Friday, you wish you were dead. On Saturday you are able to swallow a little beef tea, and to sit up on deck, and answer with a wan, sweet smile when kind-hearted people ask you how you feel now. On Sunday, you begin to walk about again, and take solid food. And on Monday morning, as, with your bag and umbrella in your hand, you stand by the gunwale, waiting to step ashore, you begin to thoroughly like it.

I remember my brother-in-law going for a short sea trip once, for the benefit of his health. He took a return berth from London to

Liverpool; and when he got to Liverpool, the only thing he was anxious about was to sell that return ticket.

It was offered round the town at a tremendous reduction, so I am told; and was eventually sold for eighteenpence to a bilious-looking youth who had just been advised by his medical men to go to the seaside, and take exercise.

"Seaside!" said my brother-in-law, pressing the ticket affectionately into his hand; "why, you'll have enough to last you a lifetime; and as for exercise! Why, you'll get more exercise, sitting down on that ship, than you would turning somersaults on dry land."

He himself—my brother-in-law—came back by train. He said the North-Western Railway was healthy enough for him.

Another fellow I knew went for a week's voyage round the coast, and, before they started the steward came to him to ask whether he would pay for each meal as he had it, or arrange beforehand for the whole series.

The steward recommended the latter course, as it would come so much cheaper. He said they would do him for the whole week at two-pounds-five. He said for breakfast there would be fish, followed by a grill. Lunch was at one, and consisted of four courses. Dinner at six—soup, fish, entrée, joint, poultry, salad, sweets, cheese, and dessert. And a light meat supper at ten.

My friend thought he would close on the two-pound-five job (he is a hearty eater), and did so.

Lunch came just as they were off Sheerness. He didn't feel so hungry as he thought he should, and so contented himself with a bit of boiled beef, and some strawberries and cream. He pondered a good deal during the afternoon, and at one time it seemed to him that he had been eating nothing but boiled beef for weeks, and at other times it seemed that he must have been living on strawberries and cream for years.

Neither the beef nor the strawberries and cream seemed happy, either—seemed discontented like.

At six, they came and told him dinner was ready. The announcement aroused no enthusiasm within him, but he felt that there was some of that two-pound-five to be worked off, and he held on to ropes and things and went down. A pleasant odour of onions and hot ham, mingled with fried fish and greens, greeted him at the bottom of the ladder; and then the steward came up with an oily smile, and said:

"What can I get you, sir?"

"Get me out of this," was the feeble reply.

And they ran him up quick, and propped him up, over to leeward, and left him.

For the next four days he lived a simple and blameless life on thin captain's biscuits (I mean that the biscuits were thin, not the captain) and soda-water; but, towards Saturday, he got uppish, and went in for weak tea and dry toast, and on Monday he was gorging himself on chicken broth. He left the ship on Tuesday, and as it steamed away from the landing-stage he gazed after it regretfully.

"There she goes," he said, "there she goes, with two pounds' worth of food on board that belongs to me, and that I haven't had."

He said that if they had given him another day he thought he could have put it straight.

So I set my face against the sea trip. Not, as I explained, upon my own account. I was never queer. But I was afraid for George. George said he should be all right, and would rather like it, but he would advise Harris and me not to think of it, as he felt sure we should both be ill. Harris said that, to himself, it was always a mystery how people managed to get sick at sea—said he thought people must do it on purpose, from affectation—said he had often wished to be, but had never been able.

Then he told us anecdotes of how he had gone across the Channel when it was so rough that the passengers had to be tied into their berths, and he and the captain were the only two living souls on board who were not ill. Sometimes it was he and the second mate who were not ill; but it was generally he and one other man. If not he and another man, then it was he by himself.

It is a curious fact, but nobody ever is sea-sick—on land. At sea, you come across plenty of people very bad indeed, whole boatloads of them; but I never met a man yet, on land, who had ever known at all what it was to be sea-sick. Where the thousands upon thousands of bad sailors that swarm in every ship hide themselves when they are on land is a mystery.

If most men were like a fellow I saw on the Yarmouth boat one day, I could account for the seeming enigma easily enough. It was just off Southend Pier, I recollect, and he was leaning out through one of the portholes in a very dangerous position. I went up to him to try and save him.

"Hi! Come further in," I said, shaking him by the shoulder. "You'll be overboard."

"Oh my'! I wish I was," was the only answer I could get; and there I had to leave him.

Three weeks afterwards, I met him in the coffee-room of a Bath hotel, talking about his voyages, and explaining, with enthusiasm, how he loved the sea.

"Good sailor!" he replied in answer to a mild young man's envious query; "well, I did feel a little queer *once*, I confess. It was off Cape Horn. The vessel was wrecked the next morning."

I said:

"Weren't you a little shaky by Southend Pier one day, and wanted to be thrown overboard?"

"Southend Pier!" he replied, with a puzzled expression.

"Yes; going down to Yarmouth, last Friday three weeks."

"Oh, ah—yes," he answered, brightening up; "I remember now. I did have a headache that afternoon. It was the pickles, you know. They were the most disgraceful pickles I ever tasted in a respectable boat. Did *you* have any?"

For myself, I have discovered an excellent preventive against sea-sickness, in balancing myself. You stand in the centre of the deck, and, as the ship heaves and pitches, you move your body about, so as to keep it always straight. When the front of the ship rises, you lean forward, till the deck almost touches your nose; and when its back end gets up, you lean backwards. This is all very well for an hour or two; but you can't balance yourself for a week.

George said:

"Let's go up the river."

He said we should have fresh air, exercise and quiet; the constant change of scene would occupy our minds (including what there was of Harris'); and the hard work would give us a good appetite, and make us sleep well.

Harris said he didn't think George ought to do anything that would have a tendency to make him sleepier than he always was, as it might be dangerous. He said he didn't very well understand how George was going to sleep anymore than he did now, seeing that there were only twenty-four hours in each day, summer and winter alike; but thought that if he *did* sleep anymore, he might just as well be dead and so save his board and lodging.

Harris said, however, that the river would suit him to a "T." I don't know what a "T" is (except a six-penny one, which includes bread-and-butter and cake *ad lib.*, and is cheap at the price, if you haven't had any dinner). It seems to suit everybody, however, which is greatly to its credit.

It suited me to a "T" too, and Harris and I both said it was a good idea of George's; and we said it in a tone that seemed to somehow imply that we were surprised that George should have come out so sensible.

The only one who was not struck with the suggestion was Montmorency. He never did care for the river, did Montmorency.

"It's all very well for you fellows," he says; "you like it, but *I* don't. There's nothing for me to do. Scenery is not in my line, and I don't smoke. If I see a rat, you won't stop; and if I go to sleep, you get fooling about with the boat, and slop me overboard. If you ask me, I call the whole thing bally foolishness."

We were three to one, however, and the motion was carried.

CHAPTER II

Plans discussed • Pleasures of "camping out," on fine nights • Ditto, wet nights • Compromise decided on • Montmorency, first impressions of • Fears lest he is too good for this world, fears subsequently dismissed as groundless • Meeting adjourns

WE PULLED OUT THE MAPS, AND DISCUSSED PLANS.

We arranged to start on the following Saturday from Kingston. Harris and I would go down in the morning, and take the boat up to Chertsey, and George, who would not be able to get away from the City till the afternoon (George goes to sleep at a bank from ten to four each day, except Saturdays, when they wake him up and put him outside at two), would meet us there.

Should we "camp out" or sleep at inns?

George and I were for camping out. We said it would be so wild and free, so patriarchal like.

Slowly the golden memory of the dead sun fades from the hearts of the cold, sad clouds. Silent, like sorrowing children, the birds have ceased their song, and only the moorhen's plaintive cry and the harsh croak of the corncrake stirs the awed hush around the couch of waters, where the dying day breathes out her last.

From the dim woods on either bank, Night's ghostly army, the grey shadows, creep out with noiseless tread to chase away the lingering rearguard of the light, and pass, with noiseless, unseen feet, above the waving river-grass, and through the sighing rushes; and Night, upon her sombre throne, folds her black wings above the darkening world, and, from her phantom palace, lit by the pale stars, reigns in stillness.

Then we run our little boat into some quiet nook, and the tent is pitched, and the frugal supper cooked and eaten. Then the big pipes are filled and lighted, and the pleasant chat goes round in musical undertone; while, in the pauses of our talk, the river, playing round the boat, prattles strange old tales and secrets, sings low the old child's song that it has sung so many thousand years—will sing so many thousand years to come, before its voice grows harsh and old—a song that we, who have learnt to love its changing face, who have so often nestled on its yielding bosom, think, somehow, we understand, though we could not tell you in mere words the story that we listen to.

And we sit there, by its margin, while the moon, who loves it too, stoops down to kiss it with a sister's kiss, and throws her silver arms around it clingingly; and we watch it as it flows, ever singing, ever whispering, out to meet its king, the sea—till our voices die away in silence, and the pipes go out—till we, commonplace, everyday young men enough, feel strangely full of thoughts, half sad, half sweet, and do not care or want to speak—till we laugh, and, rising, knock the ashes from our burnt-out pipes, and say "Goodnight," and, lulled by the lapping water, and the rustling trees, we fall asleep beneath the great, still stars, and dream that the world is young again—young and sweet as she used to be ere the centuries of fret and care had furrowed her fair face, ere her children's sins and follies had made old her loving heart—sweet as she was in those bygone days when, a new-made mother, she nursed us, her children, upon her own deep breast—ere the wiles of painted civilisation had lured us away from her fond arms, and the poisoned sneers of artificiality had made us ashamed of the simple life we led with her, and the simple, stately home where mankind was born so many thousands of years ago.

Harris said:

"How about when it rained?"

You can never rouse Harris. There is no poetry about Harris—no wild yearning for the unattainable. Harris never "weeps, he knows not why." If Harris' eyes fill with tears, you can bet it is because Harris has been eating raw onions, or has put too much Worcester over his chop.

If you were to stand at night by the seashore with Harris, and say:

"Hark! Do you not hear? Is it but the mermaids singing deep below the waving waters; or sad spirits, chanting dirges for white corpses, held by seaweed?" Harris would take you by the arm, and say:

"I know what it is, old man; you've got a chill. Now, you come along with me. I know a place round the corner here, where you can get a

drop of the finest Scotch whisky you ever tasted—put you right in less than no time."

Harris always does know a place round the corner where you can get something brilliant in the drinking line. I believe that if you met Harris up in Paradise (supposing such a thing likely), he would immediately greet you with:

"So glad you've come, old fellow; I've found a nice place round the corner here, where you can get some really first-class nectar."

In the present instance, however, as regarded the camping out, his practical view of the matter came as a very timely hint. Camping out in rainy weather is not pleasant.

It is evening. You are wet through, and there is a good two inches of water in the boat, and all the things are damp. You find a place on the banks that is not quite so puddly as other places you have seen, and you land and lug out the tent, and two of you proceed to fix it.

It is soaked and heavy, and it flops about, and tumbles down on you, and clings round your head and makes you mad. The rain is pouring steadily down all the time. It is difficult enough to fix a tent in dry weather: in wet, the task becomes herculean. Instead of helping you, it seems to you that the other man is simply playing the fool. Just as you get your side beautifully fixed, he gives it a hoist from his end, and spoils it all.

"Here! What are you up to?" you call out.

"What are *you* up to?" he retorts; "leggo, can't you?"

"Don't pull it; you've got it all wrong, you stupid ass!" you shout.

"No, I haven't," he yells back; "let go your side!"

"I tell you you've got it all wrong!" you roar, wishing that you could get at him; and you give your ropes a lug that pulls all his pegs out.

"Ah, the bally idiot!" you hear him mutter to himself; and then comes a savage haul, and away goes your side. You lay down the mallet and start to go round and tell him what you think about the whole business, and, at the same time, he starts round in the same direction to come and explain his views to you. And you follow each other round and round, swearing at one another, until the tent tumbles down in a heap, and leaves you looking at each other across its ruins, then you both indignantly exclaim, in the same breath:

"There you are! What did I tell you?"

Meanwhile the third man, who has been baling out the boat, and who has spilled the water down his sleeve, and has been cursing away to himself steadily for the last ten minutes, wants to know what the thundering blazes you're playing at, and why the blarmed tent isn't up yet.

At last, somehow or other, it does get up, and you land the things. It is hopeless attempting to make a wood fire, so you light the methylated spirit stove, and crowd round that.

Rainwater is the chief article of diet at supper. The bread is two-thirds rainwater, the beefsteak-pie is exceedingly rich in it, and the jam, and the butter, and the salt, and the coffee have all combined with it to make soup.

After supper, you find your tobacco is damp, and you cannot smoke. Luckily you have a bottle of the stuff that cheers and inebriates, if taken in proper quantity, and this restores to you sufficient interest in life to induce you to go to bed.

There you dream that an elephant has suddenly sat down on your chest, and that the volcano has exploded and thrown you down to the bottom of the sea—the elephant still sleeping peacefully on your bosom. You wake up and grasp the idea that something terrible really has happened. Your first impression is that the end of the world has come; and then you think that this cannot be, and that it is thieves and murderers, or else fire, and this opinion you express in the usual method. No help comes, however, and all you know is that thousands of people are kicking you, and you are being smothered.

Somebody else seems in trouble, too. You can hear his faint cries coming from underneath your bed. Determining, at all events, to sell your life dearly, you struggle frantically, hitting out right and left with arms and legs, and yelling lustily the while, and at last something gives way, and you find your head in the fresh air. Two feet off, you dimly observe a half-dressed ruffian, waiting to kill you, and you are preparing for a life-and-death struggle with him, when it begins to dawn upon you that it's Jim.

"Oh, it's you, is it?" he says, recognizing you at the same moment.

"Yes," you answer, rubbing your eyes; "what's happened?"

"Bally tent's blown down, I think," he says. "Where's Bill?"

Then you both raise up your voices and shout for "Bill!" and the ground beneath you heaves and rocks, and the muffled voice that you heard before replies from out the ruin:

"Get off my head, can't you?"

And Bill struggles out, a muddy, trampled wreck, and in an unnecessarily aggressive mood—he being under the evident belief that the whole thing has been done on purpose.

In the morning you are all three speechless, owing to having caught severe colds in the night; you also feel very quarrelsome, and you swear at each other in hoarse whispers during the whole of breakfast time.

We therefore decided that we would sleep out on fine nights; and hotel it, and inn it, and pub. it, like respectable folks, when it was wet, or when we felt inclined for a change.

Montmorency hailed this compromise with much approval. He does not revel in romantic solitude. Give him something noisy; and if a trifle low, so much the jollier. To look at Montmorency you would imagine that he was an angel sent upon the earth, for some reason withheld from mankind, in the shape of a small fox-terrier. There is a sort of Oh-what-a-wicked-world-this-is-and-how-I-wish-I-could-do-something-to-make-it-better-and-nobler expression about Montmorency that has been known to bring the tears into the eyes of pious old ladies and gentlemen.

When first he came to live at my expense, I never thought I should be able to get him to stop long. I used to sit down and look at him, as he sat on the rug and looked up at me, and think: "Oh, that dog will never live. He will be snatched up to the bright skies in a chariot, that is what will happen to him."

But, when I had paid for about a dozen chickens that he had killed; and had dragged him, growling and kicking, by the scruff of his neck, out of a hundred and fourteen street fights; and had had a dead cat brought round for my inspection by an irate female, who called me a murderer; and had been summoned by the man next door but one for having a ferocious dog at large, that had kept him pinned up in his own tool-shed, afraid to venture his nose outside the door for over two hours on a cold night; and had learned that the gardener, unknown to myself, had won thirty shillings by backing him to kill rats against time, then I began to think that maybe they'd let him remain on earth for a bit longer, after all.

To hang about a stable, and collect a gang of the most disreputable dogs to be found in the town, and lead them out to march round the slums to fight other disreputable dogs, is Montmorency's idea of "life"; and so, as I before observed, he gave to the suggestion of inns, and pubs., and hotels his most emphatic approbation.

Having thus settled the sleeping arrangements to the satisfaction of all four of us, the only thing left to discuss was what we should take with us; and this we had begun to argue, when Harris said he'd had enough oratory for one night, and proposed that we should go out and have a smile, saying that he had found a place, round by the square where you could really get a drop of Irish worth drinking.

 George said he felt thirsty (I never knew George when he didn't); and, as I had a presentiment that a little whisky, warm, with a slice of lemon, would do my complaint good, the debate was, by common assent, adjourned to the following night; and the assembly put on its hats and went out.

CHAPTER III

Arrangements settled • Harris' method of doing work • How the elderly, family-man puts up a picture • George makes a sensible remark • Delights of early morning bathing • Provisions for getting upset

So, ON THE FOLLOWING EVENING, WE AGAIN ASSEMBLED, TO DISCUSS and arrange our plans. Harris said:

"Now, the first thing to settle is what to take with us. Now, you get a bit of paper and write down, J., and you get the grocery catalogue, George, and somebody give me a bit of pencil, and then I'll make out a list."

That's Harris all over—so ready to take the burden of everything himself, and put it on the backs of other people.

He always reminds me of my poor Uncle Podger. You never saw such a commotion up and down a house, in all your life, as when my Uncle Podger undertook to do a job. A picture would have come home from the frame-maker's, and be standing in the dining room, waiting to be put up; and Aunt Podger would ask what was to be done with it, and Uncle Podger would say:

"Oh, you leave that to *me*. Don't you, any of you, worry yourselves about that. *I'll* do all that."

And then he would take off his coat, and begin. He would send the girl out for sixpence'orth of nails, and then one of the boys after her to tell her what size to get; and, from that, he would gradually work down, and start the whole house.

"Now you go and get me my hammer, Will," he would shout; "and you bring me the rule, Tom; and I shall want the stepladder, and I had better have a kitchen-chair, too; and, Jim! You run round to Mr. Goggles, and tell him, 'Pa's kind regards, and hopes his leg's better; and will he lend him his spirit-level?' And don't you go, Maria, because I shall want somebody to hold me the light; and when the girl comes back, she must go out again for a bit of picture-cord; and Tom! Where's Tom? Tom, you come here; I shall want you to hand me up the picture."

And then he would lift up the picture, and drop it, and it would come out of the frame, and he would try to save the glass, and cut himself; and then he would spring round the room, looking for his handkerchief. He could not find his handkerchief, because it was in the pocket of the coat he had taken off, and he did not know where he had put the coat, and all the house had to leave off looking for his tools, and start looking for his coat; while he would dance round and hinder them.

 "Doesn't anybody in the whole house know where my coat is? I never came across such a set in all my life—upon my word I didn't. Six of you! And you can't find a coat that I put down not five minutes ago! Well, of all the—"

Then he'd get up, and find that he had been sitting on it, and would call out:

"Oh, you can give it up! I've found it myself now. Might just as well ask the cat to find anything as expect you people to find it."

And, when half an hour had been spent in tying up his finger, and a new glass had been got, and the tools, and the ladder, and the chair, and the candle had been brought, he would have another go, the whole family, including the girl and the charwoman, standing round in a semicircle, ready to help. Two people would have to hold the chair, and a third would help him up on it, and hold him there, and a fourth would hand him a nail, and a fifth would pass him up the hammer, and he would take hold of the nail, and drop it.

"There!" he would say, in an injured tone, "now the nail's gone."

And we would all have to go down on our knees and grovel for it, while he would stand on the chair, and grunt, and want to know if he was to be kept there all the evening.

The nail would be found at last, but by that time he would have lost the hammer.

"Where's the hammer? What did I do with the hammer? Great heavens! Seven of you, gaping round there, and you don't know what I did with the hammer!"

We would find the hammer for him, and then he would have lost sight of the mark he had made on the wall, where the nail was to go in, and each of us had to get up on the chair, beside him, and see if we could find it; and we would each discover it in a different place, and he would call us all fools, one after another, and tell us to get down. And he would take the rule, and re-measure, and find that he wanted half thirty-one and three-eighths inches from the corner, and would try to do it in his head, and go mad.

And we would all try to do it in our heads, and all arrive at different results, and sneer at one another. And in the general row, the original number would be forgotten, and Uncle Podger would have to measure it again.

He would use a bit of string this time, and at the critical moment, when the old fool was leaning over the chair at an angle of forty-five, and trying to reach a point three inches beyond what was possible for him to reach, the string would slip, and down he would slide on to the piano, a really fine musical effect being produced by the suddenness with which his head and body struck all the notes at the same time.

And Aunt Maria would say that she would not allow the children to stand round and hear such language.

At last, Uncle Podger would get the spot fixed again, and put the point of the nail on it with his left hand, and take the hammer in his right hand. And, with the first blow, he would smash his thumb, and drop the hammer, with a yell, on somebody's toes.

Aunt Maria would mildly observe that, next time Uncle Podger was going to hammer a nail into the wall, she hoped he'd let her know in time, so that she could make arrangements to go and spend a week with her mother while it was being done.

"Oh! You women, you make such a fuss over everything," Uncle Podger would reply, picking himself up. "Why, I *like* doing a little job of this sort."

And then he would have another try, and, at the second blow, the nail would go clean through the plaster, and half the hammer after it, and Uncle Podger be precipitated against the wall with force nearly sufficient to flatten his nose.

Then we had to find the rule and the string again, and a new hole was made; and, about midnight, the picture would be up—very crooked and insecure, the wall for yards round looking as if it had been smoothed down with a rake, and everybody dead beat and wretched—except Uncle Podger.

"There you are," he would say, stepping heavily off the chair on to the charwoman's corns, and surveying the mess he had made with evident pride. "Why, some people would have had a man in to do a little thing like that!"

Harris will be just that sort of man when he grows up, I know, and I told him so. I said I could not permit him to take so much labour upon himself. I said:

"No; *you* get the paper, and the pencil, and the catalogue, and George write down, and I'll do the work."

The first list we made out had to be discarded. It was clear that the upper reaches of the Thames would not allow of the navigation of a boat sufficiently large to take the things we had set down as indispensable; so we tore the list up, and looked at one another!

George said:

"You know we are on a wrong track altogether. We must not think of the things we could do with, but only of the things that we can't do without."

George comes out really quite sensible at times. You'd be surprised. I call that downright wisdom, not merely as regards the present case, but with reference to our trip up the river of life, generally. How many people, on that voyage, load up the boat till it is ever in danger of swamping with a store of foolish things which they think essential to the pleasure and comfort of the trip, but which are really only useless lumber.

How they pile the poor little craft mast-high with fine clothes and big houses; with useless servants, and a host of swell friends that do not care twopence for them, and that they do not care three ha'pence for; with expensive entertainments that nobody enjoys, with formalities and fashions, with pretence and ostentation, and with—oh, heaviest, maddest lumber of all! The dread of what will my neighbour think, with luxuries that only cloy, with pleasures that bore, with empty show that, like the criminal's iron crown of yore, makes to bleed and swoon the aching head that wears it!

It is lumber, man—all lumber! Throw it overboard. It makes the boat so heavy to pull, you nearly faint at the oars. It makes it so cumbersome and dangerous to manage, you never know a moment's freedom from anxiety and care, never gain a moment's rest for dreamy laziness—no time to watch the windy shadows skimming lightly o'er the shallows, or the glittering sunbeams flitting in and out among the ripples, or the great trees by the margin looking down at their own image, or the woods all green and golden, or the lilies white and yellow, or the sombre-waving rushes, or the sedges, or the orchids, or the blue forget-me-nots.

Throw the lumber over, man! Let your boat of life be light, packed with only what you need—a homely home and simple pleasures, one or two friends, worth the name, someone to love and someone to love you, a cat, a dog, and a pipe or two, enough to eat and enough to wear, and a little more than enough to drink; for thirst is a dangerous thing.

You will find the boat easier to pull then, and it will not be so liable to upset, and it will not matter so much if it does upset; good, plain merchandise will stand water. You will have time to think as well as to work. Time to drink in life's sunshine—time to listen to the Æolian music that the wind of God draws from the human heartstrings around us—time to—

I beg your pardon, really. I quite forgot.

Well, we left the list to George, and he began it.

"We won't take a tent," suggested George; "we will have a boat with a cover. It is ever so much simpler, and more comfortable."

It seemed a good thought, and we adopted it. I do not know whether you have ever seen the thing I mean. You fix iron hoops up over the

boat, and stretch a huge
canvas over them, and
fasten it down all round,
from stem to stern, and
it converts the boat into a
sort of little house, and it
is beautifully cosy, though

a trifle stuffy; but there, everything has its drawbacks, as the man said
when his mother-in-law died, and they came down upon him for the
funeral expenses.

George said that in that case we must take a rug each, a lamp,
some soap, a brush and comb (between us), a toothbrush (each), a
basin, some toothpowder, some shaving tackle (sounds like a French
exercise, doesn't it)? And a couple of big towels for bathing. I notice
that people always make gigantic arrangements for bathing when they
are going anywhere near the water, but that they don't bathe much
when they are there.

It is the same when you go to the seaside. I always determine—
when thinking over the matter in London—that I'll get up early every
morning, and go and have a dip before breakfast, and I religiously
pack up a pair of drawers and a bath towel. I always get red bathing
drawers. I rather fancy myself in red drawers. They suit my complexion so. But when I get to the sea I don't feel somehow that I want that
early morning bathe nearly so much as I did when I was in town.

On the contrary, I feel more that I want to stop in bed till the
last moment, and then come down and have my breakfast. Once or
twice virtue has triumphed, and I have got out at six and half-dressed
myself, and have taken my drawers and towel, and stumbled dismally
off. But I haven't enjoyed it. They seem to keep a specially cutting
east wind, waiting for me, when I go to bathe in the early morning;
and they pick out all the three-cornered stones, and put them on the
top, and they sharpen up the rocks and cover the points over with a
bit of sand so that I can't see them, and they take the sea and put it
two miles out, so that I have to huddle myself up in my arms and hop,
shivering, through six inches of water. And when I do get to the sea,
it is rough and quite insulting.

One huge wave catches me up and chucks me in a sitting posture, as hard as ever it can, down on to a rock which has been put there for me. And, before I've said "Oh! Ugh!" and found out what has gone, the wave comes back and carries me out to mid-ocean. I begin to strike out frantically for the shore, and wonder if I shall ever see home and friends again, and wish I'd been kinder to my little sister when a boy (when *I* was a boy, I mean). Just when I have given up all hope, a wave retires and leaves me sprawling like a starfish on the sand, and I get up and look back and find that I've been swimming for my life in two feet of water. I hop back and dress, and crawl home, where I have to pretend I liked it.

In the present instance, we all talked as if we were going to have a long swim every morning. George said it was so pleasant to wake up in the boat in the fresh morning, and plunge into the limpid river. Harris said there was nothing like a swim before breakfast to give you an appetite. He said it always gave him an appetite. George said that if it was going to make Harris eat more than Harris ordinarily ate, then he should protest against Harris having a bath at all. He said there would be quite enough hard work in towing sufficient food for Harris up against stream, as it was.

I urged upon George, however, how much pleasanter it would be to have Harris clean and fresh about the boat, even if we did have to take a few more hundredweight of provisions; and he got to see it in my light, and withdrew his opposition to Harris' bath.

Agreed, finally, that we should take *three* bath towels, so as not to keep each other waiting.

For clothes, George said two suits of flannel would be sufficient, as we could wash them ourselves, in the river, when they got dirty. We asked him if he had ever tried washing flannels in the river, and he replied: "No, not exactly himself like; but he knew some fellows who had, and it was easy enough"; and Harris and I were weak enough to fancy he knew what he was talking about, and that three respectable young men, without position or influence, and with no experience in washing, could really clean their own shirts and trousers in the river Thames with a bit of soap.

We were to learn in the days to come, when it was too late, that George was a miserable impostor, who could evidently have known nothing whatever about the matter. If you had seen these clothes after—but, as the shilling shockers say, we anticipate.

George impressed upon us to take a change of under-things and plenty of socks, in case we got upset and wanted a change; also plenty of handkerchiefs, as they would do to wipe things, and a pair of leather boots as well as our boating shoes, as we should want them if we got upset.

CHAPTER IV

The food question • Objections to paraffine oil as an
atmosphere • Advantages of cheese as a travelling companion •
A married woman deserts her home • Further provision for getting
upset • I pack • Cussedness of toothbrushes • George and Harris
pack • Awful behaviour of Montmorency • We retire to rest

THEN WE DISCUSSED THE FOOD QUESTION. GEORGE SAID:

"Begin with breakfast" (George is so practical). "Now for breakfast we shall want a frying pan"—(Harris said it was indigestible; but
we merely urged him not to be an ass, and George went on)—"a teapot and a kettle, and a methylated spirit stove."

"No oil," said George, with a significant look; and Harris and
I agreed.

We had taken up an oil-stove once, but "never again." It had been
like living in an oil-shop that week. It oozed. I never saw such a thing
as paraffine oil is to ooze. We kept it in the nose of the boat, and,
from there, it oozed down to the rudder, impregnating the whole
boat and everything in it on its way, and it oozed over the river,
and saturated the scenery and spoilt the atmosphere. Sometimes a
westerly oily wind blew, and at other times an easterly oily wind, and
sometimes it blew a northerly oily wind, and maybe a southerly oily
wind; but whether it came from the Arctic snows, or was raised in the
waste of the desert sands, it came alike to us laden with the fragrance
of paraffine oil.

And that oil oozed up and ruined the sunset; and as for the moon-
beams, they positively reeked of paraffine.

We tried to get away from it at Marlow. We left the boat by the bridge, and took a walk through the town to escape it, but it followed us. The whole town was full of oil. We passed through the church-yard, and it seemed as if the people had been buried in oil. The High Street stunk of oil; we wondered how people could live in it. And we walked miles upon miles out Birmingham way; but it was no use, the country was steeped in oil.

At the end of that trip we met together at midnight in a lonely field, under a blasted oak, and took an awful oath (we had been swearing for a whole week about the thing in an ordinary, middle-class way, but this was a swell affair)—an awful oath never to take paraffine oil with us in a boat again—except, of course, in case of sickness.

Therefore, in the present instance, we confined ourselves to meth-ylated spirit. Even that is bad enough. You get methylated pie and methylated cake. But methylated spirit is more wholesome when taken into the system in large quantities than paraffine oil.

For other breakfast things, George suggested eggs and bacon, which were easy to cook, cold meat, tea, bread and butter, and jam. For lunch, he said, we could have biscuits, cold meat, bread and but-ter, and jam—but *no cheese*. Cheese, like oil, makes too much of itself. It wants the whole boat to itself. It goes through the hamper, and gives a cheesy flavour to everything else there. You can't tell whether you are eating apple pie or German sausage, or strawberries and cream. It all seems cheese. There is too much odour about cheese.

I remember a friend of mine buying a couple of cheeses at Liverpool. Splendid cheeses they were, ripe and mellow, and with a two hundred horsepower scent about them that might have been war-ranted to carry three miles, and knock a man over at two hundred yards. I was in Liverpool at the time, and my friend said that if I didn't mind he would get me to take them back with me to London, as he should not be coming up for a day or two himself, and he did not think the cheeses ought to be kept much longer.

"Oh, with pleasure, dear boy," I replied, "with pleasure."

I called for the cheeses, and took them away in a cab. It was a ramshackle affair, dragged along by a knock kneed, broken-winded somnambulist, which his owner, in a moment of enthusiasm, during conversation, referred to as a horse. I put the cheeses on the top, and we started off at a shamble that would have done credit to the swiftest steamroller ever built, and all went merry as a funeral bell, until we turned the corner. There, the wind carried a whiff from the cheeses full on to our steed. It woke him up, and, with a snort of terror, he dashed off at three miles an hour. The wind still blew in his direction, and before we reached the end of the street he was laying himself out at the rate of nearly four miles an hour, leaving the cripples and stout old ladies simply nowhere.

It took two porters as well as the driver to hold him in at the station; and I do not think they would have done it, even then, had not one of the men had the presence of mind to put a handkerchief over his nose, and to light a bit of brown paper.

I took my ticket, and marched proudly up the platform, with my cheeses, the people falling back respectfully on either side. The train was crowded, and I had to get into a carriage where there were already seven other people. One crusty old gentleman objected, but I got in, notwithstanding; and, putting my cheeses upon the rack, squeezed down with a pleasant smile, and said it was a warm day. A few moments passed, and then the old gentleman began to fidget.

"Very close in here," he said.

"Quite oppressive," said the man next him.

And then they both began sniffing, and, at the third sniff, they caught it right on the chest, and rose up without another word and went out. And then a stout lady got up, and said it was disgraceful that a respectable married woman should be harried about in this way, and gathered up a bag and eight parcels and went. The remaining four passengers sat on for a while, until a solemn-looking man in the corner, who, from his dress and general appearance, seemed to belong to the undertaker class, said it put him in mind of a dead baby; and the other three passengers tried to get out of the door at the same time, and hurt themselves.

I smiled at the black gentleman, and said I thought we were going to have the carriage to ourselves; and he laughed pleasantly, and said that some people made such a fuss over a little thing. But even he grew strangely depressed after we had started, and so, when we reached

Crewe, I asked him to come and have a drink. He accepted, and we forced our way into the buffet, where we yelled, and stamped, and waved our umbrellas for a quarter of an hour; and then a young lady came and asked us if we wanted anything.

"What's yours?" I said, turning to my friend.

"I'll have half-a-crown's worth of brandy, neat, if you please, miss," he responded.

And he went off quietly after he had drunk it and got into another carriage, which I thought mean.

From Crewe I had the compartment to myself, though the train was crowded. As we drew up at the different stations, the people, seeing my empty carriage, would rush for it. "Here y' are, Maria; come along, plenty of room." "All right, Tom; we'll get in here," they would shout. And they would run along, carrying heavy bags, and fight round the door to get in first. And one would open the door and mount the steps, and stagger back into the arms of the man behind him; and they would all come and have a sniff, and then droop off and squeeze into other carriages, or pay the difference and go first.

From Euston, I took the cheeses down to my friend's house. When his wife came into the room she smelt round for an instant. Then she said:

"What is it? Tell me the worst."

I said:

"It's cheeses. Tom bought them in Liverpool, and asked me to bring them up with me."

And I added that I hoped she understood that it had nothing to do with me; and she said that she was sure of that, but that she would speak to Tom about it when he came back.

My friend was detained in Liverpool longer than he expected; and, three days later, as he hadn't returned home, his wife called on me. She said:

"What did Tom say about those cheeses?"

I replied that he had directed they were to be kept in a moist place, and that nobody was to touch them.

She said:

"Nobody's likely to touch them. Had he smelt them?"

I thought he had, and added that he seemed greatly attached to them.

"You think he would be upset," she queried, "if I gave a man a sovereign to take them away and bury them?"

I answered that I thought he would never smile again.

An idea struck her. She said:

"Do you mind keeping them for him? Let me send them round to you."

"Madam," I replied, "for myself I like the smell of cheese, and the journey the other day with them from Liverpool I shall ever look back upon as a happy ending to a pleasant holiday. But, in this world, we must consider others. The lady under whose roof I have the honour of residing is a widow, and, for all I know, possibly an orphan too. She has a strong, I may say an eloquent, objection to being what she terms 'put upon.' The presence of your husband's cheeses in her house she would, I instinctively feel, regard as a 'put upon'; and it shall never be said that I put upon the widow and the orphan."

"Very well, then," said my friend's wife, rising, "all I have to say is, that I shall take the children and go to an hotel until those cheeses are eaten. I decline to live any longer in the same house with them."

She kept her word, leaving the place in charge of the charwoman, who, when asked if she could stand the smell, replied, "What smell?" and who, when taken close to the cheeses and told to sniff hard, said she could detect a faint odour of melons. It was argued from this that little injury could result to the woman from the atmosphere, and she was left.

The hotel bill came to fifteen guineas; and my friend, after reckoning everything up, found that the cheeses had cost him eight-and-sixpence a pound. He said he dearly loved a bit of cheese, but it was beyond his means; so he determined to get rid of them. He threw them into the canal; but had to fish them out again, as the bargemen complained. They said it made them feel quite faint. And, after that, he took them one dark night and left them in the parish mortuary. But the coroner discovered them, and made a fearful fuss.

He said it was a plot to deprive him of his living by waking up the corpses.

My friend got rid of them, at last, by taking them down to a seaside town, and burying them on the beach. It gained the place quite a reputation. Visitors said they had never noticed before how strong the air was, and weak-chested and consumptive people used to throng there for years afterwards.

Fond as I am of cheese, therefore, I hold that George was right in declining to take any.

"We shan't want any tea," said George (Harris' face fell at this); "but we'll have a good round, square, slap-up meal at seven—dinner, tea, and supper combined."

Harris grew more cheerful. George suggested meat and fruit pies, cold meat, tomatoes, fruit, and green stuff. For drink, we took some wonderful sticky concoction of Harris', which you mixed with water and called lemonade, plenty of tea, and a bottle of whisky, in case, as George said, we got upset.

It seemed to me that George harped too much on the getting-upset idea. It seemed to me the wrong spirit to go about the trip in.

But I'm glad we took the whisky.

We didn't take beer or wine. They are a mistake up the river. They make you feel sleepy and heavy. A glass in the evening, when you are doing a mouch round the town and looking at the girls is all right enough; but don't drink when the sun is blazing down on your head, and you've got hard work to do.

We made a list of the things to be taken, and a pretty lengthy one it was, before we parted that evening. The next day, which was Friday, we got them all together, and met in the evening to pack. We got a big Gladstone for the clothes, and a couple of hampers for the victuals and the cooking utensils. We moved the table up against the window, piled everything in a heap in the middle of the floor, and sat round and looked at it.

I said I'd pack.

I rather pride myself on my packing. Packing is one of those many things that I feel I know more about than any other person living. (It surprises me myself, sometimes, how many of these subjects there are.) I impressed the fact upon George and Harris, and told them that they had better leave the whole matter entirely to me. They fell into the suggestion with a readiness that had something uncanny about it. George put on a pipe and spread himself over the easy chair, and Harris cocked his legs on the table and lit a cigar.

This was hardly what I intended. What I had meant, of course, was, that I should boss the job, and that Harris and George should potter about under my directions, I pushing them aside every now and then with, "Oh, you!" "Here, let me do it." "There you are, simple enough!" really teaching them, as you might say. Their taking it in the way they did irritated me. There is nothing does irritate me more than seeing other people sitting about doing nothing when I'm working.

I lived with a man once who used to make me mad that way. He would loll on the sofa and watch me doing things by the hour together, following me round the room with his eyes, wherever I went. He said it did him real good to look on at me, messing about. He said it made him feel that life was not an idle dream to be gaped and yawned through, but a noble task, full of duty and stern work. He said he often wondered now how he could have gone on before he met me, never having anybody to look at while they worked.

Now, I'm not like that. I can't sit still and see another man slaving and working. I want to get up and superintend, and walk round with my hands in my pockets, and tell him what to do. It is my energetic nature. I can't help it.

However, I did not say anything, but started the packing. It seemed a longer job than I had thought it was going to be; but I got the bag finished at last, and I sat on it and strapped it.

"Ain't you going to put the boots in?" said Harris.

And I looked round, and found I had forgotten them. That's just like Harris. He couldn't have said a word until I'd got the bag shut and strapped, of course. And George laughed—one of those irritating, senseless, chuckle-headed, crack-jawed laughs of his. They do make me so wild.

I opened the bag and packed the boots in; and then, just as I was going to close it, a horrible idea occurred to me. Had I packed my toothbrush? I don't know how it is, but I never do know whether I've packed my toothbrush.

My toothbrush is a thing that haunts me when I'm travelling, and makes my life a misery. I dream that I haven't packed it, and wake up in a cold perspiration, and get out of bed and hunt for it. And, in the morning, I pack it before I have used it, and have to unpack again to get it, and it is always the last thing I turn out of the bag; and then I repack and forget it, and have to rush upstairs for it at the last moment and carry it to the railway station, wrapped up in my pocket-handkerchief.

 Of course I had to turn every mortal thing out now, and, of course, I could not find it. I rummaged the things up into much the same state that they must have been before the world was created, and when chaos reigned. Of course, I found George's and Harris' eighteen times over, but I couldn't find my own. I put the things back one by one, and held everything up and shook it. Then I found it inside a boot. I repacked once more.

When I had finished, George asked if the soap was in. I said I didn't care a hang whether the soap was in or whether it wasn't; and I slammed the bag to and strapped it, and found that I had packed my tobacco-pouch in it, and had to re-open it. It got shut up finally at 10:05 PM, and then there remained the hampers to do. Harris said that we should be wanting to start in less than twelve hours' time, and thought that he and George had better do the rest; and I agreed and sat down, and they had a go.

They began in a light-hearted spirit, evidently intending to show me how to do it. I made no comment; I only waited. When George is hanged, Harris will be the worst packer in this world; and I looked at the piles of plates and cups, and kettles, and bottles and jars, and pies, and stoves, and cakes, and tomatoes, &c., and felt that the thing would soon become exciting.

It did. They started with breaking a cup. That was the first thing they did. They did that just to show you what they *could* do, and to get you interested.

Then Harris packed the strawberry jam on top of a tomato and squashed it, and they had to pick out the tomato with a teaspoon.

And then it was George's turn, and he trod on the butter. I didn't say anything, but I came over and sat on the edge of the table and watched them. It irritated them more than anything I could have said. I felt that. It made them nervous and excited, and they stepped on things, and put things behind them, and then couldn't find them when they wanted them; and they packed the pies at the bottom, and put heavy things on top, and smashed the pies in.

They upset salt over everything, and as for the butter! I never saw two men do more with one-and-twopence worth of butter in my whole life than they did. After George had got it off his slipper, they tried to put it in the kettle. It wouldn't go in, and what *was* in wouldn't come out. They did scrape it out at last, and put it down on a chair, and Harris sat on it, and it stuck to him, and they went looking for it all over the room.

"I'll take my oath I put it down on that chair," said George, staring at the empty seat.

"I saw you do it myself, not a minute ago," said Harris.

Then they started round the room again looking for it; and then they met again in the centre, and stared at one another.

"Most extraordinary thing I ever heard of," said George.

"So mysterious!" said Harris.

Then George got round at the back of Harris and saw it.

"Why, here it is all the time," he exclaimed, indignantly.

"Where?" cried Harris, spinning round.

"Stand still, can't you!" roared George, flying after him.

And they got it off, and packed it in the teapot.

Montmorency was in it all, of course. Montmorency's ambition in life, is to get in the way and be sworn at. If he can squirm in anywhere where he particularly is not wanted, and be a perfect nuisance, and make people mad, and have things thrown at his head, then he feels his day has not been wasted.

To get somebody to stumble over him, and curse him steadily for an hour, is his highest aim and object; and, when he has succeeded in accomplishing this, his conceit becomes quite unbearable.

He came and sat down on things, just when they were wanted to be packed; and he laboured under the fixed belief that, whenever

Harris or George reached out their hand for anything, it was his cold, damp nose that they wanted. He put his leg into the jam, and he worried the teaspoons, and he pretended that the lemons were rats, and got into the hamper and killed three of them before Harris could land him with the frying pan.

Harris said I encouraged him. I didn't encourage him. A dog like that don't want any encouragement. It's the natural, original sin that is born in him that makes him do things like that.

The packing was done at 12.50; and Harris sat on the big hamper, and said he hoped nothing would be found broken. George said that if anything was broken it *was* broken, which reflection seemed to comfort him. He also said he was ready for bed. We were all ready for bed. Harris was to sleep with us that night, and we went upstairs.

We tossed for beds, and Harris had to sleep with me. He said:

"Do you prefer the inside or the outside, J.?"

I said I generally preferred to sleep *inside* a bed.

Harris said it was old.

George said:

"What time shall I wake you fellows?"

Harris said:

"Seven."

I said:

"No—six," because I wanted to write some letters.

Harris and I had a bit of a row over it, but at last split the difference, and said half-past six.

"Wake us at 6.30, George," we said.

George made no answer, and we found, on going over, that he had been asleep for some time; so we placed the path where he could tumble into it on getting out in the morning, and went to bed ourselves.

CHAPTER V

Mrs. P. arouses us • George, the sluggard • The "weather forecast" swindle • Our luggage • Depravity of the small boy • The people gather round us • We drive off in great style, and arrive at Waterloo • Innocence off South Western Officials concerning such worldly things as trains • We are afloat, afloat in an open boat

IT WAS MRS. POPPETS THAT WOKE ME UP NEXT morning.

She said:

"Do you know that it's nearly nine o'clock, sir?"

"Nine o' what?" I cried, starting up.

"Nine o'clock," she replied, through the keyhole. "I thought you was a-oversleeping yourselves."

I woke Harris, and told him. He said:

"I thought you wanted to get up at six?"

"So I did," I answered; "why didn't you wake me?"

"How could I wake you, when you didn't wake me?" he retorted. "Now we shan't get on the water till after twelve. I wonder you take the trouble to get up at all."

"Um," I replied, "lucky for you that I do. If I hadn't woke you, you'd have lain there for the whole fortnight."

We snarled at one another in this strain for the next few minutes, when we were interrupted by a defiant snore from George. It reminded us, for the first time since our being called, of his existence. There he lay—the man who had wanted to know what time he should wake us—on his back, with his mouth wide open, and his knees stuck up.

I don't know why it should be, I am sure; but the sight of  another man asleep in bed when I am up, maddens me. It seems to me so shocking to see the precious hours of a man's life—the priceless moments that will never come back to him again—being wasted in mere brutish sleep.

There was George, throwing away in hideous sloth the inestimable gift of time; his valuable life, every second of which he would have to account for hereafter, passing away from him, unused. He might have been up stuffing himself with eggs and bacon, irritating the dog, or flirting with the slavey, instead of sprawling there, sunk in soul-clogging oblivion.

It was a terrible thought. Harris and I appeared to be struck by it at the same instant. We determined to save him, and, in this noble resolve, our own dispute was forgotten. We flew across and slung the clothes off him, and Harris landed him one with a slipper, and I shouted in his ear, and he awoke.

"Wasermarrer?" he observed, sitting up.

"Get up, you fat-headed chunk!" roared Harris. "It's quarter to ten."

"What!" he shrieked, jumping out of bed into the bath; "——Who the thunder put this thing here?"

We told him he must have been a fool not to see the bath.

We finished dressing, and, when it came to the extras, we remembered that we had packed the toothbrushes and the brush and comb (that toothbrush of mine will be the death of me, I know) and we had to go downstairs, and fish them out of the bag. And when we had done that George wanted the shaving tackle. We told him that he would have to go without shaving that morning, as we weren't going to unpack that bag again for him, nor for anyone like him.

He said:

"Don't be absurd. How can I go into the City like this?"

It was certainly rather rough on the City, but what cared we for human suffering? As Harris said, in his common, vulgar way, the City would have to lump it.

We went downstairs to breakfast. Montmorency had invited two other dogs to come and see him off, and they were whiling away the time by fighting on the doorstep. We calmed them with an umbrella, and sat down to chops and cold beef.

Harris said:

"The great thing is to make a good breakfast," and he started with a couple of chops, saying that he would take these while they were hot, as the beef could wait.

George got hold of the paper, and read us out the boating fatalities, and the weather forecast, which latter prophesied "rain, cold, wet to fine" (whatever more than usually ghastly thing in weather that may be), "occasional local thunderstorms, east wind, with general depression over the Midland Counties (London and Channel). Bar. falling."

I do think that, of all the silly, irritating tom-foolishness by which we are plagued, this "weather-forecast" fraud is about the most aggravating. It "forecasts" precisely what happened yesterday or the day before, and precisely the opposite of what is going to happen today.

I remember a holiday of mine being completely ruined one late autumn by our paying attention to the weather report of the local newspaper. "Heavy showers, with thunderstorms, may be expected today," it would say on Monday, and so we would give up our picnic, and stop indoors all day, waiting for the rain. And people would pass the house, going off in wagonettes and coaches as jolly and merry as could be, the sun shining out, and not a cloud to be seen.

"Ah!" we said, as we stood looking out at them through the window, "won't they come home soaked!"

And we chuckled to think how wet they were going to get, and came back and stirred the fire, and got our books, and arranged our specimens of seaweed and cockle shells. By twelve o'clock, with the sun pouring into the room, the heat became quite oppressive, and we wondered when those heavy showers and occasional thunderstorms were going to begin.

"Ah! They'll come in the afternoon, you'll find," we said to each other. "Oh, *won't* those people get wet. What a lark!"

At one o'clock the landlady would come in to ask if we weren't going out, as it seemed such a lovely day.

"No, no," we replied, with a knowing chuckle, "not we. *We* don't mean to get wet—no, no."

And when the afternoon was nearly gone, and still there was no sign of rain, we tried to cheer ourselves up with the idea that it would come down all at once, just as the people had started for home, and were out of the reach of any shelter, and that they would thus get more drenched than ever. But not a drop ever fell, and it finished a grand day, and a lovely night after it.

The next morning we would read that it was going to be a "warm, fine to set-fair day; much heat"; and we would dress ourselves in flimsy things, and go out, and, half-an-hour after we had started, it would commence to rain hard, and a bitterly cold wind would spring up, and both would keep on steadily for the whole day, and we would come home with colds and rheumatism all over us, and go to bed.

The weather is a thing that is beyond me altogether. I never can understand it. The barometer is useless: it is as misleading as the newspaper forecast.

There was one hanging up in a hotel at Oxford at which I was staying last spring, and, when I got there, it was pointing to "set fair." It was simply pouring with rain outside, and had been all day; and I couldn't quite make matters out. I tapped the barometer, and it jumped up and pointed to "very dry." The Boots stopped as he was passing and said he expected it meant tomorrow. I fancied that maybe it was thinking of the week before last, but Boots said, No, he thought not.

I tapped it again the next morning, and it went up still higher, and the rain came down faster than ever. On Wednesday I went and hit it again, and the pointer went round towards "set fair," "very dry," and "much heat," until it was stopped by the peg, and couldn't go any further. It tried its best, but the instrument was built so that it couldn't prophesy fine weather any harder than it did without breaking itself. It evidently wanted to go on, and prognosticate drought, and water famine, and sunstroke, and simooms, and such things, but the peg prevented it, and it had to be content with pointing to the mere commonplace "very dry."

Meanwhile, the rain came down in a steady torrent, and the lower part of the town was under water, owing to the river having overflowed.

Boots said it was evident that we were going to have a prolonged spell of grand weather *some time*, and read out a poem which was printed over the top of the oracle, about

Long foretold, long last;
Short notice, soon past.

The fine weather never came that summer. I expect that machine must have been referring to the following spring.

Then there are those new style of barometers, the long straight ones. I never can make head or tail of those. There is one side for 10 AM yesterday, and one side for 10 AM today; but you can't always get there as early as ten, you know. It rises or falls for rain and fine, with much or less wind, and one end is "Nly" and the other "Ely" (what's Ely got to do with it?). And if you tap it, it doesn't tell you anything. And you've got to correct it to sea-level, and reduce it to Fahrenheit, and even then I don't know the answer.

But who wants to be foretold the weather? It is bad enough when it comes, without our having the misery of knowing about it beforehand. The prophet we like is the old man who, on the particularly gloomy-looking morning of some day when we particularly want it to be fine, looks round the horizon with a particularly knowing eye, and says:

"Oh no, sir, I think it will clear up all right. It will break all right enough, sir."

"Ah, he knows," we say, as we wish him good morning, and start off; "wonderful how these old fellows can tell!"

And we feel an affection for that man which is not at all lessened by the circumstances of its *not* clearing up, but continuing to rain steadily all day.

"Ah, well," we feel, "he did his best."

For the man that prophesies us bad weather, on the contrary, we entertain only bitter and revengeful thoughts.

"Going to clear up, d'ye think?" we shout, cheerily, as we pass.

"Well, no, sir; I'm afraid it's settled down for the day," he replies, shaking his head.

"Stupid old fool!" we mutter, "what's *he* know about it?" And, if his portent proves correct, we come back feeling still more angry against him, and with a vague notion that, somehow or other, he has had something to do with it.

It was too bright and sunny on this especial morning for George's blood-curdling readings about "Bar. failing," "atmospheric disturbance, passing in an oblique line over Southern Europe," and "pressure increasing," to very much upset us: and so, finding that he could not make us wretched, and was only wasting his time, he sneaked the cigarette that I had carefully rolled up for myself, and went.

Then Harris and I, having finished up the few things left on the table, carted out our luggage on to the doorstep, and waited for a cab.

There seemed a good deal of luggage, when we put it all together. There was the Gladstone and the small handbag, and the two hampers, and a large roll of rugs, and some four or five overcoats and mackintoshes, and a few umbrellas, and then there was a melon by itself in a bag, because it was too bulky to go in anywhere, and a couple of pounds of grapes in another bag, and a Japanese paper umbrella, and a frying pan, which, being too long to pack, we had wrapped round with brown paper.

It did look a lot, and Harris and I began to feel rather ashamed of it, though why we should be, I can't see. No cab came by, but the street boys did, and got interested in the show, apparently, and stopped.

Biggs' boy was the first to come round. Biggs is our greengrocer, and his chief talent lies in securing the services of the most abandoned and unprincipled errand-boys that civilisation has as yet produced. If anything more than usually villainous in the boy-line crops up in our neighbourhood, we know that it is Biggs' latest. I was told that, at the time of the Great Coram Street murder, it was promptly concluded by our street that Biggs' boy (for that period)

was
at the bot-
tom of it, and had he not
been able, in reply to the severe cross-
examination to which he was subjected by No. 19, when he called
there for orders the morning after the crime (assisted by No. 21,
who happened to be on the step at the time), to prove a complete
alibi, it would have gone hard with him. I didn't know Biggs' boy at
that time, but, from what I have seen of them since, I should not
have attached much importance to that *alibi* myself.

Biggs' boy, as I have said, came round the corner. He was evidently
in a great hurry when he first dawned upon the vision, but, on catching sight of Harris and me, and Montmorency, and the things, he
eased up and stared. Harris and I frowned at him. This might have
wounded a more sensitive nature, but Biggs' boys are not, as a rule,
touchy. He came to a dead stop, a yard from our step, and, leaning up
against the railings, and selecting a straw to chew, fixed us with his
eye. He evidently meant to see this thing out.

In another moment, the grocer's boy passed on the opposite side
of the street. Biggs' boy hailed him:

"Hi! Ground floor o' 42's a-moving."

The grocer's boy came across, and took up a position on the other side of the step. Then the young gentleman from the boot-shop stopped, and joined Biggs' boy; while the empty-can superintendent from "The Blue Posts" took up an independent position on the curb.

"They ain't a-going to starve, are they?" said the gentleman from the boot-shop.

"Ah! You'd want to take a thing or two with *you*," retorted "The Blue Posts," "if you was a-going to cross the Atlantic in a small boat."

"They ain't a-going to cross the Atlantic," struck in Biggs' boy; "they're a-going to find Stanley."

By this time, quite a small crowd had collected, and people were asking each other what was the matter. One party (the young and giddy portion of the crowd) held that it was a wedding, and pointed out Harris as the bridegroom; while the elder and more thoughtful among the populace inclined to the idea that it was a funeral, and that I was probably the corpse's brother.

At last, an empty cab turned up (it is a street where, as a rule, and when they are not wanted, empty cabs pass at the rate of three a minute, and hang about, and get in your way), and packing ourselves and our belongings into it, and shooting out a couple of Montmorency's friends, who had evidently sworn never to forsake him, we drove away amidst the cheers of the crowd, Biggs' boy shying a carrot after us for luck.

We got to Waterloo at eleven, and asked where the eleven-five started from. Of course nobody knew; nobody at Waterloo ever does know where a train is going to start from, or where a train when it does start is going to, or anything about it. The porter who took our things thought it would go from number two platform, while another porter, with whom he discussed the question, had heard a rumour that it would go from number one. The station-master, on the other hand, was convinced it would start from the local.

To put an end to the matter, we went upstairs, and asked the traffic superintendent, and he told us that he had just met a man, who said he had seen it at number three platform. We went to number three platform, but the authorities there said that they rather thought that train was the Southampton express, or else the Windsor loop.

But they were sure it wasn't the Kingston train, though why they were sure it wasn't they couldn't say.

Then our porter said he thought that must be it on the high-level platform; said he thought he knew the train. So we went to the high-level platform, and saw the engine-driver, and asked him if he was going to Kingston. He said he couldn't say for certain of course, but that he rather thought he was. Anyhow, if he wasn't the 11:05 for Kingston, he said he was pretty confident he was the 9:32 for Virginia Water, or the 10 AM express for the Isle of Wight, or somewhere in that direction, and we should all know when we got there. We slipped half-a-crown into his hand, and begged him to be the 11:05 for Kingston.

"Nobody will ever know, on this line," we said, "what you are, or where you're going. You know the way, you slip off quietly and go to Kingston."

"Well, I don't know, gents," replied the noble fellow, "but I suppose *some* train's got to go to Kingston; and I'll do it. Gimme the half-crown."

Thus we got to Kingston by the London and South-Western Railway.

We learnt, afterwards, that the train we had come by was really the Exeter mail, and that they had spent hours at Waterloo, looking for it, and nobody knew what had become of it.

Our boat was waiting for us at Kingston just below bridge, and to it we wended our way, and round it we stored our luggage, and into it we stepped.

"Are you all right, sir?" said the man.

"Right it is," we' answered; and with Harris at the sculls and I at the tiller-lines, and Montmorency, unhappy and deeply suspicions, in the prow, out we shot on to the waters which, for a fortnight, were to be our home.

CHAPTER VI

Kingston • Instructive remarks on early English history • Instructive observations on carved oak and life in general • Sad case of Stivvings, junior • Musings on antiquity • I forget that I am steering • Interesting result • Hampton Court Maze • Harris as a guide

IT WAS A GLORIOUS MORNING, LATE SPRING OR EARLY SUMMER, AS YOU care to take it, when the dainty sheen of grass and leaf is blushing to a deeper green; and the year seems like a fair young maid, trembling with strange, wakening pulses on the brink of womanhood.

The quaint back streets of Kingston, where they came down to the water's edge, looked quite picturesque in the flashing sunlight, the glinting river with its drifting barges, the wooded towpath, the trim-kept villas on the other side, Harris, in a red and orange blazer, grunting away at the sculls, the distant glimpses of the grey old palace of the Tudors, all made a sunny picture, so bright but calm, so full of life, and yet so peaceful, that, early in the day though it was, I felt myself being dreamily lulled off into a musing fit.

I mused on Kingston, or "Kyningestun," as it was once called in the days when Saxon "kinges" were crowned there. Great Cæsar crossed the river there, and the Roman legions camped upon its sloping uplands. Cæsar, like, in later years, Elizabeth, seems to have stopped everywhere: only he was more respectable than good Queen Bess; he didn't put up at the public houses.

She was nuts on public houses, was England's Virgin Queen. There's scarcely a pub of any attractions within ten miles of London that she does not seem to have looked in at, or stopped at, or slept at, some time or other. I wonder now, supposing Harris, say, turned over a new leaf, and became a great and good man, and got to be Prime Minister, and died, if they would put up signs over the public houses that he had patronised: "Harris had a glass of bitter in this house"; "Harris had two of Scotch cold here in the summer of '88"; "Harris was chucked from here in December, 1886."

No, there would be too many of them! It would be the houses that he had never entered that would become famous. "Only house in South London that Harris never had a drink in!" The people would flock to it to see what could have been the matter with it.

How poor weak-minded King Edwy must have hated Kyningestun! The coronation feast had been too much for him. Maybe boar's head stuffed with sugar-plums did not agree with him (it wouldn't with me, I know), and he had had enough of sack and mead; so he slipped from the noisy revel to steal a quiet moonlight hour with his beloved Elgiva.

Perhaps from the casement, standing hand-in-hand, they were watching the calm moonlight on the river, while from the distant halls the boisterous revelry floated in broken bursts of faint-heard din and tumult.

Then brutal Odo and St. Dunstan force their rude way into the quiet room, and hurl coarse insults at the sweet-faced Queen, and drag poor Edwy back to the loud clamour of the drunken brawl.

Years later, to the crash of battle music, Saxon kings and Saxon revelry were buried side by side, and Kingston's greatness passed away for a time, to rise once more when Hampton Court became the palace of the Tudors and the Stuarts, and the royal barges strained at their moorings on the river's bank, and bright-cloaked gallants swaggered down the water-steps to cry: "What Ferry, ho! Gadzooks, gramercy."

Many of the old houses, round about, speak very plainly of those days when Kingston was a royal borough, and nobles and courtiers lived there, near their King, and the long road to the palace gates was gay all day with clanking steel and prancing palfreys, and rustling silks and velvets, and fair faces. The large and spacious houses, with their oriel, latticed windows, their huge fireplaces, and their gabled roofs, breathe of the days of hose and doublet, of pearl-embroidered stomachers, and complicated oaths. They were upraised in the days "when men knew how to build." The hard red bricks have only grown more firmly set with time, and their oak stairs do not creak and grunt when you try to go down them quietly.

Speaking of oak staircases reminds me that there is a magnificent carved oak staircase in one of the houses in Kingston. It is a shop now, in the marketplace, but it was evidently once the mansion of some great personage. A friend of mine, who lives at Kingston, went in there to buy a hat one day, and, in a thoughtless moment, put his hand in his pocket and paid for it then and there.

The shopman (he knows my friend) was naturally a little staggered at first; but, quickly recovering himself, and feeling that something ought to be done to encourage this sort of thing, asked our hero if he would like to see some fine old carved oak. My friend said he would, and the shopman, thereupon, took him through the shop, and up the staircase of the house. The balusters were a superb piece of workmanship, and the wall all the way up was oak-panelled, with carving that would have done credit to a palace.

From the stairs they went into the drawing room, which was a large, bright room, decorated with a somewhat startling though cheerful paper of a blue ground. There was nothing, however, remarkable about the apartment, and my friend wondered why he had been brought there. The proprietor went up to the paper, and tapped it. It gave forth a wooden sound.

"Oak," he explained. "All carved oak, right up to the ceiling, just the same as you saw on the staircase."

"But, great Cæsar! Man," expostulated my friend; "you don't mean to say you have covered over carved oak with blue wallpaper?"

"Yes," was the reply: "it was expensive work. Had to match-board it all over first, of course. But the room looks cheerful now. It was awful gloomy before."

I can't say I altogether blame the man (which is doubtless a great relief to his mind). From his point of view, which would be that of the average householder, desiring to take life as lightly as possible, and not that of the old curiosity-shop maniac, there is reason on his side. Carved oak is very pleasant to look at, and to have a little of, but it is no doubt somewhat depressing to live in, for those whose fancy does not lie that way. It would be like living in a church.

No, what was sad in his case was that he, who didn't care for carved oak, should have his drawing room panelled with it, while people who do care for get have to pay enormous prices to get it. It seems to be the rule of this world. Each person has what he doesn't want, and other people have what he does want.

Married men have wives, and don't seem to want them; and young single fellows cry out that they can't get them. Poor people who can hardly keep themselves have eight hearty children. Rich old couples, with no one to leave their money to, die childless.

Then there are girls with lovers. The girls that have lovers never want them. They say they would rather be without them, that they bother them, and why don't they go and make love to Miss Smith and Miss Brown, who are plain and elderly, and haven't got any lovers? They themselves don't want lovers. They never mean to marry.

It does not do to dwell on these things; it makes one so sad.

There was a boy at our school, we used to call him Sandford and Merton. His real name was Stivvings. He was the most extraordinary lad I ever came across. I believe he really liked study. He used to get into awful rows for sitting up in bed and reading Greek; and as for French irregular verbs there was simply no keeping him away from them. He was full of weird and unnatural notions about being a credit to his parents and an honour to the school; and he yearned to win prizes, and grow up and be a clever man, and had all those sorts or weak-minded ideas. I never knew such a strange creature, yet harmless, mind you, as the babe unborn.

Well, that boy used to get ill about twice a week, so that he couldn't go to school. There never was such a boy to get ill as that Sandford and Merton. If there was any known disease going within ten miles of him, he had it, and had it badly. He would take bronchitis in the dog-days, and have hay-fever at Christmas. After a six weeks' period of drought, he would be stricken down with rheumatic fever; and he would go out in a November fog and come home with a sunstroke.

They put him under laughing-gas one year, poor lad, and drew all his teeth, and gave him a false set, because he suffered so terribly with toothache; and then it turned to neuralgia and earache. He was never without a cold, except once for nine weeks while he had scarlet fever; and he always had chilblains. During the great cholera scare of 1871, our neighbourhood was singularly free from it. There was only one reputed case in the whole parish: that case was young Stivvings.

He had to stop in bed when he was ill, and eat chicken and custards and hothouse grapes; and he would lie there and sob, because they wouldn't let him do Latin exercises, and took his German grammar away from him.

And we other boys, who would have sacrificed ten terms of our school-life for the sake of being ill for a day, and had no desire whatever to give our parents any excuse for being stuck-up about us, couldn't catch so much as a stiff neck. We fooled about in draughts, and it did us good, and freshened us up; and we took things to make us sick, and they made us fat, and gave us an appetite. Nothing we could think of seemed to make us ill until the holidays began. Then, on the breaking-up day, we caught colds, and whooping cough, and all kinds of disorders, which lasted till the term recommenced; when, in spite of everything we could manœuvre to the contrary, we would get suddenly well again, and be better than ever.

Such is life; and we are but as grass that is cut down, and put into the oven and baked.

To go back to the carved-oak question, they must have had very fair notions of the artistic and the beautiful, our great-great-grandfathers. Why, all our art treasures of today are only the dug-up commonplaces of three or four hundred years ago. I wonder if there is any real intrinsic beauty in the old soup-plates, beer-mugs, and candle-snuffers that we prize so now, or if it is only the halo of age glowing around them that gives them their charms in our eyes. The "old blue" that we hang about our walls as ornaments were the common everyday household utensils of a few centuries ago; and the pink shepherds and the yellow shepherdesses that we hand round now for all our friends to gush over, and pretend they understand, were the unvalued mantel-ornaments that the mother of the eighteenth century would have given the baby to suck when he cried.

Will it be the same in the future? Will the prized treasures of today always be the cheap trifles of the day before? Will rows of our willow-pattern dinner plates be ranged above the chimneypieces of the great in the years 2000 and odd? Will the white cups with the gold rim and the beautiful gold flower inside (species unknown), that our Sarah Janes now break in sheer light-heartedness of spirit, be carefully mended, and stood upon a bracket and dusted only by the lady of the house?

That china dog that ornaments the bedroom of my furnished lodgings. It is a white dog. Its eyes are blue. Its nose is a delicate red, with black spots. Its head is painfully erect, and  its expression is amiability carried to the verge of imbecility. I do not admire it myself. Considered as a work of art, I may say it irritates me. Thoughtless friends jeer at it, and even my landlady herself has no admiration for it, and excuses its presence by the circumstance that her aunt gave it to her.

But in 200 years' time it is more than probable that that dog will be dug up from somewhere or other, minus its legs, and with its tail broken, and will be sold for old china, and put in a glass cabinet. And people will pass it round, and admire it. They will be struck by the wonderful depth of the colour on the nose, and speculate as to how beautiful the bit of the tail that is lost no doubt was.

We, in this age, do not see the beauty of that dog. We are too familiar with it. It is like the sunset and the stars: we are not awed by their loveliness because they are common to our eyes. So it is with that china dog. In 2288 people will gush over it. The making of such dogs will have become a lost art. Our descendants will wonder how we did it, and say how clever we were. We shall be referred to lovingly as "those grand old artists that flourished in the nineteenth century, and produced those china dogs."

The "sampler" that the eldest daughter did at school will be spoken of as "tapestry of the Victorian era," and be almost priceless. The blue-and-white mugs of the present-day roadside inn will be hunted up, all cracked and chipped, and sold for their weight in gold, and rich people will use them for claret cups; and travellers from Japan will buy up all the "Presents from Ramsgate," and "Souvenirs of Margate," that may have escaped destruction, and take them back to Jedo as ancient English curios.

At this point Harris threw away the sculls, got up and left his seat, and sat on his back, and stuck his legs in the air. Montmorency howled, and turned a somersault, and the top hamper jumped up, and all the things came out.

I was somewhat surprised, but I did not lose my temper. I said, pleasantly enough:

"Hulloa! What's that for?"

"What's that for? Why—"

No, on second thoughts, I will not repeat what Harris said. I may have been to blame, I admit it; but nothing excuses violence of language and coarseness of expression, especially in a man who has been carefully brought up, as I know Harris has been. I was thinking of other things, and forgot, as anyone might easily understand, that I was steering, and the consequence was that we had got mixed up a good deal with the towpath. It was difficult to say, for the moment, which was us and which was the Middlesex bank of the river; but we found out after a while, and separated ourselves.

Harris, however, said he had done enough for a bit, and proposed that I should take a turn; so, as we were in, I got out and took the towline, and ran the boat on past Hampton Court. What a dear old wall that is that runs along by the river there! I never pass it without feeling better for the sight of it. Such a mellow, bright, sweet old wall; what a charming picture it would make, with the lichen creeping here and the moss growing there, a shy young vine peeping over the top at this spot, to see what is going on upon the busy river, and the sober old ivy clustering a little farther down! There are fifty shades and tints and hues in every ten yards of that old wall. If I could only draw, and knew how to paint, I could make a lovely sketch of that old wall, I'm sure. I've often thought I should like to live at Hampton Court. It looks so peaceful and so quiet, and it is such a dear old place to ramble round in the early morning before many people are about.

But, there, I don't suppose I should really care for it when it came to actual practice. It would be so ghastly dull and depressing in the evening, when you lamp cast uncanny shadows on the panelled walls, and the echo of distant feet rang through the cold stone corridors, and now drew nearer, and now died away, and all was deathlike silence, save the beating of one's own heart.

We are creatures of the sun, we men and women. We love light and life. That is why we crowd into the towns and cities, and the country grows more and more deserted every year. In the sunlight—in the daytime, when Nature is alive and busy all around us, we like the open hillsides and the deep woods well enough: but in the night, when our Mother Earth has gone to sleep, and left us waking, oh! The world seems so lonesome, and we get frightened, like children in a silent house. Then we sit and sob, and long for the gas-lit streets, and the sound of human voices, and the answering throb of human life. We feel so helpless and so little in the great stillness, when the dark

trees rustle in the night-wind. There are so many ghosts about, and their silent sighs make us feel so sad. Let us gather together in the great cities, and light huge bonfires of a million gasjets, and shout and sing together and feel brave.

Harris asked me if I'd ever been in the maze at Hampton Court. He said he went in once to show somebody else the way.

He had studied it up in a map, and it was so simple that it seemed foolish—hardly worth the twopence charged for admission. Harris said he thought that map must have been got up as a practical joke, because it wasn't a bit like the real thing, and only misleading. It was a country cousin that Harris took in. He said:

"We'll just go in here, so that you can say you've been, but it's very simple. It's absurd to call it a maze. You keep on taking the first turning to the right. We'll just walk round for ten minutes, and then go and get some lunch."

They met some people soon after they had got inside, who said they had been there for three-quarters of an hour, and had had about enough of it. Harris told them they could follow him, if they liked; he was just going in, and then should turn round and come out again. They said it was very kind of him, and fell behind, and followed.

They picked up various other people who wanted to get it over, as they went along, until they had absorbed all the persons in the maze. People who had given up all hopes of ever getting either in or out, or of ever seeing their home and friends again, plucked up courage at the sight of Harris and his party, and joined the procession, blessing him. Harris said he should judge there must have been twenty people, following him, in all; and one woman with a baby, who had been there all the morning, insisted on taking his arm, for fear of losing him.

Harris kept on turning to the right, but it seemed a long way, and his cousin said he supposed it was a very big maze.

"Oh, one of the largest in Europe," said Harris.

"Yes, it must be," replied the cousin, "because we've walked a good two miles already."

Harris began to think it rather strange himself, but he held on until, at last, they passed the half of a penny bun on the ground that Harris' cousin swore he had noticed there seven minutes ago. Harris said: "Oh, impossible!" but the woman with the baby said, "Not at all," as she herself had taken it from the child, and thrown it down there, just before she met Harris. She also added that she wished she never had met Harris, and expressed an opinion that he was an impostor.

That made Harris mad, and he produced his map, and explained his theory.

"The map may be all right enough," said one of the party, "if you know whereabouts in it we are now."

Harris didn't know, and suggested that the best thing to do would be to go back to the entrance, and begin again. For the beginning again part of it there was not much enthusiasm; but with regard to the advisability of going back to the entrance there was complete unanimity, and so they turned, and trailed after Harris again, in the opposite direction. About ten minutes more passed, and then they found themselves in the centre.

Harris thought at first of pretending that that was what he had been aiming at; but the crowd looked dangerous, and he decided to treat it as an accident.

Anyhow, they had got something to start from then. They did know where they were, and the map was once more consulted, and the thing seemed simpler than ever, and off they started for the third time.

And three minutes later they were back in the centre again.

After that, they simply couldn't get anywhere else. Whatever way they turned brought them back to the middle. It became so regular at length, that some of the people stopped there, and waited for the others to take a walk round, and come back to them. Harris drew out his map again, after a while, but the sight of it only infuriated the mob, and they told him to go and curl his hair with it. Harris said that he couldn't help feeling that, to a certain extent, he had become unpopular.

They all got crazy at last, and sang out for the keeper, and the man came and climbed up the ladder outside, and shouted out directions to them. But all their heads were, by this time, in such a confused whirl that they were incapable of grasping anything, and so the man told them to stop where they were, and he would come to them. They huddled together, and waited; and he climbed down, and came in.

He was a young keeper, as luck would have it, and new to the business; and when he got in, he couldn't get to them, and then *he* got lost. They caught sight of him, every now and then, rushing about the other side of the hedge, and he would see them, and rush to get to them, and they would wait there for about five minutes, and then he would reappear again in exactly the same spot, and ask them where they had been.

They had to wait until one of the old keepers came back from his dinner before they got out.

Harris said he thought it was a very fine maze, so far as he was a judge; and we agreed that we would try to get George to go into it, on our way back.

CHAPTER VII

The river in its Sunday garb • Dress on the river • A chance
for the men • Absence of taste in Harris • George's blazer • A day
with the fashion-plate young lady • Mrs. Thomas's tomb • The man
who loves not graves and coffins and skulls • Harris mad • His views
on George and Banks and lemonade • He performs tricks

IT WAS WHILE PASSING THROUGH MOULSEY LOCK THAT HARRIS TOLD
me about his maze experience. It took us some time to pass through,
as we were the only boat, and it is a big lock. I don't think I ever
remember to have seen Moulsey Lock, before, with only one boat in
it. It is, I suppose, Boulter's not even excepted, the busiest lock on
the river.

I have stood and watched it, sometimes, when you could not see
any water at all, but only a brilliant tangle of bright blazers, and gay
caps, and saucy hats, and many-coloured parasols, and silken rugs,
and cloaks, and streaming ribbons, and dainty whites; when looking
down into the lock from the quay, you might fancy it was a huge box
into which flowers of every hue and shade had been thrown pell-mell,
and lay piled up in a rainbow heap, that covered every corner.

On a fine Sunday it presents this appearance nearly all day long,
while, up the stream, and down the stream, lie, waiting their turn,
outside the gates, long lines of still more boats; and boats are drawing near and passing away, so that the sunny river, from the Palace
up to Hampton Church, is dotted and decked with yellow, and blue,
and orange, and white, and red, and pink. All the inhabitants of

Hampton and Moulsey dress themselves up in boating costume, and come and mouch round the lock with their dogs, and flirt, and smoke, and watch the boats; and, altogether, what with the caps and jackets of the men, the pretty coloured dresses of the women, the excited dogs, the moving boats, the white sails, the pleasant landscape, and the sparkling water, it is one of the gayest sights I know of near this dull old London town.

The river affords a good opportunity for dress. For once in a way, we men are able to show *our* taste in colours, and I think we come out very natty, if you ask me. I always like a little red in my things—red and black. You know my hair is a sort of golden brown, rather a pretty shade I've been told, and a dark red matches it beautifully; and then I always think a light-blue necktie goes so well with it, and a pair of those Russian-leather shoes and a red silk handkerchief round the waist—a handkerchief looks so much better than a belt.

Harris always keeps to shades or mixtures of orange or yellow, but I don't think he is at all wise in this. His complexion is too dark for yellows. Yellows don't suit him: there can be no question about it. I want him to take to blue as a background, with white or cream for relief; but, there! the less taste a person has in dress, the more obstinate he always seems to be. It is a great pity, because he will never be a success as it is, while there are one or two colours in which he might not really look so bad, with his hat on.

George has bought some new things for this trip, and I'm rather vexed about them. The blazer is loud. I should not like George to know that I thought so, but there really is no other word for it. He brought it home and showed it to us on Thursday evening. We asked him what colour he called it, and he said he didn't know. He didn't think there was a name for the colour. The man had told him it was an Oriental design. George put it on, and asked us what we thought of it. Harris said that, as an object to hang over a flower-bed in early spring to frighten the birds away, he should respect it; but that, considered as an article of dress for any human being, except a Margate nigger, it made him ill. George got quite huffy; but, as Harris said, if he didn't want his opinion, why did he ask for it?

What troubles Harris and myself, with regard to it, is that we are afraid it will attract attention to the boat.

Girls, also, don't look half bad in a boat, if prettily dressed. Nothing is more fetching, to my thinking, than a tasteful boating costume. But a "boating costume," it would be as well if all ladies would understand, ought to be a costume that can be worn in a boat, and not merely under a glass-case. It utterly spoils an excursion if you have folk in the boat who are thinking all the time a good deal more of their dress than of the trip. It was my misfortune once to go for a water picnic with two ladies of this kind. We did have a lively time!

They were both beautifully got up—all lace and silky stuff, and flowers, and ribbons, and dainty shoes, and light gloves. But they were dressed for a photographic studio, not for a river picnic. They were the "boating costumes" of a French fashion-plate. It was ridiculous, fooling about in them anywhere near real earth, air, and water.

The first thing was that they thought the boat was not clean. We dusted all the seats for them, and then assured them that it was, but they didn't believe us. One of them rubbed the cushion with the fore-finger of her glove, and showed the result to the other, and they both sighed, and sat down, with the air of early Christian martyrs trying to make themselves comfortable up against the stake. You are liable to occasionally splash a little when sculling, and it appeared that a drop of water ruined those costumes. The mark never came out, and a stain was left on the dress forever.

I was stroke. I did my best. I feathered some two feet high, and I paused at the end of each stroke to let the blades drip before return-ing them, and I picked out a smooth bit of water to drop them into again each time. (Bow said, after a while, that he did not feel himself a sufficiently accomplished oarsman to pull with me, but that he would sit still, if I would allow him, and study my stroke. He said it interested him.) But, notwithstanding all this, and try as I would,

I could not help an occasional flicker of water from going over those dresses.

The girls did not complain, but they huddled up close together, and set their lips firm, and everytime a drop touched them, they visibly shrank and shuddered. It was a noble sight to see them suffering thus in silence, but it unnerved me altogether. I am too sensitive. I got wild and fitful in my rowing, and splashed more and more, the harder I tried not to.

I gave it up at last; I said I'd row bow. Bow thought the arrangement would be better too, and we changed places. The ladies gave an involuntary sigh of relief when they saw me go, and quite brightened up for a moment. Poor girls! They had better have put up with me. The man they had got now was a jolly, light-hearted, thick-headed sort of a chap, with about as much sensitiveness in him as there might be in a Newfoundland puppy. You might look daggers at him for an hour and he would not notice it, and it would not trouble him if he did. He set a good, rollicking, dashing stroke that sent the spray playing all over the boat like a fountain, and made the whole crowd sit up straight in no time. When he spread more than a pint of water over one of those dresses, he would give a pleasant little laugh, and say:

"I beg your pardon, I'm sure"; and offer them his handkerchief to wipe it off with.

"Oh, it's of no consequence," the poor girls would murmur in reply, and covertly draw rugs and coats over themselves, and try and protect themselves with their lace parasols.

At lunch they had a very bad time of it. People wanted them to sit on the grass, and the grass was dusty; and the tree-trunks, against which they were invited to lean, did not appear to have been brushed for weeks; so they spread their handkerchiefs on the ground and sat on those, bolt upright. Somebody, in walking about with a plate of beef-steak pie, tripped up over a root, and sent the pie flying. None of it went over them, fortunately, but the accident suggested a fresh danger to them, and agitated them; and, whenever anybody moved about after that, with anything in his hand that could fall and make a mess, they watched that person with growing anxiety until he sat down again.

"Now then, you girls," said our friend Bow to them, cheerily, after it was all over, "come along, you've got to wash up!"

They didn't understand him at first. When they grasped the idea, they said they feared they did not know how to wash up.

"Oh, I'll soon show you," he cried; "it's rare fun! You lie down on your—I mean you lean over the bank, you know, and sloush the things about in the water."

The elder sister said that she was afraid that they hadn't got on dresses suited to the work.

"Oh, they'll be all right," said he light-heartedly; "tuck 'em up."

And he made them do it, too. He told them that that sort of thing was half the fun of a picnic. They said it was very interesting.

Now I come to think it over, was that young man as dense-headed as we thought? Or was he—no, impossible! There was such a simple, child-like expression about him!

Harris wanted to get out at Hampton Church, to go and see Mrs. Thomas' tomb.

"Who is Mrs. Thomas?" I asked.

"How should I know?" replied Harris. "She's a lady that's got a funny tomb, and I want to see it."

I objected. I don't know whether it is that I am built wrong, but I never did seem to hanker after tombstones myself. I know that the proper thing to do, when you get to a village or town, is to rush off to the churchyard and enjoy the graves; but it is a recreation that I always deny myself. I take no interest in creeping round dim and chilly churches behind wheezy old men, and reading epitaphs. Not even the sight of a bit of cracked brass let into a stone affords me what I call real happiness.

I shock respectable sextons by the imperturbability I am able to assume before exciting inscriptions, and by my lack of enthusiasm for the local family history, while my ill-concealed anxiety to get outside wounds their feelings.

One golden morning of a sunny day, I leant against the low stone wall that guarded a little village church, and I smoked, and drank in deep, calm gladness from the sweet, restful scene—the grey old church with its clustering ivy and its quaint carved wooden porch, the white lane winding down the hill between tall rows of elms, the thatched-roof cottages peeping above their trim-kept hedges, the silver river in the hollow, the wooded hills beyond!

It was a lovely landscape. It was idyllic, poetical, and it inspired me. I felt good and noble. I felt I didn't want to be sinful and wicked anymore. I would come and live here, and never do any more wrong, and lead a blameless, beautiful life, and have silver hair when I got old, and all that sort of thing.

In that moment I forgave all my friends and relations for their wickedness and cussedness, and I blessed them. They did not know that I blessed them. They went their abandoned way all unconscious of what I, far away in that peaceful village, was doing for them; but I did it, and I wished that I could let them know that I had done it, because I wanted to make them happy. I was going on thinking away all these grand, tender thoughts, when my reverie was broken in upon by a shrill piping voice crying out:

"All right, sur, I'm a-coming, I'm a-coming. It's all right, sur; don't you be in a hurry."

I looked up, and saw an old bald-headed man hobbling across the churchyard towards me, carrying a huge bunch of keys in his hand that shook and jingled at every step.

I motioned him away with silent dignity, but he still advanced, screeching out the while:

"I'm a-coming, sur, I'm a-coming. I'm a little lame. I ain't as spry as I used to be. This way, sur."

"Go away, you miserable old man," I said.

"I've come as soon as I could, sur," he replied. "My missis never see you till just this minute. You follow me, sur"

"Go away," I repeated; "leave me before I get over the wall, and slay you."

He seemed surprised.

"Don't you want to see the tombs?" he said.

"No," I answered, "I don't. I want to stop here, leaning up against this gritty old wall. Go away, and don't disturb me. I am chock full of beautiful and noble thoughts, and I want to stop like it, because it feels nice and good. Don't you come fooling about, making me mad, chivying away all my better feelings with this silly tombstone nonsense of yours. Go away, and get somebody to bury you cheap, and I'll pay half the expense."

He was bewildered for a moment. He rubbed his eyes, and looked hard at me. I seemed human enough on the outside: he couldn't make it out.

He said:

"Yuise a stranger in these parts? You don't live here?"

"No," I said, "I don't. *You* wouldn't if *I* did."

"Well then," he said, "you want to see the tombs— graves—folks been buried, you know—coffins!"

"You are an untruther," I replied, getting roused; "I do not want to see tombs—not your tombs. Why should I? We have graves of our own, our family has. Why my Uncle Podger has a tomb in Kensal Green Cemetery, that is the pride of all that country-side; and my grandfather's vault at Bow is capable of accommodating eight visitors, while my great-aunt Susan has a brick grave in Finchley Churchyard, with a headstone with a coffee-pot sort of thing in bas-relief upon it, and a six-inch best white stone coping all the way round, that cost pounds. When I want graves, it is to those places that I go and revel. I do not want other folk's. When you yourself are buried, I will come and see yours. That is all that I can do for you."

He burst into tears. He said that one of the tombs had a bit of stone upon the top of it that had been said by some to be probably part of the remains of the figure of a man, and that another had some words, carved upon it, that nobody had ever been able to decipher.

I still remained obdurate, and, in broken-hearted tones, he said:

"Well, won't you come and see the memorial window?"

I would not even see that, so he fired his last shot. He drew near, and whispered hoarsely:

"I've got a couple of skulls down in the crypt," he said; "come and see those. Oh, do come and see the skulls! You are a young man out for a holiday, and you want to enjoy yourself. Come and see the skulls!"

Then I turned and fled, and as I sped I heard him calling to me: "Oh, come and see the skulls; come back and see the skulls!"

Harris, however, revels in tombs, and graves, and epitaphs, and monumental inscriptions, and the thought of not seeing Mrs. Thomas's grave made him crazy. He said he had looked forward to seeing Mrs. Thomas' grave from the first moment that the trip was proposed—said he wouldn't have joined if it hadn't been for the idea of seeing Mrs. Thomas' tomb.

I reminded him of George, and how we had to get the boat up to Shepperton by five o'clock to meet him, and then he went for George. Why was George to fool about all day, and leave us to lug this lumbering old top-heavy barge up and down the river by ourselves to meet him? Why couldn't George come and do some work? Why couldn't he have got the day off, and come down with us? Bank be blowed! What good was he at the bank?

"I never see him doing any work there," continued Harris, "whenever I go in. He sits behind a bit of glass all day, trying to look as if he was doing something. What's the good of a man behind a bit of glass? I have to work for my living. Why can't he work. What use is he there, and what's the good of their banks? They take your money, and then, when you draw a cheque, they send it back smeared all over with 'No effects,' 'Refer to drawer.' What's the good of that? That's the sort of trick they served me twice last week. I'm not going to stand it much longer. I shall withdraw my account. If he was here, we could go and see that tomb. I don't believe he's at the bank at all. He's larking about somewhere, that's what he's doing, leaving us to do all the work. I'm going to get out, and have a drink."

I pointed out to him that we were miles away from a pub; and then he went on about the river, and what was the good of the river, and was everyone who came on the river to die of thirst?

It is always best to let Harris have his head when he gets like this. Then he pumps himself out, and is quiet afterwards.

I reminded him that there was concentrated lemonade in the hamper, and a gallon-jar of water in the nose of the boat, and that the two only wanted mixing to make a cool and refreshing beverage.

Then he flew off about lemonade, and "such-like Sunday-school slops," as he termed them, ginger-beer, raspberry syrup, &c., &c. He said they all produced dyspepsia, and ruined body and soul alike, and were the cause of half the crime in England.

He said he must drink something, however, and climbed upon the seat, and leant over to get the bottle. It was right at the bottom of the hamper, and seemed difficult to find, and he had to lean over farther and farther, and, in trying to steer at the same time, from a topsy-turvy point of view, he pulled the wrong line, and sent the boat into the bank, and the shock upset him, and he dived down right into the hamper, and stood there on his head, holding on to the sides of the boat like grim death, his legs sticking up into the air. He dared not move for fear of going over, and had to stay there till I could get hold of his legs, and haul him back, and that made him madder than ever.

CHAPTER VIII

Blackmailing • The proper course to pursue • Selfish boorishness
of river-side landowner • "Notice" boards • Unchristianlike feelings
of Harris • How Harris sings a comic song • A high-class
party • Shameful conduct of two abandoned young men • Some
useless information • George buys a banjo

WE STOPPED UNDER THE WILLOWS BY KEMPTON PARK, AND LUNCHED.
It is a pretty little spot there: a pleasant grass plateau, running along
by the water's edge, and overhung by willows. We had just commenced the third course—the bread and jam—when a gentleman
in shirt sleeves and a short pipe came along, and wanted to know if
we knew that we were trespassing. We said we hadn't given the matter sufficient consideration as yet to enable us to arrive at a definite
conclusion on that point, but that, if he assured us on his word as a
gentleman that we *were* trespassing, we would, without further hesita-
tion, believe it.

He gave us the required assurance, and we thanked him, but he
still hung about, and seemed to be dissatisfied, so we asked him if
there was anything further that we could do for him, and Harris, who
is of a chummy disposition, offered him a bit of bread and jam.

I fancy he must have belonged to some society sworn to abstain
from bread and jam; for he declined it quite gruffly, as if he were
vexed at being tempted with it, and he added that it was his duty to
turn us off.

Harris said that if it was a duty it ought to be done, and asked the man what was his idea with regard to the best means for accomplishing it. Harris is what you would call a well-made man of about number one size, and looks hard and bony, and the man measured him up and down, and said he would go and consult his master, and then come back and chuck us both into the river.

Of course, we never saw him anymore, and, of course, all he really wanted was a shilling. There are a certain number of riverside roughs who make quite an income during the summer, by slouching about the banks and blackmailing weak-minded noodles in this way. They represent themselves as sent by the proprietor. The proper course to pursue is to offer your name and address, and leave the owner, if he really has anything to do with the matter, to summon you, and prove what damage you have done to his land by sitting down on a bit of it. But the majority of people are so intensely lazy and timid, that they prefer to encourage the imposition by giving in to it rather than put an end to it by the exertion of a little firmness.

Where it is really the owners that are to blame, they ought to be shown up. The selfishness of the riparian proprietor grows with every year. If these men had their way they would close the river Thames altogether. They actually do this along the minor tributary streams and in the backwaters. They drive posts into the bed of the stream, and draw chains across from bank to bank, and nail huge notice-boards on every tree. The sight of those notice-boards rouses every evil instinct in my nature. I feel I want to tear each one down, and hammer it over the head of the man who put it up, until I have killed him, and then I would bury him, and put the board up over the grave as a tombstone.

I mentioned these feelings of mine to Harris, and he said he had them worse than that. He said he not only felt he wanted to kill the man who caused the board to be put up, but that he should like to slaughter the whole of his family and all his friends and relations, and then burn down his house. This seemed to me to be going too far, and I said so to Harris; but he answered:

"Not a bit of it. Serve 'em all jolly well right, and I'd go and sing comic songs on the ruins."

I was vexed to hear Harris go on in this blood-thirsty strain. We never ought to allow our instincts of justice to degenerate into mere vindictiveness. It was a long while before I could get Harris to take a more Christian view of the subject, but I succeeded at last, and he promised me that he would spare the friends and relations at all events, and would not sing comic songs on the ruins.

You have never heard Harris sing a comic song, or you would understand the service I had rendered to mankind. It is one of Harris's fixed ideas that he *can* sing a comic song; the fixed idea, on the contrary, among those of Harris's friends who have heard him try, is that he *can't*, and never will be able to, and that he ought not to be allowed to try.

When Harris is at a party, and is asked to sing, he replies: "Well, I can only sing a *comic* song, you know"; and he says it in a tone that implies that his singing of *that*, however, is a thing that you ought to hear once, and then die.

"Oh, that *is* nice," says the hostess. "Do sing one, Mr. Harris"; and Harris gets up, and makes for the piano, with the beaming cheeriness of a generous-minded man who is just about to give somebody something.

"Now, silence, please, everybody," says the hostess, turning round; "Mr. Harris is going to sing a comic song!"

"Oh, how jolly!" they murmur; and they hurry in from the conservatory, and come up from the stairs, and go and fetch each other from all over the house, and crowd into the drawing room, and sit round, all smirking in anticipation.

Then Harris begins.

Well, you don't look for much of a voice in a comic song. You don't expect correct phrasing or vocalization. You don't mind if a man does find out, when in the middle of a note, that he is too high, and comes down with a jerk. You don't bother about time. You don't mind a man being two bars in front' of the accompaniment, and easing up in the middle of a line to argue it out with the pianist, and then starting the verse afresh. But you do expect the words.

You don't expect a man to never remember more than the first three lines of the first verse, and to keep on repeating these until it is time to begin the chorus. You don't expect a man to break off in the middle of a line, and snigger, and say, it's very funny, but he's blest if he can think of the rest of it, and then try and make it up for himself, and, afterwards, suddenly recollect it, when he has got to an entirely different part of the song, and break off without a word of warning, to go back and let you have it then and there. You don't—well, I will just give you an idea of Harris' comic singing, and then you can judge of it for yourself.

HARRIS (*standing up in front of piano and addressing the expectant mob*): "I'm afraid it's a very old thing, you know. I expect you all know it, you know. But it's the only thing I know. It's the Judge's song out of *Pinafore*—no, I don't mean *Pinafore*—I mean—you know what I mean— the other thing, you know. You must all join in the chorus, you know."

Murmurs of delight and anxiety to join in the chorus. Brilliant performance of prelude to the Judge's song in "Trial by Jury" by nervous pianist. Moment arrives for Harris to join in. Harris takes no notice of it. Nervous pianist commences prelude over again, and Harris, commencing singing at the same time, dashes off the first two lines of the First Lord's song out of "Pinafore." Nervous pianist tries to push on with prelude, gives it up, and tries to follow Harris with accompaniment to Judge's song out of "Trial by Jury," finds that doesn't answer, and tries to recollect what he is doing, and where he is, feels his mind giving way, and stops short.

HARRIS (*with kindly encouragement*): "It's all right. You're doing it very well, indeed—go on."

NERVOUS PIANIST: "I'm afraid there's a mistake somewhere. What are you singing?"

HARRIS (*promptly*): "Why the Judge's song out of *Trial by Jury*. Don't you know it?"

SOME FRIEND OF HARRIS' (*from the back of the room*): "No, you're not, you chuckle-head, you're singing the Admiral's song from *Pinafore*."

Long argument between Harris and Harris' friend as to what Harris is really singing. Friend finally suggests that it does't matter what Harris is singing so long as Harris gets on and sings it, and Harris, with an evident sense of injustice rankling inside him, requests pianist to begin again. Pianist, thereupon, starts prelude to the Admiral's song, and Harris, seizing what he considers to be a favourable opening in the music, begins.

HARRIS:

"When I was young and called to the Bar."

General roar of laughter, taken by Harris as a compliment. Pianist, thinking of his wife and family, gives up the unequal contest and retires; his place being taken by a stronger-nerved man.

THE NEW PIANIST (*cheerily*): "Now then, old man, you start off, and I'll follow. We won't bother about any prelude."

HARRIS (*upon whom the explanation of matters has slowly dawned—laughing*): "By Jove! I beg your pardon. Of course—I've been mixing up the two songs. It was Jenkins confused me, you know. Now then."

Singing; his voice appearing to come from the cellar, and suggesting the first low warnings of an approaching earthquake.

"When I was young I served a term
As office-boy to an attorney's firm."

(Aside to pianist): "It is too low, old man; we'll have that over again, if you don't mind."

Sings first two lines over again, in a high falsetto this time. Great surprise on the part of the audience. Nervous old lady near the fire begins to cry, and has to be led out.

HARRIS (*continuing*):

"I swept the windows and I swept the door,
And I——"

"No—no, I cleaned the windows of the big front door. And I polished up the floor—no, dash it—I beg your pardon—funny thing, I can't think of that line. And I—and I—Oh, well, we'll get on to the chorus, and chance it" (*sings*):

"And I diddle-diddle-diddle-diddle-diddle-diddle-de,
Till now I am ruler of the Queen's navee."

"Now then, chorus—it's the last two lines repeated, you know."

GENERAL CHORUS:

"And he diddle-diddle-diddle-diddle-diddle-diddle-dēē'd,
Till now he is ruler of the Queen's navēē."

And Harris never sees what an ass he is making of himself, and how he is annoying a lot of people who never did him any harm. He honestly imagines that he has given them a treat, and says he will sing another comic song after supper.

Speaking of comic songs and parties, reminds me of a rather curious incident at which I once assisted; which, as it throws much light upon the inner mental working of human nature in general, ought, I think, to be recorded in these pages.

We were a fashionable and highly cultured party. We had on our best clothes, and we talked pretty, and were very happy—all except two young fellows, students, just returned from Germany, commonplace young men, who seemed restless and uncomfortable, as if they found the proceedings slow. The truth was, we were too clever for them. Our brilliant but polished conversation, and our high-class tastes, were beyond them. They were out of place, among us. They never ought to have been there at all. Everybody agreed upon that, later on.

We played *morceaux* from the old German masters. We discussed philosophy and ethics. We flirted with graceful dignity. We were even humorous—in a high-class way.

Somebody recited a French poem after supper, and we said it was beautiful; and then a lady sang a sentimental ballad in Spanish, and it made one or two of us weep—it was so pathetic.

And then those two young men got up, and asked us if we had ever heard Herr Slossenn Boschen (who had just arrived, and was then down in the supper room) sing his great German comic song.

None of us had heard it, that we could remember.

The young men said it was the funniest song that had ever been written, and that, if we liked, they would get Herr Slossenn Boschen, whom they knew very well, to sing it. They said it was so funny that, when Herr Slossenn Boschen had sung it once before the German Emperor, he (the German Emperor) had had to be carried off to bed.

They said nobody could sing it like Herr Slossenn Boschen; he was so intensely serious all through it that you might fancy he was reciting a tragedy, and that, of course, made it all the funnier. They said he never once suggested by his tone or manner that he was singing anything funny—that would spoil it. It was his air of seriousness, almost of pathos, that made it so irresistibly amusing.

We said we yearned to hear it, that we wanted a good laugh; and they went downstairs, and fetched Herr Slossenn Boschen.

He appeared to be quite pleased to sing it, for he came up at once, and sat down to the piano without another word.

"Oh, it will amuse you. You will laugh," whispered the two young men, as they passed through the room, and took up an unobtrusive position behind the Professor's back.

Herr Slossenn Boschen accompanied himself. The prelude did not suggest a comic song exactly. It was a weird, soulful air. It quite made one's flesh creep; but we murmured to one another that it was the German method, and prepared to enjoy it.

I don't understand German myself. I learned it at school, but forgot every word of it two years after I had left, and have felt much better ever since. Still, I did not want the people there to guess my ignorance: so I hit upon what I thought to be rather a good idea. I kept my eye on the two young students, and followed them. When they tittered, I tittered; when they roared, I roared; and I also threw in a little snigger all by myself now and then, as if I had seen a bit of humour that had escaped the others. I considered this particularly artful on my part.

I noticed, as the song progressed, that a good many other people seemed to have their eye fixed on the two young men, as well as myself. These other people also tittered when the young men tittered, and roared when the young men roared; and, as the two young men tittered and roared and exploded with laughter pretty continuously all through the song, it went exceedingly well.

And yet that German Professor did not seem happy. At first, when we began to laugh the expression of his face was one of intense surprise, as if laughter were the very last thing he had expected to be greeted with. We thought this very funny: we said his earnest manner was half the humour. The slightest hint on his part that he knew how funny he was would have completely ruined it all. As we continued to laugh, his surprise gave way to an air of annoyance and indignation, and he scowled fiercely round upon us all (except upon the two young men who, being behind him, he could not see). That sent us into convulsions. We told each other that it would be the death of us, this thing. The words alone, we said, were enough to send us into fits, but added to his mock seriousness—oh, it was too much!

In the last verse, he surpassed himself. He glowered round upon us with a look of such concentrated ferocity that, but for our being forewarned as to the German method of comic singing, we should have been nervous; and he threw such a wailing note of agony into the weird music that, if we had not known it was a funny song, we might have wept.

He finished amid a perfect shriek of laughter. We said it was the funniest thing we had ever heard in all our lives. We said how strange it was that, in the face of things like these, there should be a popular notion that the Germans hadn't any sense of humour. And we asked the Professor why he didn't translate the song into English, so that the common people could understand it, and hear what a real comic song was like.

Then Herr Slossenn Boschen got up, and went on awful. He swore at us in German (which I should judge to be a singularly effective language for that purpose), and he danced, and shook his fists, and called us all the English he knew. He said he had never been so insulted in all his life.

It appeared that the song was not a comic song at all. It was about a young girl who lived in the Hartz Mountains, and who had given up her life to save her lover's soul; and he died, and met her spirit in the air; and then, in the last verse, he jilted her spirit, and went off with another spirit—I'm not quite sure of the details, but it was something very sad, I know. Herr Boschen said he had sung it once before the German Emperor, and he (the German Emperor) had sobbed like a little child. He (Herr Boschen) said it was generally acknowledged to be one of the most tragic and pathetic songs in the German language.

It was a trying situation for us—very trying. There seemed to be no answer. We looked around for the two young men who had done this thing, but they had left the house in an unostentatious manner immediately after the end of the song.

That was the end of that party. I never saw a party break up so quietly, and with so little fuss. We never said goodnight even to one another. We came downstairs one at a time, walking softly, and keeping the shady side. We asked the servant for our hats and coats in whispers, and opened the door for ourselves, and slipped out, and got round the corner quickly, avoiding each other as much as possible.

I have never taken much interest in German songs since then.

We reached Sunbury Lock at half-past three. The river is sweetly pretty just there before you come to the gates, and the backwater is charming; but don't attempt to row up it.

I tried to do so once. I was sculling, and asked the fellows who were steering if they thought it could be done, and they said, oh, yes, they thought so, if I pulled hard. We were just under the little foot-bridge that crosses it between the two weirs, when they said this, and I bent down over the sculls, and set myself up, and pulled.

I pulled splendidly. I got well into a steady rhythmical swing. I put my arms, and my legs, and my back into it. I set myself a good, quick, dashing stroke, and worked in really grand style. My two friends said it was a pleasure to watch me. At the end of five minutes, I thought we ought to be pretty near the weir, and I looked up. We were under the bridge, in exactly the same spot that we were when I began, and there were those two idiots, injuring themselves by violent laughing. I had been grinding away like mad to keep that boat stuck still under that bridge. I let other people pull up backwaters against strong streams now.

We sculled up to Walton, a rather large place for a riverside town. As with all riverside places, only the tiniest corner of it comes down to the water, so that from the boat you might fancy it was a village of some half-dozen houses, all told. Windsor and Abingdon are the only towns between London and Oxford that you can really see anything of from the stream. All the others hide round corners, and merely peep at the river down one street: my thanks to them for being so considerate, and leaving the riverbanks to woods and fields and waterworks.

Even Reading, though it does its best to spoil and sully and make hideous as much of the river as it can reach, is good-natured enough to keep its ugly face a good deal out of sight.

Cæsar, of course, had a little place at Walton—a camp, or an entrenchment, or something of that sort. Cæsar was a regular upriver man. Also Queen Elizabeth, she was there, too. You can never get away from that woman, go where you will. Cromwell and Bradshaw (not the guide man, but the King Charles' head man) likewise sojourned here. They must have been quite a pleasant little party, altogether.

There is an iron "scold's bridle" in Walton Church. They used these things in ancient days for curbing women's tongues. They have given up the attempt now. I suppose iron was getting scarce, and nothing else would be strong enough.

There are also tombs of note in the church, and I was afraid I should never get Harris past them; but he didn't seem to think of them, and we went on. Above the bridge the river winds tremendously. This makes it look picturesque; but it irritates you from a towing or sculling point of view, and causes argument between the man who is pulling and the man who is steering.

You pass Oatlands Park on the right bank here. It is a famous old place. Henry VIII stole it from someone or the other, I forget whom now, and lived in it. There is a grotto in the park which you can see for a fee, and which is supposed to be very wonderful; but I cannot see much in it myself. The late Duchess of York, who lived at Oatlands, was very fond of dogs, and kept an immense number. She had a special graveyard made, in which to bury them when they died, and there they lie, about fifty of them, with a tombstone over each, and an epitaph inscribed thereon.

Well, I dare say they deserve it quite as much as the average Christian does.

At "Corway Stakes"—the first bend above Walton Bridge—was fought a battle between Cæsar and Cassivelaunus. Cassivelaunus had prepared the river for Cæsar, by planting it full of stakes (and had, no doubt, put up a notice-board). But Cæsar crossed in spite of this. You couldn't choke Cæsar off that river. He is the sort of man we want round the backwaters now.

Halliford and Shepperton are both pretty little spots where they touch the river; but there is nothing remarkable about either of them. There is a tomb in Shepperton churchyard, however, with a poem on it, and I was nervous lest Harris should want to get out and fool round it. I saw him fix a longing eye on the landing-stage as we drew near it, so I managed, by an adroit movement, to jerk his cap into the water, and in the excitement of recovering that, and his indignation at my clumsiness, he forgot all about his beloved graves.

At Weybridge, the Wey (a pretty little stream, navigable for small boats up to Guildford, and one which I have always been making up my mind to explore, and never have), the Bourne, and the Basingstoke Canal all enter the Thames together. The lock is just opposite the town, and the first thing that we saw, when we came in view of it, was George's blazer on one of the lock gates, closer inspection showing that George was inside it.

Montmorency set up a furious barking, I shrieked, Harris roared; George waved his hat, and yelled back. The lock-keeper rushed out with a drag, under the impression that somebody had fallen into the lock, and appeared annoyed at finding that no one had.

George had rather a curious oilskin-covered parcel in his hand. It was round and flat at one end, with a long straight handle sticking out of it.

"What's that?" said Harris, "a frying-pan?"

"No," said George, with a strange, wild look glittering in his eyes; "they are all the rage this season; everybody has got them up the river. It's a banjo."

"I never knew you played the banjo!" cried Harris and I, in one breath.

"Not exactly," replied George: "but it's very easy, they tell me; and I've got the instruction book!"

Chapter ix

George is introduced to work • Heathenish instincts of
towlines • Ungrateful conduct of a double-sculling skiff • Towers
and towed • A use discovered for lovers • Strange disappearance
of an elderly lady • Much haste, less speed • Being towed by
girls: exciting sensation • The missing lock or the haunted
river • Music • Saved!

We made George work, now we had got him. He did not want
to work, of course; that goes without saying. He had had a hard time
in the City, so he explained. Harris, who is callous in his nature, and
not prone to pity, said:

"Ah! And now you are going to have a hard time on the river for a
change; change is good for everyone. Out you get!"

He could not in conscience—not even George's conscience—
object, though he did suggest that, perhaps, it would be better for
him to stop in the boat, and get tea ready, while Harris and I towed,
because getting tea was such a worrying work, and Harris and I
looked tired. The only reply we made to this, however, was to pass
him over the towline, and he took it, and stepped out.

There is something very strange and unaccountable about a towline. You roll it up with as much patience and care as you would take
to fold up a new pair of trousers, and five minutes afterwards, when
you pick it up, it is one ghastly, soul-revolting tangle.

I do not wish to be insulting, but I firmly believe that if you took
an average towline, and stretched it out straight across the middle of
a field, and then turned your back on it for thirty seconds, that, when

you looked round again, you would find that it had got itself alto-gether in a heap in the middle of the field, and had twisted itself up, and tied itself into knots, and lost its two ends, and become all loops; and it would take a good half-hour, sitting down there on the grass and swearing all the while, to disentangle it again.

That is my opinion of towlines in general. Of course, there may be hon-ourable exceptions; I do not say that there are not. There may be towlines that are a credit to their profession—conscientious, respectable towlines—towlines that do not imagine they are crochet-work, and try to knit themselves up into antimacassars the instant they are left to themselves. I say there *may* be such towlines; I sincerely hope there are. But I have not met with them.

This towline I had taken in myself just before we had got to the lock. I would not let Harris touch it, because he is careless. I had looped it round slowly and cautiously, and tied it up in the middle, and folded it in two, and laid it down gently at the bottom of the boat. Harris had lifted it up scientifically, and had put it into George's hand. George had taken it firmly, and held it away from him, and had begun to unravel it as if he were taking the swaddling clothes off a newborn infant; and, before he had unwound a dozen yards, the thing was more like a badly made doormat than anything else.

It is always the same, and the same sort of thing always goes on in connection with it. The man on the bank, who is trying to disen-tangle it, thinks all the fault lies with the man who rolled it up; and when a man up the river thinks a thing, he says it.

"What have you been trying to do with it, make a fishing-net of it? You've made a nice mess you have; why couldn't you wind it up prop-erly, you silly dummy?" he grunts from time to time as he struggles wildly with it, and lays it out flat on the towpath, and runs round and round it, trying to find the end.

On the other hand, the man who wound it up thinks the whole cause of the muddle rests with the man who is trying to unwind it.

"It was all right when you took it!" he exclaims indignantly. "Why don't you think what you are doing? You go about things in such a slap-dash style. You'd get a scaffolding pole entangled *you* would!"

And they feel so angry with one another that they would like to hang each other with the thing. Ten minutes go by, and the first man gives a yell and goes mad, and dances on the rope, and tries to pull it straight by seizing hold of the first piece that comes to his hand and hauling at it. Of course, this only gets it into a tighter tangle than ever. Then the second man climbs out of the boat and comes to help him, and they get in each other's way, and hinder one another. They both get hold of the same bit of line, and pull at it in opposite directions, and wonder where it is caught. In the end, they do get it clear, and then turn round and find that the boat has drifted off, and is making straight for the weir.

This really happened once to my own knowledge. It was up by Boveney, one rather windy morning. We were pulling down stream, and, as we came round the bend, we noticed a couple of men on the bank. They were looking at each other with as bewildered and help-lessly miserable expression as I have ever witnessed on any human countenance before or since, and they held a long towline between them. It was clear that something had happened, so we eased up and asked them what was the matter.

"Why, our boat's gone off!" they replied in an indignant tone. "We just got out to disentangle the towline, and when we looked round, it was gone!"

And they seemed hurt at what they evidently regarded as a mean and ungrateful act on the part of the boat.

We found the truant for them half a mile further down, held by some rushes, and we brought it back to them. I bet they did not give that boat another chance for a week.

I shall never forget the picture of those two men walking up and down the bank with a towline, looking for their boat.

One sees a good many funny incidents up the river in connection with towing. One of the most common is the sight of a couple of tow-ers, walking briskly along, deep in an animated discussion, while the man in the boat, a hundred yards behind them, is vainly shrieking to them to stop, and making frantic signs of distress with a scull. Something has gone wrong; the rudder has come off, or the boat-hook has slipped overboard, or his hat has dropped into the water and is floating rapidly down stream. He calls to them to stop, quite gently and politely at first.

"Hi! Stop a minute, will you?" he shouts cheerily. "I've dropped my hat overboard."

Then: "Hi! Tom—Dick! Can't you hear?" not quite so affably this time.

Then: "Hi! Confound *you*, you dunder-headed idiots! Hi! Stop! Oh you—!"

After that he springs up, and dances about, and roars himself red in the face, and curses everything he knows. And the small boys on the bank stop and jeer at him, and pitch stones at him as he is pulled along past them, at the rate of four miles an hour, and can't get out.

Much of this sort of trouble would be saved if those who are towing would keep remembering that they *are* towing, and give a pretty frequent look round to see how their man is getting on. It is best to let one person tow. When two are doing it, they get chattering, and forget, and the boat itself, offering, as it does, but little resistance, is of no real service in reminding them of the fact.

As an example of how utterly oblivious a pair of towers can be to their work, George told us, later on in the evening, when we were discussing the subject after supper, of a very curious instance.

He and three other men, so he said, were sculling a very heavily laden boat up from Maidenhead one evening, and a little above Cookham lock they noticed a fellow and a girl, walking along the towpath, both deep in an apparently interesting and absorbing conversation. They were carrying a boat-hook between them, and attached to the boat-hook was a towline, which trailed behind them, its end in the water. No boat was near, no boat was in sight. There must have been a boat attached to that towline at some time or other, that was certain; but what had become of it, what ghastly fate had overtaken it, and those who had been left in it, was buried in mystery. Whatever the accident may have been, however, it had in no way disturbed the young lady and gentleman, who were towing. They had the boat-hook and they had the line, and that seemed to be all that they thought necessary to their work.

George was about to call out and wake them up, but, at that moment, a bright idea flashed across him, and he didn't. He got the hitcher instead, and reached over, and drew in the end of the towline; and they made a loop in it, and put it over their mast, and then they tidied up the sculls, and went and sat down in the stern, and lit their pipes.

And that young man and young woman towed those four hulking chaps and a heavy boat up to Marlow.

George said he never saw so much thoughtful sadness concentrated into one glance before, as when, at the lock, that young couple grasped the idea that, for the last two miles, they had been towing the wrong boat. George fancied that, if it had not been for the restraining influence of the sweet woman at his side, the young man might have given way to violent language.

The maiden was the first to recover from her surprise, and, when she did, she clasped her hands and said, wildly:

"Oh, Henry, then *where* is auntie?"

"Did they ever recover the old lady?" asked Harris.

George replied he did not know.

Another example of the dangerous want of sympathy between tower and towed was witnessed by George and myself once up near Walton. It was where the towpath shelves gently down into the water, and we were camping on the opposite bank, noticing things in general. By-and-by a small boat came in sight, towed through the water at a tremendous pace by a powerful barge horse, on which sat a very small boy. Scattered about the boat, in dreamy and reposeful attitudes, lay five fellows, the man who was steering having a particularly restful appearance.

"I should like to see him pull the wrong line," murmured George, as they passed. And at that precise moment the man did it, and the boat rushed up the bank with a noise like the ripping up of forty thousand linen sheets. Two men, a hamper, and three oars immediately left the boat on the larboard side, and reclined on the bank, and one and a half moments afterwards, two other men disembarked from the starboard, and sat down among boat-hooks and sails and

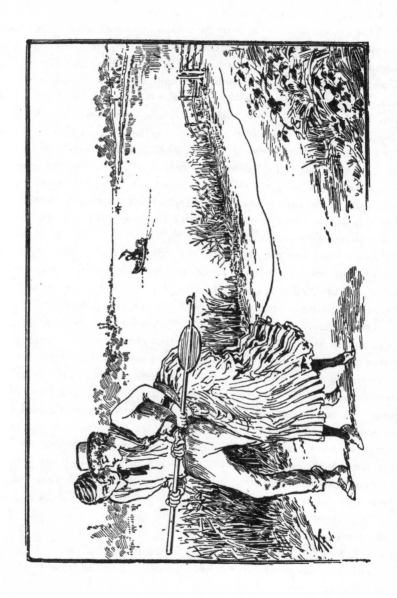

carpet-bags and bottles. The last man went on twenty yards further, and then got out on his head.

This seemed to sort of lighten the boat, and it went on much easier, the small boy shouting at the top of his voice, and urging his steed into a gallop. The fellows sat up and stared at one another. It was some seconds before they realised what had happened to them, but, when they did, they began to shout lustily for the boy to stop. He, however, was too much occupied with the horse to hear them, and we watched them flying after him, until the distance hid them from view.

I cannot say I was sorry at their mishap. Indeed, I only wish that all the young fools who have their boats towed in this fashion—and plenty do—could meet with similar misfortunes. Besides the risk they run themselves, they become a danger and an annoyance to every other boat they pass. Going at the pace they do, it is impossible for them to get out of anybody else's way, or for anybody else to get out of theirs. Their line gets hitched across your mast, and overturns you, or it catches somebody in the boat, and either throws them into the water, or cuts their face open. The best plan is to stand your ground, and be prepared to keep them off with the butt-end of a mast.

Of all experiences in connection with towing, the most exciting is being towed by girls. It is a sensation that nobody ought to miss. It takes three girls to tow always; two hold the rope, and the other one runs round and round and giggles. They generally begin by getting themselves tied up. They get the line round their legs, and have to sit down on the path and undo each other, and then they twist it round their necks, and are nearly strangled. They fix it straight, however, at last, and start off at a run, pulling the boat along at quite a danger-ous pace. At the end of a hundred yards they are naturally breathless, and suddenly stop, and all sit down on the grass and laugh, and your boat drifts out to mid-stream and turns round, before you know what has happened, or can get hold of a scull. Then they stand up, and are surprised.

"Oh, look!" they say; "he's gone right out into the middle."

They pull on pretty steadily for a bit, after this, and then it all at once occurs to one of them that she will pin up her frock, and they ease up for the purpose, and the boat runs aground.

You jump up and push it off, and you shout to them not to stop.

"Yes. What's the matter?" they shout back.

"Don't stop," you roar.

"Don't what?"

"Don't stop—go on—go on!"

"Go back, Emily, and see what it is they want," says one; and Emily comes back, and asks what it is.

"What do you want?" she says; "anything happened?"

"No," you reply, "it's all right; only go on, you know—don't stop."

"Why not?"

"Why, we can't steer, if you keep stopping. You must keep some way on the boat."

"Keep some what?"

"Some way—you must keep the boat moving."

"Oh, all right, I'll tell 'em. Are we doing it all right?"

"Oh, yes, very nicely, indeed, only don't stop."

"It doesn't seem difficult at all. I thought it was so hard."

"Oh, no, it's simple enough. You want to keep on steady at it, that's all."

"I see. Give me out my red shawl, it's under the cushion."

You find the shawl, and hand it out, and by this time another has come back and thinks she will have hers too, and they take Mary's on chance, and Mary does not want it, so they bring it back and have a pocket-comb instead. It is about twenty minutes before they get off again, and, at the next corner, they see a cow, and you have to leave the boat to chivy the cow out of their way.

There is never a dull moment in the boat while girls are towing it.

George got the line right after a while, and towed us steadily on to Penton Hook. There we discussed the important question of camping. We had decided to sleep on board that night, and we had either to lay up just about there, or go on past Staines. It seemed early to think about shutting up then, however, with the sun still in the heavens, and we settled to push straight on for Runnymead, three and a half miles further, a quiet wooded part of the river, and where there is good shelter.

We all wished, however, afterward that we had stopped at Penton Hook. Three or four miles up stream is a trifle, early in the morning, but it is a weary pull at the end of a long day. You take no interest in the scenery during these last few miles. You do not chat and laugh. Every half-mile you cover seems like two. You can hardly believe you are only where you are, and you are convinced that the map must be wrong; and, when you have trudged along for what seems to you at least ten miles, and still the lock is not in sight, you begin to seriously fear that somebody must have sneaked it, and run off with it.

I remember being terribly upset once up the river (in a figurative sense, I mean). I was out with a young lady—cousin on my mother's side—and we were pulling down to Goring. It was rather late, and we were anxious to get in—at least *she* was anxious to get in. It was half-past six when we reached Benson's lock, and dusk was drawing on, and she began to get excited then. She said she must be in to supper. I said it was a thing I felt I wanted to be in at, too; and I drew out a map I had with me to see exactly how far it was. I saw it was just a mile and a half to the next lock—Wallingford—and five on from there to Cleeve.

"Oh, it's all right!" I said. "We'll be through, the next lock before seven, and then there is only one more"; and I settled down and pulled steadily away.

We passed the bridge, and soon after that I asked if she saw the lock. She said no, she did not see any lock; and I said, "Oh!" and pulled on. Another five minutes went by, and then I asked her to look again.

"No," she said; "I can't see any signs of a lock."

"You—you are sure you know a lock, when you do see one?" I asked hesitatingly, not wishing to offend her.

The question did not offend her, however, and she suggested that I had better look for myself; so I laid down the sculls, and took a view. The river stretched out straight before us in the twilight for about a mile; not a ghost of a lock was to be seen.

"You don't think we have lost our way, do you?" asked my companion.

I did not see how that was possible; though, as I suggested, we might have somehow got into the weir stream, and be making for the falls.

This idea did not comfort her in the least, and she began to cry. She said we should both be drowned, and that it was a judgment on her for coming out with me.

It seemed an excessive punishment, I thought; but my cousin thought not, and hoped it would all soon be over.

I tried to reassure her, and to make light of the whole affair. I said that the fact evidently was that I was not rowing as fast as I fancied I was, but that we should soon reach the lock now; and I pulled on for another mile.

Then I began to get nervous myself. I looked again at the map. There was Wallingford lock, clearly marked, a mile and a half below Benson's. It was a good, reliable map; and, besides, I recollected the lock myself. I had been through it twice. Where were we? What had happened to us? I began to think it must be all a dream, and that I was really asleep in bed, and should wake up in a minute, and be told it was past ten.

I asked my cousin if she thought it could be a dream, and she replied that she was just about to ask me the same question; and then we both wondered if we were both asleep, and if so, who was the real one that was dreaming, and who was the one that was only a dream; it got quite interesting.

I still went on pulling, however, and still no lock came in sight, and the river grew more and more gloomy and mysterious under the gathering shadows of night, and things seemed to be getting weird and uncanny. I thought of hobgoblins and banshees, and will-o'-the-wisps, and those wicked girls who sit up all night on rocks, and lure people into whirlpools and things; and I wished I had been a better man, and knew more hymns; and in the middle of these reflections I heard the blessed strains of "He's got 'em on," played, badly, on a concertina, and knew that we were saved.

I do not admire the tones of a concertina, as a rule; but, oh! How beautiful the music seemed to us both then—far, far more beautiful than the voice of Orpheus or the lute of Apollo, or anything of that sort could have sounded. Heavenly melody, in our then state of mind, would only have still further harrowed us. A soul-moving harmony, correctly performed, we should have taken as a spirit-warning, and have given up all hope. But about the strains of "He's got 'em on," jerked spasmodically, and with involuntary variations, out of a wheezy accordion, there was something singularly human and reassuring.

The sweet sounds drew nearer, and soon the boat from which they were worked lay alongside us.

It contained a party of provincial 'Arrys and 'Arriets, out for a moonlight sail. (There was not any moon, but that was not their fault.) I never saw more attractive, lovable people in all my life. I hailed them, and asked if they could tell me the way to Wallingford lock; and I explained that I had been looking for it for the last two hours.

"Wallingford lock!" they answered. "Lor' love you, sir, that's been done away with for over a year. There ain't no Wallingford lock now, sir. You're close to Cleeve now. Blow me tight if 'ere ain't a gentleman been looking for Wallingford lock, Bill!"

I had never thought of that. I wanted to fall upon all their necks and bless them; but the stream was running too strong just there to allow of this, so I had to content myself with mere cold-sounding words of gratitude.

We thanked them over and over again, and we said it was a lovely night, and we wished them a pleasant trip, and, I think, I invited them all to come and spend a week with me, and my cousin said her mother would be so pleased to see them. And we sang the "Soldiers' Chorus" out of *Faust*, and got home in time for supper, after all.

CHAPTER X

Our first night • Under canvas • An appeal for help • Contrariness
of teakettles, how to overcome • Supper • How to feel
virtuous • Wanted! A comfortably appointed, well-drained desert
island, neighbourhood of South Pacific Ocean preferred • Funny
thing that happened to George's father • A restless night

HARRIS AND I BEGAN TO THINK THAT BELL WEIR LOCK MUST HAVE
been done away with after the same manner. George had towed us
up to Staines, and we had taken the boat from there, and it seemed
that we were dragging fifty tons after us, and were walking forty
miles. It was half-past seven when we were through, and we all got in,
and sculled up close to the left bank, looking out for a spot to haul
up in.

We had originally intended to go on to Magna Charta Island, a
sweetly pretty part of the river, where it winds through a soft, green
valley, and to camp in one of the many picturesque inlets to be
found round that tiny shore. But, somehow, we did not feel that we
yearned for the picturesque nearly so much now as we had earlier in
the day. A bit of water between a coal-barge and a gasworks would
have quite satisfied us for that night. We did not want scenery. We
wanted to have our supper and go to bed. However, we did pull up to
the point—"Picnic Point," it is called—and dropped into a very pleasant nook under a great elm tree, to the spreading roots of which we
fastened the boat.

Then we thought we were going to have supper (we had dispensed with tea, so as to save time), but George said no; that we had better get the canvas up first, before it got quite dark, and while we could see what we were doing. Then, he said, all our work would be done, and we could sit down to eat with an easy mind.

That canvas wanted more putting up than I think any of us had bargained for. It looked so simple in the abstract. You took five iron arches, like gigantic croquet hoops, and fitted them up over the boat, and then stretched the canvas over them, and fastened it down: it would take quite ten minutes, we thought.

That was an underestimate.

We took up the hoops, and began to drop them into the sockets placed for them. You would not imagine this to be dangerous work; but, looking back now, the wonder to me is that any of us are alive to tell the tale. They were not hoops, they were demons. First they would not fit into their sockets at all, and we had to jump on them, and kick them, and hammer at them with the boat-hook; and, when they were in, it turned out that they were the wrong hoops for those particular sockets, and they had to come out again.

But they would not come out, until two of us had gone and struggled with them for five minutes, when they would jump up suddenly, and try and throw us into the water and drown us. They had hinges in the middle, and, when we were not looking, they nipped us with these hinges in delicate parts of the body; and, while we were wrestling with one side of the hoop, and endeavouring to persuade it to do its duty, the other side would come behind us in a cowardly manner, and hit us over the head.

We got them fixed at last, and then all that was to be done was to arrange the covering over them. George unrolled it, and fastened one end over the nose of the boat. Harris stood in the middle to take it from George and roll it on to me, and I kept by the stern to receive it. It was a long time coming down to me. George did his part all right, but it was new work to Harris, and he bungled it.

How he managed it I do not know, he could not explain himself; but by some mysterious process or other he succeeded, after ten minutes of superhuman effort, in getting himself completely rolled up in it. He was so firmly wrapped round and tucked in and folded over, that he could not get out. He, of course, made frantic struggles for freedom—the birthright of every Englishman—and, in doing so (I learned this afterwards), knocked over George; and then George, swearing at Harris, began to struggle too, and got *himself* entangled and rolled up.

I knew nothing about all this at the time. I did not understand the business at all myself. I had been told to stand where I was, and wait till the canvas came to me, and Montmorency and I stood there and waited both as good as gold. We could see the canvas being violently jerked and tossed about, pretty considerably; but we supposed this was part of the method, and did not interfere.

We also heard much smothered language coming from underneath it, and we guessed that they were finding the job rather troublesome, and concluded that we would wait until things had got a little simpler before we joined in.

We waited some time, but matters seemed to get only more and more involved, until, at last, George's head came wriggling out over the side of the boat, and spoke up.

It said:

"Give us a hand here, can't you, you cuckoo; standing there like a stuffed mummy, when you see we are both being suffocated, you dummy!"

I never could withstand an appeal for help, so I went and undid them; not before it was time, either, for Harris was nearly black in the face.

It took us half an hour's hard labour, after that, before it was properly up, and then we cleared the decks, and got out supper. We put the kettle on to boil, up in the nose of the boat, and went down to the stern and pretended to take no notice of it, but set to work to get the other things out.

That is the only way to get a kettle to boil up the river. If it sees that you are waiting for it and are anxious, it will never even sing. You have to go away and begin your meal, as if you were not going to have any tea at all. You must not even look round at it. Then you will soon hear it sputtering away, mad to be made into tea.

It is a good plan, too, if you are in a great hurry, to talk very loudly to each other about how you don't need any tea, and are not going to have any. You get near the kettle, so that it can overhear you, and then you shout out, "I don't want any tea; do you, George?" to which George shouts back, "Oh, no, I don't like tea; we'll have lemonade instead—tea's so indigestible." Upon which the kettle boils over, and puts the stove out.

We adopted this harmless bit of trickery, and the result was that, by the time everything else was ready, the tea was waiting. Then we lit the lantern, and squatted down to supper.

We wanted that supper.

For five-and-thirty minutes not a sound was heard throughout the length and breadth of that boat, save the clank of cutlery and crockery, and the steady grinding of four sets of molars. At the end of five-and-thirty minutes, Harris said, "Ah!" and took his left leg out from under him and put his right one there instead.

Five minutes afterwards, George said, "Ah!" too, and threw his plate out on the bank; and, three minutes later than that, Montmorency gave the first sign of contentment he had exhibited since we had started, and rolled over on his side, and spread his legs out; and then I said,"Ah!"and bent my head back, and bumped it against one of the hoops, but I did not mind it. I did not even swear.

How good one feels when one is full—how satisfied with ourselves and with the world! People who have tried it, tell me that a clear conscience makes you very happy and contented; but a full stomach does the business quite as well, and is cheaper, and more easily obtained. One feels so forgiving and generous after a substantial and well-digested meal—so noble-minded, so kindly hearted.

It is very strange, this domination of our intellect by our digestive organs. We cannot work, we cannot think, unless our stomach wills so. It dictates to us our emotions, our passions. After eggs and bacon, it says, "Work!" After beefsteak and porter, it says, "Sleep!" After a cup of tea (two spoonsful for each cup, and don't let it stand more than three minutes), it says to the brain. "Now, rise, and show your strength. Be eloquent, and deep, and tender; see, with a clear eye, into Nature and into life; spread your white wings of quivering thought, and soar, a god-like spirit, over the whirling world beneath you, up through long lanes of flaming stars to the gates of eternity!"

After hot muffins, it says, "Be dull and soulless, like a beast of the field—a brainless animal, with listless eye, unlit by any ray of fancy, or of hope, or fear, or love, or life." And after brandy, taken in suf-ficient quantity, it says, "Now, come, fool, grin and tumble, that your fellow-men may laugh—drivel in folly, and splutter in senseless sounds, and show what a helpless ninny is poor man whose wit and will are drowned, like kittens, side by side, in half an inch of alcohol."

We are but the veriest, sorriest slaves of our stomach. Reach not after morality and righteousness, my friends; watch vigilantly your stomach, and diet it with care and judgment. Then virtue and con-tentment will come and reign within your heart, unsought by any effort of your own; and you will be a good citizen, a loving husband, and a tender father—a noble, pious man.

Before our supper, Harris and George and I were quarrelsome and snappy and ill-tempered; after our supper, we sat and beamed on one another, and we beamed upon the dog, too. We loved each other, we loved everybody. Harris, in moving about, trod on George's corn. Had this happened before supper, George would have expressed wishes and desires concerning Harris' fate in this world and the next that would have made a thoughtful man shudder.

As it was, he said, "Steady, old man; 'ware wheat."

And Harris, instead of merely observing, in his most unpleas-ant tones, that a fellow could hardly help treading on some bit of George's foot, if he had to move about at all within ten yards of where George was sitting, suggesting that George never ought to come into an ordinary sized boat with feet that length, and advising him to hang them over the side, as he would have done before supper, now said: "Oh, I'm so sorry, old chap; I hope I haven't hurt you."

And George said: "Not at all"; that it was his
fault; and Harris said no, it was his.

It was quite pretty to hear them.

We lit our pipes, and sat, looking out on the
quiet night, and talked.

George said why could not we be always like
this—away from the world, with its sin and temp-
tation, leading sober, peaceful lives, and doing
good. I said it was the sort of thing I had often
longed for myself; and we discussed the possibil-
ity of our going away, we four, to some handy,
well-fitted desert island, and living there in the woods.

Harris said that the danger about desert islands, as far as he had
heard, was that they were so damp; but George said no, not if prop-
erly drained.

And then we got on to drains, and that put George in mind of a
very funny thing that happened to his father once. He said his father
was travelling with another fellow through Wales, and, one night,
they stopped at a little inn, where there were some other fellows,
and they joined the other fellows, and spent the evening with them.

They had a very jolly evening, and sat up late, and, by the
time they came to go to bed, they (this was when George's father was
a very young man) were slightly jolly, too. They (George's father and
George's father's friend) were to sleep in the same room, but in different beds. They took the candle, and went up. The candle lurched
up against the wall when they got into the room, and went out, and
they had to undress and grope into bed in the dark. This they did;
but, instead of getting into separate beds, as they thought they
were doing, they both climbed into the same one without knowing
it—one getting in with his head at the top, and the other crawling
in from the opposite side of the compass, and lying with his feet on
the pillow.

There was silence for a moment, and then George's father said:
"Joe!"

"What's the matter, Tom?" replied Joe's voice from the other end
of the bed.

"Why, there's a man in my bed," said George's father; "here's his feet on my pillow."

"Well, it's an extraordinary thing, Tom," answered the other; "but I'm blest if there isn't a man in my bed, too!"

"What are you going to do?" asked George's father.

"Well, I'm going to chuck him out," replied Joe.

"So am I," said George's father, valiantly.

There was a brief struggle, followed by two heavy bumps on the floor, and then a rather doleful voice said:

"I say, Tom!"

"Yes!"

"How have you got on?"

"Well, to tell you the truth, my man's chucked *me* out."

"So's mine! I say, I don't think much of this inn, do you?"

"What was the name of that inn?" said Harris.

"The 'Pig and Whistle,'" said George. "Why?"

"Ah, no, then it isn't the same," replied Harris.

"What do you mean?" queried George.

"Why it's so curious," murmured Harris, "but precisely that very same thing happened to *my* father once at a country inn. I've often heard him tell the tale. I thought it might have been the same inn."

We turned in at ten that night, and I thought I should sleep well, being tired; but I didn't. As a rule, I undress and put my head on the pillow, and then somebody bangs at the door, and says it is half-past eight: but, tonight, everything seemed against me; the novelty of it all, the hardness of the boat, the cramped position (I was lying with my feet under one seat, and my head on another), the sound of the lapping water round the boat, and the wind among the branches, kept me restless and disturbed.

I did get to sleep for a few hours, and then some part of the boat which seemed to have grown up in the night—for it certainly was not there when we started, and it had disappeared by the morning—kept digging into my spine. I slept through it for a while, dreaming that I had swallowed a sovereign, and that they were cutting a hole in my back with a gimlet, so as to try and get it out. I thought it very unkind of them, and I told them I would owe them the money, and they should have it at the end of the month. But they would not hear of that, and said it would be much better if they had it then, because otherwise the interest would accumulate so. I got quite cross with them after a bit, and told them what I thought of them, and then they gave the gimlet such an excruciating wrench that I woke up.

The boat seemed stuffy, and my head ached; so I thought I would step out into the cool night-air. I slipped on what clothes I could find about—some of my own, and some of George's and Harris'—and crept under the canvas on to the bank.

It was a glorious night. The moon had sunk and left the quiet earth alone with the stars. It seemed as if, in the silence and the hush, while we her children slept, they were talking with her, their sister—conversing of mighty mysteries in voices too vast and deep for childish human ears to catch the sound.

They awe us, these strange stars, so cold, so clear. We are as children whose small feet have strayed into some dim-lit temple of the god they have been taught to worship but know not; and, standing where the echoing dome spans the long vista of the shadowy light, glance up, half hoping, half afraid to see some awful vision hovering there.

And yet it seems so full of comfort and of strength, the night. In its great presence, our small sorrows creep away, ashamed. The day has been so full of fret and care, and our hearts have been so full of evil and of bitter thoughts, and the world has seemed so hard and wrong, to us. Then Night, like some great loving mother, gently lays her hand upon our fevered head, and turns our little tear-stained face up to hers, and smiles, and, though she does not speak, we know what she would say, and lay our hot flushed cheek against her bosom, and the pain is gone.

Sometimes, our pain is very deep and real, and we stand before her very silent, because there is no language for our pain, only a moan. Night's heart is full of pity for us: she cannot ease our aching; she takes our hand in hers, and the little world grows very small and very far away beneath us, and, borne on her dark wings, we pass for a moment into a mightier Presence than her own, and in the wondrous light of that great Presence, all human life lies like a book before us, and we know that Pain and Sorrow are but the angels of God.

Only those who have worn the crown of suffering can look upon that wondrous light; and they, when they return, may not speak of it, or tell the mystery they know.

Once upon a time, through a strange country, there rode some goodly knights, and their path lay by a deep wood, where tangled briars grew very thick and strong, and tore the flesh of them that lost their way therein. And the leaves of the trees that grew in the wood were very dark and thick, so that no ray of light came through the branches to lighten the gloom and sadness.

And, as they passed by that dark wood, one knight of those that rode, missing his comrades, wandered far away, and returned to them no more; and they, sorely grieving, rode on without him, mourning him as one dead.

Now, when they reached the fair castle towards which they had been journeying, they stayed there many days, and made merry; and one night, as they sat in cheerful ease around the logs that burned in the great hall, and drank a loving measure, there came the comrade they had lost, and greeted them. His clothes were ragged, like a beggar's, and many sad wounds were on his sweet flesh, but upon his face there shone a great radiance of deep joy.

And they questioned him, asking him what had befallen him: and he told them how in the dark wood he had lost his way, and had wandered many days and nights, till, torn and bleeding, he had lain him down to die.

Then, when he was nigh unto death, lo! Through the savage gloom there came to him a stately maiden, and took him by the hand and led him on through devious paths, unknown to any man, until upon the darkness of the wood there dawned a light such as the light of day was unto but as a little lamp unto the sun; and, in that wondrous light, our way-worn knight saw as in a dream a vision, and so glorious, so fair the vision seemed, that of his bleeding wounds he thought no more, but stood as one entranced, whose joy is deep as is the sea, whereof no man can tell the depth.

And the vision faded, and the knight, kneeling upon the ground, thanked the good saint who into that sad wood had strayed his steps, so he had seen the vision that lay there hid.

And the name of the dark forest was Sorrow; but of the vision that the good knight saw therein we may not speak nor tell.

CHAPTER XI

How George, once upon a time, got up early in the
morning • George, Harris, and Montmorency do not like
the look of the cold water • Heroism and determination
on the part of J. • George and his shirt: story with a moral •
Harris as cook • Historical retrospect, specially inserted for
the use of schools

I WOKE AT SIX THE NEXT MORNING; AND FOUND GEORGE AWAKE TOO.
We both turned round, and tried to go to sleep again, but we could
not. Had there been any particular reason why we should *not* have
gone to sleep again, but have got up and dressed then and there, we
should have dropped off while we were looking at our watches, and
have slept till ten. As there was no earthly necessity for our getting up
under another two hours at the very least, and our getting up at that
time was an utter absurdity, it was only in keeping with the natural
cussedness of things in general that we should both feel that lying
down for five minutes more would be death to us.

George said that the same kind of thing, only worse, had happened to him some eighteen months ago, when he was lodging by
himself in the house of a certain Mrs. Gippings. He said his watch
went wrong one evening, and stopped at a quarter-past eight. He did
not know this at the time because, for some reason or other, he forgot
to wind it up when he went to bed (an unusual occurrence with him),
and hung it up over his pillow without ever looking at the thing.

It was in the winter when this happened, very near the shortest
day, and a week of fog into the bargain, so the fact that it was still

very dark when George woke in the morning was no guide to him as to the time. He reached up, and hauled down his watch. It was a quarter-past eight.

"Angels and ministers of grace defend us!" exclaimed George; "and here have I got to be in the City by nine. Why didn't somebody call me? Oh, this is a shame!" And he flung the watch down, and sprang out of bed, and had a cold bath, and washed himself, and dressed himself, and shaved himself in cold water because there was not time to wait for the hot and then rushed and had another look at the watch.

Whether the shaking it had received in being thrown down on the bed had started it, or how it was, George could not say, but certain it was that from a quarter-past eight it had begun to go, and now pointed to twenty minutes to nine.

George snatched it up, and rushed downstairs. In the sitting-room, all was dark and silent: there was no fire, no breakfast. George said it was a wicked shame of Mrs. G., and he made up his mind to tell her what he thought of her when he came home in the evening. Then he dashed on his great-coat and hat, and, seizing his umbrella, made for the front door. The door was not even unbolted. George anathematized Mrs. G. for a lazy old woman, and thought it was very strange that people could not get up at a decent, respectable time, unlocked and unbolted the door, and ran out.

He ran hard for a quarter of a mile, and at the end of that distance it began to be borne in upon him as a strange and curious thing that there were so few people about, and that there were no shops open. It was certainly a very dark and foggy morning, but still it seemed an unusual course to stop all business on that account. *He* had to go to business: why should other people stop in bed merely because it was dark and foggy?

At length he reached Holborn. Not a shutter was down! Not a bus was about! There were three men in sight, one of whom was a policeman; a market-cart full of cabbages, and a dilapidated looking cab. George pulled out his watch and looked at it: it was five minutes to nine! He stood still and counted his pulse. He stooped down and felt his legs. Then, with his watch still in his hand, he went up to the policeman, and asked him if he knew what the time was.

"What's the time?" said the man, eyeing George up and down with evident suspicion; "why, if you listen you will hear it strike."

George listened, and a neighbouring clock immediately obliged.

"But it's only gone three!" said George in an injured tone, when it had finished.

"Well, and how many did you want it to go?" replied the constable.

"Why, nine," said George, showing his watch.

"Do you know where you live?" said the guardian of public order severely.

George thought, and gave the address.

"Oh! That's where it is, is it?" replied the man "well, you take my advice and go there quietly, and take that watch of yours with you; and don't let's have anymore of it."

And George went home again, musing as he walked along, and let himself in.

At first, when he got in, he determined to undress and go to bed again; but when he thought of the redressing and rewashing, and the having of another bath, he determined he would not, but would sit up and go to sleep in the easy chair.

But he could not get to sleep: he never felt more wakeful in his life; so he lit the lamp and got out the chessboard, and played himself a game of chess. But even that did not enliven him: it seemed slow somehow; so he gave chess up and tried to read. He did not seem able to take any sort of interest in reading either, so he put on his coat again and went out for a walk.

It was horribly lonesome and dismal, and all the policemen he met regarded him with undisguised suspicion, and turned their lanterns on him and followed him about, and this had such an effect upon him at last that he began to feel as if he really had done something, and he got to slinking down the by-streets and hiding in dark doorways when he heard the regulation flip-flop approaching.

Of course, this conduct made the force only more distrustful of him than ever, and they would come and rout him out and ask him what he was doing there; and when he answered, "Nothing," he had merely come out for a stroll (it was then four o'clock in the morning), they looked as though they did not believe him, and two plain-clothes constables came home with him to see if he really did live where he had said he did. They saw him go in with his key, and then they took up a position opposite and watched the house.

He thought he would light a fire when he got inside, and make himself some breakfast, just to pass away the time; but he did not seem able to handle anything from a scuttleful of coals to a teaspoon without dropping it or falling over it, and making such a noise that he was in mortal fear that it would wake Mrs. G. up, and that she would think it was burglars and open the window and call "Police!" and then these two detectives would rush in and handcuff him, and march him off to the police-court.

He was in a morbidly nervous state by this time, and he pictured the trial, and his trying to explain the circumstances to the jury, and nobody believing him, and his being sentenced to twenty years' penal servitude, and his mother dying of a broken heart. So he gave up trying to get breakfast, and wrapped himself up in his overcoat, and sat in the easy chair till Mrs. G. came down at half-past seven.

He said he had never got up too early since that morning: it had been such a warning to him.

We had been sitting huddled up in our rugs while George had been telling me this true story, and on his finishing it I set to work to wake up Harris with a scull. The third prod did it: and he turned over on the other side, and said he would be down in a minute, and that he would have his lace-up boots. We soon let him know where he was, however, by the aid of the hitcher, and he sat up suddenly, sending Montmorency, who had been sleeping the sleep of the just right on the middle of his chest, sprawling across the boat.

Then we pulled up the canvas, and all four of us poked our heads out over the offside, and looked down at the water and shivered. The idea, overnight, had been that we should get up early in the morning, fling off our rugs and shawls, and, throwing back the canvas, spring into the river with a joyous shout, and revel in a long delicious swim. Somehow, now the morning had come, the notion seemed less tempting. The water looked damp and chilly: the wind felt cold.

"Well, who's going to be first in?" said Harris at last.

There was no rush for precedence. George settled the matter so far as he was concerned by retiring into the boat and pulling on his socks. Montmorency gave vent to an involuntary howl, as if merely thinking of the thing had given him the horrors; and Harris said it would be so difficult to get into the boat again, and went back and sorted out his trousers.

I did not altogether like to give in, though I did not relish the plunge. There might be snags about, or weeds, I thought. I meant to compromise matters by going down to the edge and just throwing the water over myself; so I took a towel and crept out on the bank and wormed my way along on to the branch of a tree that dipped down into the water.

It was bitterly cold. The wind cut like a knife. I thought I would not throw the water over myself after all. I would go back into the boat and dress; and I turned to do so; and, as I turned, the silly branch gave way, and I and the towel went in together with a tremendous splash,

and I was out mid-stream with a gallon of Thames water inside me before I knew what had happened.

"By Jove! Old J.'s gone in," I heard Harris say, as I came blowing to the surface. "I didn't think he'd have the pluck to do it. Did you?"

"Is it all right?" sung out George.

"Lovely," I spluttered back. "You are duffers not to come in. I wouldn't have missed this for worlds. Why won't you try it? It only wants a little determination."

But I could not persuade them.

Rather an amusing thing happened while dressing that morning. I was very cold when I got back into the boat, and, in my hurry to get my shirt on, I accidentally jerked it into the water. It made me awfully wild, especially as George burst out laughing. I could not see anything to laugh at, and I told George so, and he only laughed the more. I never saw a man laugh so much. I quite lost my temper with him at last, and I pointed out to him what a drivelling maniac of an imbecile idiot he was; but he only roared the louder. And then, just as I was landing the shirt, I noticed that it was not my shirt at all, but George's, which I had mistaken for mine; whereupon the humour of the thing struck me for the first time, and *I* began to laugh. And the more I looked from George's wet shirt to George, roaring with laughter, the more I was amused, and I laughed so much that I had to let the shirt fall back into the water again.

"Ar'n't you—you—going to get it out?" said George between his shrieks.

I could not answer him at all for a while, I was laughing so, but, at last, between my peals I managed to jerk out:

"It isn't my shirt—it's *yours!*"

I never saw a man's face change from lively to severe so suddenly in all my life before.

"What!" he yelled, springing up. "You silly cuckoo! Why can't you be more careful what you're doing? Why the deuce don't you go and dress on the bank? You're not fit to be in a boat, you're not. Gimme the hitcher."

I tried to make him see the fun of the thing, but he could not. George is very dense at seeing a joke sometimes.

Harris proposed that we should have scrambled eggs for breakfast. He said he would cook them. It seemed, from his account, that he was very good at doing scrambled eggs. He often did them at picnics and when out on yachts. He was quite famous for them. People who had once tasted his scrambled eggs, so we gathered from his conversation, never cared for any other food afterwards, but pined away and died when they could not get them.

It made our mouths water to hear him talk about the things, and we handed him out the stove and the frying pan and all the eggs that had not smashed and gone over everything in the hamper, and begged him to begin.

He had some trouble in breaking the eggs—or rather not so much trouble in breaking them exactly as in getting them into the frying pan when broken, and keeping them off his trousers, and preventing them from running up his sleeve; but he fixed some half-a-dozen into the pan at last, and then squatted down by the side of the stove and chivied them about with a fork.

It seemed harassing work, so far as George and I could judge. Whenever he went near the pan he burned himself, and then he would drop everything and dance round the stove, flicking his fingers about and cursing the things. Indeed, everytime George and I looked round at him he was sure to be performing this feat. We thought at first that it was a necessary part of the culinary arrangements.

We did not know what scrambled eggs were, and we fancied that it must be some Red Indian or Sandwich Islands sort of dish that required dances and incantations for its proper cooking. Montmorency went and put his nose over it once, and the fat spluttered up and scalded him, and then *he* began dancing and cursing. Altogether it was one of the most interesting and exciting operations I have ever witnessed. George and I were both quite sorry when it was over.

The result was not altogether the success that Harris had anticipated. There seemed so little to show for the business. Six eggs had gone into the frying pan, and all that came out was a teaspoonful of burnt and unappetizing looking mess.

Harris said it was the fault of the frying pan, and thought it would have gone better if we had had a fish-kettle and a gas-stove; and we decided not to attempt the dish again until we had those aids to housekeeping by us.

The sun had got more powerful by the time we had finished breakfast, and the wind had dropped, and it was as lovely a morning as one could desire. Little was in sight to remind us of the nineteenth century; and, as we looked out upon the river in the morning sunlight, we could almost fancy that the centuries between us and that ever-to-be-famous June morning of 1215 had been drawn aside, and that we, English yeomen's sons in homespun cloth, with dirk at belt, were waiting there to witness the writing of that stupendous page of history, the meaning whereof was to be translated to the common people some four hundred and odd years later by one Oliver Cromwell, who had deeply studied it.

It is a fine summer morning—sunny, soft, and still. But through the air there runs a thrill of coming stir. King John has slept at Duncroft Hall, and all the day before the little town of Staines has echoed to the clang of armed men, and the clatter of great horses over its rough stones, and the shouts of captains, and the grim oaths and surly jests of bearded bowmen, billmen, pikemen, and strange-speaking foreign spearmen.

Gay-cloaked companies of knights and squires have ridden in, all travel-stained and dusty. And all the evening long the timid towns-men's doors have had to be quick opened to let in rough groups of soldiers, for whom there must be found both board and lodging, and the best of both, or woe betide the house and all within; for the sword is judge and jury, plaintiff and executioner, in these tempestuous times, and pays for what it takes by sparing those from whom it takes it, if it pleases it to do so.

Round the campfire in the market place gather still more of the Barons' troops, and eat and drink deep, and bellow forth roistering drinking songs, and gamble and quarrel as the evening grows and deepens into night. The firelight sheds quaint shadows on their piled-up arms and on their uncouth forms. The children of the town steal round to watch them, wondering; and brawny country wenches, laugh-ing, draw near to bandy alehouse jest and jibe with the swaggering troopers so unlike the village swains, who, now despised, stand apart behind, with vacant grins upon their broad, peering faces. And out from the fields around, glitter the faint lights of more distant camps, as here some great lord's followers lie mustered, and there false John's French mercenaries hover like crouching wolves without the town.

And so, with sentinel in each dark street, and twinkling watch-fires on each height around, the night has worn away, and over this fair valley of old Thames has broken the morning of the great day that is to close so big with the fate of ages yet unborn.

Ever since grey dawn, in the lower of the two islands, just above where we are standing, there has been great clamour, and the sound of many workmen. The great pavilion brought there yester eve is being raised, and carpenters are busy nailing tiers of seats, while 'prentices from London town are there with many-coloured stuffs and silks and cloth of gold and silver.

And now, lo! Down upon the road that winds along the river's bank from Staines there come towards us, laughing and talking together in deep guttural bass, a half-a-score of stalwart halbert-men —Barons' men, these—and halt at a hundred yards or so above us, on the other bank, and lean upon their arms, and wait.

And so, from hour to hour, march up along the road ever fresh groups and bands of armed men, their casques and breastplates flashing back the long low lines of morning sunlight, until, as far as eye can reach, the way seems thick with glittering steel and prancing steeds. And shouting horsemen are galloping from group to group, and little banners are fluttering lazily in the warm breeze, and every now and then there is a deeper stir as the ranks make way on either side, and some great Baron on his war-horse, with his guard of squires around him, passes along to take his station at the head of his serfs and vassals.

And up the slope of Cooper's Hill, just opposite, are gathered the wondering rustics and curious townsfolk, who have run from Staines, and none are quite sure what the bustle is about, but each one has a different version of the great event that they have come to see; and some say that much good to all the people will come from this day's work; but the old men shake their heads, for they have heard such tales before.

And all the river down to Staines is dotted with small craft and boats and tiny coracles—which last are growing out of favour now, and are used only by the poorer folk. Over the rapids, where in after years trim Bell Weir lock will stand, they have been forced or dragged by their sturdy rowers, and now are crowding up as near as they dare come to the great covered barges, which lie in readiness to bear King John to where the fateful Charter waits his signing.

It is noon, and we and all the people have been waiting patient for many an hour, and the rumour has run round that slippery John has again escaped from the Barons' grasp, and has stolen away from Duncroft Hall with his mercenaries at his heels, and will soon be doing other work than signing charters for his people's liberty.

Not so! This time the grip upon him has been one of iron, and he has slid and wriggled in vain. Far down the road a little cloud of dust has risen, and draws nearer and grows larger, and the pattering of many hoofs grows louder, and in and out between the scattered groups of drawn-up men, there pushes on its way a brilliant cavalcade of gay-dressed lords and knights. And front and rear, and either flank, there ride the yeomen of the Barons, and in the midst King John.

He rides to where the barges lie in readiness, and the great Barons step forth from their ranks to meet him. He greets them with a smile and laugh, and pleasant honeyed words, as though it were some feast in his honour to which he had been invited. But as he rises to dismount, he casts one hurried glance from his own French mercenaries drawn up in the rear to the grim ranks of the Barons' men that hem him in.

Is it too late? One fierce blow at the unsuspecting horseman at his side, one cry to his French troops, one desperate charge upon the unready lines before him, and these rebellious Barons might rue the day they dared to thwart his plans! A bolder hand might have turned the game even at that point. Had it been a Richard there! The cup of liberty might have been dashed from England's lips, and the taste of freedom held back for a hundred years.

But the heart of King John sinks before the stern faces of the English fighting men, and the arm of King John drops back on to his rein, and he dismounts and takes his seat in the foremost barge. And the Barons follow in, with each mailed hand upon the sword-hilt, and the word is given to let go.

Slowly the heavy, bright-decked barges leave the shore of Runningmede. Slowly against the swift current they work their ponderous way, till, with a low grumble, they grate against the bank of the little island that from this day will bear the name of Magna Charta Island. And King John has stepped upon the shore, and we wait in breathless silence till a great shout cleaves the air, and the great cornerstone in England's temple of liberty has, now we know, been firmly laid.

CHAPTER XII

Henry VIII and Anne Boleyn • Disadvantages of living in same house with pair of lovers • A trying time for the English nation • A night search for the picturesque • Homeless and houseless • Harris prepares to die • An angel comes along • Effect of sudden joy on Harris • A little supper • Lunch • High price for mustard • A fearful battle • Maidenhead • Sailing • Three fishers • We are cursed

I WAS SITTING ON THE BANK, CONJURING UP THIS SCENE TO MYSELF, when George remarked that when I was quite rested, perhaps I would not mind helping to wash up; and, thus recalled from the days of the glorious past to the prosaic present, with all its misery and sin, I slid down into the boat and cleaned out the frying pan with a stick of wood and a tuft of grass, polishing it up finally with George's wet shirt.

We went over to Magna Charta Island, and had a look at the stone which stands in the cottage there and on which the great Charter is said to have been signed; though, as to whether it really was signed there, or, as some say, on the other bank at "Runningmede," I decline to commit myself. As far as my own personal opinion goes, however, I am inclined to give weight to the popular island theory. Certainly, had I been one of the Barons, at the time, I should have strongly urged upon my comrades the advisability of our getting such a slippery customer as King John on to the island, where there was less chance of surprises and tricks.

There are the ruins of an old priory in the grounds of Ankerwyke House, which is close to Picnic Point, and it was round about the grounds of this old priory that Henry VIII is said to have waited for and met Anne Boleyn. He also used to meet her at Hever Castle in Kent, and also somewhere near St. Albans. It must have been difficult for the people of England in those days to have found a spot where these thoughtless young folk were *not* spooning.

Have you ever been in a house where there are a couple courting? It is most trying. You think you will go and sit in the drawing room, and you march off there. As you open the door, you hear a noise as if somebody had suddenly recollected something, and, when you get in, Emily is over by the window, full of interest in the opposite side of the road, and your friend, John Edward, is at the other end of the room with his whole soul held in thrall by photographs of other people's relatives.

"Oh!" you say, pausing at the door, "I didn't know anybody was here."

"Oh! Didn't you?"says Emily, coldly, in a tone which implies that she does not believe you.

You hang about for a bit, then you say:

"It's very dark. Why don't you light the gas?"

John Edward says, "Oh!" he hadn't noticed it; and Emily says that papa does not like the gas lit in the afternoon.

You tell them one or two items of news, and give them your views and opinions on the Irish question; but this does not appear to inter-est them. All they remark on any subject is, "Oh!" "Is it?" "Did he?" "Yes," and "You don't say so!" And, after ten minutes of such style of conversation, you edge up to the door, and slip out, and are surprised to find that the door immediately closes behind you, and shuts itself, without your having touched it.

Half an hour later, you think you will try a pipe in the conser-vatory. The only chair in the place is occupied by Emily; and John Edward, if the language of clothes can be relied upon, has evidently been sitting on the floor. They do not speak, but they give you a look that says all that can be said in a civilised community; and you back out promptly and shut the door behind you.

You are afraid to poke your nose into any room in the house now; so, after walking up and down the stairs for a while, you go and sit in your own bedroom. This becomes uninteresting, however, after a time, and so you put on your hat and stroll out into the garden. You walk down the path, and as you pass the summerhouse you glance in, and there are those two young idiots, huddled up into one corner of it; and they see you, and are evidently under the idea that, for some wicked purpose of your own, you are following them about.

"Why don't they have a special room for this sort of thing, and make people keep to it?" you mutter; and you rush back to the hall and get your umbrella and go out.

It must have been much like this when that foolish boy Henry VIII was courting his little Anne. People in Buckinghamshire would have come upon them unexpectedly when they were mooning round Windsor and Wraysbury, and have exclaimed, "Oh! You here!" and Henry would have blushed and said, "Yes; he'd just come over to see a man"; and Anne would have said, "Oh, I'm so glad to see you! Isn't it funny? I've just met Mr. Henry VIII in the lane, and he's going the same way I am."

Then those people would have gone away and said to themselves: "Oh! We'd better get out of here while this billing and cooing is on. We'll go down to Kent."

And they would go to Kent, and the first thing they would see in Kent, when they got there, would be Henry and Anne fooling round Hever Castle.

"Oh, drat this!" they would have said. "Here, let's go away. I can't stand anymore of it. Let's go to St. Albans—nice quiet place, St. Albans."

And when they reached St. Albans, there would be that wretched couple, kissing under the Abbey walls. Then these folks would go and be pirates until the marriage was over.

From Picnic Point to Old Windsor Lock is a delightful bit of the river. A shady road, dotted here and there with dainty little cottages, runs by the bank up to the "Bells of Ouseley," a picturesque inn, as most upriver inns are, and a place where a very good glass of ale may be drunk—so Harris says; and on a matter of this kind you can take

Harris' word. Old Windsor is a famous spot in its way. Edward the Confessor had a palace here, and here the great Earl Godwin was proved guilty by the justice of that age of having encompassed the death of the King's brother. Earl Godwin broke a piece of bread and held it in his hand.

"If I am guilty," said the Earl, "may this bread choke me when I eat it!"

Then he put the bread into his mouth and swallowed it, and it choked him, and he died.

After you pass Old Windsor, the river is somewhat uninteresting, and does not become itself again until you are nearing Boveney. George and I towed up past the Home Park, which stretches along the right bank from Albert to Victoria Bridge; and as we were passing Datchet, George asked me if I remembered our first trip up the river, and when we landed at Datchet at ten o'clock at night, and wanted to go to bed.

I answered that I did remember it. It will be some time before I forget it.

It was the Saturday before the August Bank Holiday. We were tired and hungry, we same three, and when we got to Datchet we took out the hamper, the two bags, and the rugs and coats, and such like things, and started off to look for diggings. We passed a very pretty little hotel, with clematis and creeper over the porch; but there was no honeysuckle about it, and, for some reason or other, I had got my mind fixed on honeysuckle, and I said:

"Oh, don't let's go in there! Let's go on a bit further, and see if there isn't one with honeysuckle over it."

So we went on till we came to another hotel. That was a very nice hotel, too, and it had honeysuckle on it, round at the side; but Harris did not like the look of a man who was leaning against the front door. He said he didn't look a nice man at all, and he wore ugly boots: so we went on further. We went a goodish way without coming across any more hotels, and then we met a man, and asked him to direct us to a few.

He said:

"Why, you are coming away from them. You must turn right round and go back, and then you will come to the Stag."

We said:

"Oh, we had been there, and didn't like it—no honeysuckle over it."

"Well, then," he said, "there's the Manor House, just opposite. Have you tried that?"

Harris replied that we did not want to go there—didn't like the looks of a man who was stopping there—Harris did not like the colour of his hair, didn't like his boots, either.

"Well, I don't know what you'll do, I'm sure," said our informant; "because they are the only two inns in the place."

"No other inns!" exclaimed Harris.

"None," replied the man.

"What on earth are we to do?" cried Harris.

Then George spoke up. He said Harris and I could get an hotel built for us, if we liked, and have some people made to put in. For his part, he was going back to the Stag.

The greatest minds never realise their ideals in any matter; and Harris and I sighed over the hollowness of all earthly desires, and followed George.

We took our traps into the Stag, and laid them down in the hall. The landlord came up and said:

"Good evening, gentlemen."

"Oh, good evening," said George; "we want three beds, please."

"Very sorry, sir," said the landlord; "but I'm afraid we can't manage it."

"Oh, well, never mind," said George, "two will do. Two of us can sleep in one bed, can't we?" he continued, turning to Harris and me.

Harris said, "Oh, yes"; he thought George and I could sleep in one bed very easily.

"Very sorry, sir," again repeated the landlord: "but we really haven't got a bed vacant in the whole house. In fact, we are putting two, and even three gentlemen in one bed, as it is."

This staggered us for a bit.

But Harris, who is an old traveller, rose to the occasion, and, laughing cheerily, said:

"Oh, well, we can't help it. We must rough it. You must give us a shakedown in the billiard-room."

"Very sorry, sir. Three gentlemen sleeping on the billiard-table already, and two in the coffee-room. Can't possibly take you in tonight."

We picked up our things, and went over to the Manor House. It was a pretty little place. I said I thought I should like it better than the other house; and Harris said, "Oh, yes," it would be all right, and we needn't look at the man with the red hair; besides, the poor fellow couldn't help having red hair.

Harris spoke quite kindly and sensibly about it.

The people at the Manor House did not wait to hear us talk. The landlady met us on the doorstep with the greeting that we were the fourteenth party she had turned away within the last hour and a half. As for our meek suggestions of stables, billiard-room, or coal-cellars, she laughed them all to scorn: all these nooks had been snatched up long ago.

Did she know of any place in the whole village where we could get shelter for the night?

"Well, if we didn't mind roughing it—she did not recommend it, mind—but there was a little beershop half a mile down the Eton Road——"

We waited to hear no more; we caught up the hamper and the bags, and the coats and rugs, and parcels, and ran. The distance seemed more like a mile than half a mile, but we reached the place at last, and rushed, panting, into the bar.

The people at the beershop were rude. They merely laughed at us. There were only three beds in the whole house, and they had seven single gentlemen and two married couples sleeping there already. A kind-hearted bargeman, however, who happened to be in the taproom, thought we might try the grocer's, next door to the Stag, and we went back.

The grocer's was full. An old woman we met in the shop then kindly took us along with her for a quarter of a mile, to a lady friend of hers, who occasionally let rooms to gentlemen.

This old woman walked very slowly, and we were twenty minutes getting to her lady friend's. She enlivened the journey by describing to us, as we trailed along, the various pains she had in her back.

Her lady friend's rooms were let. From there we were recommended to No. 27. No. 27 was full, and sent us to No. 32, and 32 was full.

Then we went back into the high road, and Harris sat down on the hamper and said he would go no further. He said it seemed a quiet spot, and he would like to die there. He requested George and me to kiss his mother for him, and to tell all his relations that he forgave them and died happy.

At that moment an angel came by in the disguise of a small boy (and I cannot think of anymore effective disguise an angel could have assumed), with a can of beer in one hand, and in the other something at the end of a string, which he let down on to every flat stone he came across, and then pulled up again, this producing a peculiarly unattractive sound, suggestive of suffering.

We asked this heavenly messenger (as we discovered him afterwards to be) if he knew of any lonely house, whose occupants were few and feeble (old ladies or paralysed gentlemen preferred), who could be easily frightened into giving up their beds for the night to three desperate men; or, if not this, could he recommend us to an empty pigstye, or a disused limekiln, or anything of that sort. He did not know of any such place—at least, not one handy; but he said that, if we liked to come with him, his mother had a room to spare, and could put us up for the night.

We fell upon his neck there in the moonlight and blessed him, and it would have made a very beautiful picture if the boy himself had not been so overpowered by our emotion as to be unable to sustain himself under it, and sunk to the ground, letting us all down on top of him. Harris was so overcome with joy that he fainted, and had to seize the boy's beer can and half empty it before he could recover consciousness, and then he started off at a run, and left George and me to bring on the luggage.

It was a little four-roomed cottage where the boy lived, and his mother good soul! Gave us hot bacon for supper, and we ate it all—five pounds—and a jam tart afterwards, and two pots of tea, and then we went to bed. There were two beds in the room; one was a 2 ft. 6 in. truckle bed, and George and I slept in that, and kept in by tying ourselves together with a sheet; and the other was the little boy's bed, and Harris had that all to himself, and we found him, in the morning, with two feet of bare leg sticking out at the bottom, and George and I used it to hang the towels on while we bathed.

We were not so uppish about what sort of hotel we would have, next time we went to Datchet.

To return to our present trip: nothing exciting happened, and we tugged steadily on to a little below Monkey Island, where we drew up and lunched. We tackled the cold beef for lunch, and then we found that we had forgotten to bring any mustard. I don't think I ever in my life, before or since, felt I wanted mustard as badly as I felt I wanted it then. I don't care for mustard as a rule, and it is very seldom that I take it at all, but I would have given worlds for it then.

I don't know how many worlds there may be in the universe, but anyone who had brought me a spoonful of mustard at that precise moment could have had them all. I grow reckless like that when I want a thing and can't get it.

Harris said he would have given worlds for mustard too. It would have been a good thing for anybody who had come up to that spot with a can of mustard, then: he would have been set up in worlds for the rest of his life.

But there! I dare say both Harris and I would have tried to back out of the bargain after we had got the mustard. One makes these extravagant offers in moments of excitement, but, of course, when one comes to think of it, one sees how absurdly out of proportion they are with the value of the required article. I heard a man, going up a mountain in Switzerland, once say he would give worlds for a glass of beer, and, when he came to a little shanty where they kept it, he kicked up a most fearful row because they charged him five francs for a bottle of Bass. He said it was a scandalous imposition, and he wrote to *The Times* about it.

It cast a gloom over the boat, there being no mustard. We ate our beef in silence. Existence seemed hollow and uninteresting. We thought of the happy days of childhood, and sighed. We brightened up a bit, however, over the apple-tart, and, when George drew out a tin of pineapple from the bottom of the hamper, and rolled it into the middle of the boat we felt that life was worth living after all.

We are very fond of pineapple, all three of us. We looked at the picture on the tin; we thought of the juice. We smiled at one another, and Harris got a spoon ready.

Then we looked for the knife to open the tin with. We turned out everything in the hamper. We turned out the bags. We pulled up the boards at the bottom of the boat. We took everything out on to the bank and shook it. There was no tin-opener to be found.

Then Harris tried to open the tin with a pocketknife, and broke the knife and cut himself badly; and George tried a pair of scissors, and the scissors flew up, and nearly put his eye out. While they were dressing their wounds, I tried to make a hole in the thing with the spiky end of the hitcher, and the hitcher slipped and jerked me out between the boat and the bank into two feet of muddy water, and the tin rolled over, uninjured, and broke a teacup.

Then we all got mad. We took that tin out on the bank, and Harris went up into a field and got a big sharp stone, and I went back into the boat and brought out the mast, and George held the tin and Harris held the sharp end of his stone against the top of it, and I took the mast and poised it high up in the air, and gathered up all my strength and brought it down.

It was George's straw hat that saved his life that day. He keeps that hat now (what is left of it), and, of a winter's evening, when the pipes are lit and the boys are telling stretchers about the dangers they have passed through, George brings it down and shows it round, and the stirring tale is told anew, with fresh exaggerations everytime.

Harris got off with merely a flesh wound.

After that, I took the tin off myself, and hammered at it with the mast till I was worn out and sick at heart, whereupon Harris took it in hand.

We beat it out flat; we beat it back square; we battered it into every form known to geometry—but we could not make a hole in it. Then George went at it, and knocked it into a shape, so strange, so weird, so unearthly in its wild hideousness, that he got frightened and threw away the mast. Then we all three sat round it on the grass and looked at it.

There was one great dent across the top that had the appearance of a mocking grin, and it drove us furious, so that Harris rushed at the thing, and caught it up, and flung it far into the middle of the river, and as it sank we hurled our curses at it, and we got into the boat and rowed away from the spot, and never paused till we reached Maidenhead.

Maidenhead itself is too snobby to be pleasant. It is the haunt of the river swell and his overdressed female companion. It is the town of showy hotels, patronised chiefly by dudes and ballet girls. It is the witch's kitchen from which go forth those demons of the river—steam-launches. The *London Journal* duke always has his "little place" at Maidenhead; and the heroine of the three-volume novel always dines there when she goes out on the spree with somebody else's husband.

We went through Maidenhead quickly, and then eased up, and took leisurely that grand reach beyond Boulter's and Cookham locks. Clieveden Woods still wore their dainty dress of spring, and rose up, from the water's edge, in one long harmony of blended shades of fairy green. In its unbroken loveliness this is, perhaps, the sweetest stretch of all the river, and lingeringly we slowly drew our little boat away from its deep peace.

We pulled up in the backwater, just below Cookham, and had tea; and, when we were through the lock, it was evening. A stiffish breeze had sprung up—in our favour, for a wonder; for, as a rule on the river, the wind is always dead against you whatever way you go. It is against you in the morning, when you start for a day's trip, and you pull a long distance, thinking how easy it will be to come back with the sail. Then, after tea, the wind veers round, and you have to pull hard in its teeth all the way home.

When you forget to take the sail at all, then the wind is consistently in your favour both ways. But there! This world is only a probation, and man was born to trouble as the sparks fly upward.

This evening, however, they had evidently made a mistake, and had put the wind round at our back instead of in our face. We kept very quiet about it, and got the sail up quickly before they found it out, and then we spread ourselves about the boat in thoughtful attitudes, and the sail bellied out, and strained, and grumbled at the mast, and the boat flew.

I steered.

There is no more thrilling sensation I know of than sailing. It comes as near to flying as man has got to yet—except in dreams. The wings of the rushing wind seem to be bearing you onward, you know not where. You are no longer the slow, plodding, puny thing of clay, creeping tortuously upon the ground; you are a part of Nature! Your heart is throbbing against hers. Her glorious arms are round you, raising you up against her heart! Your spirit is at one with hers; your limbs grow light! The voices of the air are singing to you. The earth seems far away and little; and the clouds so close above your head, are brothers, and you stretch your arms to them.

We had the river to ourselves, except that, far in the distance, we could see a fishing-punt, moored in mid-stream, on which three fishermen sat; and we skimmed over the water, and passed the wooded banks, and no one spoke.

I was steering.

As we drew nearer, we could see that the three men fishing seemed old and solemn-looking men. They sat on three chairs in the punt, and watched intently their lines. And the red sunset threw a mystic light upon the waters, and tinged with fire the towering woods, and made a golden glory of tile piled-up clouds. It was an hour of deep enchantment, of ecstatic hope and longing. The little sail stood out against the purple sky, the gloaming lay around us, wrapping the world in rainbow shadows; and, behind us, crept the night.

We seemed like knights of some old legend, sailing across some mystic lake into the unknown realm of twilight, unto the great land of the sunset.

We did not go into the realm of twilight; we went slap into that punt, where those three old men were fishing. We did not know what had happened at first, because the sail shut out the view, but from the nature of the language that rose up upon the evening air, we gathered that we had come into the neighbourhood of human beings, and that they were vexed and discontented.

Harris let the sail down, and then we saw what had happened. We had knocked those three old gentlemen off their chairs into a general heap at the bottom of the boat, and they were now slowly and painfully sorting themselves out from each other, and picking fish off themselves; and as they worked, they cursed us—not with a common cursory curse, but with long, carefully-thought-out, comprehensive curses, that embraced the whole of our career, and went away into the distant future, and included all our relations, and covered everything connected with us—good, substantial curses.

Harris told them they ought to be grateful for a little excitement, sitting there fishing all day, and he also said that he was shocked and grieved to hear men their age give way to temper so.

But it did not do any good.

George said he would steer, after that. He said a mind like mine ought not to be expected to give itself away in steering boats—better let a mere commonplace human being see after that boat, before we jolly well all got drowned; and he took the lines, and brought us up to Marlow.

And at Marlow we left the boat by the bridge, and went and put up for the night at the "Crown."

CHAPTER XIII

Marlow • Bisham Abbey • The Medmenham Monks • Montmorency thinks he will murder an old Tom cat • But eventually decides that he will let it live • Shameful conduct of a fox terrier at the Civil Service Stores • Our departure from Marlow • An imposing procession • The steam launch, useful recipes for annoying and hindering it • We decline to drink the river • A peaceful dog • Strange disappearance of Harris and a pie

MARLOW IS ONE OF THE PLEASANTEST RIVER CENTRES I KNOW OF. IT is a bustling, lively little town; not very picturesque on the whole, it is true, but there are many quaint nooks and corners to be found in it, nevertheless—standing arches in the shattered bridge of Time, over which our fancy travels back to the days when Marlow Manor owned Saxon Altar for its lord, ere conquering William seized it to give to Queen Matilda, ere it passed to the Earls of Warwick or to worldly wise Lord Paget, the councillor of four successive sovereigns.

There is lovely country round about it, too, if, after boating, you are fond of a walk, while the river itself is at its best here. Down to Cookham, past the Quarry Woods and the meadows, is a lovely reach. Dear old Quarry Woods! With your narrow, climbing paths, and little winding glades, how scented to this hour you seem with memories of sunny summer days! How haunted are your shadowy vistas with the ghosts of laughing faces! How from your whispering leaves there softly fall the voices of long ago!

From Marlow up to Sonning is even fairer yet. Grand old Bisham Abbey, whose stone walls have rung to the shouts of the  Knights Templars, and which, at one time, was the home of Anne of Cleves and at another of Queen Elizabeth, is passed on the right bank just half a mile above Marlow Bridge. Bisham Abbey is rich in melodramatic properties. It contains a tapestry bedchamber, and a secret room hid high up in the thick walls. The ghost of the Lady Holy, who beat her little boy to death, still walks there at night, trying to wash its ghostly hands clean in a ghostly basin.

Warwick, the king-maker, rests there, careless now about such trivial things as earthly kings and earthly kingdoms; and Salisbury, who did good service at Poictiers. Just before you come to the abbey, and right on the river's bank, is Bisham Church, and, perhaps, if any tombs are worth inspecting, they are the tombs and monuments in Bisham Church. It was while floating in his boat under the Bisham beeches that Shelley, who was then living at Marlow (you can see his house now, in West Street), composed *The Revolt of Islam*.

By Hurley Weir, a little higher up, I have often thought that I could stay a month without having sufficient time to drink in all the beauty of the scene. The village of Hurley, five minutes' walk from the lock, is as old a little spot as there is on the river, dating, as it does, to quote the quaint phraseology of those dim days, "from the times of King Sebert and King Offa." Just past the weir (going up) is Danes' Field, where the invading Danes once encamped, during their march to Gloucestershire; and a little further still, nestling by a sweet corner of the stream, is what is left of Medmenham Abbey.

The famous Medmenham monks, or "Hell Fire Club," as they were commonly called, and of whom the notorious Wilkes was a member, were a fraternity whose motto was "Do as you please," and that invitation still stands over the ruined doorway of the abbey. Many years before this bogus abbey, with its congregation of irreverent jesters, was founded, there stood upon this same spot a monastery of a sterner kind, whose monks were of a somewhat different type to the revellers that were to follow them, five hundred years afterwards.

The Cistercian monks, whose abbey stood there in the thirteenth century, wore no clothes but rough tunics and cowls, and ate no flesh, nor fish, nor eggs. They lay upon straw, and they rose at midnight to mass. They spent the day in labour, reading, and prayer; and over all their lives there fell a silence, as of death, for no one spoke.

A grim fraternity, passing grim lives in that sweet spot, that God had made so bright! Strange that Nature's voices all around them—the soft singing of the waters, the whisperings of the river grass, the music of the rushing wind—should not have taught them a truer meaning of life than this. They listened there, through the long days, in silence, waiting for a voice from heaven; and all day long and through the solemn night it spoke to them in myriad tones, and they heard it not.

From Medmenham to sweet Hambledon Lock the river is full of peaceful beauty, but, after it passes Greenlands, the rather uninteresting looking river residence of my newsagent—a quiet unassuming old gentleman, who may often be met with about these regions, during the summer months, sculling himself along in easy vigorous style, or chatting genially to some old lock-keeper, as he passes through—until well the other side of Henley, it is somewhat bare and dull.

We got up tolerably early on the Monday morning at Marlow, and went for a bathe before breakfast; and, coming back, Montmorency made an awful ass of himself. The only subject on which Montmorency and I have any serious difference of opinion is cats. I like cats; Montmorency does not.

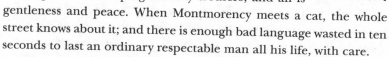

When I meet a cat, I say, "Poor Pussy!" and stoop down and tickle the side of its head; and the cat sticks up its tail in a rigid, cast-iron manner, arches its back, and wipes its nose up against my trousers; and all is gentleness and peace. When Montmorency meets a cat, the whole street knows about it; and there is enough bad language wasted in ten seconds to last an ordinary respectable man all his life, with care.

I do not blame the dog (contenting myself, as a rule, with merely clouting his head or throwing stones at him), because I take it that it is his nature. Fox-terriers are born with about four times as much original sin in them as other dogs are, and it will take years and years of patient effort on the part of us Christians to bring about any appreciable reformation in the rowdiness of the fox-terrier nature.

I remember being in the lobby of the Haymarket Stores one day, and all round about me were dogs, waiting for the return of their owners, who were shopping inside. There were a mastiff, and one or two collies, and a St. Bernard, a few retrievers and Newfoundlands, a boar-hound, a French poodle, with plenty of hair round its head, but mangy about the middle; a bulldog, a few Lowther Arcade sort of animals, about the size of rats, and a couple of Yorkshire tykes.

There they sat, patient, good, and thoughtful. A solemn peacefulness seemed to reign in that lobby. An air of calmness and resignation—of gentle sadness pervaded the room.

Then a sweet young lady entered, leading a meek-looking little fox-terrier, and left him, chained up there, between the bulldog and the poodle. He sat and looked about him for a minute. Then he cast up his eyes to the ceiling, and seemed, judging from his expression, to be thinking of his mother. Then he yawned. Then he looked round at the other dogs, all silent, grave, and dignified.

He looked at the bulldog, sleeping dreamlessly on his right. He looked at the poodle, erect and haughty, on his left. Then, without a word of warning, without the shadow of a provocation, he bit that poodle's near foreleg, and a yelp of agony rang through the quiet shades of that lobby.

The result of his first experiment seemed highly satisfactory to him, and he determined to go on and make things lively all round. He sprang over the poodle and vigorously attacked a collie, and the collie woke up, and immediately commenced a fierce and noisy contest with the poodle. Then Foxey came back to his own place, and caught the bulldog by the ear, and tried to throw him away; and the bulldog, a curiously impartial animal, went for everything he could reach, including the hall-porter, which gave that dear little terrier the opportunity to enjoy an uninterrupted fight of his own with an equally willing Yorkshire tyke.

Anyone who knows canine nature need hardly be told that, by this time, all the other dogs in the place were fighting as if their hearths and homes depended on the fray. The big dogs fought each other indiscriminately; and the little dogs fought among themselves, and filled up their spare time by biting the legs of the big dogs.

The whole lobby was a perfect pandemonium, and the din was terrific. A crowd assembled outside in the Haymarket, and asked if it was a vestry meeting; or, if not, who was being murdered, and why? Men came with poles and ropes, and tried to separate the dogs, and the police were sent for.

And in the midst of the riot that sweet young lady returned, and snatched up that sweet little dog of hers (he had laid the tyke up for a month, and had on the expression, now, of a newborn lamb) into her arms, and kissed him, and asked him if he was killed, and what these great nasty brutes of dogs had been doing to him; and he nestled up against her, and gazed up into her face with a look that seemed to say: "Oh, I'm so glad you've come to take me away from this disgraceful scene!"

She said that the people at the Stores had no right to allow great savage things like those other dogs to be put with respectable people's dogs, and that she had a great mind to summon somebody.

Such is the nature of fox-terriers; and, therefore, I do not blame Montmorency for his tendency to row with cats; but he wished he had not given way to it that morning.

We were, as I have said, returning from a dip, and halfway up the High Street a cat darted out from one of the houses in front of us, and began to trot across the road. Montmorency gave a cry of joy—the cry of a stern warrior who sees his enemy given over to his hands—the sort of cry Cromwell might have uttered when the Scots came down the hill—and flew after his prey.

His victim was a large black Tom. I never saw a larger cat, nor a more disreputable-looking cat. It had lost half its tail, one of its ears, and a fairly appreciable proportion of its nose. It was a long, sinewy-looking animal. It had a calm, contented air about it.

Montmorency went for that poor cat at the rate of twenty miles an hour; but the cat did not hurry up—did not seem to have grasped the idea that its life was in danger. It trotted quietly on until its would-be assassin was within a yard of it, and then it turned round and sat down in the middle of the road, and looked at Montmorency with a gentle, inquiring expression, that said:

"Yes! You want me?"

Montmorency does not lack pluck; but there was something about the look of that cat that might have chilled the heart of the boldest dog. He stopped abruptly, and looked back at Tom.

Neither spoke; but the conversation that one could imagine was clearly as follows:

THE CAT: "Can I do anything for you?"

MONTMORENCY: "No—no, thanks."

THE CAT: "Don't you mind speaking, if you really want anything, you know."

MONTMORENCY (*backing down the High Street*):"Oh, no—not at all—certainly—don't you trouble. I—I am afraid I've made a mistake. I thought I knew you. Sorry I disturbed you."

THE CAT: "Not at all—quite a pleasure. Sure you don't want anything, now?"

MONTMORENCY (*still backing*): "Not at all, thanks—not at all—very kind of you. Good morning."

THE CAT: "Good morning."

Then the cat rose, and continued his trot; and Montmorency, fitting what he calls his tail carefully into its groove, came back to us, and took up an unimportant position in the rear.

To this day, if you say the word "Cats!" to Montmorency, he will visibly shrink and look up piteously at you, as if to say:

"Please don't."

We did our marketing after breakfast, and revictualled the boat for three days. George said we ought to take vegetables—that it was unhealthy not to eat vegetables. He said they were easy enough to cook, and that he would see to that; so we got ten pounds of potatoes, a bushel of peas, and a few cabbages. We got a beefsteak pie, a couple of gooseberry tarts, and a leg of mutton from the hotel; and fruit, and cakes, and bread and butter, and jam, and bacon and eggs, and other things we foraged round about the town for.

Our departure from Marlow I regard as one of our greatest successes. It was dignified and impressive, without being ostentatious. We had insisted at all the shops we had been to that the things should be sent with us then and there. None of your "Yes, sir, I will send them off at once: the boy will be down there before you are, sir!" and then fooling about on the landing-stage, and going back to the shop twice to have a row about them, for us. We waited while the basket was packed, and took the boy with us.

We went to a good many shops, adopting this principle at each one; and the consequence was that, by the time we had finished, we had as fine a collection of boys with baskets following us around as heart could desire; and our final march down the middle of the High Street, to the river, must have been as imposing a spectacle as Marlow had seen for many a long day.

The order of the procession was as follows:

Montmorency, carrying a stick.
Two disreputable-looking curs, friends of Montmorency's.
George, carrying coats and rugs, and smoking a short pipe.
Harris, trying to walk with easy grace, while carrying a
bulged-out Gladstone bag in one hand and a bottle of
lime-juice in the other.
Greengrocer's boy and baker's boy,with baskets.
Boots from the hotel, carrying hamper.
Confectioner's boy, with basket.
Grocer's boy, with basket.
Long-haired dog.
Cheesemonger's boy, with basket.
Odd man, carrying a bag.
Bosom companion of odd man, with his hands in his pockets,
smoking a short clay.
Fruiterer's boy, with basket.
Myself, carrying three hats and a pair of boots, and trying to
look as if I didn't know it.
Six small boys, and four stray dogs.

When we got down to the landing-stage, the boatman said:

"Let me see, sir; was yours a steam-launch or a houseboat?"

On our informing him it was a double-sculling skiff, he seemed surprised.

We had a good deal of trouble with steam launches that morning. It was just before the Henley week, and they were going up in large numbers; some by themselves some to by houseboats. I do hate steam launches: I suppose every rowing man does. I never see a steam launch but I feel I should like to lure it to a lonely part of the river, and there, in the silence and the solitude, strangle it.

There is a blatant bumptiousness about a steam launch that has the knack of rousing every evil instinct in my nature, and I yearn for the good old days, when you could go about and tell people what you thought of them with a hatchet and a bow and arrows. The expression on the face of the man who, with his hands in his pockets, stands by the stern, smoking a cigar, is sufficient to excuse a breach of the peace by itself; and the lordly whistle for you to get out of the way would, I am confident, ensure a verdict of "justifiable homicide" from any jury of river men.

They used to *have* to whistle for us to get out of their way. If I may do so, without appearing boastful, I think I can honestly say that our one small boat, during that week, caused more annoyance and delay and aggravation to the steam launches that we came across than all the other craft on the river put together.

"Steam launch, coming!" one of us would cry out, on sighting the enemy in the distance; and in an instant, everything was got ready to receive her. I would take the lines, and Harris and George would sit down beside me, all of us with our backs to the launch, and the boat would drift out quietly into mid-stream.

On would come the launch, whistling, and on we would go, drifting. At about a hundred yards off, she would start whistling like mad, and the people would come and lean over the side, and roar at us; but we never heard them! Harris would be telling us an anecdote about his mother, and George and I would not have missed a word of it for worlds.

Then that launch would give one final shriek of a whistle that would nearly burst the boiler, and she would reverse her engines, and blow off steam, and swing round and get aground; everyone on board of it would rush to the bow and yell at us, and the people on the bank would stand and shout to us, and all the other passing boats would stop and join in, till the whole river for miles up and down was in a state of frantic commotion. And then Harris would break off in the most interesting part of his narrative, and look up with mild surprise, and say to George:

"Why, George, bless us, if here isn't a steam launch!"

And George would answer:

"Well, do you know, I *thought* I heard something!"

Upon which we would get nervous and confused, and not know how to get the boat out of the way, and the people in the launch would crowd round and instruct us:

"Pull your right—you, you idiot! Back with your left. No, not *you*—the other one—leave the lines alone, can't you—now, both together. NOT *that* way. Oh, you——!"

Then they would lower a boat and come to our assistance; and, after quarter of an hour's effort, would get us clean out of their way, so that they could go on; and we would thank them so much, and ask them to give us a tow. But they never would.

Another good way we discovered of irritating the aristocratic type of steam launch, was to mistake them for a beanfeast, and ask them if they were Messrs. Cubit's lot or the Bermondsey Good Templars, and could they lend us a saucepan.

Old ladies, not accustomed to the river, are always intensely nervous of steam launches. I remember going up once from Staines to Windsor—a stretch of water peculiarly rich in these mechanical monstrosities—with a party containing three ladies of this description. It was very exciting. At the first glimpse of every steam launch that came in view, they insisted on landing and sitting down on the bank until it was out of sight again. They said they were very sorry, but that they owed it to their families not to be fool-hardy.

We found ourselves short of water at Hambledon Lock; so we took our jar and went up to the lock-keeper's house to beg for some.

George was our spokesman. He put on a winning smile, and said: "Oh, please could you spare us a little water?"

"Certainly," replied the old gentleman; "take as much as you want, and leave the rest."

"Thank you so much," murmured George, looking about him. "Where—where do you keep it?"

"It's always in the same place, my boy," was the stolid reply: "just behind you."

"I don't see it," said George, turning round.

"Why, bless us, where's your eyes?" was the man's comment, as he twisted George round and pointed up and down the stream. "There's enough of it to see, ain't there?"

"Oh!" exclaimed George, grasping the idea; "but we can't drink the river, you know!"

"No; but you can drink *some* of it," replied the old fellow. "It's what *I've* drunk for the last fifteen years."

George told him that his appearance, after the course, did not seem a sufficiently good advertisement for the brand; and that he would prefer it out of a pump.

We got some from a cottage a little higher up. I daresay *that* was only river water, if we had known. But we did not know, so it was all right. What the eye does not see, the stomach does not get upset over.

We tried river water once, later on in the season, but it was not a success. We were coming down stream, and had pulled up to have tea in a backwater near Windsor. Our jar was empty, and it was a case of going without our tea or taking water from the river. Harris was for chancing it. He said it must be all right if we boiled the water. He said that the various germs of poison present in the water would be killed by the boiling. So we filled our kettle with Thames backwater, and boiled it; and very careful we were to see that it did boil.

We had made the tea, and were just settling down comfortably to drink it, when George, with his cup halfway to his lips, paused and exclaimed:

"What's that?"

"What's what?" asked Harris and I.

"Why that!" said George, looking westward.

Harris and I followed his gaze, and saw, coming down towards us on the sluggish current, a dog. It was one of the quietest and peace-fullest dogs I have ever seen. I never met a dog who seemed more contented—more easy in its mind. It was floating dream-ily on its back, with its four legs stuck up straight into the air. It was what I should call a full-bodied dog, with a well-

developed chest. On he came, serene, dignified, and calm, until he was abreast of our boat, and there, among the rushes, he eased up, and settled down cosily for the evening.

George said he didn't want any tea, and emptied his cup into the water. Harris did not feel thirsty, either, and followed suit. I had drunk half mine, but I wished I had not.

I asked George if he thought I was likely to have typhoid.

He said: "Oh, no"; he thought I had a very good chance indeed of escaping it. Anyhow, I should know in about a fortnight, whether I had or had not.

We went up the backwater to Wargrave. It is a short cut, leading out of the right-hand bank about half a mile above Marsh Lock, and is well worth taking, being a pretty, shady little piece of stream, besides saving nearly half a mile of distance.

Of course, its entrance is studded with posts and chains, and surrounded with notice boards, menacing all kinds of torture, impris-onment, and death to everyone who dares set scull upon its waters—I wonder some of these riparian boors don't claim the air of the river and threaten everyone with forty shillings fine who breathes it—but the posts and chains a little skill will easily avoid; and as for the boards, you might, if you have five minutes to spare, and there is nobody about, take one or two of them down and throw them into the river.

Halfway up the backwater, we got out and lunched; and it was during this lunch that George and I received rather a trying shock.

Harris received a shock, too; but I do not think Harris' shock could have been anything like so bad as the shock that George and I had over the business.

You see, it was in this way: we were sitting in a meadow, about ten yards from the water's edge, and we had just settled down comfortably to feed. Harris had the beefsteak pie between his knees, and was carving it, and George and I were waiting with our plates ready.

"Have you got a spoon there?" says Harris; "I want a spoon to help the gravy with."

The hamper was close behind us, and George and I both turned round to reach one out. We were not five seconds getting it. When we looked round again, Harris and the pie were gone!

It was a wide, open field. There was not a tree or a bit of hedge for hundreds of yards. He could not have tumbled into the river, because we were on the water side of him, and he would have had to climb over us to do it.

George and I gazed all about. Then we gazed at each other.

"Has he been snatched up to heaven?" I queried.

"They'd hardly have taken the pie too," said George.

There seemed weight in this objection, and we discarded the heavenly theory.

"I suppose the truth of the matter is," suggested George, descending to the commonplace and practicable, "that there has been an earthquake."

And then he added, with a touch of sadness in his voice: "I wish he hadn't been carving that pie."

With a sigh, we turned our eyes once more towards the spot where Harris and the pie had last been seen on earth; and there, as our blood froze in our veins and our hair stood up on end, we saw Harris' head—and nothing but his head—sticking bolt upright among the tall grass, the face very red, and bearing upon it an expression of great indignation!

George was the first to recover.

"Speak!" he cried, "and tell us whether you are alive or dead—and where is the rest of you?"

"Oh, don't be a stupid ass!" said Harris' head. "I believe you did it on purpose."

"Did what?" exclaimed George and I.

"Why, put me to sit here—darn silly trick! Here, catch hold of the pie."

And out of the middle of the earth, as it seemed to us, rose the pie—very much mixed up and damaged; and, after it, scrambled Harris—tumbled, grubby, and wet.

He had been sitting, without knowing it, on the very verge of a small gully, the long grass hiding it from view; and in leaning a little back he had shot over, pie and all.

He said he had never felt so surprised in all his life, as when he first felt himself going, without being able to conjecture in the slightest what had happened. He thought at first that the end of the world had come.

Harris believes to this day that George and I planned it all beforehand. Thus does unjust suspicion follow even the most blameless; for, as the poet says, "Who shall escape calumny?"

Who, indeed!

CHAPTER XIV

WE CAUGHT A BREEZE, AFTER LUNCH, WHICH TOOK US GENTLY UP past Wargrave and Shiplake. Mellowed in the drowsy sunlight of a summer's afternoon, Wargrave, nestling where the river bends, makes a sweet old picture as you pass it, and one that lingers long upon the retina of memory.

The "George and Dragon" at Wargrave boasts a sign, painted on the one side by Leslie, R.A., and on the other by Hodgson of that ilk. Leslie has depicted the fight; Hodgson has imagined the scene, "After the Fight"—George, the work done, enjoying his pint of beer.

Day, the author of *Sandford and Merton*, lived and—more credit to the place still—was killed at Wargrave. In the church is a memorial to Mrs. Sarah Hill, who bequeathed *&pound*; 1 annually, to be divided at Easter, between two boys and two girls who "have never been undutiful to their parents; who have never been known to swear or to tell untruths, to steal, or to break windows." Fancy giving up all that for five shillings a year! It is not worth it.

It is rumoured in the town that once, many years ago, a boy appeared who really never had done these things—or at all events, which was all that was required or could be expected, had never been *known* to do them—and thus won the crown of glory. He was exhibited for three weeks afterwards in the Town Hall, under a glass case.

What has become of the money since no one knows. They say it is always handed over to the nearest waxworks show.

Shiplake is a pretty village, but it cannot be seen from the river, being upon the hill. Tennyson was married in Shiplake Church.

The river up to Sonning winds in and out through many islands, and is very placid, hushed, and lonely. Few folk, except at twilight, a pair or two of rustic lovers, walk along its banks. Arry and Lord Fitznoodle have been left behind at Henley, and dismal, dirty Reading is not yet reached. It is a part of the river in which to dream of bygone days, and vanished forms and faces, and things that might have been, but are not, confound them.

We got out at Sonning, and went for a walk round the village. It is the most fairylike little nook on the whole river. It is more like a stage village than one built of bricks and mortar. Every house is smothered in roses, and now, in early June, they were bursting forth in clouds of dainty splendour. If you stop at Sonning, put up at the "Bull," behind the church. It is a veritable picture of an old country inn, with green, square courtyard in front, where, on seats beneath the trees, the old men group of an evening to drink their ale and gossip over village politics; with low, quaint rooms and latticed windows, and awkward stairs and winding passages.

We roamed about sweet Sonning for an hour or so, and then, it being too late to push on past Reading, we decided to go back to one of the Shiplake islands, and put up there for the night. It was still early when we got settled, and George said that, as we had plenty of time, it would be a splendid opportunity to try a good, slap-up supper. He said he would show us what could be done up the river in the way of cooking, and suggested that, with the vegetables and the remains of the cold beef and general odds and ends, we should make an Irish stew.

It seemed a fascinating idea. George gathered wood and made a fire, and Harris and I started to peel the potatoes. I should never have thought that peeling potatoes was such an undertaking. The job turned out to be the biggest thing of its kind that I had ever been in. We began cheerfully, one might almost say skittishly, but our light-heartedness was gone by the time the first potato was finished. The more we peeled, the more peel there seemed to be left on; by the time we had got all the peel off and all the eyes out, there was no potato left—at least none worth speaking of. George came and had a look at it—it was about the size of a peanut. He said:

"Oh, that won't do! You're wasting them. You must scrape them."

So we scraped them, and that was harder work than peeling. They are such an extraordinary shape, potatoes—all bumps and warts and hollows. We worked steadily for five-and-twenty minutes, and did four potatoes. Then we struck. We said we should require the rest of the evening for scraping ourselves.

I never saw such a thing as potato-scraping for making a fellow in a mess. It seemed difficult to believe that the potato-scrapings in which Harris and I stood, half-smothered, could have come off four potatoes. It shows you what can be done with economy and care.

George said it was absurd to have only four potatoes in an Irish stew, so we washed half-a-dozen or so more, and put them in without peeling. We also put in a cabbage and about half a peck of peas. George stirred it all up, and then he said that there seemed to be a lot of room to spare, so we overhauled both the hampers, and picked out all the odds and ends and the remnants, and added them to the stew. There were half a pork pie and a bit of cold boiled bacon left, and we put them in. Then George found half a tin of potted salmon, and he emptied that into the pot.

He said that was the advantage of Irish stew: you got rid of such a lot of things. I fished out a couple of eggs that had got cracked, and we put those in. George said they would thicken the gravy.

I forget the other ingredients, but I know nothing was wasted; and I remember that, towards the end, Montmorency, who had evinced great interest in the proceedings throughout, strolled away with an earnest and thoughtful air, reappearing, a few minutes afterwards, with a dead water-rat in his mouth, which he evidently wished to present as his contribution to the dinner whether in a sarcastic spirit, or with a genuine desire to assist, I cannot say.

We had a discussion as to whether the rat should go in or not. Harris said that he thought it would be all right, mixed up with the other things, and that every little helped; but George stood up for precedent. He said he had never heard of water-rats in Irish stew, and he would rather be on the safe side, and not try experiments.

Harris said:

"If you never try a new thing, how can you tell what it's like? It's men such as you that hamper the world's progress. Think of the man who first tried German sausage!"

It was a great success, that Irish stew. I don't think I ever enjoyed a meal more. There was something so fresh and piquant about it. One's palate gets so tired of the old hackneyed things: here was a dish with a new flavour, with a taste like nothing else on earth.

And it was nourishing, too. As George said, there was good stuff in it. The peas and potatoes might have been a bit softer, but we all had good teeth, so that did not matter much: and as for the gravy, it was a poem—a little too rich, perhaps, for a weak stomach, but nutritious.

We finished up with tea and cherry tart. Montmorency had a fight with the kettle during tea-time, and came off a poor second.

Throughout the trip, he had manifested great curiosity concerning the kettle. He would sit and watch it, as it boiled, with a puzzled expression, and would try and rouse it every now and then by growling at it. When it began to splutter and steam, he regarded it as a challenge, and would want to fight it, only, at that precise moment, someone would always dash up and bear off his prey before he could get at it.

Today he determined he would be beforehand. At the first sound the kettle made, he rose, growling, and advanced towards it in a threatening attitude. It was only a little kettle, but it was full of pluck, and it up and spit at him.

"Ah! Would ye!" growled Montmorency, showing his teeth; "I'll teach ye to cheek a hard-working, respectable dog; ye miserable, long-nosed, dirty-looking scoundrel, ye. Come on!"

And he rushed at that poor little kettle, and seized it by the spout. Then, across the evening stillness, broke a blood-curdling yelp, and

 Montmorency left the boat, and did a constitutional three times round the island at the rate of thirty-five miles an hour, stopping every now and then to bury his nose in a bit of cool mud.

From that day Montmorency regarded the kettle with a mixture of awe, suspicion, and hate. Whenever he saw it he would growl and back at a rapid rate, with his tail shut down, and the moment it was put upon the stove he would promptly climb out of the boat, and sit on the bank, till the whole tea business was over.

George got out his banjo after supper, and wanted to play it, but Harris objected: he said he had got a headache, and did not feel strong enough to stand it. George thought the music might do him good—said music often soothed the nerves and took away a headache; and he twanged two or three notes, just to show Harris what it was like.

Harris said he would rather have the headache.

George has never learned to play the banjo to this day. He has had too much all-round discouragement to meet. He tried on two or three evenings, while we were up the river, to get a little practice, but it was never a success. Harris' language used to be enough to unnerve any man; added to which, Montmorency would sit and howl steadily, right through the performance. It was not giving the man a fair chance.

"What's he want to howl like that for when I'm playing?" George would exclaim indignantly, while taking aim at him with a boot.

"What do you want to play like that for when he is howling?" Harris would retort, catching the boot. "You let him alone. He can't help howling. He's got a musical ear, and your playing *makes* him howl."

So George determined to postpone study of the banjo until he reached home. But he did not get much opportunity even there. Mrs. P. used to come up and say she was very sorry—for herself, she liked to hear him—but the lady upstairs was in a very delicate state, and the doctor was afraid it might injure the child.

Then George tried taking it out with him late at night and practising round the square. But the inhabitants complained to the police about it, and a watch was set for him one night, and he was captured. The evidence against him was very clear, and he was bound over to keep the peace for six months.

He seemed to lose heart in the business after that. He did make one or two feeble efforts to take up the work again when the six months had elapsed, but there was always the same coldness—the same want of sympathy on the part of the world to fight against; and, after awhile, he despaired altogether, and advertised the instrument for sale at a great sacrifice—"owner having no further use for same"—and took to learning card tricks instead.

It must be disheartening work learning a musical instrument. You would think that Society, for its own sake, would do all it could to assist a man to acquire the art of playing a musical instrument. But it doesn't!

I knew a young fellow once, who was studying to play the bagpipes, and you would be surprised at the amount of opposition he had to contend with. Why, not even from the members of his own family did he receive what you could call active encouragement. His father was dead against the business from the beginning, and spoke quite unfeelingly on the subject.

My friend used to get up early in the morning to practise, but he had to give that plan up, because of his sister. She was somewhat religiously inclined, and she said it seemed such an awful thing to begin the day like that.

So he sat up at night instead, and played after the family had gone to bed, but that did not do, as it got the house such a bad name. People, going home late, would stop outside to listen, and then put it about all over the town, the next morning, that a fearful murder had been committed at Mr. Jefferson's the night before; and would describe how they had heard the victim's shrieks and the brutal oaths and curses of the murderer, followed by the prayer for mercy, and the last dying gurgle of the corpse.

So they let him practise in the daytime, in the back-kitchen with all the doors shut; but his more successful passages could generally be heard in the sitting room, in spite of these precautions, and would affect his mother almost to tears.

She said it put her in mind of her poor father (he had been swallowed by a shark, poor man, while bathing off the coast of New Guinea—where the connection came in, she could not explain).

Then they knocked up a little place for him at the bottom of the garden, about quarter of a mile from the house, and made him take the machine down there when he wanted to work it; and sometimes a visitor would come to the house who knew nothing of the matter, and they would forget to tell him all about it, and caution him, and he would go out for a stroll round the garden and suddenly get within earshot of those bagpipes without being prepared for it, or knowing what it was. If he were a man of strong mind, it only gave him fits; but a person of mere average intellect it usually sent mad.

There is, it must be confessed, something very sad about the early efforts of an amateur in bagpipes. I have felt that myself when listening to my young friend. They appear to be a trying instrument to perform upon. You have to get enough breath for the whole tune before you start—at least, so I gathered from watching Jefferson.

He would begin magnificently with a wild, full, come-to-the-battle sort of a note, that quite roused you. But he would get more and more piano as he went on, and the last verse generally collapsed in the middle with a splutter and a hiss.

You want to be in good health to play the bagpipes.

Young Jefferson only learnt to play one tune on those bagpipes: but I never heard any complaints about the insufficiency of his repertoire—none whatever. This tune was "The Campbells are Coming, Hooray—Hooray!" so he said, though his father always held that it was "The Blue Bells of Scotland." Nobody seemed quite sure what it was exactly, but they all agreed that it sounded Scotch.

Strangers were allowed three guesses, and most of them guessed a different tune each time.

Harris was disagreeable after supper—I think it must have been the stew that had upset him: he is not used to high living—so George and I left him in the boat, and settled to go for a mouch round Henley. He said he should have a glass of whisky and a pipe, and fix things up for the night. We were to shout when we returned, and he would row over from the island and fetch us.

"Don't go to sleep, old man," we said as we started.

"Not much fear of that while this stew's on," he grunted, as he pulled back to the island.

Henley was getting ready for the regatta, and was full of bustle. We met a goodish number of men we knew about the town, and in their pleasant company the time slipped by somewhat quickly; so that it was nearly eleven o'clock before we set off on our four-mile walk home—as we had learned to call our little craft by this time.

It was a dismal night, coldish, with a thin rain falling; and as we trudged through the dark, silent fields, talking low to each other, and wondering if we were going right or not, we thought of the cosy boat, with the bright light streaming through the tight-drawn canvas; of Harris and Montmorency, and the whisky, and wished that we were there.

We conjured up the picture of ourselves inside, tired and a little hungry; of the gloomy river and the shapeless trees; and, like a giant glowworm underneath them, our dear old boat, so snug and warm and cheerful. We could see ourselves at supper there, pecking away at cold meat, and passing each other chunks of bread; we could hear the cheery clatter of our knives, the laughing voices, filling all the space, and overflowing through the opening out into the night. And we hurried on to realise the vision.

We struck the towpath at length, and that made us happy; because prior to this we had not been sure whether we were walking towards the river or away from it, and when you are tired and want to go to bed uncertainties like that worry you. We passed Shiplake as the clock was striking the quarter to twelve; and then George said, thoughtfully:

"You don't happen to remember which of the islands it was, do you?"

"No," I replied, beginning to grow thoughtful too, "I don't. How many are there?"

"Only four," answered George. "It will be all right, if he's awake."

"And if not?" I queried; but we dismissed that train of thought.

We shouted when we came opposite the first island, but there was no response; so we went to the second, and tried there, and obtained the same result.

"Oh! I remember now," said George; "it was the third one."

And we ran on hopefully to the third one, and hallooed.

No answer!

The case was becoming serious. It was now past midnight. The hotels at Shiplake and Henley would be crammed; and we could not go round, knocking up cottagers and householders in the middle of the night, to know if they let apartments! George suggested walking back to Henley and assaulting a policeman, and so getting a night's lodging in the stationhouse. But then there was the thought, "Suppose he only hits us back and refuses to lock us up!"

We could not pass the whole night fighting policemen. Besides, we did not want to overdo the thing and get six months.

We despairingly tried what seemed in the darkness to be the fourth island, but met with no better success. The rain was coming down fast now, and evidently meant to last. We were wet to the skin, and cold and miserable. We began to wonder whether there were only four islands or more, or whether we were near the islands at all, or whether we were anywhere within a mile of where we ought to be, or in the wrong part of the river altogether; everything looked so strange and different in the darkness. We began to understand the sufferings of the Babes in the Wood.

Just when we had given up all hope—yes, I know that is always the time that things do happen in novels and tales; but I can't help it. I resolved when I began to write this book, that I would be strictly truthful in all things; and so I will be, even if I have to employ hackneyed phrases for the purpose.

It *was* just when we had given up all hope, and I must therefore say so. Just when we had given up all hope, then, I suddenly caught sight, a little way below us, of a strange, weird sort of glimmer flickering among the trees on the opposite bank. For an instant I thought of ghosts: it was such a shadowy, mysterious light. The next moment it flashed across me that it was our boat, and I sent up such a yell across the water that made the night seem to shake in its bed.

We waited breathless for a minute, and then—oh! Divinest music of the darkness! We heard the answering bark of Montmorency. We shouted back loud enough to wake the Seven Sleepers—I never could understand myself why it should take more noise to wake seven sleepers than one—and, after what seemed an hour, but what was really, I suppose, about five minutes, we saw the lighted boat creeping slowly over the blackness, and heard Harris' sleepy voice asking where we were.

There was an unaccountable strangeness about Harris. It was something more than mere ordinary tiredness. He pulled the boat against a part of the bank from which it was quite impossible for us to get into it, and immediately went to sleep. It took us an immense amount of screaming and roaring to wake him up again, and put some sense into him; but we succeeded at last, and got safely on board.

Harris had a sad expression on him, so we noticed, when we got into the boat. He gave you the idea of a man who had been through trouble. We asked him if anything had happened, and he said—

"Swans!"

It seemed we had moored close to a swan's nest, and, soon after George and I had gone, the female swan came back, and kicked up a row about it. Harris had chivied her off, and she had gone away, and fetched up her old man. Harris said he had had quite a fight with these two swans; but courage and skill had prevailed in the end, and he had defeated them.

Half-an-hour afterwards they returned with eighteen other swans! It must have been a fearful battle, so far as we could understand Harris' account of it. The swans had tried to drag him and Montmorency out of the boat and drown them; and he had defended himself like a hero for four hours, and had killed the lot, and they had all paddled away to die.

"How many swans did you say there were?" asked George.

"Thirty-two," replied Harris, sleepily.

"You said eighteen just now," said George.

"No, I didn't," grunted Harris; "I said twelve. Think I can't count?"

What were the real facts about these swans we never found out. We questioned Harris on the subject in the morning, and he said, "What swans?" and seemed to think that George and I had been dreaming.

Oh, how delightful it was to be safe in the boat, after our trials and fears! We ate a hearty supper, George and I, and we should have had some toddy after it, if we could have found the whisky, but we could not. We examined Harris as to what he had done with it; but he did not seem to know what we meant by "whisky," or what we were talking about at all. Montmorency looked as if he knew something, but said nothing.

I slept well that night, and should have slept better if it had not been for Harris. I have a vague recollection of having been woke up at least a dozen times during the night by Harris wandering about the boat with the lantern, looking for his clothes. He seemed to be worrying about his clothes all night.

Twice he routed up George and myself to see if we were lying on his trousers. George got quite wild the second time.

"What the thunder do you want your trousers for, in the middle of the night?" he asked indignantly. "Why don't you lie down, and go to sleep?"

I found him in trouble, the next time I awoke, because he could not find his socks; and my last hazy remembrance is of being rolled over on my side, and of hearing Harris muttering something about its being an extraordinary thing where his umbrella could have got to.

CHAPTER XV

WE WOKE LATE THE NEXT MORNING, AND, AT HARRIS' EARNEST desire, partook of a plain breakfast, with "non dainties." Then we cleaned up, and put everything straight (a continual labour, which was beginning to afford me a pretty clear insight into a question that had often posed me—namely, how a woman with the work of only one house on her hands manages to pass away her time), and, at about ten, set out on what we had determined should be a good day's journey.

We agreed that we would pull this morning, as a change from towing; and Harris thought the best arrangement would be that George and I should scull, and he steer. I did not chime in with this idea at all; I said I thought Harris would have been showing a more proper spirit if he had suggested that he and George should work, and let me rest a bit. It seemed to me that I was doing more than my fair share of the work on this trip, and I was beginning to feel strongly on the subject.

It always does seem to me that I am doing more work than I should do. It is not that I object to the work, mind you; I like work: it fascinates me. I can sit and look at it for hours. I love to keep it by me: the idea of getting rid of it nearly breaks my heart.

You cannot give me too much work; to accumulate work has almost become a passion with me: my study is so full of it now, that there is hardly an inch of room for anymore. I shall have to throw but a wing soon.

And I am careful of my work, too. Why, some of the work that I have by me now has been in my possession for years and years, and there isn't a finger mark on it. I take a great pride in my work; I take it down now and then and dust it. No man keeps his work in a better state of preservation than I do.

But, though I crave for work, I still like to be fair. I do not ask for more than my proper share.

But I get it without asking for it—at least, so it appears to me—and this worries me.

George says he does not think I need trouble myself on the subject. He thinks it is only my over scrupulous nature that makes me fear I am having more than my due; and that, as a matter of fact, I don't have half as much as I ought. But I expect he only says this to comfort me.

In a boat, I have always noticed that it is the fixed idea of each member of the crew that he is doing everything. Harris' notion was, that it was he alone who had been working, and that both George and I had been imposing upon him. George, on the other hand, ridiculed the idea of Harris' having done anything more than eat and sleep, and had a cast-iron opinion that it was he—George himself—who had done all the labour worth speaking of.

He said he had never been out with such a couple of lazily skulks as Harris and I.

That amused Harris.

"Fancy old George talking about work!" he laughed; "why, about half-an-hour of it would kill him. Have you ever seen George work?" he added, turning to me.

I agreed with Harris that I never had—most certainly not since we had started on this trip.

"Well, I don't see how *you* can know much about it, one way or the other," George retorted on Harris; "for I'm blest if you haven't been asleep half the time. Have you ever seen Harris fully awake, except at mealtime?" asked George, addressing me.

Truth compelled me to support George. Harris had been very little good in the boat, so far as helping was concerned, from the beginning.

"Well, hang it all, I've done more than old J., anyhow," rejoined Harris.

"Well, you couldn't very well have done less," added George.

"I suppose J. thinks he is the passenger," continued Harris.

And that was their gratitude to me for having brought them and their wretched old boat all the way up from Kingston, and for having superintended and managed everything for them, and taken care of them, and slaved for them. It is the way of the world.

We settled the present difficulty by arranging that Harris and George should scull up past Reading, and that I should tow the boat on from there. Pulling a heavy boat against a strong stream has few attractions for me now. There was a time, long ago, when I used to clamour for the hard work: now I like to give the youngsters a chance.

I notice that most of the old river hands are similarly retiring, whenever there is any stiff pulling to be done. You can always tell the old river hand by the way in which he stretches himself out upon the cushions at the bottom of the boat, and encourages the rowers by telling them anecdotes about the marvellous feats he performed last season.

"Call what you're doing hard work!" he drawls, between his contented whiffs, addressing the two perspiring novices, who have been grinding away steadily up stream for the last hour and a half; "why, Jim Biffles and Jack and I, last season, pulled up from Marlow to Goring in one afternoon—never stopped once. Do you remember that, Jack?"

Jack, who has made himself a bed up in the prow of all the rugs and coats he can collect, and who has been lying there asleep for the last two hours, partially wakes up on being thus appealed to, and recollects all about the matter, and also remembers that there was an unusually strong stream against them all the way—likewise a stiff wind.

"About thirty-four miles, I suppose, it must have been," adds the first speaker, reaching down another cushion to put under his head.

"No—no; don't exaggerate, Tom," murmurs Jack, reprovingly; "thirty-three at the outside."

And Jack and Tom, quite exhausted by this conversational effort, drop off to sleep once more. And the two simpleminded youngsters at the sculls feel quite proud of being allowed to row such wonderful oarsmen as Jack and Tom, and strain away harder than ever.

When I was a young man, I used to listen to these tales from my elders, and take them in, and swallow them, and digest every word of them, and then come up for more; but the new generation does not seem to have the simple faith of the old times. We—George, Harris, and myself—took a "raw'un" up with us once last season, and we plied him with the customary stretchers about the wonderful things we had done all the way up.

We gave him all the regular ones—the time-honoured lies that have done duty up the river with every boating-man for years past—and added seven entirely original ones that we had invented for ourselves, including a really quite likely story, founded, to a certain extent, on an all but true episode, which had actually happened in a modified degree some years ago to friends of ours—a story that a mere child could have believed without injuring itself, much.

And that young man mocked at them all, and wanted us to repeat the feats then and there, and to bet us ten to one that we didn't.

We got to chatting about our rowing experiences this morning, and to recounting stories of our first efforts in the art of oarsmanship. My own earliest boating recollection is of five of us contributing threepence each and taking out a curiously constructed craft on the Regent's Park lake, drying ourselves subsequently in the park-keeper's lodge.

After that, having acquired a taste for the water, I did a good deal of rafting in various suburban brickfields—an exercise providing more interest and excitement than might be imagined, especially when you are in the middle of the pond and the proprietor of the materials of which the raft is constructed suddenly appears on the bank, with a big stick in his hand.

Your first sensation on seeing this gentleman is that, somehow or other, you don't feel equal to company and conversation, and that, if you could do so without appearing rude, you would rather avoid meeting him; and your object is, therefore, to get off on the opposite side of the pond to which he is, and to go home quietly and quickly, pretending not to see him. He, on the contrary, is yearning to take you by the hand, and talk to you.

It appears that he knows your father, and is intimately acquainted with yourself, but this does not draw you towards him. He says he'll teach you to take his boards and make a raft of them; but, seeing that you know how to do this pretty well already, the offer, though doubtless kindly meant, seems a superfluous one on his part, and you are reluctant to put him to any trouble by accepting it.

His anxiety to meet you, however, is proof against all your coolness, and the energetic manner in which he dodges up and down the pond so as to be on the spot to greet you when you land is really quite flattering.

If he be of a stout and short-winded build, you can easily avoid his advances; but, when he is of the youthful and long-legged type, a meeting is inevitable. The interview is, however, extremely brief, most of the conversation being on his part, your remarks being mostly of an exclamatory and monosyllabic order, and as soon as you can tear yourself away you do so.

I devoted some three months to rafting, and, being then as proficient as there was any need to be at that branch of the art, I determined to go in for rowing proper, and joined one of the Lea boating clubs.

Being out in a boat on the river Lea, especially on Saturday afternoons, soon makes you smart at handling a craft, and spry at escaping being run down by roughs or swamped by barges; and it also affords plenty of opportunity for acquiring the most prompt and graceful method of lying down flat at the bottom of the boat so as to avoid being chucked out into the river by passing towlines.

But it does not give you style. It was not till I came to the Thames that I got style. My style of rowing is very much admired now. People say it is so quaint.

George never went near the water until he was sixteen. Then he and eight other gentlemen of about the same age went down in a body to Kew one Saturday, with the idea of hiring a boat there, and pulling to Richmond and back; one of their number, a shock-headed youth, named Joskins, who had once or twice taken out a boat on the Serpentine, told them it was jolly fun, boating!

The tide was running out pretty rapidly when they reached the landing-stage, and there was a stiff breeze blowing across the river, but this did not trouble them at all, and they proceeded to select their boat.

There was an eight-oared racing outrigger drawn up on the stage; that was the one that took their fancy. They said they'd have that one, please. The boatman was away, and only his boy was in charge. The boy tried to damp their ardour for the outrigger, and showed them two or three very comfortable-looking boats of the family-party build, but those would not do at all; the outrigger was the boat they thought they would look best in.

So the boy launched it, and they took off their coats and prepared to take their seats. The boy suggested that George, who, even in those days, was always the heavy man of any party, should be number four. George said he should be happy to be number four, and promptly stepped into bow's place and sat down with his back to the stern. They got him into his proper position at last, and then the others followed.

A particularly nervous boy was appointed cox, and the steering principle explained to him by Joskins. Joskins himself took stroke. He told the others that it was simple enough; all they had to do was to follow him.

They said they were ready, and the boy on the landing-stage took a boat-hook and shoved him off.

What then followed George is unable to describe in detail. He has a confused recollection of having, immediately on starting, received a violent blow in the small of the back from the butt-end of number five's scull, at the same time that his own seat seemed to disappear from under him by magic, and leave him sitting on the boards. He also noticed, as a curious circumstance, that number two was at the same instant lying on his back at the bottom of the boat, with his legs in the air, apparently in a fit.

They passed under Kew Bridge, broadside, at the rate of eight miles an hour. Joskins being the only one who was rowing. George, on recovering his seat, tried to help him, but, on dipping his oar into the water, it immediately, to his intense surprise, disappeared under the boat, and nearly took him with it.

And the "cox" threw both rudder lines overboard and burst into tears.

How they got back George never knew, but it took them just forty minutes. A dense crowd watched the entertainment from Kew Bridge with much interest, and everybody shouted out to them different directions. Three times they managed to get the boat back through the arch, and three times they were carried under it again, and everytime "cox" looked up and saw the bridge above him he broke out into renewed sobs.

George said he little thought that afternoon that he should ever come to really like boating.

Harris is more accustomed to sea rowing than to river work, and says that, as an exercise, he prefers it. I don't. I remember taking a small boat out at Eastbourne last summer: I used to do a good deal of sea rowing years ago, and I thought I should be all right; but I found I had forgotten the art entirely. When one scull was deep down underneath the water, the other would be flourishing wildly about in the air. To get a grip of the water with both at the same time I had to stand up. The parade was crowded with the nobility and gentry, and I had to pull past them in this ridiculous fashion. I landed halfway down the beach, and secured the services of an old boatman to take me back.

I like to watch an old boatman rowing, especially one who has been hired by the hour. There is something so beautifully calm and restful about his method. It is so free from that fretful haste, that vehement striving, that is everyday becoming more and more the bane of nineteenth-century life. He is not forever straining himself to pass all the other boats. If another boat overtakes him and passes him it does not annoy him; as a matter of fact, they all do overtake him and pass him—all those that are going his way. This would trouble and irritate some people; the sublime equanimity of the hired boatman under the ordeal affords us a beautiful lesson against ambition and uppishness.

Plain practical rowing of the get-the-boat-along order is not a very difficult art to acquire, but it takes a good deal of practice before a man feels comfortable when rowing past girls. It is the "time" that worries a youngster. "It's jolly funny," he says, as for the twentieth time within five minutes he disentangles his sculls from yours; "I can get on all right when I'm by myself!"

To see two novices try to keep time with one another is very amusing. Bow finds it impossible to keep pace with stroke, because stroke rows in such an extraordinary fashion. Stroke is intensely indignant at this, and explains that what he has been endeavouring to do for

the last ten minutes is to adapt his method to bow's limited capacity. Bow, in turn, then becomes insulted, and requests stroke not to trouble his head about him (bow), but to devote his mind to setting a sensible stroke.

"Or, shall *I* take stroke?" he adds, with the evident idea that that would at once put the whole matter right.

They splash along for another hundred yards with still moderate success, and then the whole secret of their trouble bursts upon stroke like a flash of inspiration.

"I tell you what it is: you've got my sculls," he cries, turning to bow; "pass yours over."

"Well, do you know, I've been wondering how it was I couldn't get on with these," answers bow, quite brightening up, and most willingly assisting in the exchange. "*Now* we shall be all right."

But they are not—not even then. Stroke has to stretch his arms nearly out of their sockets to reach his sculls now; while bow's pair, at each recovery, hit him a violent blow in the chest. So they change back again, and come to the conclusion that the man has given them the wrong set altogether; and over their mutual abuse of this man they become quite friendly and sympathetic.

George said he had often longed to take to punting for a change. Punting is not as easy as it looks. As in rowing, you soon learn how to get along and handle the craft, but it takes long practice before you can do this with dignity and without getting the water all up your sleeve.

One young man I knew had a very sad accident happen to him the first time he went punting. He had been getting on so well that he had grown quite cheeky over the business, and was walking up and down the punt, working his pole with a careless grace that was quite fascinating to watch. Up he would march to the head of the punt, plant his pole, and then run along right to the other end, just like an old punter. Oh! It was grand.

And it would all have gone on being grand if he had not unfortunately, while looking round to enjoy the scenery, taken just one step more than there was any necessity for, and walked off the punt altogether. The pole was firmly fixed in the mud, and he was left clinging to it while the punt drifted away. It was an undignified position for him. A rude boy on the bank immediately yelled out to a lagging chum to "hurry up and see a real monkey on a stick."

I could not go to his assistance, because, as ill-luck would have it, we had not taken the proper precaution to bring out a spare pole with us. I could only sit and look at him. His expression as the pole slowly sank with him I shall never forget; there was so much thought in it.

I watched him gently let down into the water, and saw him scramble out, sad and wet. I could not help laughing, he looked such a ridiculous figure. I continued to chuckle to myself about it for some time, and then it was suddenly forced upon me that really I had got very little to laugh at when I came to think of it. Here was I, alone in a punt, without a pole, drifting helplessly down mid-stream—possibly towards a weir.

I began to feel very indignant with my friend for having stepped overboard and gone off in that way. He might, at all events, have left me the pole.

I drifted on for about a quarter of a mile, and then I came in sight of a fishing-punt moored in mid-stream, in which sat two old fishermen. They saw me bearing down upon them, and they called out to me to keep out of their way.

"I can't," I shouted back.

"But you don't try," they answered.

I explained the matter to them when I got nearer, and they caught me and lent me a pole. The weir was just fifty yards below. I am glad they happened to be there.

The first time I went punting was in company with three other fellows; they were going to show me how to do it. We could not all start together, so I said I would go down first and get out the punt, and then I could potter about and practise a bit until they came.

I could not get a punt out that afternoon, they were all engaged; so I had nothing else to do but to sit down on the bank, watching the river, and waiting for my friends.

I had not been sitting there long before my attention became attracted to a man in a punt who, I noticed with some surprise, wore a jacket and cap exactly like mine. He was evidently a novice at punting, and his performance was most interesting. You never knew what was going to happen when he put the pole in; he evidently did not know himself. Sometimes he shot up stream and sometimes he shot down stream, and at other times he simply spun round and came up the other side of the pole. And with every result he seemed equally surprised and annoyed.

The people about the river began to get quite absorbed in him after a while, and to make bets with one another as to what would be the outcome of his next push.

In the course of time my friends arrived on the opposite bank, and they stopped and watched him too. His back was towards them, and they only saw his jacket and cap. From this they immediately jumped to the conclusion that it was I, their beloved companion, who was making an exhibition of himself, and their delight knew no bounds. They commenced to chaff him unmercifully.

I did not grasp their mistake at first, and I thought, "How rude of them to go on like that, with a perfect stranger, too!" But before I could call out and reprove them, the explanation of the matter occurred to me, and I withdrew behind a tree.

Oh, how they enjoyed themselves, ridiculing that young man! For five good minutes they stood there, shouting ribaldry at him, deriding him, mocking him, jeering at him. They peppered him with stale jokes, they even made a few new ones and threw at him. They hurled at him all the private family jokes belonging to our set, and which must have been perfectly unintelligible to him. And then, unable to stand their brutal jibes any longer, he turned round on them, and they saw his face!

I was glad to notice that they had sufficient decency left in them to look very foolish. They explained to him that they had thought he was someone they knew. They said they hoped he would not deem them capable of so insulting anyone except a personal friend of their own.

Of course their having mistaken him for a friend excused it. I remember Harris telling me once of a bathing experience he had at Boulogne. He was swimming about there near the beach, when he felt himself suddenly seized by the neck from behind, and forcibly plunged under water. He struggled violently, but whoever had got hold of him seemed to be a perfect Hercules in strength, and all his efforts to escape were unavailing. He had given up kicking, and was trying to turn his thoughts upon solemn things, when his captor released him.

He regained his feet, and looked round for his would-be murderer. The assassin was standing close by him, laughing heartily, but the moment he caught sight of Harris's face, as it emerged from the water, he started back and seemed quite concerned.

"I really beg your pardon," he stammered confusedly, "but I took you for a friend of mine!"

Harris thought it was lucky for him the man had not mistaken him for a relation, or he would probably have been drowned outright.

Sailing is a thing that wants knowledge and practice too—though, as a boy, I did not think so. I had an idea it came natural to a body, like rounders and touch. I knew another boy who held this view likewise, and so, one windy day, we thought we would try the sport. We were stopping down at Yarmouth, and we decided we would go for a trip up the Yare. We hired a sailing boat at the yard by the bridge, and started off.

"It's rather a rough day," said the man to us, as we put off: "better take in a reef and luff sharp when you get round the bend."

We said we would make a point of it, and left him with a cheery "Good morning," wondering to ourselves how you "luffed," and where we were to get a "reef" from, and what we were to do with it when we had got it.

We rowed until we were out of sight of the town, and then, with a wide stretch of water in front of us, and the wind blowing a perfect hurricane across it, we felt that the time had come to commence operations.

Hector—I think that was his name—went on pulling while I unrolled the sail. It seemed a complicated job, but I accomplished it at length, and then came the question, which was the top end?

By a sort of natural instinct, we, of course, eventually decided that the bottom was the top, and set to work to fix it upside-down. But it was a long time before we could get it up, either that way or any other way. The impression on the mind of the sail seemed to be that we were playing at funerals and that I was the corpse and itself was the winding sheet.

When it found that this was not the idea, it hit me over the head with the boom, and refused to do anything.

"Wet it," said Hector; "drop it over and get it wet."

He said people in ships always wetted the sails before they put them up. So I wetted it; but that only made matters worse than they were before. A dry sail clinging to your legs and wrapping itself round your head is not pleasant, but, when the sail is sopping wet, it becomes quite vexing.

We did get the thing up at last, the two of us together. We fixed it, not exactly upside down—more sideways like—and we tied it up to the mast with the painter, which we cut off for the purpose.

That the boat did not upset I simply state as a fact. Why it did not upset I am unable to offer any reason. I have often thought about the matter since, but I have never succeeded in arriving at any satisfactory explanation of the phenomenon.

Possibly the result may have been brought about by the natural obstinacy of all things in this world. The boat may possibly have come to the conclusion, judging from a cursory view of our behaviour, that we had come out for a morning's suicide, and had thereupon determined to disappoint us. That is the only suggestion I can offer.

By clinging like grim death to the gunwale, we just managed to keep inside the boat, but it was exhausting work. Hector said that pirates and other seafaring people generally lashed the rudder to something or other, and hauled in the main top-jib, during severe squalls, and thought we ought to try to do something of the kind; but I was for letting her have her head to the wind.

As my advice was by far the easiest to follow, we ended by adopting it, and contrived to embrace the gunwale and give her her head.

The boat travelled up stream for about a mile at a pace I have never sailed at since, and don't want to again. Then, at a bend, she heeled over till half her sail was under water. Then she righted herself by a miracle and flew for a long low bank of soft mud.

That mud-bank saved us. The boat ploughed its way into the middle of it and then stuck. Finding that we were once more able to move according to our ideas, instead of being pitched and thrown about like peas in a bladder, we crept forward, and cut down the sail.

We had had enough sailing. We did not want to overdo the thing and get a surfeit of it. We had had a sail—a good all-round exciting, interesting sail—and now we thought we would have a row, just for a change like.

We took the sculls and tried to push the boat off the mud, and, in doing so, we broke one of the sculls. After that we proceeded with great caution, but they were a wretched old pair, and the second one cracked almost easier than the first, and left us helpless.

The mud stretched out for about a hundred yards in front of us, and behind us was the water. The only thing to be done was to sit and wait until some one came by.

It was not the sort of day to attract people out on the river, and it was three hours before a soul came in sight. It was an old fisherman who, with immense difficulty, at last rescued us, and we were towed back in an ignominious fashion to the boat-yard.

What between tipping the man who had brought us home, and paying for the broken sculls, and for having been out four hours and a half, it cost us a pretty considerable number of weeks' pocket-money, that sail. But we learned experience, and they say that is always cheap at any price.

CHAPTER XVI

Reading • We are towed by steam launch • Irritating behaviour of small boats • How they get in the way of steam launches • George and Harris again shirk their work • Rather a hackneyed story • Streatley and Goring

WE CAME IN SIGHT OF READING ABOUT ELEVEN. THE RIVER IS DIRTY and dismal here. One does not linger in the neighbourhood of Reading. The town itself is a famous old place, dating from the dim days of King Ethelred, when the Danes anchored their warships in the Kennet, and started from Reading to ravage all the land of Wessex; and here Ethelred and his brother Alfred fought and defeated them, Ethelred doing the praying and Alfred the fighting.

In later years, Reading seems to have been regarded as a handy place to run down to, when matters were becoming unpleasant in London. Parliament generally rushed off to Reading whenever there was a plague on at Westminster; and, in 1625, the Law followed suit, and all the courts were held at Reading. It must have been worth while having a mere ordinary plague now and then in London to get rid of both the lawyers and the Parliament.

During the Parliamentary struggle, Reading was besieged by the Earl of Essex, and, a quarter of a century later, the Prince of Orange routed King James' troops there.

Henry I lies buried at Reading, in the Benedictine abbey founded by him there, the ruins of which may still be seen; and, in this same abbey, great John of Gaunt was married to the Lady Blanche.

At Reading Lock we came up with a steam launch, belonging to some friends of mine, and they towed us up to within about a mile of Streatley. It is very delightful being towed up by a launch. I prefer it myself to rowing. The run would have been more delightful still, if it had not been for a lot of wretched small boats that were continually getting in the way of our launch, and, to avoid running down which, we had to be continually easing and stopping. It is really most annoying, the manner in which these rowing boats get in the way of one's launch up the river; something ought to be done to stop it.

And they are so confoundedly impertinent, too, over it. You can whistle till you nearly burst your boiler before they will trouble themselves to hurry. I would have one or two of them run down now and then, if I had my way, just to teach them all a lesson.

The river becomes very lovely from a little above Reading. The railway rather spoils it near Tilehurst, but from Mapledurham up to Streatley it is glorious. A little above Mapledurham Lock you pass Hardwick House, where Charles I played bowls. The neighbourhood of Pangbourne, where the quaint little Swan Inn stands, must be as familiar to the *habitués* of the Art Exhibitions as it is to its own inhabitants.

My friends' launch cast us loose just below the grotto, and then Harris wanted to make out that it was my turn to pull. This seemed to me most unreasonable. It had been arranged in the morning that I should bring the boat up to three miles above Reading. Well, here we were, ten miles above Reading! Surely it was now their turn again.

I could not get either George or Harris to see the matter in its proper light, however; so, to save argument, I took the sculls. I had not been pulling for more than a minute or so, when George noticed something black floating on the water, and we drew up to it. George leant over, as we neared it, and laid hold of it. And then he drew back with a cry, and a blanched face.

It was the dead body of a woman. It lay very lightly on the water, and the face was sweet and calm. It was not a beautiful face; it was too prematurely aged-looking, too thin and drawn, to be that; but it was a gentle, lovable face, in spite of its stamp of pinch and poverty, and upon it was that look of restful peace that comes to the faces of the sick sometimes when at last the pain has left them.

Fortunately for us—we having no desire to be kept hanging about coroners' courts—some men on the bank had seen the body too, and now took charge of it from us.

We found out the woman's story afterwards. Of course it was the old, old vulgar tragedy. She had loved and been deceived—or had deceived herself. Anyhow, she had sinned—some of us do now and then—and her family and friends, naturally shocked and indignant, had closed their doors against her.

Left to fight the world alone, with the millstone of her shame around her neck, she had sunk ever lower and lower. For a while she had kept both herself and the child on the twelve shillings a week that twelve hours' drudgery a day procured her, paying six shillings out of it for the child, and keeping her own body and soul together on the remainder.

Six shillings a week does not keep body and soul together very unitedly. They want to get away from each other when there is only such a very slight bond as that between them; and one day, I suppose, the pain and the dull monotony of it all had stood before her eyes plainer than usual, and the mocking spectre had frightened her. She had made one last appeal to friends, but, against the chill wall of their respectability, the voice of the erring outcast fell unheeded; and then she had gone to see her child—had held it in her arms and kissed it, in a weary, dull sort of way, and without betraying any particular emotion of any kind, and had left it, after putting into its hand a penny box of chocolate she had bought it, and afterwards, with her last few shillings, had taken a ticket and come down to Goring.

It seemed that the bitterest thoughts of her life must have centred about the wooded reaches and the bright green meadows around Goring; but women strangely hug the knife that stabs them, and, perhaps, amidst the gall, there may have mingled also sunny memories of sweetest hours, spent upon those shadowed deeps over which the great trees bend their branches down so low.

She had wandered about the woods by the river's brink all day, and then, when evening fell and the grey twilight spread its dusky robe upon the waters, she stretched her arms out to the silent river

that had known her sorrow and her joy. And the old river had taken her into its gentle arms, and had laid her weary head upon its bosom, and had hushed away the pain.

Thus had she sinned in all things—sinned in living and in dying. God help her! And all other sinners, if anymore there be.

Goring on the left bank and Streatley on the right are both or either charming places to stay at for a few days. The reaches down to Pangbourne woo one for a sunny sail or for a moonlight row, and the country round about is full of beauty. We had intended to push on to Wallingford that day, but the sweet smiling face of the river here lured us to linger for a while; and so we left our boat at the bridge, and went up into Streatley, and lunched at the "Bull," much to Montmorency's satisfaction.

They say that the hills on each side of the stream here once joined and formed a barrier across what is now the Thames, and that then the river ended there above Goring in one vast lake. I am not in a position either to contradict or affirm this statement. I simply offer it.

It is an ancient place, Streatley, dating back, like most riverside towns and villages, to British and Saxon times. Goring is not nearly so pretty a little spot to stop at as Streatley, if you have your choice; but it is passing fair enough in its way, and is nearer the railway in case you want to slip off without paying your hotel bill.

CHAPTER XVII

Washing day • Fish and fishers • On the art of
angling • A conscientious fly-fisher • A fishy story

WE STAYED TWO DAYS AT STREATLEY, AND GOT OUR CLOTHES
washed. We had tried washing them ourselves, in the river, under
George's superintendence, and it had been a failure. Indeed, it had

been more than a fail-
ure, because we were
worse off after we had
washed our clothes
than we were before.
Before we had washed
them, they had been
very, very dirty, it is
true; but they were
just wearable. *After* we
had washed them—well, the river between Reading and Henley was
much cleaner, after we had washed our clothes in it, than it was before.
All the dirt contained in the river between Reading and Henley we
collected, during that wash, and worked it into our clothes.

The washerwoman at Streatley said she felt she owed it to herself
to charge us just three times the usual prices for that wash. She
said it had not been like washing, it had been more in the nature
of excavating.

We paid the bill without a murmur.

The neighbourhood of Streatley and Goring is a great fishing centre. There is some excellent fishing to be had here. The river abounds in pike, roach, dace, gudgeon, and eels, just here; and you can sit and fish for them all day.

Some people do. They never catch them. I never knew anybody catch anything, up the Thames, except minnows and dead cats, but that has nothing to do, of course, with fishing! The local fisherman's guide doesn't say a word about catching anything. All it says is the place is "a good station for fishing"; and, from what I have seen of the district, I am quite prepared to bear out this statement.

There is no spot in the world where you can get more fishing, or where you can fish for a longer period. Some fishermen come here and fish for a day, and others stop and fish for a month. You can hang on and fish for a year, if you want to: it will be all the same.

The *Angler's Guide to the Thames* says that "jack and perch are also to be had about here," but there the *Angler's Guide* is wrong. Jack and perch may *be* about there. Indeed, I know for a fact that they are. You can *see* them there in shoals, when you are out for a walk along the banks: they come and stand half out of the water with their mouths open for biscuits. And, if you go for a bathe, they crowd round, and get in your way and irritate you. But they are not to be "had" by a bit of worm on the end of a hook, nor anything like it—not they!

I am not a good fisherman myself. I devoted a considerable amount of attention to the subject at one time, and was getting on, as I thought, fairly well; but the old hands told me that I should never be any real good at it, and advised me to give it up. They said that I was an extremely neat thrower, and that I seemed to have plenty of gumption for the thing, and quite enough constitutional laziness. But they were sure I should never make anything of a fisherman. I had not got sufficient imagination.

They said that as a poet, or a shilling shocker, or a reporter, or anything of that kind, I might be satisfactory, but that, to gain any position as a Thames angler, would require more play of fancy, more power of invention than I appeared to possess.

Some people are under the impression that all that is required to make a good fisherman is the ability to tell lies easily and without blushing; but this is a mistake. Mere bald fabrication is useless; the veriest tyro can manage that. It is in the circumstantial detail, the embellishing touches of probability, the general air of scrupulous— almost of pedantic—veracity, that the experienced angler is seen.

Anybody can come in and say, "Oh, I caught fifteen dozen perch yesterday evening"; or "Last Monday I landed a gudgeon, weighing eighteen pounds, and measuring three feet from the tip to the tail."

There is no art, no skill, required for that sort of thing. It shows pluck, but that is all.

No; your accomplished angler would scorn to tell a lie, that way. His method is a study in itself.

He comes in quietly with his hat on, appropriates the most comfortable chair, lights his pipe, and commences to puff in silence. He lets the youngsters brag away for a while, and then, during a momentary lull, he removes the pipe from his mouth, and remarks, as he knocks the ashes out against the bars:

"Well, I had a haul on Tuesday evening that it's not much good my telling anybody about."

"Oh! Why's that?" they ask.

"Because I don't expect anybody would believe me if I did," replies the old fellow calmly, and without even a tinge of bitterness in his tone, as he refills his pipe, and requests the landlord to bring him three of Scotch, cold.

There is a pause after this, nobody feeling sufficiently sure of himself to contradict the old gentleman. So he has to go on by himself without any encouragement.

"No," he continues thoughtfully; "I shouldn't believe it myself if anybody told it to me, but it's a fact, for all that. I had been sitting there all the afternoon and had caught literally nothing—except a few dozen dace and a score of jack; and I was just about giving it up as a bad job when I suddenly felt a rather smart pull at the line. I thought it was another little one, and I went to jerk it up. Hang me, if I could move the rod! It took me half-an-hour—half-an-hour, sir! To land that fish; and every moment I thought the line was going to snap! I reached him at last, and what do you think it was? A sturgeon! A forty pound sturgeon! Taken on a line, sir!

Yes, you may well look surprised—I'll have another three of Scotch, landlord, please."

And then he goes on to tell of the astonishment of everybody who saw it; and what his wife said, when he got home, and of what Joe Buggles thought about it.

I asked the landlord of an inn up the river once, if it did not injure him, sometimes, listening to the tales that the fishermen about there told him; and he said:

"Oh, no; not now, sir. It did used to knock me over a bit at first, but, or love you! Me and the missus we listens to 'em all day now. It's what you're used to, you know. It's what you're used to."

I knew a young man once, he was a most conscientious fellow, and, when he took to fly-fishing, he determined never to exaggerate his hauls by more than twenty-five percent.

"When I have caught forty fish," said he, "then I will tell people that I have caught fifty, and so on. But I will not lie anymore than that, because it is sinful to lie."

But the twenty-five percent plan did not work well at all. He never was able to use it. The greatest number of fish he ever caught in one day was three, and you can't add twenty-five per cent to three—at least, not in fish.

So he increased his percentage to thirty-three-and-a-third, but that, again, was awkward, when he had only caught one or two; so, to simplify matters, he made up his mind to just double the quantity.

He stuck to this arrangement for a couple of months, and then he grew dissatisfied with it. Nobody believed him when he told them that he only doubled, and he, therefore, gained no credit that way whatever, while his moderation put him at a disadvantage among the other anglers. When he had really caught three small fish, and said he had caught six, it used to make him quite jealous to hear a man, whom he knew for a fact had only caught one, going about telling people he had landed two dozen.

So, eventually he made one final arrangement with himself, which he has religiously held to ever since, and that was to count each fish that he caught as ten, and to assume ten to begin with. For example, if he did not catch any fish at all, then he said he had caught ten fish—you could never catch less than ten fish by his system; that was the foundation of it. Then, if by any chance he really did catch one fish, he called it twenty, while two fish would count thirty, three forty, and so on.

It is a simple and easily worked plan, and there as been some talk lately of its being made use of by the angling fraternity in general. Indeed, the Committee of the Thames Anglers' Association did recommend its adoption about two years ago, but some of the older members opposed it. They said they would consider the idea if the number were doubled, and each fish counted as twenty.

If ever you have an evening to spare, up the river, I should advise you to drop into one of the little village inns, and take a seat in the taproom. You will be nearly sure to meet one or two old rodmen, sipping their toddy there, and they will tell you enough fishy stories, in half an hour, to give you indigestion for a month.

George and I—I don't know what had become of Harris; he had gone out and had a shave, early in the afternoon, and had then come back and spent full forty minutes in pipeclaying his shoes, we had not seen him since—George and I, therefore, and the dog, left to ourselves, went for a walk to Wallingford on the second evening, and, coming home, we called in at a little riverside inn, for a rest, and other things.

We went into the parlour and sat down. There was an old fellow there, smoking a long clay pipe, and we naturally began chatting.

He told us that it had been a fine day today, and we told him that it had been a fine day yesterday, and then we all told each other that we thought it would be a fine day tomorrow; and George said the crops seemed to be coming up nicely.

After that it came out, somehow or other, that we were strangers

in the neighbourhood, and that we were going away the next morning.

Then a pause ensued in the conversation, during which our eyes wandered round the room. They finally rested upon a dusty old glass-case, fixed very high up above the chimneypiece, and containing a trout. It rather fascinated me, that trout; it was such a monstrous fish. In fact, at first glance, I thought it was a cod.

"Ah!" said the old gentleman, following the direction of my gaze, "fine fellow that, ain't he?"

"Quite uncommon," I murmured; and George asked the old man how much he thought it weighed.

"Eighteen pounds six ounces," said our friend, rising and taking down his coat. "Yes," he continued, "it wur sixteen year ago, come the third o' next month, that I landed him. I caught him just below the bridge with a minnow. They told me he wur in the river, and I said I'd have him, and so I did. You don't see many fish that size about here now, I'm thinking. Goodnight, gentlemen, goodnight."

And out he went, and left us alone.

We could not take our eyes off the fish after that. It really was a remarkably fine fish. We were still looking at it, when the local carrier, who had just stopped at the inn, came to the door of the room with a pot of beer in his hand, and he also looked at the fish.

"Good-sized trout, that," said George, turning round to him.

"Ah! You may well say that, sir," replied the man; and then, after a pull at his beer, he added, "Maybe you wasn't here, sir, when that fish was caught?"

"No," we told him. We were strangers in the neighbourhood.

"Ah!" said the carrier, "then, of course, how should you? It was nearly five years ago that I caught that trout."

"Oh! Was it you who caught it, then?" said I.

"Yes, sir," replied the genial old fellow. "I caught him just below the lock—leastways, what was the lock then—one Friday afternoon; and the remarkable thing about it is that I caught him with a fly. I'd gone out pike fishing, bless you, never thinking of a trout, and when I saw that whopper on the end of my line, blest if it didn't quite take me aback. Well, you see, he weighed twenty-six pound. Goodnight, gentlemen, goodnight."

Five minutes afterwards, a third man came in, and described how *he* had caught it early one morning, with bleak; and then he left, and a stolid, solemn-looking, middle-aged individual came in, and sat down over by the window.

None of us spoke for a while; but, at length, George turned to the new comer, and said:

"I beg your pardon, I hope you will forgive the liberty that we—perfect strangers in the neighbourhood—are taking, but my friend here and myself would be so much obliged if you would tell us how you caught that trout up there."

"Why, who told you I caught that trout!" was the surprised query.

We said that nobody had told us so, but somehow or other we felt instinctively that it was he who had done it.

"Well, it's a most remarkable thing—most remarkable," answered the stolid stranger, laughing; "because, as a matter of fact, you are quite right. I did catch it. But fancy your guessing it like that. Dear me, it's really a most remarkable thing."

And then he went on, and told us how it had taken him half an hour to land it, and how it had broken his rod. He said he had weighed it carefully when he reached home, and it had turned the scale at thirty-four pounds.

He went in his turn, and when he was gone, the landlord came in to us. We told him the various histories we had heard about his trout, and he was immensely amused, and we all laughed very heartily.

"Fancy Jim Bates and Joe Muggles and Mr. Jones and old Billy Maunders all telling you that they had caught it. Ha! ha! ha! Well, that is good," said the honest old fellow, laughing heartily. "Yes, they are the sort to give it *me*, to put up in *my* parlour, if *they* had caught it, they are! Ha! ha! ha!"

And then he told us the real history of the fish. It seemed that he had caught it himself, years ago, when he was quite a lad; not by any art or skill, but by that unaccountable luck that appears to always wait upon a boy when he plays the wag from school, and goes out fishing on a sunny afternoon, with a bit of string tied on to the end of a tree.

He said that bringing home that trout had saved him from a whacking, and that even his schoolmaster had said it was worth the rule-of-three and practice put together.

He was called out of the room at this point, and George and I again turned our gaze upon the fish.

It really was a most astonishing trout. The more we looked at it, the more we marvelled at it.

It excited George so much that he climbed up on the back of a chair to get a better view of it.

And then the chair slipped, and George clutched wildly at the trout-case to save himself, and down it came with a crash, George and the chair on top of it.

"You haven't injured the fish, have you?" I cried in alarm, rushing up.

"I hope not," said George, rising cautiously and looking about.

But he had. That trout lay shattered into a thousand fragments—I say a thousand, but they may have only been nine hundred. I did not count them.

We thought it strange and unaccountable that a stuffed trout should break up into little pieces like that.

And so it would have been strange and unaccountable, if it had been a stuffed trout, but it was not.

That trout was plaster-of-Paris.

CHAPTER XVIII

Locks • George and I are photographed • Wallingford • Dorchester
• Abingdon • A family man • A good spot for drowning • A difficult
bit of water • Demoralizing effect of river air

WE LEFT STREATLEY EARLY THE NEXT MORNING, AND PULLED UP TO
Culham, and slept under the canvas, in the backwater there.

The river is not extraordinarily interesting between Streatley and
Wallingford. From Cleve you get a stretch of six and a half miles
without a lock. I believe this is the longest uninterrupted stretch
anywhere above Teddington, and the Oxford Club make use of it for
their trial eights.

But however satisfactory this absence of locks may be to rowing-
men, it is to be regretted by the mere pleasure-seeker.

For myself, I am fond of locks. They pleasantly break the monotony of the pull. I like sitting in the boat and slowly rising out of the
cool depths up into new reaches and fresh views; or sinking down,
as it were, out of the world, and then waiting, while tile gloomy gates
creak, and the narrow strip of daylight between them widens till the
fair smiling river lies full before you, and you push your little boat out
from its brief prison on to the welcoming waters once again.

They are picturesque little spots, these locks. The stout old lock-
keeper, or his cheerful-looking wife, or bright-eyed daughter, are
pleasant folk to have a passing chat with.[1] You meet other boats there,
and river gossip is exchanged. The Thames would not be the fairy-
land it is without its flower-decked locks.

Talking of locks reminds me of an accident George and I very nearly had one summer's morning at Hampton Court.

It was a glorious day, and the lock was crowded; and, as is a common practice up the river, a speculative photographer was taking a picture of us all as we lay upon the rising waters.

I did not catch what was going on at first, and was, therefore, extremely surprised at noticing George hurriedly smooth out his trousers, ruffle up his hair, and slick his cap on in a rakish manner at the back of his head, and then, assuming an expression of mingled affability and sadness, sit down in a graceful attitude, and try to hide his feet.

My first idea was that he had suddenly caught sight of some girl he knew, and I looked about to see who it was. Everybody in the lock seemed to have been suddenly struck wooden. They were all standing or sitting about in the most quaint and curious attitudes I have ever seen off a Japanese fan. All the girls were smiling. Oh, they did look so sweet! And all the fellows were frowning, and looking stern and noble.

And then, at last, the truth flashed across me, and I wondered if I should be in time. Ours was the first boat, and it would be unkind of me to spoil the man's picture, I thought.

So I faced round quickly, and took up a position in the prow, where I leant with careless grace upon the hitcher, in an attitude suggestive of agility and strength. I arranged my hair with a curl over the forehead, and threw an air of tender wistfulness into my expression, mingled with a touch of cynicism, which I am told suits me.

As we stood, waiting for the eventful moment, I heard someone behind call out:

"Hi! Look at your nose."

I could not turn round to see what was the matter, and whose nose it was that was to be looked at. I stole a side-glance at George's nose! It was all right—at all events, there was nothing wrong with it that could be altered. I squinted down at my own, and that seemed all that could be expected also.

"Look at your nose, you stupid ass!" came the same voice again, louder:

And then another voice cried:

"Push your nose out, can't you, you—you two with the dog!"

Neither George nor I dared to turn round. The man's hand was on the cap, and the picture might be taken any moment. Was it us they were calling to? What was the matter with our noses? Why were they to be pushed out!

But now the whole lock started yelling, and a stentorian voice from the back shouted:

"Look at your boat, sir; you in the red and black caps. It's your two corpses that will get taken in that photo, if you ain't quick."

We looked then, and saw that the nose of our boat had got fixed under the woodwork of the lock, while the in-coming water was rising all around it, and tilting it up. In another moment we should be over. Quick as thought, we each seized an oar, and a vigorous blow against the side of the lock with the butt-ends released the boat, and sent us sprawling on our backs.

We did not come out well in that photograph, George and I.

Of course, as was to be expected, our luck ordained it, that the man should set his wretched machine in motion at the precise moment that we were both lying on our backs with a wild expression of "Where am I? and what is it?" on our faces, and our four feet waving madly in the air.

Our feet were undoubtedly the leading article in that photograph. Indeed, very little else was to be seen. They filled up the foreground entirely. Behind them, you caught glimpses of the other boats, and bits of the surrounding scenery; but everything and everybody else in the lock looked so utterly insignificant and paltry compared with our feet, that all the other people felt quite ashamed of themselves, and refused to subscribe to the picture.

The owner of one steam launch, who had bespoke six copies, rescinded the order on seeing the negative. He said he would take them if anybody could show him his launch, but nobody could. It was somewhere behind George's right foot.

There was a good deal of unpleasantness over the business. The photographer thought we ought to take a dozen copies each, seeing that the photo was about nine-tenths us, but we declined. We said we had no objection to being photo'd full-length, but we preferred being taken the right way up.

Wallingford, six miles above Streatley, is a very ancient town, and has been an active centre for the making of English History. It was a rude, mud-built town in the time of the Britons, who squatted there, until the Roman legions evicted them; and replaced their clay-baked walls by mighty fortifications, the trace of which Time has not yet succeeded in sweeping away, so well those old-world masons knew how to build.

But Time, though he halted at Roman walls, soon crumbled Romans to dust; and on the ground, in later years, fought savage Saxons and huge Danes, until the Normans came.

It was a walled and fortified town up to the time of the Parliamentary War, when it suffered a long and bitter siege from Fairfax. It fell at last, and then the walls were razed.

From Wallingford up to Dorchester the neighbourhood of the river grows more hilly, varied, and picturesque. Dorchester stands half a mile from the river. It can be reached by paddling up the Thames if you have a small boat; but the best way is to leave the river at Day's Lock, and take a walk across the fields. Dorchester is a delightfully peaceful old place, nestling in stillness and silence and drowsiness.

Dorchester, like Wallingford, was a city in ancient British times; it was then called Caer Doren, "the city on the water." In more recent times the Romans formed a great camp here, the fortifications surrounding which now seem like low, even hills. In Saxon days it was the capital of Wessex. It is very old, and it was very strong and great once. Now it sits aside from the stirring world, and nods and dreams.

Round Clifton Hampden, itself a wonderfully pretty village, old-fashioned, peaceful, and dainty with flowers, the river scenery is rich and beautiful. If you stay the night on land at Clifton, you cannot do better than put up at the "Barley Mow." It is, without exception, I should say, the quaintest, most old-world inn up the river. It stands on the right of the bridge, quite away from the village. Its low-pitched gables and thatched roof and latticed windows give it quite a story-book appearance, while inside it is even still more once-upon-a-timeyfied.

It would not be a good place for the heroine of a modern novel to stay at. The heroine of a modern novel is always "divinely tall," and she is ever "drawing herself up to her full height." At the "Barley Mow" she would bump her head against the ceiling each time she did this.

It would also be a bad house for a drunken man to put up at. There are too many surprises in the way of unexpected steps down into this room and up into that; and as for getting upstairs to his bedroom, or ever finding his bed when he got up, either operation would be an utter impossibility to him.

We were up early the next morning, as we wanted to be in Oxford by the afternoon. It is surprising how early one *can* get up, when camping out. One does not yearn for "just another five minutes" nearly so much, lying wrapped up in a rug on the boards of a boat, with a Gladstone bag for a pillow, as one does in a feather-bed. We had finished breakfast, and were through Clifton Lock by half-past eight.

From Clifton to Culham the river banks are flat, monotonous, and uninteresting, but, after you get through Culham Lock—the coldest and deepest lock on the river—the landscape improves.

At Abingdon, the river passes by the streets. Abingdon is a typical country town of the smaller order—quiet, eminently respectable, clean, and desperately dull. It prides itself on being old, but whether it can compare in this respect with Wallingford and Dorchester seems doubtful. A famous abbey stood here once, and within what is left of its sanctified walls they brew bitter ale nowadays.

In St. Nicholas Church, at Abingdon, there is a monument to John Blackwall and his wife Jane, who both, after leading a happy married life, died on the very same day, August 21, 1625; and in St. Helen's Church, it is recorded that W. Lee, who died in 1637, "had in his lifetime issue from his loins two hundred lacking but three." If you work this out you will find that Mr. W. Lee's family numbered one hundred and ninety-seven. Mr. W. Lee—five times Mayor of Abingdon—was,

no doubt, a benefactor to his generation, but I hope there are not many of his kind about in this overcrowded nineteenth century.

From Abingdon to Nuneham Courtenay is a lovely stretch. Nuneham Park is well worth a visit. It can be viewed on Tuesdays and Thursdays. The house contains a fine collection of pictures and curiosities, and the grounds are very beautiful.

The pool under Sandford lasher, just behind the lock, is a very good place to drown yourself in. The undercurrent is terribly strong, and if you once get down into it you are all right. An obelisk marks the spot where two men have already been drowned, while bathing there; and the steps of the obelisk are generally used as a diving-board by young men now who wish to see if the place really is dangerous.

Iffley Lock and Mill, a mile before you reach Oxford, is a favourite subject with the river-loving brethren of the brush. The real article, however, is rather disappointing, after the pictures. Few things, I have noticed, come quite up to the pictures of them, in this world.

We passed through Iffley Lock at about half-past twelve, and then, having tidied up the boat and made all ready for landing, we set to work on our last mile.

Between Iffley and Oxford is the most difficult bit of the river I know. You want to be born on that bit of water, to understand it. I have been over it a fairish number of times, but I have never been able to get the hang of it. The man who could row a straight course from Oxford to Iffley ought to be able to live comfortably, under one roof, with his wife, his mother-in-law, his eldest sister, and the old servant who was in the family when he was a baby.

First the current drives you on to the right bank, and then on to the left, then it takes you out into the middle, turns you round three times, and carries you up stream again, and always ends by trying to smash you up against a college barge.

Of course, as a consequence of this, we got in the way of a good many other boats, during the mile, and they in ours, and, of course, as a consequence of that, a good deal of bad language occurred.

I don't know why it should be, but everybody is always so exceptionally irritable on the river. Little mishaps, that you would hardly notice on dry land, drive you nearly frantic with rage, when they occur on the water. When Harris or George makes an ass of himself on dry land, I smile indulgently; when they behave in a chuckle-head way on the river, I use the most blood-curdling language to them. When another boat gets in my way, I feel I want to take an oar and kill all the people in it.

The mildest tempered people, when on land, become violent and bloodthirsty when in a boat. I did a little boating once with a young lady. She was naturally of the sweetest and gentlest disposition imaginable but on the river it was quite awful to hear her.

"Oh, drat the man!" she would exclaim, when some unfortunate sculler would get in her way; "why don't he look where he's going?"

And, "Oh, bother the silly old thing!" she would say indignantly, when the sail would not go up properly. And she would catch hold of it, and shake it quite brutally.

Yet, as I have said, when on shore she was kind-hearted and amiable enough.

The air of the river has a demoralising effect upon one's temper, and this it is, I suppose, which causes even bargemen to be sometimes rude to one another, and to use language which, no doubt, in their calmer moments they regret.

CHAPTER XIX

Oxford • Montmorency's idea of heaven • The hired upriver river
boat, its beauties and advantages • "The Pride of the Thames" •
The weather changes • The river under different aspects • Not a
cheerful evening • Yearnings for the unattainable • The cheery
chat goes round • George performs upon the banjo • A mournful
melody • Another wet day • Flight • A little supper and a toast

WE SPENT TWO VERY PLEASANT DAYS AT OXFORD. THERE ARE PLENTY
of dogs in the town of Oxford. Montmorency had eleven fights on the
first day, and fourteen on the second, and evidently
thought he had got to heaven.

Among folk too constitutionally weak, or too
constitutionally lazy, whichever it may be, to relish
upstream work, it is a common practice to get a boat at
Oxford, and row down. For the energetic, however, the upstream jour-

ney is certainly to be preferred. It does not seem good to
be always going with the current. There is more satisfaction in squaring one's back, and fighting against it, and
winning one's way forward in spite of it—at least, so I feel,
when Harris and George are sculling and I am steering.

To those who do contemplate making Oxford their starting-place,
I would say, take your own boat—unless, of course, you can take
someone else's without any possible danger of being found out. The
boats that, as a rule, are let for hire on the Thames above Marlow,
are very good boats. They are fairly water-tight; and so long as
they are handled with care, they rarely come to pieces, or sink. There

are places in them to sit down on, and they are complete with all the necessary arrangements—or nearly all—to enable you to row them and steer them.

But they are not ornamental. The boat you hire up the river above Marlow is not the sort of boat in which you can flash about and give yourself airs. The hired upriver boat very soon puts a stop to any nonsense of that sort on the part of its occupants. That is its chief—one may say, its only recommendation.

The man in the hired upriver boat is modest and retiring. He likes to keep on the shady side underneath the trees, and to do most of his travelling early in the morning or late at night, when there are not many people about on the river to look at him.

When the man in the hired upriver boat sees anyone he knows, he gets out on to the bank, and hides behind a tree.

I was one of a party who hired an upriver boat one summer, for a few days' trip. We had none of us ever seen the hired upriver boat before; and we did not know what it was when we did see it.

We had written for a boat—a double sculling skiff; and when we went down with our bags to the yard, and gave our names, the man said:

"Oh, yes; you're the party that wrote for a double sculling skiff. It's all right. Jim, fetch round *The Pride of the Thames.*"

The boy went, and reappeared five minutes afterwards, struggling with an antediluvian chunk of wood, that looked as though it had been recently dug out of somewhere and dug out carelessly, so as to have been unnecessarily damaged in the process.

My own idea, on first catching sight of the object, was that it was a Roman relic of some sort, relic of *what* I do not know, possibly of a coffin.

The neighbourhood of the upper Thames is rich in Roman relics, and my surmise seemed to me a very probable one; but our serious young man, who is a bit of a geologist, pooh-poohed my Roman relic theory, and said it was clear to the meanest intellect (in which category he seemed to be grieved that he could not conscientiously include mine) that the thing the boy had found was the fossil of a whale; and he pointed out to us various evidences proving that it must have belonged to the preglacial period.

To settle the dispute, we appealed to the boy. We told him not to be afraid, but to speak the plain truth: Was it the fossil of a pre-Adamite whale, or was it an early Roman coffin?

The boy said it was *The Pride of the Thames*.

We thought this a very humorous answer on the part of the boy at first, and somebody gave him twopence as a reward for his ready wit; but when he persisted in keeping up the joke, as we thought, too long, we got vexed with him.

"Come, come, my lad!" said our captain sharply, "don't let us have any nonsense. You take your mother's washing-tub home again, and bring us a boat."

The boat-builder himself came up then, and assured us, on his word, as a practical man, that the thing really was a boat—was, in fact, *the* boat, the "double sculling skiff" selected to take us on our trip down the river.

We grumbled a good deal. We thought he might, at least, have had it whitewashed or tarred—had *something* done to it to distinguish it from a bit of a wreck; but he could not see any fault in it.

He even seemed offended at our remarks. He said he had picked us out the best boat in all his stock, and he thought we might have been more grateful.

He said it, *The Pride of the Thames*, had been in use, just as it now stood (or rather as it now hung together), for the last forty years, to *his* knowledge, and nobody had complained of it before, and he did not see why we should be the first to begin.

We argued no more.

We fastened the so-called boat together with some pieces of string, got a bit of wallpaper and pasted over the shabbier places, said our prayers, and stepped on board.

They charged us thirty-five shillings for the loan of the remnant for six days; and we could have bought the thing out-and-out for four-and-sixpence at any sale of driftwood round the coast.

The weather changed on the third day—Oh! I am talking about our present trip now—and we started from Oxford upon our home-ward journey in the midst of a steady drizzle.

The river—with the sunlight flashing from its dancing wavelets, gilding gold the grey-green beech-trunks, glinting through the dark, cool wood paths, chasing shadows o'er the shallows, flinging dia-monds from the mill-wheels, throwing kisses to the lilies, wantoning with the weirs' white waters, silvering moss-grown walls and bridges, brightening every tiny townlet, making sweet each lane and meadow, lying tangled in the rushes, peeping, laughing, from each inlet, gleaming gay on many a far sail, making soft the air with glory—is a golden fairy stream.

But the river—chill and weary, with the ceaseless raindrops falling on its brown and sluggish waters, with the sound as of a woman, weep-ing low in some dark chamber; while the woods, all dark and silent, shrouded in their mists of vapour, stand like ghosts upon the margin; silent ghosts with eyes reproachful, like the ghosts of evil actions, like the ghosts of friends neglected—is a spirit-haunted water through the land of vain regrets.

Sunlight is the life-blood of Nature. Mother Earth looks at us with such dull, soulless eyes, when the sunlight has died away from out of her. It makes us sad to be with her then; she does not seem to know us or to care for us. She is as a widow who has lost the husband she loved; and her children touch her hand, and look up into her eyes, but gain no smile from her.

We rowed on all that day through the rain, and very melancholy work it was. We pretended, at first, that we enjoyed it. We said it was a change, and that we liked to see the river under all its different aspects. We said we could not expect to have it all sunshine, nor should we wish it. We told each other that Nature was beautiful, even in her tears.

Indeed, Harris and I were quite enthusiastic about the business, for the first few hours. And we sang a song about a gipsy's life, and

how delightful a gipsy's existence was! Free to storm and sunshine, and to every wind that blew! And how he enjoyed the rain, and what a lot of good it did him; and how he laughed at people who didn't like it.

George took the fun more soberly, and stuck to the umbrella.

We hoisted the cover before we had lunch, and kept it up all the afternoon, just leaving a little space in the bow, from which one of us could paddle and keep a lookout. In this way we made nine miles, and pulled up for the night a little below Day's Lock.

I cannot honestly say that we had a merry evening. The rain poured down with quiet persistency. Everything in the boat was damp and clammy. Supper was not a success. Cold veal pie, when you don't feel hungry, is apt to cloy. I felt I wanted whitebait and a cutlet; Harris babbled of soles and white-sauce, and passed the remains of his pie to Montmorency, who declined it, and, apparently insulted by the offer, went and sat over at the other end of the boat by himself.

George requested that we would not talk about these things, at all events until he had finished his cold boiled beef without mustard.

We played penny nap after supper. We played for about an hour and a half, by the end of which time George had won fourpence—George always is lucky at cards—and Harris and I had lost exactly twopence each.

We thought we would give up gambling then. As Harris said, it breeds an unhealthy excitement when carried too far. George offered to go on and give us our revenge; but Harris and I decided not to battle any further against Fate.

After that, we mixed ourselves some toddy, and sat round and talked. George told us about a man he had known, who had come up the river two years ago, and who had slept out in a damp boat on just such another night as that was, and it had given him rheumatic fever, and nothing was able to save him, and he had died in great agony ten days afterwards. George said he was quite a young man, and was engaged to be married. He said it was one of the saddest things he had ever known.

And that put Harris in mind of a friend of his, who had been in the Volunteers, and who had slept out under canvas one wet night down at Aldershot, "on just such another night as this," said Harris; and he had woke up in the morning a cripple for life. Harris said he would introduce us both to the man when we got back to town; it would make our hearts bleed to see him.

This naturally led to some pleasant chat about sciatica, fevers, chills, lung diseases, and bronchitis; and Harris said how very awkward it would be if one of us were taken seriously ill in the night, seeing how far away we were from a doctor.

There seemed to be a desire for something frolicsome to follow upon this conversation, and in a weak moment I suggested that George should get out his banjo, and see if he could not give us a comic song.

I will say for George that he did not want any pressing. There was no nonsense about having left his music at home, or anything of that sort. He at once fished out his instrument, and commenced to play "Two Lovely Black Eyes."

I had always regarded "Two Lovely Black Eyes" as rather a commonplace tune until that evening. The rich vein of sadness that George extracted from it quite surprised me.

The desire that grew upon Harris and myself, as the mournful strains progressed, was to fall upon each other's necks and weep; but by great effort we kept back the rising tears, and listened to the wild yearnful melody in silence.

When the chorus came we even made a desperate effort to be merry. We re-filled our glasses and joined in; Harris, in a voice trembling with emotion, leading, and George and I following a few words behind:

> Two lovely black eyes;
> Oh! What a surprise!
> Only for telling a man he was wrong,
> Two——

There we broke down. The unutterable pathos of George's accompaniment to that "two" we were, in our then state of depression, unable to bear. Harris sobbed like a little child, and the dog howled till I thought his heart or his jaw must surely break.

George wanted to go on with another verse. He thought that when he had got a little more into the tune, and could throw more "abandon," as it were, into the rendering, it might not seem so sad. The feeling of the majority, however, was opposed to the experiment.

There being nothing else to do, we went to bed—that is, we undressed ourselves, and tossed about at the bottom of the boat for some three or four hours. After which, we managed to get some fitful slumber until five AM, when we all got up and had breakfast.

The second day was exactly like the first. The rain continued to pour down, and we sat, wrapped up in our mackintoshes, underneath the canvas, and drifted slowly down.

One of us—I forget which one now, but I rather think it was myself—made a few feeble attempts during the course of the morning to work up the old gipsy foolishness about being children of Nature and enjoying the wet; but it did not go down well at all. That—

> I care not for the rain, not I!

was so painfully evident, as expressing the sentiments of each of us, that to sing it seemed unnecessary.

On one point we were all agreed, and that was that, come what might, we would go through with this job to the bitter end. We had come out for a fortnight's enjoyment on the river, and a fortnight's enjoyment on the river we meant to have. If it killed us! Well, that would be a sad thing for our friends and relations, but it could not be helped. We felt that to give in to the weather in a climate such as ours would be a most disastrous precedent.

"It's only two days more," said Harris, "and we are young and strong. We may get over it all right, after all."

At about four o'clock we began to discuss our arrangements for the evening. We were a little past Goring then, and we decided to paddle on to Pangbourne, and put up there for the night.

"Another jolly evening!" murmured George.

We sat and mused on the prospect. We should be in at Pangbourne by five. We should finish dinner at, say, half-past six. After that we could walk about the village in the pouring rain until bedtime; or we could sit in a dimly lit bar-parlour and read the almanac.

"Why, the Alhambra would be almost more lively," said Harris, venturing his head outside the cover for a moment and taking a survey of the sky.

"With a little supper at the——² to follow," I added, half unconsciously.

"Yes, it's almost a pity we've made up our minds to stick to this boat," answered Harris; and then there was silence for awhile.

"If we *hadn't* made up our minds to contract our certain deaths in this bally old coffin," observed George, casting a glance of intense malevolence over the boat, "it might be worth while to mention that there's a train leaves Pangbourne, I know, soon after five, which would just land us in town in comfortable time to get a chop, and then go on to the place you mentioned afterwards."

Nobody spoke. We looked at one another, and each one seemed to see his own mean and guilty thoughts reflected in the faces of the others. In silence, we dragged out and overhauled the Gladstone. We looked up the river and down the river; not a soul was in sight!

Twenty minutes later, three figures, followed by a shamed-looking dog, might have been seen creeping stealthily from the boat-house at the "Swan" towards the railway station, dressed in the following neither neat nor gaudy costume:

Black leather shoes, dirty; suit of boating flannels, very dirty; brown felt hat, much battered; mackintosh, very wet; umbrella.

We had deceived the boatman at Pangbourne. We had not had the face to tell him that we were running away from the rain. We had left the boat, and all it contained, in his charge, with instructions that it was to be ready for us at nine the next morning. If, we said—*if* anything unforeseen should happen, preventing our return, we would write to him.

We reached Paddington at seven, and drove direct to the restaurant I have before described, where we partook of a light meal, left Montmorency, together with suggestions for a supper to be ready at half-past ten, and then continued our way to Leicester Square.

We attracted a good deal of attention at the Alhambra. On our presenting ourselves at the pay-box we were gruffly directed to go round to Castle Street, and were informed that we were half-an-hour behind our time.

We convinced the man, with some difficulty, that we were *not* "the world-renowned contortionists from the Himalaya Mountains," and he took our money and let us pass.

Inside we were a still greater success. Our fine bronzed countenances and picturesque clothes were followed round the place with admiring gaze. We were the cynosure of every eye.

It was a proud moment for us all.

We adjourned soon after the first ballet, and wended our way back to the restaurant, where supper was already awaiting us.

I must confess to enjoying that supper. For about ten days we seemed to have been living, more or less, on nothing but cold meat, cake, and bread and jam. It had been a simple, a nutritious diet; but there had been nothing exciting about it, and the odour of Burgundy, and the smell of French sauces, and the sight of clean napkins and long loaves, knocked as a very welcome visitor at the door of our inner man.

We pegged and quaffed away in silence for a while, until the time came when, instead of sitting bolt upright, and grasping the knife and fork firmly, we leant back in our chairs and worked slowly and carelessly—when we stretched out our legs beneath the table, let our napkins fall, unheeded, to the floor, and found time to more critically examine the smoky ceiling than we had hitherto been able to do—when we rested our glasses at arm's-length upon the table, and felt good, and thoughtful, and forgiving.

Then Harris, who was sitting next the window, drew aside the curtain and looked out upon the street.

It glistened darkly in the wet, the dim lamps flickered with each gust, the rain splashed steadily into the puddles and trickled down the water-spouts into the running gutters. A few soaked wayfarers hurried past, crouching beneath their dripping umbrellas, the women holding up their skirts.

"Well," said Harris, reaching his hand out for his glass, "we have had a pleasant trip, and my hearty thanks for it to old Father Thames—but I think we did well to chuck it when we did. Here's to Three Men well out of a Boat!"

And Montmorency, standing on his hind legs, before the window, peering out into the night, gave a short bark of decided concurrence with the toast.

ENDNOTES

CHAPTER XVIII

[1] Or rather *were*. The Conservancy of late seems to have constituted itself into a society for the employment of idiots. A good many of the new lock-keepers, especially in the more crowded portions of the river, are excitable, nervous old men quite unfitted for their post.

[2] A capital little out-of-the-way restaurant, in the neighborhood of——, where you can get one of the best-cooked and cheapest little French dinners or suppers that I know of, with an excellent bottle of Beaune, for three-and-six; and which I am not going to be idiot enough to advertise.

SUGGESTED READING

BOLLAND, R. R. *In the Wake of Three Men in a Boat.* London: Parapress, 1995.

CONNOLLY, JOSEPH. *Jerome K. Jerome.* London: Orbis, 1982.

FAUROT, RUTH MARIE. *Jerome K. Jerome.* New York: Twayne, 1974.

JEROME, JEROME K. *My Life and Times.* London: Hodder & Stoughton, 1926.

———. *On the Stage—and Off: The Brief Career of a Would-Be Actor (1885).* Stroud Glous.: Sutton, 1991.

———. *Paul Kelver.* New York: Dodd Mead, 1902.

———. *The Idle Thoughts of an Idle Fellow (1886).* Stroud Glous.: Sutton, 1991.

———. *The Passing of a Third Floor Back: An Idle Fancy in a Prologue, a Play and an Epilogue.* New York: Samuel French, 1921.

———. *Three Men on a Bummel (1900).* Stroud Glous.: Sutton, 1990.

WOHLGELERNTER, MAURICE. *Israel Zangwill.* New York: Columbia University Press, 1964.

Look for the following titles, available now from The Barnes & Noble Library of Essential Reading.

Visit your Barnes & Noble bookstore,
or shop online at *www.bn.com/loer*

NONFICTION

Age of Revolution, The	Winston S. Churchill	0760768595
Alexander	Theodore Ayrault Dodge	0760773491
American Democrat, The	James Fenimore Cooper	0760761981
American Indian Stories	Zitkala-Ša	0760765502
Ancient Greek Historians, The	J. B. Bury	0760776350
Ancient History	George Rawlinson	0760773580
Antichrist, The	Friedrich Nietzsche	0760777705
Autobiography of Benjamin Franklin, The	Benjamin Franklin	0760768617
Autobiography of Charles Darwin, The	Charles Darwin	0760769087
Babylonian Life and History	E. A. Wallis Budge	0760765499
Beyond the Pleasure Principle	Sigmund Freud	0760774919
Birth of Britain, The	Winston S. Churchill	0760768579
Boots and Saddles	Elizabeth B. Custer	076077370X
Characters and Events of Roman History	Guglielmo Ferrero	0760765928
Chemical History of a Candle, The	Michael Faraday	0760765227
Civil War, The	Julius Caesar	0760768943
Common Law, The	Oliver Wendell Holmes	0760754985
Confessions	Jean-Jacques Rousseau	0760773599
Conquest of Gaul, The	Julius Caesar	0760768951
Consolation of Philosophy, The	Boethius	0760769796
Conversations with Socrates	Xenophon	0760770441

Creative Evolution	Henri Bergson	0760765480
Critique of Judgment	Immanuel Kant	0760762023
Critique of Practical Reason	Immanuel Kant	0760760942
Critique of Pure Reason	Immanuel Kant	0760755949
Dark Night of the Soul, The	St. John of the Cross	0760765871
Democracy and Education	John Dewey	0760765863
Democracy in America	Alexis de Tocqueville	0760752303
Descent of Man and Selection in Relation to Sex, The	Charles Darwin	0760763119
Dialogues concerning Natural Religion	David Hume	0760777713
Discourse on Method	René Descartes	0760756023
Discourses on Livy	Niccolò Machiavelli	0760771731
Dolorous Passion of Our Lord Jesus Christ, The	Anne Catherine Emmerich	0760771715
Early History of Rome, The	Titus Livy	0760770239
Ecce Homo	Friedrich Nietzsche	0760777721
Edison: His Life and Inventions	Frank Lewis Dyer	0760765820
Egyptian Book of the Dead, The	E. A. Wallis Budge	0760768382
Elements, The	Euclid	0760763127
Emile	Jean-Jacques Rousseau	0760773513
Eminent Victorians	Lytton Strachey	0760749930
Encheiridion	Epictetus	0760770204
Enquiry concerning Human Understanding, An	David Hume	0760755922
Essay concerning Human Understanding, An	John Locke	0760760497
Essays, The	Francis Bacon	0760770182
Essence of Christianity, The	Ludwig Feuerbach	076075764X
Ethics and On the Improvement of the Understanding	Benedict de Spinoza	0760768374
Extraordinary Popular Delusions and the Madness of Crowds	Charles Mackay	0760755825
Fall of Troy, The	Quintus of Smyrna	0760768366
Fifteen Decisive Battles of the Western World	Edward Shepherd Creasy	0760754950
Florentine History	Niccolò Machiavelli	0760756015
From Manassas to Appomattox	James Longstreet	0760759200
From Ritual to Romance	Jessie L. Weston	0760773548
Great Democracies, The	Winston S. Churchill	0760768609
Guide for the Perplexed, The	Moses Maimonides	0760757577
Hannibal	Theodore Ayrault Dodge	076076896X
Happy Hunting-Grounds, The	Kermit Roosevelt	0760755817
History of Atlantis, The	Lewis Spence	076077045X

History of the Conquest of Mexico, The	William H. Prescott	0760759227
History of the Conquest of Peru, The	William H. Prescott	076076137X
History of the Donner Party, The	Charles F. McGlashan	0760752427
History of the English Church and People, The	Bede	0760765510
History of Wales, A	J. E. Lloyd	0760752419
How the Other Half Lives	Jacob A. Riis	0760755892
How to Sing	Lilli Lehmann	0760752311
How We Think	John Dewey	0760770387
Hunting the Grisly and Other Sketches	Theodore Roosevelt	0760752338
Imitation of Christ, The	Thomas À. Kempis	0760755914
In His Steps	Charles M. Sheldon	0760755779
Influence of Sea Power upon History, The, 1660–1783	Alfred Thayer Mahan	0760754993
Interesting Narrative of the Life of Olaudah Equiano, The	Olaudah Equiano	0760773505
Interior Castle, The	St. Teresa of Avila	0760770247
Introduction to Logic	Immanuel Kant	0760770409
Introduction to Mathematical Philosophy	Bertrand Russell	0760773408
Introduction to Mathematics	Alfred North Whitehead	076076588X
Investigation of the Laws of Thought, An	George Boole	0760765847
Kingdom of God is Within You, The	Leo Tolstoy	0760765529
Lady's Life in the Rockies, A	Isabella Bird	0760763135
Leonardo da Vinci and a Memory of His Childhood	Sigmund Freud	0760749922
Letters and Saying of Epicurus	Epicurus	0760763283
Leviathan, The	Thomas Hobbes	0760755930
Life of Johnson	James Boswell	0760773483
Lives of the Caesars, The	Suetonius	0760757585
Manners, Customs, and History of the Highlanders of Scotland	Walter Scott	0760758697
Meditations	Marcus Aurelius	076075229X
Memoirs	William T. Sherman	0760773688
Metaphysics	Aristotle	0760773637
Montcalm and Wolfe	Francis Parkman	0760768358
Montessori Method, The	Maria Montessori	0760749957
Mosby's Memoirs	John Singleton Mosby	0760773726

THE BARNES & NOBLE
LIBRARY OF ESSENTIAL READING

This newly developed series has been established to provide affordable access to books of literary, academic, and historic value—works of both well-known writers and those who deserve to be rediscovered. Selected and introduced by scholars and specialists with an intimate knowledge of the works, these volumes present complete, original texts in a modern, readable typeface—welcoming a new generation of readers to influential and important books of the past. With more than 100 titles already in print and more than 100 forthcoming, the Library of Essential Reading offers an unrivaled variety of thought, scholarship, and entertainment. Best of all, these handsome and durable paperbacks are priced to be exceptionally affordable. For a full list of titles, visit *www.bn.com/loer*.

The Skin You're In

Other books in the growing Faithgirlz!™ library

The Faithgirlz!™ Bible
NIV Faithgirlz!™ Backpack Bible
My Faithgirlz!™ Journal

The Sophie Series

Sophie's World (Book One)
Sophie's Secret (Book Two)
Sophie Under Pressure (Book Three)
Sophie Steps Up (Book Four)
Sophie's First Dance (Book Five)
Sophie's Stormy Summer (Book Six)
Sophie's Friendship Fiasco (Book Seven)
Sophie and the New Girl (Book Eight)
Sophie Flakes Out (Book Nine)
Sophie Loves Jimmy (Book Ten)
Sophie's Drama (Book Eleven)
Sophie Gets Real (Book Twelve)

Nonfiction

Everybody Tells Me to Be Myself but I Don't Know Who I Am
Girl Politics
Body Talk
No Boys Allowed: Devotions for Girls
Girlz Rock: Devotions for Girls
Chick Chat: Devotions for Girls
Shine On, Girl!: Devotions for Girls

Check out www.faithgirlz.com

faiThGirLz!

The Skin You're In

Discovering True Beauty

Nancy Rue

ZONDERkidz

ZONDERVAN.com/
AUTHORTRACKER
follow your favorite authors

We want to hear from you. Please send your comments
about this book to us in care of zreview@zondervan.com. Thank you.

ZONDERKIDZ

The Skin You're In
Previously titled *Beauty Lab*
Copyright © 2007, 2010 by Nancy Rue
Illustrations © 2007, 2010 by Zondervan

Requests for information should be addressed to:

Zonderkidz, *Grand Rapids, Michigan* 49530

Library of Congress Cataloging-in-Publication Data

Rue, Nancy N.
    [Beauty lab]
        The skin you're in : discovering true beauty / by Nancy Rue.
            p. cm. — (Faithgirlz!)
        Previously published as: Beauty lab.
        ISBN 978-0-310-71999-1 (softcover)
    1. Grooming for girls — Juvenile literature. 2. Beauty, Personal — Juvenile literature. 3.
    Beauty, Personal — Religious aspects — Christianity — Juvenile literature. I. Title.
    RA777.25.R84 2009
        646.7'042 — dc22   2009023119

Published in association with the literary agency of Alive Communications, Inc., 7680
Goddard Street, Suite 200, Colorado Springs, CO 80920, www.alivecommunications.com.

Zonderkidz is a trademark of Zondervan.

Editor: Barbara Scott
Interior Design: Sherri L. Hoffman
Art Direction & Cover Design: Merit Kathan

Printed in the United States of America

11 12 13 14 15 /QG/ 25 24 23 22 21 20 19 18 17 16 15 14 13 12 11 10 9 8 7 6 5 4

Contents

Many thanks to the most beautiful young woman I know,
my daughter Marijean Rue. Her hard work and wonderful
ideas have helped shape this book. Her wisdom and love
have shown me what real beauty is.

chapter one

You've Got It
GOIN' ON

The morning Betsy Honeycutt turned eleven, she took a big ol' long look in the mirror, and she didn't like what she saw.

That was pretty weird, since she had seen the very same face the day before (and the day before that and the day before — well, you get the idea), and she hadn't thought much about her freckles or her blue eyes or her honey-brown bob one way or the other. Yesterday she was just Betsy. But today — yikes!

Has my nose always been that long? she thought. *Gross! It looks like a fishhook!*

And what about my eyes? They've gotten closer together — I know they have!

Betsy watched her upper lip curl. Her very thin lip — not plump and luscious like the girls' mouths in the magazines that she'd just fanned across her bed. In fact, there was nothing about her that was even remotely like a model, or, come to think of it, like any of the girls at school that everybody was imitating. She narrowed her eyes at her reflection.

Her hair wasn't long and shiny and thick like Madison's.

Her teeth weren't perfectly white and straight like Taylor's.

And where in the *world* had that *zit* come from? Ashleigh didn't have *zits!*

Betsy gasped right out loud and shoved her face closer to the mirror. It was a pimple between her eyebrows, all right, red and ugly and growing bigger by the millisecond.

She stepped back, hoping it wouldn't look so hideous from farther away, but it was like there was a spotlight shining on it so the entire world could check it out. And not only that, but now she could see her whole self in all her glory.

"Uh, I am *so not* glorious," Betsy said.

The girl in the mirror looked to her like a shapeless blob, dressed in a too-small T-shirt and a too-big pair of shorts that revealed legs hairier than her cocker spaniel's. When she put her hand up to her mouth in disgust, all she saw was the froggy green nail polish she'd put on at last week's sleepover and had been steadily gnawing away at ever since.

"And this is before I turned the lights on," Betsy told the stranger-self. "EWWWWW!"

She turned away from the mirror and looked down at the clear-skinned faces of the perfect girls on the magazine covers. *Will I ever be that pretty?* she thought.

She didn't see how the answer could ever be yes.

now what?

Which of these comes closest to what you were you
thinking as you read Betsy's story?

___ I don't get it. I hardly ever hang out looking in the mirror.
___ Um, I kind of like what I see when I look in the mirror.
___ Hello-o! I know exactly how she feels!

Just about every girl between the ages of eight and twelve
starts to think—at least a little bit—about the way she looks. But
did you know that the minute you're aware that your appearance
is a big part of yourself, you're on a journey?

It can be a lifetime of visits to the mirror where you can
always find something *wrong.* Or . . . it can be an adventure of
discovering the true, absolute, no-denying-it beauty that every girl
has—that *you* have.

The choice is pretty much a no-brainer, which is why you have
this book in your hand. This book is here to help you set out on
the way-fun path to finding your beautiful self. And not just the
hair-and-skin-and-clothes outside self, but the unique, one-of-a-
kind inside you, which is where real beauty comes from. More on
that later.

Before you begin the adventure, it's good to know where
you are right now. Write in the space on the next page what you
would say to Betsy if you were in her bedroom, watching her
suffer in front of the mirror. Look back at what you checked off
above to help you. There are no right or wrong answers, so be
free and real as you write. If, as you read on in this book, you
change your mind about what you want to say to Betsy, you'll
have a chance to express that when we get to the end.

Dear Betsy...

When it comes to thinking about the way you look, you're probably somewhere between "What's a mirror?" and "I want to put a bag over my head!" Whatever you think about your beauty, chances are you've gotten some ideas about what beautiful is by looking around and listening. Maybe you've heard things like this:

> "She's so thin. I wish I looked like her."
> "Her skin is perfect. Look at that! I bet she's never had a pimple."
> "Long blonde hair and big blue eyes — now *that's* what I'm talking about."
> "Train to be a model or just look like one! Call now! Operators are standing by!"

To hear people talk, you'd think the only girls who could be considered beautiful are pencil skinny with flawless complexions, long blonde hair, and big blue eyes; and they dress only in the trends that just started this morning. But think about all the girls and women you know that you consider beautiful. Do they all look like that?

What about

- ❀ your best friend?
- ❀ your favorite female teacher?
- ❀ your cool aunt, the cousin you want to be like, and your mom?
- ❀ And, hey — what about *you?*

Yeah, you. If you counted up all the people who like you and love you, you'd run out of fingers. Ask any one of them if he or she thinks you're a beautiful person, and you'll hear, "Honey, you're drop-dead gorgeous," or something like that.

The point is, no matter what people say about being beautiful, when you get right down to it, the ones who count in your life know real, true, unique beauty when they see it. So how do girls get the idea that they have to look like the cover girl on *Seventeen* to be pretty?

Simple.

(Important Thing):

Don't ask a boy younger than twenty-five. He can't handle questions like that yet. You're sure to get a variation of, "Yeah, if you like baboons," which probably means he likes you — but don't even go there.

From the media. That's TV, movies, billboards, magazines — anything that a lot of people see. The beauties there are all different, but they have one thing in common: they're perfect. Oops — wait. They *look* perfect. But if you met one of them outside the studio, you'd see right away that she has flaws just like everybody else: A piece of hair that won't stay out of her eye; the retainer she just popped in; maybe even a zit — yikes! You don't see those things in an ad or on the movie screen because (1) a team of makeup artists, personal trainers, and wardrobe consultants were all over her before she went before the camera, and (2) film editors can do amazing things with digital enhancing, just the way you can in Photoshop. A couple of clicks and that piece of flyaway hair or that enormous pimple disappears. The eyes are darker. The dress fits better. Get it? A famous model named Cindy Crawford once said, "Even I don't wake up looking like Cindy Crawford."

From models. You may have seen a professional model in person, and she did look pretty perfect to you. There wasn't an ounce of fat on her body! Before you consider yourself a hippo because at ten years old you weigh more than she does at twenty, remember this: A girl who becomes a model tends to be naturally thin and very tall to begin with. Then it becomes part of her job to keep her weight low so the curves of her body don't take attention away from the clothes she's modeling. Many models diet constantly, practically living on water and celery, and they work out daily for hours on end. Don't even think about doing that. You have healthy growing to do.

From what boys say. Like you care, right? But you can't help hearing them because they're so loud. They're going through their own stuff right now, so a lot of them think they have to be funny all the time. You've probably noticed that what boys consider funny is different from what cracks up you and your friends. They think it's hilarious to call you Tinsel Teeth because you just got braces or to swat at cooties when you stand next to them. Even though you know they're just being absurd little creeps, you can get your feelings hurt. Give them a few years. They'll get nicer. Meanwhile, don't take beauty tips from them.

By comparing yourself to the "cool" girls. Sometime in elementary school, it starts to become obvious that some girls are considered "cooler" than others. We don't know who decides that. Unfortunately, it just happens. Because the cool girls get a lot of attention and have a bunch of friends, almost everybody wants to be like them. And then the comparing starts:

- "Her hair is blonder (or darker) than mine."
- "Her eyes are bigger (or bluer or sparklier) than mine."
- "My clothes aren't as cute as hers."
- "She doesn't have to wear stupid braces like I do."

It can be pretty tempting to try to change yourself to be more like the cool girl. Or you may dislike the cool girl because seeing her makes you feel so bad about yourself. Or — if you happen to be a cool girl — you may work overtime trying to *stay* cool. None of that is any fun. And none of it makes you beautiful. It makes you worried, unhappy, and resentful — but not beautiful.

Besides, here's the deal — and if you get nothing else from this book, get this — YOU ARE ALREADY BEAUTIFUL!!!! Maybe on the outside you haven't "grown into yourself" yet. Maybe you haven't learned to make the most of what you have. Maybe you have hard stuff going on in your life that keeps you from really showing your beauty. But you were made to be a beautiful person. She's in there. After all, God doesn't make ugly. Okay, so maybe roaches are ugly ... but the boy roaches think they're kinda cute.

You were made to be your unique, shining, beautiful, true self. This journey you're on is about finding that self and letting her shine.

Who says? Well, hello-o ...

GOT GOD?

You believe in God, right? You believe God's in charge because he's perfect, yes? So you agree that all the things David says about God in Psalm 139 are true:

God knows everything about you (vs. 1 – 4).
God is everywhere (vs. 5 – 12).
God created your "inmost being" (vs. 13).

If you believe that, then you can say this right along with David:

> "I praise you because I am fearfully and wonderfully made; your works are wonderful, I know that full well."
>
> —PSALM 139:14

Fearfully, by the way, doesn't mean like Frankenstein's monster (although even he turned out to have a soft spot). It means *awesomely*. You were made to be awesome and wonderful. There it is, right in the Bible. God knit you together with love in every stitch. He thought of you, and you *became*. And as David says, "How precious to me are your thoughts, O God!" (Psalm 139:17).

You are the result of God's precious thought. How cool is that! Not some modeling agency's thought (though there's nothing wrong with being a model), or a cool girl's thought (although a lot of cool girls are really nice), or that boy's thought (which he doesn't even understand himself!)—*God's* thought.

You are a beautiful person. Believe it.

God doesn't just want you to *know* you're beautiful. God wants you to *show* it—not by plastering on makeup or spending a bajillion dollars on clothes, but by shining from the inside. Jesus talked about that in his teaching.

You can—and should—let God's "precious thought" out where it can shine like a light. Be every bit the beauty God created you to be, so other people will see Christ in you and be drawn to you.

Then you can love them and show them more about God's works. No one can do that when she's hiding her beautiful self.

Okay ... go ahead and ask it ... You know you want to:

"But aren't some girls more precious than others? Don't some just naturally shine brighter?"

Okay, picture God creating a new baby girl. Imagine the God whose works are wonderful saying, "Oops, I didn't make little Megan as precious as baby Brittany. I hate it when that happens." Can you honestly imagine him saying that?

Uh ... no. Every tiny being God creates has his beautiful fingerprints on her. She's shaped with love and "breathed through" with her own gifts and special brightness. Each child is an original. Each one is God's art. Each is priceless.

And that includes you, Precious Thought. You are fearfully and wonderfully made. Your part is to uncover the beauty — inside and out. It's a journey. Are you ready to begin?

"No one lights a lamp and hides it in a jar or puts it under a bed. Instead, he puts it on a stand, so that those who come in can see the light." — Luke 8:16

There were women in the crowd when Jesus said this — Mary Magdalene, Joanna, Susanna, and many others who had been healed by Jesus and with their own money were helping to support him and his disciples. They listened to Jesus' message. So should you.

That Is SO Me

S tart by being really honest with yourself. Complete this quiz alone or with a friend you totally trust. If you're afraid a curious younger bro or sis will get those little hands on this book, keep track of your answers on another piece of paper and make confetti out of it later. This is your very private stuff.

Put a star [*] next to each thought below that you've ever had for more than, like, two seconds. Even if you don't believe the thought, if it nags you sometimes, give it a star. There's no right or wrong. No good or bad. There's just you.

___ I'm fat.

___ I'm ugly.

___ I don't look that bad except for my _____.

___ I'm too tall (or short).

___ I have my father's _____ (ex: nose, lips), which is not good.

___ I want to look like a star (model, singer, actress . . .).

___ I'll never look like a star, which is depressing.

___ Some people tell me I'm pretty, but I don't believe them.

___ Some people tell me I'm not pretty, and I believe them.

___ I don't do that much to look prettier, because it isn't gonna help.

___ I wish I were cuter, so I'd have more friends.

___ I don't care about my appearance. I'm not the girly girl type.

___ It drives me nuts to have to wear _____ (ex: glasses, braces, a school uniform). They make me look lame.

Now count your stars and put your number here: _____

If you have between 11 and 13 stars, this book is SO for you. You seem to be having a tough time seeing your own beauty. This journey is going to be especially amazing for you, because every discovery will surprise you. You're going to love the real you.

If you have between 4 and 10 stars, you're not alone. Most girls your age go back and forth between thinking they're not so bad and deciding they're total freaks. But read on, and get a true picture of yourself that gets better all the time.

If you have between 0 and 3 stars, you're in a great place to have some fun with your beauty right from the start. As you read, be aware of the things you did star, because we're going to chase those thoughts away.

Whatever your score, you're about to set out on an expedition. You won't turn into a model (unless that's what God has in mind for you). You won't suddenly become like the "cool" girls. But you *will* find your own cool—the beautiful person you were made to be.

Whatever your score says is not about whether you're practically perfect or totally messed up. That goes for all the quizzes in this book. They're just a way to show you where you are and where you might be able to go. If you were perfect already (and nobody is!), you wouldn't have the adventure of the journey ahead of you.

You're Good to Go

It's time to pack your bags for the journey. Be sure to do the following Beauty Search before you move on to chapter two.

Beauty Search

With *The Skin You're In* and a pen or pencil, go to a mirror where you can see a lot of yourself. This works best if there's no one around who's going to tease you for gazing at your reflection.

Be honest about the beautiful things you see in the mirror. Look at every detail—your nice hairline; that cute little chicken pox scar; and your big, white, shiny teeth. Look at your hair, mouth, complexion, face shape, eyebrows, smile, eyes, chin, nose, arms, legs, height, shoulders, and hands. Describe those precious things. Again, be honest, but make sure everything you include is a compliment to you.

Look in the mirror again and smile at that girl as if you want to be her best friend. Check out what happens to your face.

Now stare at her as if you totally can't stand her.

Which face looked better?

This doesn't mean you have to grin 24/7. It means look for what you can like in people, which will make you smile. That's true beauty coming out of you. It also means be a best friend to yourself. Love *you* the way you do your BFF (best friend forever) and treat yourself as kindly. It looks good on you, girl!

> Being aware of your own loveliness so you can bring it out doesn't mean you think you're all that. Pointing it out to everyone in sight ("Do I not have the cutest freckles on my nose?") would be conceited, but that's not what we're doing here. So enjoy your beauty search.

In My Beauty Search, I Discovered That I Have…

chapter two

The Skin
YOU'RE IN

B etsy dragged herself back to the mirror (after she scored an eleven on the quiz) and said about a hundred times, "I am fearfully and wonderfully made."

She actually *did* think her eyes were sparkling a little brighter than before. Her ears kind of stuck out, though. Madeline, her best friend, had nice, flat ears that didn't make her look like a Volkswagen with the doors open.

Oops, Betsy thought. *I'm not supposed to do that.*

She was actually getting better at not paying attention to the insults she gave herself, but it was still hard when other people threw them at her. Like that kid Jason ... When he asked her if that model of Mount St. Helens on her face was part of her science project, Betsy ran to the restroom in tears. She looked in the mirror and saw that Jason was wrong: There wasn't just *one* volcano-sized pimple about to erupt on her forehead, there were two! She was tempted to stick her head in one of the toilets and stay there.

But Betsy did what she was learning to do. She went to the people who really loved her and asked them, "Is it just me, or are these pimples the grossest things on the planet?"

Her father squinted at her and said, "What pimples?" Her mom told her not to worry about it, that she'd grow out of it.

She didn't mention when. Betsy's best friend said, "They're not that bad, really." Betsy loved her for lying.

None of those answers made Betsy feel any better. In fact, she even tried to get her mom to let her stay home from school the next day — and maybe the next and the next — until that science project on her face went away.

GOT GOD?

Even if your face isn't breaking out like Betsy's (and maybe it never will), taking care of your skin is a pretty huge thing, because your skin is the biggest organ your body has. It protects you, regulates your body temperature, and holds all the inner stuff in. If your skin isn't healthy, you can't be at your best, inside or out.

Since God wants you to be healthy, skin is a big thing to him too. Check out what happened to Job:

God told Satan that no matter what he did to Job, Job would never curse God. Satan took him up on the bet.

It didn't go as Satan expected. Even after Job had lost his oxen, donkeys, sheep, camels, and servants to various calamities — and all of his sons and daughters were killed when a house collapsed on them — he still didn't blame God.

So Satan said to God, "Skin for skin! ... A man will give all he has for his own life. But stretch out your hand and strike his flesh and bones, and he will surely curse you to your face" (Job 2:4–5). Satan had good reason to believe that. We human beings get very touchy about stuff happening to our bodies.

Notice that the worst thing Satan could think of was to cover Job's *skin* with painful sores — from the soles of his feet to the top of his head. He didn't give Job a series of bad hair days or grow his nose like Pinocchio. He went after that protective covering. There is something about skin funkiness that really freaks us out, partly because everybody can see it and some people don't hide the fact that it grosses them out.

So, yes, God understands how important our skin is to us. By the way, if you want the gory details about Job's skin condition, you can read about that in the book of Job. You can also read other mentions of skin care in the Bible and see that skin care is a symbol for God's love. Here are a couple of examples:

✦ Oil, which is one of the fruits of God's work, makes a person's face shine (Psalm 104:15).
✦ The woman in Bethany poured a whole container of perfume over Jesus' body as an act of devotion, a way of showing lavish love for God (Matthew 26:6 – 13).
✦ Keeping the skin clean was *really* a big deal for God's people. Ya think? In Leviticus, Moses spends four chapters (chapters 11 – 15) giving instructions for keeping clean!
✦ They were still at it in Jesus' time: "The Pharisees and all the Jews do not eat unless they give their hands a ceremonial washing, holding to the tradition of the elders. When they come from the marketplace they do not eat unless they wash" (Mark 7:3 – 4).
  This behavior was more about being clean inside than outside, but the tradition really helped them understand about being pure for God.
✦ And when someone actually had a close encounter with God, the person's face (skin) literally shone — like the sun. That happened to Moses (Exodus 34:29 – 30) and to Jesus (Matthew 17:2). It can even happen to you. When you truly believe in God's love, as Jesus showed it to us, you can "arise, shine, for your light has come" (Isaiah 60:1).

Here's the Deal

Like everything else God gives you, your skin needs to be taken care of. *Now* is the time to start, even if you haven't seen even a hint of a blemish. (That's a ladylike word for *zit*. It doesn't quite describe it, does it?)

Stuff You Totally Need to Know

Wash your face morning and night—and any other time you've worked up a sweat—with a gentle soap that contains NO acids. Rinse with at least fifteen splashes. Your skin won't shine if it still has soap on it. To block dirt, make the last few splashes cold water.

After you wash your face, smile. If your skin feels tight, put on a water-based liquid moisturizer that contains sunscreen. (We'll talk about that more below.)

Don't scrub like you would the bottom of a pot! Be gentle or you'll irritate your skin. Be sweet to yourself!

If your skin's really oily (you'll find that out below), use an oil-control lotion instead of moisturizer. That should have sunscreen in it too.

Don't forget the rest of your skin. Take regular showers or baths and wash with gentle soap, using a loofah or a washcloth so you can get rid of dead skin cells that naturally hang out. There are some really fun loofahs in stores these days with everything from frogs to rock stars on them. In the shower, pay attention to the following areas:

* neck—Dirt can gather in the little folds.
* arms—The skin on the backs of arms tends to get dry.
* elbows—A lot of people get really dark elbows, which are not attractive.
* buns—Pimples love to break out there.
* legs—Especially if you're really active, knees can get smudgy.
* feet—Obviously! Be sure to get in between toes where fungus likes to grow.

Rinse big-time, and when you get out of the shower or tub, use body lotion all over—you'll smell great and feel smooth. If that sounds like too much trouble, put some baby oil in a plastic spray bottle and squirt it on yourself while you're still wet. Then pat yourself dry with a towel. Don't rub, or it will all come off.

Make your skin-care routine as automatic as brushing your teeth. (We're hoping you're doing *that* regularly!)

Don't flop into bed at night without washing your face. It's carrying all the dirt and grime you've been exposed to all day. Yuck! If you're way tired when bedtime rolls around, ask your mom to get you some facial wipes. They're fast to use and will get you under the covers sooner.

More Stuff You Totally Need to Know

The sun's rays are great for giving you vitamins and keeping you in a good mood, but they aren't so great for your skin. No matter what anybody tells you, *a tan is not healthy!* It means you've damaged your skin.

Protect yourself now. When you're out in the sun soaking up vitamins between the hours of ten a.m. and four p.m., wear sunscreen with an SPF (sun protection factor) of at least 15 — higher if you have really fair skin — even if it's a cloudy day. Read the label to be sure it's no more than a year old — its effects do expire — and that it protects from both UVA and UBA rays.

Use it on every part of your body that's exposed, including your hands. Reapply it every two to three hours and after you've been in the water. Use SPF 15 lip balm on your lips too, since that thin skin burns easily.

Tanning beds are no safer than the sun. Instead of planning a lifetime membership at a tanning salon for your future, start getting used to the idea that your natural skin color is beautiful too, because, hello-o, it's healthy!

It seems like a pain in the neck when you're at the beach or pool having a blast, but the kind of sun damage that causes cancer usually happens before a girl is twenty years old. In fact, getting two major sunburns before age eighteen doubles your chances of getting skin cancer in your life. You don't want skin cancer. Besides, as you get older, too-tanned skin will start to look like somebody's old leather handbag.

Eat healthy food. Make sure you get veggies, fruits, whole grains, lean protein (like chicken and fish), and some dairy products. Treats are fine, but don't overdo; savor something small and exquisite rather than devouring an entire bag of chips in front of the TV. The reason? Good food has the nutrients you need for beautiful skin. The nutrients repair skin when it gets damaged (which is constantly happening in tiny ways). Your skin has to be healthy to be pretty. Sodas and candy bars will not make you pretty. Believe it or not, broccoli will!

Try eating only foods whose ingredients you can pronounce. For example, apple, versus monotyripigrossolate sodium phosphate.

Drink a lot of water, like, at least eight 8-ounce glasses a day. If that's hard to do when you're in school, try to grab a couple of swallows every time you pass the water fountain to flush out the icky stuff you take in just by breathing. Water inside gives your skin a nice glow outside.

Get the kind of exercise that makes you sweat, so that your skin is naturally cleansed. Doing some activity that you really dig for twenty minutes a day will perk your skin — and you — right up. So come on ... Off the couch! Walk the dog, get a game of screaming hide-and-seek going with your friends, practice all the cheers you know—whatever gets a smile on your face and a flush in your cheeks.

Get at least eight to ten hours of sleep every night. While you're getting your ZZZZs, your body is busy restoring itself after everything it's been through all day—and that means your skin too.

FAQs about Pimples

Q Where do pimples even come from?

A The closer you get to being a teenager, the more oil your body produces. In some girls, the oil glands really get going, and that can cause clogs of dead cells and oil that get infected. Presto—pimples.

Q Don't foods like french fries and chocolate cause zits?

A Nah. It's oil on the inside that makes skin break out. It may be, though, that white flour and sugar can make pimple problems worse, so healthy eating habits are always a good idea.

Q So how do I keep from getting them?

A The bad news is, sometimes you're going to get a pimple no matter what you do. Some people are more likely to get them because of the amount of oil they produce. Bummer. But you can prevent some breakouts by following the skin-care routine we've talked about.

Q If I get one of those evil ones that's all white and gross-looking, should I pop it?

A No! Sit on your hands if you have to but don't touch that zit. If you pop it or even pick at it, you'll spread the bacteria that has caused the infection, and more pimples just like that one are guaranteed to show up. The more you touch it, the longer it will take for it to heal. Besides, you could end up with a scar that'll be there forever. The pimple itself will go away — although the rest of the *day* may seem like forever.

Q Then what CAN I do? It's ugly!

A There are several things you can try on a pimple with a white head:

- Dab some tea tree oil on the spot with a cotton swab.

- Before you go to bed, put hot (not boiling!) water on the corner of a cloth and press it very gently on the pimple. Be patient, and it will open up and drain itself

- The next day, cover it up with a dab of a blemish stick.

Q What about those black plugs of dirt that get in my pores?

A Ah, yes, blackheads. They aren't dirt — they're skin pigment. They're created when oil and dead cells clog up a pore. They aren't infected yet, so those you can "operate on." After a hot shower, squeeze VERY gently with a finger on each side of the blackhead. Don't dig in with your fingernails, of course. If it

Your pimples always look bigger, redder, and yuckier to you than they do to anybody else. Don't remind everybody that you have them with loud wails of, "I hate my skin. I look like a pizza!" Remember, that little zit can't talk, so it says absolutely nothing about who you are.

doesn't pop out right away, leave it alone until the next time you take a shower. If you get a lot of blackheads, use a facial scrub when you wash. Rub it in with a washcloth or loofah. Be sure to be sweet with your skin while you're doing it. The grains in the scrub will do the work so you don't have to rub hard.

Q You're talking about a pimple or two. My face looks like I have big ol' boils. It even hurts. What do I do?

A That's a condition called *acne*, and it is a skin disease (though it's not catchy). The cause is complicated, but it has to do with hormones that are produced in the teen years which tell your body to produce more oil. In some people — and we don't know why — the oil gets stuck in the glands and plugs them up. The result is a face full of cysts and blackheads and pimples. Many times even after acne clears up, it leaves scars. Acne usually requires special care by a skin doctor (a dermatologist). You shouldn't have to suffer the pain. And no matter how beautiful you know you are on the inside, it's hard to feel pretty when your skin is sick. A dermatologist will tell you how to take care of your special skin and will probably prescribe medication in lotion and pill form to clear things up. You'll feel so much better. (If your mom says you'll just grow out of your acne, please show her this book.)

If you have dark skin, your skin will tend to scar easily. Don't squeeze a pimple no matter what.

That Is SO Me

Your skin is as unique as the rest of you, but you do belong to a skin *type*. Identifying your skin type can help you take extra-personalized care of You. Check out this quiz, and then be prepared to read the labels on the facial cleansers at the store.

Skin Type Quiz

Follow the flowchart on the next page to identify your skin type.

Tear a Kleenex into four small pieces. Before you wash your face in the morning, stick one piece on your forehead, one on a cheek, one on the side of your nose, and one on your chin. Keep the tissue on your face for about a minute.

If your skin gets red patches that look like a rash when you use skin-care products, you probably have sensitive skin. You can use products that are labeled "sensitive skin" or "hypoallergenic," or you can just avoid products that have fragrance in them. Be extra gentle with sensitive skin.

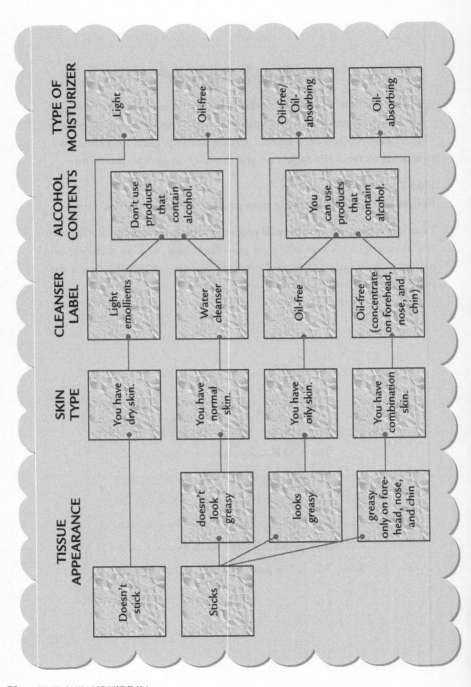

TISSUE APPEARANCE

Doesn't stick

Sticks

SKIN TYPE

You have dry skin.

You have normal skin.

You have oily skin.

You have combination skin.

doesn't look greasy

looks greasy

greasy only on forehead, nose, and chin

CLEANSER LABEL

Light emollients

Water cleanser

Oil-free

Oil-free (concentrate on forehead, nose, and chin)

ALCOHOL CONTENTS

Don't use products that contain alcohol.

You can use products that contain alcohol.

TYPE OF MOISTURIZER

Light

Oil-free

Oil-free/Oil-absorbing

Oil-absorbing

Okay, so what about makeup? It could be you haven't thought about it yet. Or you may already be telling your mom that everybody else in your class is wearing it—why can't you? Or you might fall somewhere in between. Wherever you are with the idea of blush and lip gloss and eye shadow, answers to the cosmetics questions will help you be Your Most Beautiful You at this point in your life.

When

Some girls are lingering over the lipstick displays at age eight, while others can't see the point of it even when they're teenagers. If you're younger than twelve, it's better—for the sake of your still-delicate skin—to wait to put on makeup for real. (Though you can sure have fun playing around with it—more on that later.) At around twelve, if you're dying to use makeup, talk (calmly!) to your parents about it. They have the final word. (So no sneaking on eye shadow in the girls' bathroom if their final word is "not yet.")

Why Not

Makeup can make you look older than you are. It can make you feel grown-up. But if you *aren't* older, and you *aren't* grown-up, then you're not being your true self, are you? Being real is the best beauty treatment of all. (And walking around with a scowl on your face because your dad says no to makeup will NOT be a good look for you.)

If you do wear makeup, even playing around, always, always wash it off before you go to bed. Otherwise, it can plug up your pores while you sleep. Uh, nasty!

How Much

If you and your parents agree that a little makeup would be okay, you'll still want to be "the best You at your age." You aren't trying to cover anything up or create something that isn't there, so your best look will be sheer lip colors and glosses, a little natural-looking mascara, and some blush that's the color of your skin when you exercise. That will bring out your natural beauty, and that's what makeup is always supposed to do.

How

Before you wear makeup outside your house, have someone show you how to apply it. Don't ask somebody who seems to put on her own makeup with a putty knife (or without a mirror!).

Where

You might want to start with some pretty lip gloss on special occasions. Maybe from there you could wear it on the weekends, when you and your friends are getting together—that kind of thing. Whether you break out the lip color and blush for school depends on school rules, your parents' guidelines, and how much attention you want to pay to your mirror when you have stuff to do.

What If

You really want to wear makeup and your parents won't let you. Use lip balm, which not only keeps your lips healthy but also makes them feel like you have lipstick on. Put some petroleum jelly on the tips of your eyelashes to make them look darker and longer (just don't get it in your eyes). While you're waiting for the day to come when you'll have a whole collection of shadows and blushes and other fun things in your makeup case, take great care of your skin, be your best self, and remember that you are already beautiful. Let makeup just be something fun to look forward to.

You're Good to Go

Let's have some fun with this skin thing, because being beautiful is always supposed to be fun! One or more of these activities will get you glowing and feeling like your prettiest self.

Spa Night

Do this with your mom (or another special lady if there's no mom in your life). It might even be fun to invite a friend and her mom to join you. Gather your supplies (see lists below) and set up a place where you won't be interrupted by teasing brothers, curious fathers, etc. Your mom's bedroom and bathroom are ideal, but even the kitchen will work. Make it as special as you want with candles, flowers, pretty towels, and favorite music.

Give yourselves head-to-toe spa care. These are suggestions, but you can come up with your own if you want.

HAIR — Put a deep conditioner in your hair and wrap your head in plastic wrap. Try the one under "You're Good to Go" at the end of this chapter.

FACE — Try this fun facial mask:

Ingredients: 1 cup uncooked oats, ½ cup plain yogurt, 2 tablespoons honey

Instructions: Put all the ingredients in a blender and puree. Spread the mixture on your face in an even layer and let it dry for five minutes. Wash it off with warm water and pat dry with a clean towel. Store the extra mixture in the fridge in an air-tight container for up to two weeks. You can repeat this once a day (though no more). See if you can do it once a week.

HANDS — Soak your fingers in a bowl of warm, sudsy water and your feet in a soup pot full of the same. Get some good girl talking done or listen to music.

You'll need a bowl big enough for your hands, a pot big enough for your feet, warm water, and very mild liquid soap (the best kind is made from natural ingredients).

After you rinse and style your hair, file your fingernails and toenails and maybe paint them. Then enjoy a snack feast together. Be sure it's something healthy like smoothies.

Don't forget to take pictures!

Makeup Madness

Do this with your best friend or a group of BFFs. If you don't have close buds yet, this would be a great time to invite some girls you'd like to get to know.

Ask everyone to bring any makeup that can be put on with fingers or cotton swabs. Eye shadow applicators, mascara brushes, and eyeliner used by other people carry bacteria you don't need to share. Lipstick is the exception, since that can be wiped off with a tissue. Ask your friends to bring stand-up mirrors if they have them too.

You supply lots of tissue, washcloths, cotton swabs, towels, mirrors for those who don't have them, hair thingies (for getting hair out of faces), and magazines with pix of girls in cool (or bizarre!) makeup.

Set up a place where you can spread out, get the giggles, and be able to clean up if you accidentally spill something.

Anything goes as you do makeovers on each other. Try on different looks. Experiment with techniques. Laugh. Tell each other you're gorgeous. Take pictures.

Then wash it all off and snuggle in with a healthy snack (and maybe your all-time favorite BFF movie).

Go back to your natural self with memories of fun and a glimpse of what you might look like when it IS time for sophisticated makeup.

What I've Learned About the Skin I'm in …

chapter three

Love
THE DO

Betsy stared — in horror — at the face that grinned at her through the window in the envelope. It was her worst school picture yet.

"Let's see yours!" Taylor said.

Betsy shoved the picture envelope into her binder and said, "No way. I look like a freak." By then Betsy's other friends had crowded around.

"Come on, Bets," Ashleigh said. "It can't be any worse than mine."

"Yes it can," Betsy said.

Ashleigh rolled her eyes and pulled out Betsy's packet. She looked at it for a minute and then turned to Taylor. "She's right," she said. "It IS worse."

Madison peered at it over Ashleigh's shoulder. "It's just your hair. It was doing something weird that day."

Taylor nodded. "You don't usually look like that, Bets. Really."

Betsy snatched the envelope back and waited for her friends to scatter before she sneaked another peek at herself.

"I am fearfully and wonderfully made," she said to her picture. "For a squirrel!"

Here's the Deal

Okay, so Betsy still has a long way to go on the find-your-own-beauty trail, but we hope YOU are convinced that every girl can have hair that's great for her. Let's start with some basics.

The Mane Things

Hair looks best when it's clean, so wash your hair as soon as it gets the least bit stringy. Don't wait 'til it's matted to your head, especially if your hair is becoming oily these days—which happens naturally as you grow toward teenager-hood.

Use the right kind of shampoo for your hair.

* Dry hair (especially coarse or curly)—moisturizing shampoo; baby shampoo if you wash your hair every day
* Oily hair (greasy when you skip a day of washing)—clarifying shampoo
* Normal hair (soft but not greasy)—shampoo for normal hair

It's okay to wash your hair every day, especially if it is oily or you do sports. Just get an empty shampoo bottle and fill it half-way with your shampoo and the rest of the way with warm water. Most shampoos are too strong to use everyday. Remember, you're being gentle with your beauty.

We say we're washing our hair, but we're really washing our head. Put a quarter-size glob of shampoo in the palm of your hand and work it into your wet scalp. Don't scratch with your fingernails, though. Use the pads of your fingers and massage. Enjoy. Even if you aren't a "girly" girl (like maybe your mom has to threaten you with grounding to get you to take a shower), washing your hair can still be fun. Remember when as a kid you made bunny ears with your lathered-up hair in the bathtub? Who says you can't still do that?

When you rinse, your hair will get the benefits of the shampoo. Unless you use a lot of "stuff" on your hair (mousse, gel, hairspray), you don't have to worry about the ends of your hair.

Rinse for two or three minutes. Really. If you leave shampoo in your hair, it won't shine. It's tempting to hurry to be done so you can play with your Game Boy or talk on the phone to your BFF. But let hair-washing time be your good alone time.

You probably don't have to use conditioner unless your hair gets really tangled when you wash it (or if you use products like gel when you style). A tiny dollop the size of a dime is plenty. Just apply it to the tangled places. Too much conditioner can build up on your hair so it loses its shimmer.

Always comb wet hair. Brushing it can actually break it. If you have trouble with tangles, use a comb with really big, spread-out teeth and be slow and gentle. Getting beautiful should never be painful!

Brush your hair before you go to bed at night (only if it's not wet, of course). If you have oily hair, brushing will spread the oils around to the right places. If you have dry hair (which you might if your hair is really curly or coarse), it will bring out the natural oils. Even if you have "normal" hair, brushing it is great for your scalp. It's kind of a soothing thing to do while you're thinking your end-of-the-day thoughts or listening to somebody read — whatever you do before you check out for the night.

Brush or comb your hair anytime during the day when it gets out of control — like after soccer practice or after a math test when you've been winding it around your finger while you concentrate. Just keep a small nylon-bristle brush in your backpack, give your tresses a few strokes, and you're gorgeous.

Have your hair trimmed about every six weeks. It doesn't reproduce itself like your skin does, so the ends start to look damaged if they're not cut off. If your hair is long, taking off the funky ends

Since hair is a bunch of dead cells that build up into strands that come out of your head (and your arms, legs, and arm-pits — lovely, huh?), it's very fragile. As much fun as it is to style, perm, glitter, and braid your hair, remember to be gentle with it. Accept it for what it is instead of trying to turn it into something it can't be. It will be so much more beautiful if you're nice to it.

will make it look healthier. If it's short, a trim will keep the style neat and fun. If you're trying to let it get longer, regular trims will keep it looking good. Split ends are basically dead, so they won't grow. If your hair is healthy and clean, you're going to feel good about that. After all, you're taking care of one of the gifts God gave you. When you feel good, you look good. It just happens.

Stylin'

You can stop right here if you want. But what if you'd like to do more than just wash your hair and get regular trims? First, you'll want to discover a style that suits your face. (No, Betsy. That does not mean a style that covers it up!)

If you want to be like your friends who all wear ponytails everyday, go for it. That's okay. If, on the other hand, you want to try out something that's really you . . .

- ✦ Go back to the mirror, which hopefully is now becoming your friend.
- ✦ Pull your hair back so you can really see the shape of your face.
- ✦ On a piece of paper, draw the shape you see.

It could be

very round,
oval,
square or square-ish,
long-rectangular,
triangular, or
heart-shaped.

Love that shape. It's you!

These are some ideas for hairstyles for your special face shape:

Very round — You precious thing! Long and straight is good. Or maybe a little height on top (scrunchie, anyone?) with some shape at the sides (the rest of your hair covering your ears, perhaps). If you want your face to look even rounder, go for short and curly. You get to choose.

Oval — Have at it, girl! Any style looks great on you. How fun is that?

Square or square-ish — This means your jaw and your forehead are kind of even. You can look way classy with a face like yours. Just keep your haircut above or below your jawline. Chopped off right at your jawline or poofiness going on at the corners of your forehead won't be your very best looks.

Long-rectangular — You can really look dramatic if you want to, as long as you avoid piling your hair right at the top of your head or wearing it too long and straight. You'll look fabulous with something fun and full at the sides.

Triangular — Great face for having some fun with bangs and different angles (like a ponytail that's off-center). Smooth hair at your jawline is spectacular on you.

Heart-shaped — You're a walking valentine! Curls or some- thing else soft at your jawline is made for you. Try not to go poofy on top, though.

Another thing to think about — if you're really into this hair thing — is the *texture* of your hair. This is what we mean by texture:

Straight and soft — Like, you could be in hot rollers the whole day and your hair will still be straight an hour after you take them out (if not sooner!).

Curly, maybe even frizzy — You know it if you have it!

Thick and coarse — It takes forever to dry after you wash it, and if left to its own devices, it will get bushy.

Thick and fine — You have a lot of hair, but it's really soft so it wants to lie down.

Don't even try to change the texture of your hair because it isn't going to happen. And why would you want it to? It's part of the beauty journey to discover what works — and go with it. SO . . .

Straight and soft? Try a bob, or wear your hair long and all one length.

Curly or frizzy? Have your hair cut in layers, not all one length.

Thick and coarse? Try different lengths in one style and wear it medium to long. A stylist can thin your hair with special styling shears — but not every time you get your hair cut.

Thick and fine? You'll look great with your hair all one length except for layers around your face — either very long or very short.

Your *ethnic background* is another thing to consider when you're talking hair. It's a huge part of being true to who you are.

If you're *Asian*, women all around you are probably suffering from hair-envy. (They should read this book, shouldn't they?) You are exquisite with a simple, straight cut. Don't ever let anyone talk you into getting a perm!

If you're *Latin American*, have a blast with your thick, shiny hair. You don't have to look for complicated haircuts because you're fabulous with shoulder-length or longer hair. And don't even think about changing the color.

If you blow-dry your hair every day (and especially if you use a curling iron, hot rollers, or a flat iron) towel dry your hair before you blow-dry. That will cut down on the time your hair is exposed to heat, which can make it brittle.

If you're *African American*, you have so many choices. One of the coolest ones, if you get frustrated with your hair, is to slick it back, which shows off your wonderful face. Don't fight your hair. Be proud of your heritage.

Special Hair Issues

There's never a reason to stress about your tresses, but if you want to look polished and your hair just won't cooperate, try these hints:

Does your naturally curly hair get the frizzies?

* Rub a little gel between your fingers and then run your fingers through your just-washed, wet hair. Comb your hair into place and let it air dry.

* Or if you want to blow it dry, use a diffuser — a cone shaped thing that goes over the end of your dryer. Once you're through, keep your hands out of your hair. Every time you touch it, it gets frizzier.
* Don't go outside in humid weather with damp hair.

Is your hair baby thin?

* Use a *volumizing* shampoo. It coats your hair and makes it look thicker.
* Don't use conditioner unless your hair really tangles, and then just use the tiniest bit.
* When you blow-dry, bend over at the waist, let your hair hang down, and blast away until it's almost dry. Then stand up straight and style it into place.

Do you wish your hair were another color?

* It's fun to think about, but just let your hair be its natural color for now. Once you start coloring it, you have to keep doing it unless you want funky roots. You have enough other fun stuff to do.
* Your hair may not stay the color it is. Most blondes, for example, get darker as they get older. Wait and see how it turns out.
* Because your hair is still pretty delicate at this age, eighteen is really the earliest you should consider doing any color treating. Even then, keep in mind that it's hard to keep artificially colored hair healthy unless you have it done professionally. Then you're talking some big bucks ...

With all God has to do, do you think he really cares about your hair? People in the Bible sure seemed to think so.

"Do not cut the hair at the sides of your head or clip off the edges of your beard" (Leviticus 19:27) is written as part of God's message through Moses to the entire assembly of Israel on how to be holy. Some Orthodox Jewish men still follow that rule to show total obedience to God. You'll see them with ringlets in front of their ears.

In Numbers 6:5, God said that if a man or woman wanted to make a special vow (a period of special devotion to God), one of the requirements was to not cut his or her hair. You'd know a God-devoted person by the long do.

In the New Testament, Luke (Luke 7:44) tells us about a woman who washed Jesus' feet with her tears and dried them with her hair before she kissed them and poured perfume on them.

One of the most famous people in the Bible to keep long hair was Samson. His mother was told by an angel — before Samson was even born — not to cut his hair so he would be "set apart to God from [his] birth" (Judges 13:5). As long as Samson stayed completely devoted to God — and let his hair grow as a symbol of that — he had the power to lead the Israelites in their battles against the bad guys (the Philistines). If you want to read more, his story is in Judges, chapters 13 – 16 — but be aware that it's some pretty rough stuff.

Jesus was impressed by how deeply she loved him. You *would* have to love someone a lot to dry his wet feet with your own hair.

It's the same in the Bible and now. In Matthew 10:30, Jesus says, "And even the very hairs of your head are all numbered." That is how much you are worth to God. Even if people hate you because you stand up for him, Jesus said, "*not a hair of your head will perish*" (Luke 21:18). You don't think God cares about your hair—and every other tiny part of you?

At the same time, Peter warns us women not to get so focused on our hair that we forget about being beautiful on the inside. Your beauty, he writes in 1 Peter 3:4, "should be that of your inner self, the unfading beauty of a gentle and quiet spirit, which is of great worth in God's sight."

Yes, take care of every hair God counted and put on your head. Enjoy it. And match its beauty with your actions. You won't just be *that girl with the pretty long brown hair*. You'll be *that really friendly (or nice or fun or crazy-but-I-like-her) girl with the pretty long brown hair*.

You're Good to Go

Want to do something just for fun?? Try this conditioner recipe with friends, your sisters, or—best yet—your mom. You can do it alone too. Just be sure to ask adult permission first. It's a great conditioner that feels weird in a good way and leaves your hair super shiny.

Directions:

❖ Put 1 tablespoon of oil (olive oil or any vegetable oil) in a dish that's microwave safe. Microwave it for five seconds.

❖ Add one egg yolk (not the whole egg). Ask your mom how to separate the egg.

❖ Whisk until blended, using a whisk or a fork.

* Massage the mixture into your hair. We *told* you it was going to feel weird!
* Put on a shower cap or a plastic bag (not over your face, obviously!).
* Leave it on for twenty minutes. This is why it's fun to do it with other hair-happy people. This is a great time for a snack or for starting on the next activity — or both.
* Shampoo your hair and rinse well.

You will now have the shiniest hair *ever*.

Serious about Going for a New Hairstyle?

If you haven't done it already, go back and circle the suggestions for your face shape and hair texture on pages 43 – 45.

Look through magazines for girls your age and find pictures of hair styles like the ones suggested for your shape and texture. Decide if you like any of them.

After discussing it with your mom, take this book (and a picture if you found one) to the best stylist your family can afford — and that can even be your aunt who makes everybody's hair look great. Your dad's barber — maybe not.

Explain — or have whoever takes you explain — what you want and ask the stylist if he or she thinks it's a good choice. (If you're getting a really big change and you get nervous, you can always start with a good trim, then next time go shorter.)

If you end up with the worst haircut on the planet — at least to you — remember that hair grows back. Meanwhile, get out the barrettes or headbands or clips, and use this as a chance to experiment. Wearing a hat 24/7 is not an option, because if your hair is clean and you're smiling, you're still beautiful. Got that?

What I Discovered About My God-Made Head of Hair ...

chapter four

Smooth
MOVES

B etsy had to admit she really liked her new do. Her dad
even noticed it, and he was the type to fall over the furni-
ture before he realized her mom had changed it around.

Okay, so that kid Jason in her class said her new hairstyle
made her look like a space alien. Huh. He should talk, Mr. Combs
His Hair with a Lawn Mower.

But one day in the shower, Betsy discovered some *other* hair.
When she raised her arm to wash her armpit — with the green
loofah that looked like a frog in a tutu — she noticed something
she hadn't picked up on before.

Fuzz under her arm.

Where did THAT come from? she thought. *Am I turning into Ape
Girl?*

With water still pouring down on her, Betsy examined the
rest of her body. Yikes! Her legs looked hairier too. They'd
always had kind of a blonde fuzziness, but now the little hairs
were darker, and there were more of them.

"I'm not wearing a skirt today!" Betsy said to the loofah frog.
"Not today — and maybe never again. I have hairy legs!"

That Is SO Me

Take a few minutes to figure out whether you're feeling furry, like Betsy. In EACH ROW of boxes below, put a check in the ONE that is MOST like you.

Underarm hair:
- ☐ None
- ☐ Light 'n' fuzzy
- ☐ Dark and thick

I get sweat on my shirt under my arms:
- ☐ Almost never
- ☐ When I'm way active
- ☐ Whenever I move! (almost)

Leg hair:
- ☐ Not much
- ☐ I can barely see it.
- ☐ A person across the the room can see it.

My hair 'tude:
- ☐ What body hair?
- ☐ It's not a big deal.
- ☐ I want it off!

Why I want to shave:
- ☐ I don't!
- ☐ Some of my friends do.
- ☐ I feel like an ape.

Time I spend on beauty:
- ☐ As little as possible
- ☐ The basics (almost) daily
- ☐ As much as I can

Count how many check marks you have.

Boxes on the left: _____

Boxes in the center: _____

Boxes on the right: _____

Where do you have the most checks?

If you had the most checks on the left side, you probably won't want to add shaving your legs and underarms to your beauty chart yet. Read on, though, because someday you might, and it's good to know what you're doing when you're handling a razor!

If you had the most checks in the center, you might not be up for shaving your legs yet, but it's a good idea to keep an eye on your underarms, especially if you sweat there. Hair in the pits tends to hold perspiration where it can get a little smelly. A less than lovely odor wafting from under your arms is definitely not beautiful. Read on and we'll show you how to take care of that—and your legs—when you're ready.

If you had the most checks on the right side, you may have been eyeing your dad's razor for some time, or you suddenly feel like a furry family pet. That means it's the right time to approach your mom about shaving. This chapter will tell you all the secrets of hair removal, so that once mom gives the okay, you're ready to de-fuzz.

Since taking off body hair involves a razor or a product with strong chemicals in it, you really need adult permission before you go for it. And know that once you start shaving or using a hair-removal cream or lotion, the hair you take off will grow back coarser and thicker. This means it will be important to <u>keep</u> doing it regularly, or you'll be prickly and stubbly. Just think carefully first about whether you want to add this one more thing to your routine.

Here's the Deal

Have permission to streamline your legs and/or underarms? Sure you're ready to commit to regular "defurrings"? Then get ready to feel very womanly . . .

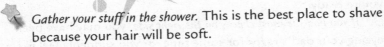

Shaving Directions

Gather your stuff in the shower. This is the best place to shave because your hair will be soft.

* Soap
* Shaving cream (the thickest you can get your hands on). Ask if you can use your dad's the first time. The men's stuff is the best. If that's not available, use hair conditioner. (Shaving dry can give you a rash.)
* A real razor with a clean blade. Disposable razors are harder to use on the bumps (like your knees). You'll be amazed at how easy it is to cut yourself and not even feel it at first. If you do use a disposable razor, throw it away after two or three times.

Wash the area you're going to shave with soap first. Since shaving cream or hair conditioner isn't soap, it won't fight bacteria. Take care of that first.

Lather up. It's really fun to cover your legs and underarms with rich, creamy shaving lather. Besides, it helps the hair stand up so the razor can catch it. Lather one underarm and shave it, then lather and shave the other, then one leg, then the other. Obviously, turn off the shower or step out of the water's stream while you're shaving or your lather will just go down the drain.

Shave. Take your time! Start at top of your armpit, and — pushing down VERY GENTLY with the razor — pull it toward the bottom in short strokes. As the shaving cream comes off, so will the hair. When shaving your legs, be sure you have a steady footing on a bathmat before propping the leg you're going to shave on the side of the bathtub or the ledge. Start at your ankle and work your way up in long, smooth strokes. Run the razor under the water when it gets goopy with shaving cream. Be extremely careful around bones that stick out. It helps to bend your knee before shaving it. Since the hair on your thighs is finer, lighter, and shorter, you don't usually have to shave them. Do not rush. Pay careful attention. If you need bandages when you get out of the shower, you were probably in too much of a hurry. Relax. This is *You* time.

Using a Hair Removal Product

Decide if that's really what you want.
* A cream or lotion may sound safer than a razor blade, but it contains strong chemicals that irritate some people's skin. No one should use one if she has even the tiniest cut or scrape. It also takes longer than shaving, because you have to leave it on for five to ten minutes. If you plan to use it on your legs, that's going to take a lot, which gets expensive. Besides all that, it can smell funky.

If you decide to go with it:
* Read the directions very carefully and follow them exactly, including the part about testing a small area

first to see if it irritates your skin. After you use it, wash your hands thoroughly before you put them near your eyes or mouth. If you get some on anything but your legs or underarms, wash it off right away.

Other ways to take hair off:
* Laser—A professional can remove hair permanently. Sounds great, but it's way expensive and takes more time than you're going to want to spend.
* Waxing—Beauty salons will gladly use warm wax to remove your hair, but, man, does it hurt. Then you have to wait two weeks before you can have it done again, which can get pretty, well, hairy.

What about Eyebrows?

You probably haven't thought much about your eyebrows, unless

* you've found yourself with one big eyebrow going all the way across, or
* you really want a polished, finished look.

If you do want to take out stray hairs or get rid of your unibrow, follow these instructions very closely.

To make a space between eyebrows:
* Take a shower or wash your face with very warm water before you start. It won't sting as much when you pull the hairs out.
* Use good tweezers with slanted ends, not the pointy kind. Save those for splinters.
* Get close to the mirror. Better yet, use a hand mirror.

Eyebrows never grow all the way back once you pull them out. That means if you plucked all of yours out right now, you would hardly have eyebrows again. You may be thinking, <u>Why</u> <u>would</u> <u>I</u> <u>do</u> <u>THAT?</u> But you'd be surprised how easy it is to get carried away once you get hold of a pair of tweezers.

* Simply pinch a hair with the tweezers and give a sharp little tug. The hair should come right out.
* Don't tweeze your brows any further back than the inside corners of your eyes. If you get one eyebrow farther in than the other, don't try to even them out. You could end up with little commas for eyebrows.

To make eyebrows look neat and groomed:
* Following the same guidelines as above, remove hairs that have popped in under your eyebrows
* Don't tweeze any above the brows at this point. It's too easy to wind up with thin lines instead of nice, velvety, healthy-looking eyebrows.
* Lots of women have their eyebrows waxed instead of tweezing them. Again, that hurts, and it costs money, and there's always the danger that too much eyebrow will be taken off. We advise you not to even go there right now.

GOT GOD?

The Bible doesn't have much to say about shaving. There's that one passage in Ezekiel where God told him, "Take a sharp sword and use it as a barber's razor to shave your head and beard" (Ezekiel 5:1). That doesn't exactly apply to you, since Ezekiel was being asked to do strange things to warn the people that they're about to go down. Do we need to even tell you not to attempt to shave your legs with a sword?

God doesn't talk about hair removal for women, because we girls didn't start going for the smooth look until it became proper for us to show our arms and legs in public, around the 1920s. Before that, what was the point? Now, being smooth and silky is considered part of good grooming for a woman in the United States. In some other countries, ladies skip the whole shaving thing and nobody bats an eye.

So basically, there's nothing bad about shaving or not shaving. It's really a matter of choice. Since your parents still have the final say in your choices, you'll have to go with theirs for a while. If your mom says you're too young to shave your legs, and you're feeling like Tarzan, try not to let it become a huge deal in your mind. Be responsible about the rest of your beauty care, and re-visit the issue with Mom in a few months. A little maturity goes a long way. God *does* say something about that: "Honor your father and your mother, so that you may live long in the land the LORD your God is giving you" (Exodus 20:12).

It doesn't get much clearer than that!

You're Good to Go

The neat thing about having leg hair to shave — or even knowing you will someday — is that it means you're turning into a young woman. What better excuse for a celebration? In each of the following balloons, choose one or more details — or come up with your own.

Who to Invite:

Your best friend

Just you and your mom

A small circle of friends

A small assortment of females who enjoy being or becoming women

Where to Party

Any place without non-women!

Decorate to Create a Feeling of Fun Femininity

Flowers and butterflies

Women's sports memorabilia

Pictures of women you admire

Everything sparkly

What to Eat

Something no boy would be caught eating

The healthiest snacks everyone can create

Frilly desserts

Be sure to include just a little chocolate.

What to Do

Have a spa night (See chapter two).

Let everyone tell what she loves about being a girl.

Everyone brings a baby picture so you can guess who's who.

Squeal over how much everyone has changed.

Watch a special chick flick together.

Whatever creative, womanly ideas you come up with, have a wonderful time celebrating that God made you girls. Be sure to include some prayer time, because God will definitely be at your party.

What I Totally Love About Being a Mini-Woman ...

chapter five

Things That Will
COME IN HANDY
... AND FOOTY!

"If you know the answer, raise your hand," Mrs. Post, Betsy's teacher said.

Betsy knew it like she knew her own name, so she waved her arm in the air. In the desk in front of her, the new girl, Caroline, stuck her hand up too. And there they were: the prettiest shell-pink fingernails, shaped like little ovals on Caroline's long, smooth fingers.

Betsy pulled her arm down and inspected her own nails — - what was left of them. She'd gnawed the last one down during that morning's math test. If they had a pop quiz in science, she planned to start chewing at the little pieces of skin that popped up around them. She decided it might be a good idea to wash her hands first, though, because there was a big old blue blob on her knuckle from the marker she'd used to color her toenails the night before when she was bored.

Suddenly, Betsy felt like all anybody could see were her chomped-off fingernails and scribbled-on toenails. She tucked her feet, which were in sandals, under her and hid her hands in her pockets. Mrs. Post called on Caroline for the right answer.

GOT GOD?

You might be wondering when poor Betsy is going to get it. Whether she's had a manicure or not shouldn't determine whether she raises her hand in class, right? Caroline sure isn't any smarter because she's wearing nail polish and doesn't have a marker blob on her index finger.

But the thing is, knowing her hands were looking pretty ragged *did* keep Betsy from showing what was really important—that she had studied, she was paying attention, and she wanted to participate because she knew she'd learn more that way. That's kind of a bummer.

It's even more of a bummer when you think about how many things God made our hands for:

Appealing to God for help—like Moses putting up his hands for God's power in battle (Exodus 17:11).

Healing—like Jesus laying hands on people to cure them (Mark 5:23), and the apostles doing it later (Acts 28:8).

Clapping—like people applauding for a new king (2 Kings 11:12).

Creating—as God's people have always done: Noah with the ark, Solomon's people with the temple, and Christians building up the church with their gifts (1 Corinthians 14:12).

Working—like the woman of noble character making clothes (Proverbs 31:24), and as Paul told the early Christians they should do (1 Thessalonians 4:11).

Helping—like that same noble woman who opens her arms to the poor and extends her hands to the needy (Proverbs 31:20)

Praying—as Paul told all Christians to do (1 Timothy 2:8).

If you stopped doing all of that because your hands didn't look like a nail-polish commercial, you'd really be letting God and yourself down. Since there are about a bajillion things you use your hands for, why not keep them looking at least clean and neat, if not downright fabulous?

That Is SO Me

When it comes to taking care of your hands, you can go from

| Cleaner than your brother's | Basically clean and neat | A little polished (and clean and neat) | A funky expression of your wild self (and clean and neat) |

Circle the look that you'd like to go for. Remember that there's no right or wrong. If you can't see yourself spending your birthday money on a bottle of Sparkling Scarlet, basically keeping your hands and nails clean is fine, even for the rest of your life. If you get really jazzed about drop-dead gorgeous nails, that's okay too.

Here's the Deal

No matter which of the four looks you circled, you'll need to follow the basics for taking care of your hands.

So here's the deal for hand health:

Wash your hands. Duh-uh, right? You'd be surprised how many people don't even think about it. Really clean your hands with warm water and soap (not just a quick run under the faucet before you take off). The bare minimum is to wash your hands when

- ❖ you've just used the bathroom;
- ❖ you're about to eat (whether it's sticking your hand in a bag of chips or sitting down to a big dinner);
- ❖ you're getting ready to fix something to eat;

- ❖ you've been touching an animal;
- ❖ you've been shopping;
- ❖ your hands feel sticky, greasy, grimy, or just a little icky;
- ❖ you have a cold (Wash your hands twice as much as usual and definitely after you've wiped your nose — hello-o!); and
- ❖ you've been around somebody who's sick.

This makes it sound like you have to have your hands in the sink all the time, but once it becomes a habit, you won't feel that way. It can be hard to get to soap and water when you're in school all day, so keep some hand sanitizer or wipes in your backpack. If somebody calls you a clean freak, pass him a Wet Wipe.

Get the dirt out from under your fingernails. Once a day, after you get out of the shower or tub, use a metal nail file (like the kind that comes on nail clippers) to gently scrape any left-over stuff from under your nails. Do it even if they don't look dirty. You'd be amazed what hides in there. (You don't really want to know . . .)

Even if you don't want glamour nails, it's way important to keep your hands clean. Since your fingers are into everything — all day long — they're the main way you pick up germs. No, you aren't picking them up between your fingertips, but they're constantly hitching a ride without your permission. Even if you can't see dirt, bacteria is there, ready to give you everything from a cold to . . . well, you get the idea.

Moisturize. Remember that from the skin chapter? When you're putting on lotion after your bath or shower, pay attention to your hands. This is especially important in cold climates where the temperatures can chap the skin on your hands just like it does your lips.

If, on *That Is SO Me*, you circled "Cleaner than your brother's," you're done.

Have a great day!

If you circled "Basically clean and neat," there are a few more steps. The good news is you don't have to do these every day. For hands and nails that say, "This girl takes good care of herself," do the following once a week:

File your nails with what's called an emery board. It's a nail file that has really fine sandpaper on it. Don't file with the metal thing, even though it's called a nail file. (Go figure!)

- Don't go back and forth like you're sawing a log. That's makes your nails weak. Start at one side of your nail and file in one direction toward the center, and then do the same from the other side.

- Since this takes time, you might do it while you're watching a movie or something.

- File until all your nails are the same length and shape, probably an oval or as close as you can get to that. You might have one or two nails that are nice and long and you're proud of them, but if the rest are way short, it's going to look funny. Say good-bye to the long ones and file away.

Take care of your cuticles. That's the skin around your nails that tends to creep onto them. It's healthier if they stay in place.

- Soak your fingers in a little bowl of hot, soapy water for a few minutes to soften up your cuticles.

Long nails look glamorous in magazines, but they probably aren't the best idea for you right now. They get in the way when you're writing, playing sports, or using the computer. They require a lot more attention. And they look as out of place when you're ten as three shades of eye shadow. Just above the tip of your finger is probably long enough. Shorter is okay too.

Using what's called an orange stick (a little wooden thing with a slanted end), or a cotton swab, gently push the cuticles off your nails. Think of it as gently persuading them to get back where they belong.

If any little pieces of cuticle stick up — like they're breaking off — you can clip them with tiny manicure scissors. Just to be on the safe side, have an experienced person (mom, big sister, etc.) show you how to do that. The broken cuticle is dead, but the skin that's still attached isn't. Nobody should bleed during a manicure!

That's it. Look at you. Nice hands, girlfriend!

If, on *That Is SO Me,* you circled "A little polished," you need to do all of the above before you move on to this part. Putting nail polish on nails that are dirty and ragged is sort of like putting frosting on a cake that hasn't been baked, you know? Once you're ready, here's what to do to look a little polished in the nail department.

Remove all old polish. You'll just need cotton balls you can dip in nail polish remover. Wipe from bottom to top until it ALL comes off.

Use a clear coat of polish first. There are special base coats, or you can just use clear. This is important if you plan to paint your nails a lot, because without it, colored polish can make them look yellow after a while.

Just use two or three strokes with the polish brush to cover your whole nail. That's all it takes. Any more and it gets gloppy. Let that dry before you move on. Don't rush. If that looks nice to you, you can stop there. Clear polish doesn't show as much when it chips off, and your nails will look shiny and pretty. If you want color . . .

Put on two layers of colored polish. Again, just use two or three strokes and let them dry completely in between. Instead of shaking the bottle to mix polish, roll it between your palms a couple of times. That away you won't get bubbles on your nails.

Apply a clear coat over that. That will help keep the color from chipping.

It only makes sense that if remover can take off nail polish, it can also take the finish off your mom's table or the color out of your jeans. Be sure you have everything covered. And do we need to mention not to get it even close to your eyes or mouth or anybody else's?

A lot of girls your age (and older!) bite their nails. You probably don't mean to; it's just that you get a little nervous or bored and before you realize it, you're chewing away. If you want to stop, pay attention for a few days to when you bite. Then, try to find a substitute for those times. If you nibble while you watch TV, take up knitting. If you tend to chow down when you're stressed out, keep a wad of Silly Putty handy to squeeze. Remember that those fingers in your mouth are feeding you germs.

Don't do anything "nail intensive" for several hours, which means you might want to do your manicure before you go to bed. Don't let water touch them. Even if you speed dry by putting your hands in the freezer for two minutes, all the coats won't be entirely dry for three hours. So if you don't go right to bed, at least don't finger paint, dig a hole, or enter a pie-eating contest!

When your polish starts to chip—and it will—remove it with nail polish remover. A flake of polish in the middle of each nail is definitely not a good look for anybody. Not a good idea to chip it off with your other nails—or (Yikes!) with your teeth. Wait until you have time to sit down with remover and cotton balls.

If on *That Is SO Me,* you circled "A funky expression of your wild self," do ALL of the above, except that when you get ready to polish, use your imagination! This is one form of makeup parents don't usually object to (although you'll want to check with yours first), and it can be a blast.

Find fun colors you like. Nail polish can be pretty cheap to buy, and a bottle lasts a while. There are so many shades that come in everything from satiny to sparkly-like-metal. There's even glitter polish, which is TOO fun. Enjoy wild, strange nail color now, because as you get older, it won't always be the thing to do.

Avoid fake nails. You know—the kind you can buy in a package that you stick on with glue? That sticky stuff really isn't good for your nails. Who wants to look fake anyway, unless you're playing the wicked witch in the school play?

GOT GOD?

Hands are one thing—but why would God care about your feet? Nobody can see them most of the time; so, when it comes right down to it, why should *you* care that much about your feet?

Let's start with God, whose people talk about feet all the time in the Bible. Most of the time, they used them as symbols. That's when an object you can see—such as a cross—helps you understand something you can't see—like faith in God. In spite of their smelliness and fuzz between the toes, feet are important symbols in God's Word (which just goes to show God can use anybody and anything).

Feet are symbols for our ability to stand up for what's right.

"He set my feet on a rock and gave me a firm place to stand." —PSALM 40:2

"For you have delivered me from death and my feet from stumbling." —PSALM 56:13

There are lots of symbols of walking a path with God.

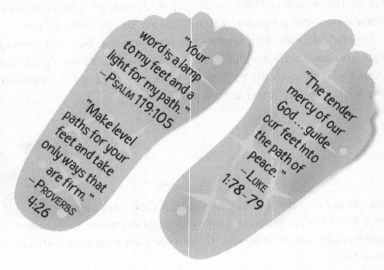

"Your word is a lamp to my feet and a light for my path."
— PSALM 119:105

"Make level paths for your feet and take only ways that are firm."
— PROVERBS 4:26

"The tender mercy of our God ... guide our feet into the path of peace."
— LUKE 1:78-79

Jesus washed the disciples' feet to symbolize how selfless God's love is, and how we have to love each other the same way.

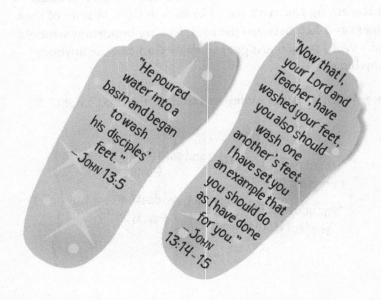

"He poured water into a basin and began to wash his disciples' feet."
— JOHN 13:5

"Now that I, your Lord and Teacher, have washed your feet, you also should wash one another's feet. I have set you an example that you should do as I have done for you."
— JOHN 13:14-15

You basically take care of your feet the same way you do your hands, with just a few special variations.

- ✤ Since toenails are tougher than fingernails, trim them with clippers instead of trying to file them.
- ✤ It's better to cut your toenails straight across instead of making ovals. Otherwise, you can get ingrown toenails. Ouch!
- ✤ While you're doing your weekly manicure, soak your feet in warm water to soften them up.
- ✤ Then use the pointed thing on the nail clippers to clean out the dirt from under your toenails. You think your *fingernails* get icky . . .
- ✤ If you're going to polish your toenails, put pieces of cotton between your toes to spread them out. That way you won't get polish all over them.

Foot Funkiness

Warts. It's common to get them on your hands too. Although they're not anybody's best look, they're harmless and usually go away. You can try treatments from the drug store, but know that it takes a while for them to shrivel up. If a wart is really bugging you, especially if it's on the bottom of your foot (a plantar wart) a doctor can "freeze" it off. And by the way, frogs and toads don't give you warts, so don't run screaming from them.

Pee-yew! Yeah, feet can definitely get smelly. Once they do, you have to wash them to get rid of the stinkiness. Here are tips to prevent them from smelling up the place to begin with:

- Wear socks made of natural fibers, like cotton or wool, that absorb sweat before it causes yuckiness.
- Your shoes should be made of natural stuff too, such as leather or canvas. Plastic tennies and sandals may be fun, but, ooh, can they smell!
- If your shoes are giving off a less-than-delicious aroma, sprinkle baking soda inside them and leave it overnight.
- Sneakers cause more of a stench than any other kind of shoe. If you have a big problem with stinky feet, switch to sandals or loafers or cute flats when you can.

If your feet are suddenly bigger than your mom's, even though you're only eleven or so, don't freak. Women's feet are commonly larger now than they were even a generation ago. There's nothing wrong with big feet. Some of the most beautiful women in the world have slipped into a size nine or larger.

Hurting feet. If you get blisters or you can't wait to take your shoes off, you're probably wearing shoes that don't fit well. Your feet are growing right now, so have your feet measured every time you go shopping for shoes. And don't beg for the pair you love if the store doesn't have your size.

You want higher heels, but your mom won't let you. You know what? You need to listen to her. In the first place, three-inch heels when you're ten are right up there with the glamour nails and the heavy eye shadow we've been talking about. You're going to look like you're playing dress up with your mom's shoes. And most important of all, high heels throw your spine completely out of line and cause all kinds of problems with hips, knees, and even necks. They're cool for special occasions as you get older, but never for all day. Be part of the generation that says, "We will NOT walk around on stilts! We will take care of our bodies!"

Between-the-toe fungus. Red, scaly patches? That's called athlete's foot, though you don't have to be an athlete to get it. To avoid it, wear flip-flops when you take a shower in a locker room or at a pool, since that's where we usually pick up the fungus. Dry your feet really well after a bath, and don't wear the same shoes all the time. If you do get athlete's foot, start treating it with a powder, spray, or cream you can get at the drugstore. It won't go away by itself, and who wants itchy feet 24/7?

You're Good to Go

By this time you might be thinking that doing the beauty thing is a lot of work. You've got your hair to take care of. Your skin. Your hands. Even your toenails. Yikes! How are you even supposed to remember all that stuff, much less do it?

What do you say we stop and take care of that right now? How about making a Beauty Chart to help you keep track of what to do and when?

What You'll Need:

- ✦ a piece of poster board, poster-sized paper, or four sheets of regular paper taped together to make one big square
- ✦ a yardstick or ruler
- ✦ a pencil
- ✦ markers, colored pencils, or crayons
- ✦ anything else you want to use to decorate your chart — stickers, stars, pictures from magazines, even photos of you doing your beauty-care thing
- ✦ tacks or that gummy stuff you use to hang posters

How to Do It

There is no right or wrong way for your chart to look, so be creative. It should include the following steps.

(The ones with stars beside them are the optional items. Include those on your chart only if you're really into them.)

Write these down the left side:

EVERY DAY
wash body
wash hair
*use conditioner
*shave legs and pits

comb wet hair
use body lotion
clean under fingernails
drink eight glasses water
get thirty minutes exercise
wash hands often

EVERY MORNING
wash face
use moisturizer with sunscreen
brush hair
*style hair

EVERY NIGHT
wash face
use moisturizer
brush hair
get eight hours sleep

WEEKLY
soak feet
*remove old nail polish
file nails
take care of cuticles
clean under toenails
clip toenails
*put on new polish

EVERY SIX WEEKS
have hair trimmed

If you live in a house where anything you display is fair game for brothers and sisters — or you just want to be more private — you can make a smaller chart in a notebook, maybe a special beauty journal, or the place you keep all your other personal writings. Make the chart the same way as described below, only in miniature.

Across the top, write two months worth of dates, so that you form columns for checking things off. (You've seen charts like this in school a bunch, right?)

Using your ruler or yardstick, draw lines across for each item and down for each date, making boxes. Decorate your chart however you want to.

Find a good place to hang your chart so you'll remember to check items off each day/week.

You can make check marks with a cool pen or marker, or you can use stars, stickers, or smiley faces—whatever makes it fun for you to keep track of what good care you are taking of yourself.

It's very cool to watch yourself form habits. Remember though, that if you miss a day doing one of your beauty tasks, it doesn't mean you're going to be ugly that day. Just get back on track tomorrow—and don't forget to enjoy!

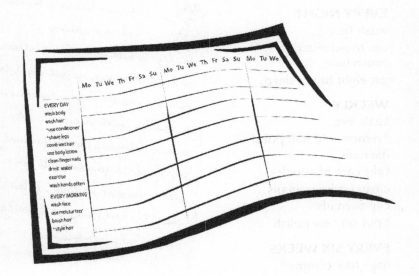

Some Cool Things About Having a Beauty Chart...

chapter six

Stylin'

It was almost as if Betsy woke up one morning and all the clothes she had worn the week before were too small. Her mom announced that it was time for a shopping trip.

Hello-o! Every girl's dream!

At first, Betsy was thrilled. Lately, she'd been focusing more on what the other girls were wearing, and she knew exactly what she wanted — which, of course, was exactly what *they* had. She raced through the store, finding jeans like Madison's and tops like Taylor's and skirts like Ashleigh's. This was going to be sweet.

But when Betsy tried on the first outfit in the dressing room and stared at herself in the mirror, she watched her mouth turn down at the corners.

"It doesn't look like it does on Madison and Taylor and Ashleigh," Betsy said to her mom.

"Of course it doesn't," her mom said. "You have longer legs than Madison and you're curvier than Taylor. Besides, your hair is darker than all of theirs, so that isn't a good color for you."

Betsy stared hard into the mirror again. "I don't care," she said stubbornly. "I want to wear clothes like my friends!"

"I'm not buying you something that doesn't look right on you," her mom said — in that voice that meant "conversation over."

That's it, Betsy thought. *My life is ruined.*

If you read all the Scripture verses about clothes, you might think God can't make up his mind about what we're supposed to wear. Let's take them one at a time and see what God really has to say.

God does want you to look your best. The woman of noble character described in Proverbs "is clothed in fine linen and purple" (Proverbs 31:22). And not only that, but in her household, "all of them are clothed in scarlet" (verse 21).

That doesn't mean you have to wear the most expensive labels and always look like you just walked out of Limited Too. It means that when you put on clothes that look good and feel great on you, *that* says, "I want people to see the real me, a person who deserves respect."

"Best," in God's eyes, is different for everyone. And not only does God create you to be one of a kind, but he watches you with loving eyes, coaxing you to be who he made you to be. "[God] forms the hearts of all ... considers everything they do" (Psalm 33:15).

Does it make sense, then, that everybody should dress exactly the same? We totally understand about wanting the clothes "everybody" is wearing. Your grandmother probably *had* to have a poodle skirt, and your mom may have begged for acid-washed, pegged jeans. It's natural to want to feel like part of a group at this point in your life.

But it's also a time for learning what makes you unique, because, of course, you are. God is amazingly creative. Even identical twins have different personalities. Your own "specialness" is what you bring to your group of friends—what makes them love you. Your best look is clothes that match that.

God doesn't want you to get all freaked out about what you're going to wear. Jesus talked about that in his famous Sermon on the Mount.

"'And why do you worry about clothes? See how the lilies of the field grow. They do not labor or spin. Yet I tell you that not even Solomon in all his splendor was dressed like one of these. If that is how God clothes the grass of the field, which is here today and tomorrow is thrown into the fire, will he not much more clothe you, O you of little faith?'" –MATTHEW 6:28-30

He wasn't saying we can just step out of the shower and God will put clothes on us. He meant that clothes shouldn't be the most important thing on the entire planet for us. It's fun to have a trendy belt or the everybody-has-one poncho. It's also fun to play board games, stay up late giggling, and make valentines for the patients at the nursing home. It's all about balance. Look good and then get on with the other stuff.

God is way more interested in how we live than how we dress, because that's what truly makes us beautiful.

"Your beauty should not come from outward adornment... Instead, it should be that of your inner self, the unfading beauty of a gentle and quiet spirit, which is of great worth in God's sight." –1 PETER 3:3-4

This is kind of a no-brainer, but which of these choices do you think is more important to God:

What shoes I wear or how I treat my mom?
Whether I have a way-cool swimsuit or whether I'm nice to the school "outcasts"?
Which top I wear with which jeans, or what I say to my friend who's having a way bad day?

Duh-uh, huh?
So what does all of that mean for your wardrobe? Pick out clothes that

+ help you feel like you're part of the group;
+ allow you to be your unique self;
+ aren't the center of your universe; and
+ allow your natural, inner beauty to shine through.

How in the *world* are you going to do all that at the same time? Fortunately God doesn't ask us to do the impossible, so let's find out!

That Is SO Me

Have you ever felt like you were wearing somebody else's clothes? That's probably because what you had on didn't tell who you were. The first step is to find your personal style.

Circle one item in each list that comes closest to something you like to do.

(a) play softball   (b) play Scrabble   (c) play a pretend game

(a) have a pillow fight   (b) do a magazine quiz   (c) giggle and talk with friends

(a) ride my bike   (b) read a book   (c) dream up a story

(a) play a computer   (b) check out a   (c) IM a friend
    game   website

(a) try snow   (b) build the perfect (c) make snow
    boarding   snowman   angels

Count up your a's, b's, and c's.

_____ a's

_____ b's

_____ c's

If you had more a's than other letters, you may prefer the sporty casual style. Who can do all the moving around you like to do in dresses and frills and pointy-toed shoes? Go with clothes that are comfortable and fun, even when you have to get dressed up. You can never tell when somebody might want to race you, or there's a tree that has to be climbed...

If you had more b's than other letters, using your mind makes you happy. You might really like a classic, tailored style. Not dull, of course, but crisp lines and cool jackets and pants and skirts you can mix 'n' match. Smart clothes!

If you had more c's than other letters, you like to laugh big and cry hard. Yours is more than likely an all-girl romantic style. It's fashion that fits your dreamy self—maybe embroidery on your jeans, spangles on your purse, beads on your flip-flops. And of course, loads of pink.

If you had an almost-equal number of each letter, you are a girl of many moods. Probably your style is creative. You like to be a tomboy one day and a girly-girl the next—and keep everybody guessing. Go ahead and combine more than one style at a time. You know—- clunky boots with a long, flowy skirt, or a baseball cap with sequins on it.

Write your style here _____

Here's the Deal

Being sporty, or tailored, or romantic, or creative doesn't mean you have to dress like that all the time. Maybe this time next year you'll change styles completely as you find out more about who you are. But since most of us don't have unlimited funds to spend on our wardrobes, it's best to make sure most of your clothes are the usual you.

Here are some suggestions to help you shop, either at the store or in your own closet.

Pants

Sporty — your favorite style jeans, fun sweats, cargo pants, easy-to-move-in shorts, slacks in great colors for dressing up

Tailored — crisp jeans, your favorite style khakis, sweats that have matching jackets, shorts with belts 'n' pockets, slacks that look fabulous with boots or slip-on flats

Romantic — jeans with pretty details such as embroidery, pastel sweats in soft fabrics like fleece, skorts, wraparound pants

Creative — funky jeans like the cropped off kind with beaded patterns, yoga pants, safari shorts, gauchos

Tops

Sporty — long- and short-sleeved straight T-shirts, zippered hoodies, tank tops, blouses that don't have to be tucked in for dressing up

Tailored — long- and short-sleeved fitted T-shirts, turtleneck and crewneck sweaters, fresh-looking sleeveless blouses, fitted blouses with details such as tucks and pleats for dress up

Romantic — long- and short-sleeved T-shirts with girly details, fancy sweaters with faux fur or crocheted collars, peasant blouses, empire-waist tops for dress up

Creative — long- and short-sleeved T-shirts with unusual designs on them, bulky knit sweaters and ponchos, tanks tops that look like two, tunic tops with fun details for dress up

Skirts and Dresses

Sporty — khaki and denim A-line skirts, skorts, simple dresses in fabrics that breathe (like 100% cotton)

Tailored — straight and pleated skirts; long skirts with simple lines; dresses with belts, pockets, and collars

Romantic — skirts that swirl when you twirl; gathered skirts; dresses with sashes, pretty sleeves, and details at the hem

Creative — skirts with unexpected features like shiny beads on denim or oversized pockets; wrap-around skirts; dresses that look like they might have come from another country

Jackets or Coats
(depending on where you live)

Sporty — jean jackets, down jackets, parkas, sweater-jackets

Tailored — blazers, peacoats, fitted ski jackets, long coats with simple lines

Romantic — short (to the waist) jackets, furry jackets and coats, pastel ponchos

Creative — funky jean jackets, colorful ponchos, bomber jackets, capes and shawls

That Is SO Me

Have you ever *really* wanted something everybody was wearing, and when you tried it on it pulled in weird places? Or made you look, well, funny?

That's because there are different **body shapes**, and not every piece of clothing looks good on every one of them. Keeping in mind that God created — and loves — all shapes and sizes of people, have some fun finding out what yours is right now.

Decide which one of these is closest to what you see when you look in a full-length mirror, wearing either your undies or clothes that fit pretty snugly.

Medium to tall and willowy, like a beautiful birch tree.
   + long and lean   + straight up and down

Short and pixie-like, like you could be a real-life Tinkerbell.
   + tiny features   + small and slim

Medium to tall and strong, like a one-woman powerhouse.
   + some muscle definition   + athletic build
   + a few curves here and there

Short and sturdy, like an undercover superhero.
   + some muscle definition   + a few curves, but not many
   + power in a small package + athletic-looking

Medium to tall and curvy, like a little woman is about to burst through.
   + a real waist, and starting to develop breasts
   + kind of like an hourglass

Short and cuddly, like a favorite teddy bear.
   + soft and round   + curves all over
   + may be starting to develop breasts

The good new is there are clothes for every body type. The bad news is ... well, there is no bad news!

You get to choose:

_____ Do you want to show your body type just as it is?
_____ Do you want to coax it to look even more beautiful?

There is no right or wrong answer to that question. It's totally up to you, as long as you like what you see when you get dressed and look in the mirror. Remember that God wants us to do our very best with what he's given us.

To play up your long, lean form — Think long and straight; don't choose belts at your waist or fabrics with big designs all over; things that flow are perfect for you.

To look taller than you are — Wear the same color from top to bottom or pick stripes and patterns that go up and down; shoes with just a little bit of a heel are smashing on you.

To play up how tiny you are — Keep your skirts above your knees (with Mom's approval); your tops can come to your waist; cropped pants, capris, and skorts are precious on you.

Since you'll be growing and changing shape a lot in these years, your body type will also probably change. Even though we suggest ways to tone down body features you aren't crazy about, try not to get freaked out about a rounded tummy or the fact that you're the tallest one in the class. Your body is becoming itself, and that is beautiful.

When you shop, buy clothes that fit you. You should never look like you've been stuffed into your outfit, no matter what the current style is. Be sure you can move around freely. Forget that your best friend wears two sizes smaller than you do. She's her size, you are yours. This is a free and exciting time in your life, so be comfy enough to have a blast!

To look shorter than you are — Keep your skirts at or below your knees; wear things that "cut you in half," like a different color on top than on the bottom or a belt at your waist; you were made for fabulous flats.

To put the focus on your strong, sturdy body — Wear clothes that cling a little, the way T-shirts and stretchy shirts do; stand-up collars and straight-leg pants are right for you; your body screams for classy athletic-looking clothes, but they don't have to be boyish.

To soften your sturdiness a little — Wear clothes that are fitted (but not tight) instead of boxy; go for a small touch of girly detail, like some embroidery on a jeans pocket or a hint of lace on a blouse; sleeves with a little bit of puff and round necklines were created just for you.

To enjoy your curves or fluffiness — Go for loose-fitting things like full blouses and wide-legged pants; pull on a bright poncho or a peasant skirt; anything really feminine will bring out your rosy girlishness.

To appear more streamlined — Wear things that just fit — not too tight, not too loose; choose tops, dresses, and jackets that curve in at the waist; you're the cutest thing on the planet in fun collars and interesting sleeves.

That Is SO Me

O ne of the most fun things about clothes is that they come in so many different colors. Since *we* come in so many different colors too, that's a good thing! It's amazing how the shades you were born to wear can make your natural beauty shine. Want to find your color code?

Take a good long look in a mirror in good light — and maybe ask your mom or another grown-up to consult with you. Then circle one description in each column that is *most* like you. (We haven't covered all the possibilities.)

Hair

red

blonde

dark

Skin

light

dark

Check your combination:

_____ red hair/light skin

_____ blonde hair/light skin

_____ blonde hair/dark skin

_____ dark hair/light skin

_____ dark hair/dark skin

Here's the Deal

❋ Of course, wear any color you want that makes you happy. God created a whole rainbow of hues for us to enjoy.

If you really want to bring out the beauty of your natural coloring, here are some suggestions. Get ready to dazzle yourself!

	Best Colors	Not So Wonderful
Red hair/ light skin	any shade of green or blue, warm red, soft gold	white, yellow, very pastel colors
Blonde hair/ light skin	pink, light blue, light green, red, green, violet, coral	black, yellow, very pastel colors
Blonde hair/ dark skin	white, pink, lavender, light green, purple	orange, fluorescent colors
Dark hair/ light skin	red, maroon, deep pink	beige, very pastel colors, orange
Dark hair/ dark skin	rich red, black, brown, purple, emerald green, bright blue, red	yellow, fluorescent colors

❋ You can't go wrong if you match your clothes to the color of your eyes.

❋ Color can have an influence on your mood and on the way people see you. How cool is that?

❖ Need a little energy or a confidence boost? Wear **red**—good for sports and times when you have to liven things up

❖ Need to feel like you have it together? **White** is your best bet — great for giving a speech in class, or playing in a piano recital.

❖ Need to state your independence? Put on your **green**. It's the perfect color for dealing with people who don't accept your "one-of-a-kind – ness."

❖ Need some calm? Clothe yourself in **light blue** — perfect for babysitting or when you're feeling jumpy.

❖ Need to be taken seriously? Get into your **dark blue**. Wear it if you're running for a class election or are determined to get that A in math.

❖ Need to be a little mysterious? **Black** is your answer. Since it's dramatic, it's just right for play tryouts, or anytime you want to keep them guessing.

❖ Need a hug or really want someone to trust you? Wear **pastels** (light shades of soft color). They're the thing on days when you feel lonely or especially loveable.

The absolutely most fun thing about putting an outfit together is adding the accessories:

hats
scarves
jewelry
belts
purses
socks, tights
shoes

Accessories are the magic in your wardrobe. They can

❖ turn a few basic items of clothing into a whole bunch of different outfits;

❖ draw attention to your best features;

❖ draw the focus away from things you're self-conscious about; and

❖ let you express your unique self in some major-fun ways.

There are certain things that draw attention wherever you put them:

❖ bright, warm colors like yellow, red, orange, and gold

❖ big designs

❖ sparkly, shiny things

❖ girly details

It's so simple to use accessories to pull someone's eye where you want it. Wear these attention getters near your best features:

Do you have great hair? Bring out the barrettes, the hair clips, and the funky scarves.

Have a tiny waist? Put on those belts, baby.

Really well-toned arms? Play them up with fun bracelets.

Nice neck? Necklaces were made for you.

Lovely legs? Go for the unique shoes, the perfect socks.

Write your own best features here:

~~~~~~

~~~~~~

~~~~~~

Use your imagination for ways to accessorize (use accessories) that will spotlight those physical gifts God gave you. Write your ideas here:

~~~~~~

~~~~~~

~~~~~~

If you have a physical feature you feel kind of funky about, keep the attention-getters away from there (but keep learning to accept that the way you were made is perfect in God's eyes):

Self-conscious about your ears? Not the best place for flashy jewelry, right?

Feeling like your hips are huge? (They probably aren't!) Don't hang a belt or scarf around them.

Always want to hide your fingernails? Stay away from rings (unless you've read chapter four).

And don't forget to show your true self when you're using accessories. Going back to your personal style, think about what is YOU. Here are some suggestions, but your own imagination is your best guide.

Sporty — ball caps, visors, pendants of your favorite sports teams, canvas shoulder bags, fun backpacks, the most perfect socks you can find, tennis shoes with personality

No matter what clothes and accessories you decide to wear, ask yourself, Does God want to see me in this? Does he want me showing a lot of skin that's better kept private? Is he going to be happy with some disrespectful saying on my T-shirt? Does he want me decked out in an outfit that makes me look way older than I am? When your mom says you can't wear your jeans that low or your top that high, she's guiding you by these questions. Try asking the questions yourself before she has to say, "You are SO not going anywhere dressed like that!"

Tailored — sleek hats, wool scarves, gloves, simple jewelry, purses to match your shoes, touches of fun in belts and buttons and socks

Romantic — sun hats, fuzzy winter caps with matching scarves and gloves, dainty jewelry (wherever you can hang it!), bows, lace, sparkly purses

Creative — berets, newsboy caps, chunky jewelry, belts and scarves galore — worn in unexpected places — funky purses, colored shoes

Although decisions about what clothes are bought for you are up to the grown-ups in your family, you can keep those decisions from turning into battles by following some of these tips. Some-day you'll be using your own money for your wardrobe, so these are good **shopping skills** to learn for the future too.

- Know how much money there is to spend and don't try to persuade your folks to go outside their budget. You can pretty much tell what the finances are at your house, so why try to wheedle an expensive pair of jeans out of your mom when you know things are tight? If this is hard for you, try earning some money to buy a few things yourself. When you have to fork over your own cash for that new have-to-have-it, you might find out you really *don't* have to have it after all.

- Ask your parents what things they will absolutely not al-low you to wear, and then don't even go to those racks in the store. They'll be impressed with how mature you are.

- Look for things that will go with what you already have. You might want new colors too, but be sure to choose things that will mix and match.

To really save money, watch for sales. Many stores have sales right after Christmas and right before school starts. Some stores have promotions, like a reward for bringing in a good report card or a coupon in the newspaper or mail. Remember that just because it's on sale doesn't mean you'll save money; be sure you're actually going to wear it.

If you're dying for something trendy, suggest to your parents that you buy it at one of the less expensive stores. That way if you only wear it until it goes out of style (like maybe **next month**), it won't be a huge waste of money.

Remember that it's better to have a few perfect-for-you, good quality pieces of clothing than a whole closet full of stuff that really isn't your best look. Don't forget that you can create different outfits with fun accessories. And besides, what rule says you have to wear something different every single day? If it's great on you this Tuesday, it will still look fabulous next Tuesday!

If there is no shopping trip planned for the near future, try "shopping" in your own closet and drawers.

Put all your clothes in two piles:
* things that don't fit you or have never been and will never be you. Ask if you can give them to charity (or your little sister!)

❀ things that fit and have possibilities for your style, body type, and coloring

Pick up each item in the I'm-keeping-it pile. Before you put it back in the closet or into a drawer, make a plan for it.

❀ See how many other things it goes with.

❀ Have fun putting surprising colors next to each other; use accessories to bring colors together. (Purple pants will go with a yellow top if you have a yellow and purple bracelet to tie them in.)

❀ If it isn't exactly your style, see what you can put with it to capture the real you. (You may not be into that romantic pink skirt, but put on a jean jacket and some clean tennies — and you're your sporty self.)

If you really love putting outfits together, write the combinations you discover on separate cards and pick one when it's time to get dressed. (You can even put different types of outfits on different color cards — pink for dressing up, yellow for school ...) If you would rather have your tonsils out than do that, just put like things together so it's easy for you to grab an outfit and go.

You're Good to Go

Whether you're jazzed about clothes, or your mom has to drag you out to shop, or you're somewhere in between, it's good to find the best wardrobe that

✦ helps you feel like you're part of the group;

✦ allows you to be your unique self;

✦ isn't the center of your universe; and

✦ allows your natural, inner beauty to shine through.

Everybody needs that! So try this "dream wardrobe" activity to head you in the right direction. (This is fun to do with a friend.)

Step 1: Gather some magazines and catalogs picturing girls your age. Or, if you're artistic, get out some paper and your drawing materials.

Step 2: Pull out or draw pictures of clothes that

* suit your style (sporty, tailored, romantic, creative);
* are right for your body shape (medium to tall and willowy, short and pixie-like, medium to tall and strong, short and sturdy, medium to tall and curvy, short and cuddly);
* bring out your natural coloring (red hair/light skin, blonde hair/light skin, blonde hair/dark skin, dark hair/light skin, dark hair/dark skin); and
* are things you need for your life (school clothes, dress-up clothes, play clothes, clothes for your special activities).

Step 3: Arrange your pictures however you want to. We suggest one of these display ideas:

* a scrapbook
* a collage
* a box of colored folders
* a bulletin board

Step 4: Look at your "dream wardrobe" every now and then and realize how uniquely beautiful you are. God really likes it when you do that.

When I Loook at My Dream Wardrobe, I See a Girl Who Is...

chapter seven

Don't You
HATE THAT?

Betsy slumped into the chair in the doctor's office and blinked back tears.

Just an hour ago she'd grinned at herself in the mirror at home because not only did she look ... well, like her own self, but she felt great. She had been planning to go shopping with her mom right after her appointment at the eye doctor — maybe pick up the new sandals she'd been saving her own money for. And then they were going to the library so she could get a book about kachina dolls, because she was totally fascinated with them, and then ...

But once again Betsy tried to keep from crying right out loud in front of the doctor and her mom, who were discussing her glasses.

Glasses! Just when she was starting to like herself, now she had to stick glasses on her face and look like an owl. She could almost hear the comments at school: Jason saying, "Hey, Four Eyes. Bet you think you're like this genius now." The mean girls saying, "Ugh. Why didn't you get contacts?" Her own friends saying, "They don't look that bad, Bets. Really. You're still pretty." *Right*, Betsy thought miserably. *Pretty as a raccoon.*

She slid further down in the chair. She didn't want to go to the shoe store or the library anymore. She just wanted to go home and hide her head under a pillow.

That Is SO Me

H ere's a list of "Beauty Bummers" some girls say they'd rather live without. Get a pencil and look at each *bummer* on the list.

Put a check mark if you have that particular thing in your life. If you do, circle the best description of how it affects you.

___ *glasses*

    a. I hate them.

    b. They're okay.

    c. They're so me!

    d. What glasses?

___ *braces*

    a. I'm counting the days until I get them off.

    b. I don't mind them most of the time.

    c. It's cool to have braces.

    d. What's the big deal?

___ *being tall*

    a. I feel like a giraffe.

    b. It's not that bad.

    c. Are you kidding? Tall girls look so good in their clothes!

    d. Who cares?

___ *being big*

    a. It's so embarrassing to be huge.

    b. I don't know—I guess it's just the way I am.

    c. There's so much more of me to love!

    d. So what?

___ *scars, birthmarks, or moles*

    a. I wish I could just put a bag over my head.

    b. People who know me just get used to it.

c. I'm one of a kind!

d. I forgot about it until just now.

____ *other physical feature kids tease you about*

a. I'm totally having plastic surgery when I turn eighteen.

b. Whatever. They'll grow up someday.

c. I inherited it and I'm proud of it!

d. I don't even get why they tease me.

If you didn't have any check marks, read on anyway. Every girl has to deal with something she doesn't like about herself at some point. Besides, this chapter will show you how to help a girlfriend who might be struggling with a "beauty bummer" right now.

If you circled any a's, you're having a hard time, aren't you? People can be mean, and as we've said, "the world" in general can make you think you have to be perfect. As you read on for help, remember that you are already beautiful, and getting more so every day.

If you circled any b's, whatever some people consider a bummer doesn't really bother you that much. Wouldn't it be fun, though, to make it one of the best things about you? Read on!

If you circled any c's, you probably could have written this chapter yourself! You have the right idea. Keep reading so you can have even more fun with your unique look and encourage other girls to do the same. You can make a difference.

If you circled any d's, you don't even see any of this as a problem. Very cool. We would tell you not to even bother with this chapter, except that it will help you understand why other girls get upset. The last thing you want to do is tell a friend who's stressing about her braces to "just get over it." But if you read on, you can help her get over it—without losing her as a friend.

Here's the Deal

No matter what letters you circled in *That Is SO Me*, there are three things everyone needs to learn in life:

* How to know what you can change and what you can't
* How to change what can be changed, or at least make it a little better
* How to accept what can't be changed, and maybe even make it work for you

For example, let's say you have what you consider to be the longest nose in the galaxy, and other kids call you Pinocchio until you want to smack somebody. Consider the three questions.

Can I change it? Not unless you have plastic surgery, and that isn't even an option at your age. Besides, who knows—your face may grow into your nose and make you look fabulous.

How can I make it a little better? Wear your hair parted on the side and not too flat on top. Choose colors that bring out the color of your eyes.

How can I accept it and make it work for me? It's probably a family trait, so be proud of that. Instead of thinking of it as "honkin' huge," find another way to describe it. Is it noble? Strong? Comical? Queenly? Call it that in your mind and it will change everything, especially when somebody thinks he's original and calls you Pinocchio for the forty-fifth time.

Get the idea? Let's see what you can do with the Basic Beauty Bummers that will bring out more of that beautiful you.

Can I change it? Not unless you want to ruin your eyesight. There's nothing beautiful about squinting your eyes to see.

How can I make it a little better? Take your time picking out frames you like that look great on you. There's a shape and color and style for every person. Ask the folks at the optical store to help you find the perfect ones. Contact lenses are a choice, and they actually help you see better than glasses do. Just remember that they require a lot of care, are easy to lose, and sometimes hard to get used to. You might want to wait until you're older.

How can I accept it and make it work for me? Think about having fewer headaches and getting better grades because you can actually see! Remember that glasses make a person look really smart. Make yours a part of your unique style, and people will say, "You look so much cuter with your glasses."

Can I change it? Probably not, especially if you really have some teeth and jaw issues that can affect your health (not to mention your looks).

How can I make it a little better? Did you know braces—and rubber bands—come in different colors as well as in clear and silver? How fun is that? You can't hide them, so why not let them sparkle? To get those braces off as fast as you can (the average time to wear them is two and a half years), brush, floss, and avoid super hard or sticky, gooey foods.

How can I accept it and make it work for me? Your teeth are going to be amazing when you get the braces off, and that will last for the rest of your life. And you certainly aren't alone. How many other girls in your grade are wearing them—and looking adorable? The best thing you can do is smile big and bright. You'll be unforgettable.

Can I change it? Not a chance.

How can I make it a little better? Remember the advice in chapter six about what to wear? You'll still be the same height, but you can look shorter.

How can I accept it and make it work for me? There are almost no minuses in being tall and lots of pluses. You look wonderful in clothes. Women who are tall are often automatically respected and considered to be leaders by other people. In a very short time, you'll really grow into your height and feel less gangly and klutzy. Meanwhile, learn to play basketball and volleyball. Dream of being a model. Enjoy the view. And most of all, stand up straight and proud.

Being Tall

Can I change it? You can't change the fact that you have big, healthy bones and a strong frame. You can keep from being overweight, but you'll probably never be skinny. (You would look pretty funny with no meat on those wonderful bones!)

Being Big

How can I make it a little better? Go back to chapter six and look at what clothes can soften your look a little. Be sure to eat good healthy stuff rather than junk and fast food. Get lots of fun exercise — at least five times a week.

How can I accept it and make it work for me? You're strong and robust. That's a great look! Go out for some sports. People seem to trust those who are bigger than they are, so let your friends have confidence in you. Be comfortable in your own skin. You can make a difference, because people will always notice you. Live large!

Can I change it? Sometimes you can. Usually removing or toning down these kinds of things involves a doctor. Talk honestly with your parents about how you feel.

How can I make it a little better? Trying to cover up things like birthmarks or moles usually only draws attention to them. If you have a scar, ask your mom if you can use a little stick foundation — in a yellow (not pink) tone — dabbed with powder.

Scars, Birthmarks, or Moles

How can I accept it and make it work for me? Think of it as a mark that gives your face character. Many models keep a mole as a trademark (and call it a beauty mark). A scar shows that you were strong enough to go through something painful. Focus on the other things that are beautiful about you. When people stare, ask if they have any questions. Remember that these things are the prints left by your life as you live it.

Even if you have the best attitude ever, there may still be kids and even adults who can't leave your glasses or your chicken pox scars or your rosy round cheeks alone. It's embarrassing. It's maddening. It's enough to make you point out *their* wart or buck teeth or bald head.

Before you hurl back an insult or run to the restroom in tears, try to remember this: When someone teases you about a "flaw," that says more about her (or him) than it does about you. A mouth full of braces or a face full of freckles tells nothing about you as a person. But a rude remark from a person's mouth announces that he or she is at that moment one of these:

* thoughtless
* careless
* insensitive
* jealous
* needing to feel better than you
* just plain mean

So what do you do about it? God says:

"Whoever corrects a mocker invites insult."
— PROVERBS 9:7

Don't argue with a teaser or you'll just be teased more.

"A fool shows his annoyance at once, but a prudent man overlooks an insult."
— PROVERBS 12:16

Ignore teasing. Don't even react in front of the teaser. (But it's okay to go away and cry if you need to.)

"Do not repay evil with evil or insult with insult, but with blessing."

— 1 Peter 3:9

Don't try to get back at the teaser with insults of your own. Be your own best self, and compliment her honestly, help her if she needs it, and refuse to talk trash about her behind her back.

"Love your enemies and pray for those who persecute you."

— Matthew 5:44

Ask God to heal whatever is causing people to tease you until it hurts. They may not change, but you will. It's hard to keep hating someone you're praying for.

You're Good to Go

Get a BIG piece of paper (the kind that comes on a roll) and lie down on it. Have someone trace an outline of you. If you can't come up with large paper, sketch an outline of yourself on the biggest piece you can find.

Using markers, crayons, or pencils in fun colors, draw in all your features that you love or that you hardly even think about. Don't use any black. Make it as beautiful as you are.

Now, using black, draw in anything you're not happy about.

Look at the final picture. There's a whole lot more color than black, isn't there? Even if you have "flaws" they have *nothing* on all that is beautiful about you.

What did you discover when you created that picture of yourself?

When I Created That Picture of Myself I Discovered...

chapter eight

What ABOUT...?

W hen Betsy took off her jacket in science class, Madison squealed. Ashley gasped. Jason said, "Dude is that *real?*"

Betsy looked down at the fake butterfly tattoo she had put on her shoulder that morning. "Do *you* think it's real?" she asked.

Jason squinted his eyes at it. "Nah — that's totally bogus."

"Your parents would never let you get a tattoo!" Madison said, mouth hanging open in horror.

Jason grunted. "Too bad. I think it looks kinda cool."

Betsy felt her cheeks get warm, and she smiled secretly to herself. Nobody had ever said anything of hers was cool before.

Was that why people got real tattoos? she wondered.

Here's the Deal

You don't have to look very far to see somebody wearing The Bad Girl Look. You know the one:

❖ pierced nose, tongue, lip, eyebrow—you name it
❖ tattoos
❖ hair colors *nobody* was born with

- clothes that scream, "I don't care who you are — you aren't the boss of me."
- accessories that suggest violence or sexiness — for example, a necklace with a skull, a belt made of bullets, a belly button ring (proudly displayed)

Most of the time, you see The Bad Girl Look on teenagers and young adults. But these days it's showing up more and more on middle schoolers and even girls your age. What's up with that?

There are probably as many reasons for wanting to tattoo and pierce as there are people who do it. These are some of the main explanations behind decking out in all black or piercing every space on an ear:

'I want to be different.'

'It's my body, and I have a right to do whatever I please with it.'

'It's my way of expressing how sick I am of everybody telling me who to be.'

'I like to weird people out, especially adults who try to control me.'

'If people really want to know the real me, they have to get past the way I look. If they judge me by my appearance, I don't want to know them.'

'I want people to look at me.'

What's wrong with that? Haven't we been saying through this whole book that you should be your unique self? That you should dress in a way that shows who you are? That you shouldn't worry about what everybody else thinks?

You're right. We have. But take a close look at each of those reasons for going for The Bad Girl Look and see why they're very different from what we've been telling you.

"I want to be different." That's totally normal. But if all your friends or half the class are also dying their hair green and piercing their eyebrows, how does that make you different? It doesn't take much imagination to fit yourself into a "look."

"It's my body, and I have the right to do whatever I please with it."

- First of all, that right doesn't kick in until you're at least eighteen *and* supporting yourself. Not only that, but no piercing is legal without a parent being present until you're sixteen, and in some states until you're eighteen or even twenty-one. Even with a parent's permission, by law a tattoo can't be done until you're eighteen. Going to someone who is willing to ignore the rules and give you a piercing or a tattoo anyway is dangerous. You can be sure he or she will ignore the safety and cleanliness rules too.

- If the piercer's instruments and hands aren't totally clean, you can get an infection. That is SO not fun, especially inside your nose or mouth.

- A tattoo involves someone injecting permanent dye under your skin. (Ouch!) If the needle isn't completely germ-free, you can get hepatitis, even AIDS. It just isn't worth the risk.

- Even if you went to the cleanest place on the planet, there are other risks with piercing:
  - It's easy to swallow a tongue ring or stud.
  - A belly button piercing can get infected just from getting caught on your jeans or the buttons on your shirt.

- If rings get torn out, it can be painful (and bloody ... EW!).
- An allergic reaction can leave a permanent ring like a tattoo on your skin.
- An infection in the hard part of your ear (not the lobe) can result in your ear losing its shape and becoming deformed.

Besides all that, who does your body really belong to? We'll talk about that more in the pages ahead.

"It's my way of expressing how sick I am of everybody telling me who to be." It's actually healthy to want to be your unique self. The trick is to truly know *you* and express *that*, not your feelings. Is *bad* who you really are? Is *angry*? You might feel like nobody gets you, but there are a whole lot of healthier and safer and less permanent ways to deal with that feeling. We'll talk about those later in this chapter.

If you do get permission to pierce your ears, it would be neat to think of it as God's ancient people did. A servant who pledged lifelong service to his beloved master had his ear pierced as a sign of devotion. Since your master is God, how cool! Be sure to go to a place approved by the Association of Professional Piercers, and keep the holes infection-free by cleaning them and your earrings with hydrogen peroxide or the stuff the store may give you.

"I like to weird people out, especially adults who try to control me." And you probably will! But what is the result? Ever noticed the way teachers watch the "bad kids"? They're always on them, ready to pounce. Teachers and other adults don't give second chances to kids who do things just to gross them out. Sometimes the rebels get in trouble for things they don't even do, just because they look like the type who would. Life's tough enough without inviting trouble.

"If people really want to know the real me, they have to get past the way I look. If they judge me by my appearance, I don't want to know them." What is that about? The whole point of looking like you is so people will see a real person and want to get to know you better. If you make people work that hard to see who you are inside, you waste a lot of time that could be spent sharing great friendships. Like it or not, when someone sees a girl who looks mean or tough or disrespectful, that person is going to assume she is, even if she isn't.

"I want people to look at me." We all want attention, and that isn't always a bad thing. If no one pays attention to you, you won't have friends, you won't be able to share what an awesome person you are, and you'll be pretty lonely. But you need the right *kind* of attention.

- ❖ The right kind of attention sounds like, "You're special." "I've never known anyone like you." "I like being around you because you don't try to be something you're not." You are communicating, "Feel free to look around all you want and let me know if I can help you."
- ❖ The wrong kind of attention sounds like, "Dude, what are you trying to prove?" "I'm not inviting you to my

party. You don't look like very nice." "I'm scared of you."

✤ Do you want to communicate, "If you aren't going to buy anything, I suggest you leave the store"?

It's hard if you don't get positive attention at home, and that can make you think that any kind of notice is better than none. But that isn't true. Just ahead, we'll talk about shining as the real you instead of making up somebody to be. First, let's see what might be pushing you to go to extremes, even in the secret places in your mind.

That Is SO Me

Put a star (*) next to each paragraph that describes you at least some of the time. If the description doesn't sound like you at all, leave it blank.

_____ A

I have to say, "Mom?" or "Dad!" like forever, before they answer me. It seems like my parents praise my brother (or sister) way more than they praise me. When I do things right, it's like no big deal, but if I mess something up, you would think I committed a crime. I don't think I'm good at anything—at least nobody says I am.

_____ B

Sometimes I feel like my own family doesn't get me. People say things like, "You sure aren't like your sister (or your mom or anybody else in the whole family)." Kids at school look at me like I'm weird. My parents are always trying to get me to be less this or more that (like less shy and more athletic). It doesn't really bother me that I'm kinda different, but it obviously bothers a lot of other people.

_____ C

I always have to keep my bedroom door open. If I just want to hang out by myself, people ask me what's wrong or try to make me "join in." I get in trouble for arguing, and when I want to do something new, I hear stuff like, "You're not old enough yet." There are things I want to decide for myself, but I'm not allowed to—things like how I wear my hair or what activities I do after school.

Here's the Deal

If you put a star next to any of the descriptions in *That Is SO Me*, you might have one of these feelings:

angry
frustrated
hurt
resentful
afraid
just constantly cranky

Even if things aren't really as bad as you think they are (since most parents are doing a pretty good job), the way you see them can still make you want to punch a pillow, bite your brother, or scream at whoever happens to be standing nearby. And sometimes those thoughts and feelings can make you want to dress like a Bad Girl, wear a big ol' stud in your lip, and dye your hair some impossible color. At the very least they can push you to hate every outfit or hairstyle your mom suggests — just because.

The thing is, lashing out at people or dressing up like a hoochie mama doesn't change those feelings. It can even make them worse, because people are going to get so focused on the way you look, they aren't going to discover how bad you feel so they can help you.

Why do something that doesn't work? Let's find out what *does*.

If you starred A on That Is SO Me, it sounds like you need *attention* — the kind that makes you smile and glow. The kind that nudges you to be *more* helpful, brave, friendly or whatever it was that got people to notice you in the first place. That doesn't mean stand on a table in the cafeteria and yell, "Look at what I did!" It does mean the following:

- ✿ Do the things you do well because you enjoy them, not so everybody will say, "Wow."
- ✿ Discover what it is about you that even one person seems to like, and go with it—whether it's the way you smile, how well you listen, or the fact that you never spread gossip.
- ✿ Give *other* people the kind of attention *you* want—praise, sympathy, a big laugh at their jokes.
- ✿ If you're feeling a little neglected by one of your parents, rather than whine or accuse, ask for some time together—even just an hour alone.
- ✿ If you don't think you do anything well, try things that sound fun or interesting to you. Have such a blast doing them that you don't worry about anyone noticing how good you are at them (although people probably will).
- ✿ Remember that God is always watching you enjoy your successes, being there the instant you need him. You have *his* undivided attention.

If you starred B on That Is SO Me, it may be that you're struggling to be *accepted for who you really are*—or you're trying to *find out* who you are. That doesn't mean that whatever you do, you think everybody should say, "That's just the way she is." It means you want that calm feeling that comes when you don't have to worry whether people think you're lame or geeky or just generally strange. Try some of these:

- ❖ Don't hang out with people who make fun of you. Don't even try to be friends with them.
- ❖ Find at least one person who appreciates your special qualities or interests—your book collection, your huge vocabulary, your total love of cats. Invite her over or ask her to sit with you at lunch.
- ❖ Show your family or your classmates that the very thing they want to change in you can really be a good thing for

them. If they say you're too quiet, listen when they have a problem. If they say you're not athletic, cheer from the sidelines when they're playing, or make a banner, or write encouraging notes if they lose. The people who love you will begin to appreciate who you are instead of trying to turn you into what they think would make you happier.

❖ Love who you are. Nobody is more appealing than a for-real person.

❖ Remember that God made your true self. He's there to help you be just that.

If you starred C on That Is SO Me, it just may be that you *want to be allowed to grow up*. Perhaps the adults in your life don't see that, or they think you're trying to be older too fast. It's sort of like walking around in shoes that are too small for you and are pinching your toes.

That doesn't mean you should ignore the limits grown-ups put on you, because you need some. But if you feel you're being treated like a baby, you can try some of these:

✳ Be mature in ways that are right for your age — doing chores without having to be reminded and not slacking off in school.

✳ Be mature in ways that will surprise people — offering to watch your little brother so your mom can take a bubble bath, refusing to exclude a girl everyone else is leaving out, putting part of your allowance in the collection plate.

✳ Make a list of things you know are not your decision — like what time you go to bed or whether you go to school. Then make a list of things you would like to decide about your life, within your parents' limits, of course — such as how you wear your hair, what books you read for fun, what sports you play. Show both lists to your parents and ask if you can make at least one of the choices on the second list.

* If you need more privacy, ask for it politely. "May I have my door closed for an hour after school?" "Could you please knock before you come in the bathroom?"
* Take care of your stuff. Keep your room at least a little bit organized. Be "together" when it's time to leave for school. Those things show that you *are* growing up.
* Dream about how you want your life to be when you're in charge of it. Keep a journal or make a scrapbook about your imagined future.
* With your friends, or alone, pretend you're grown-up. You're never too old for dress up or acting games.
* Look forward to things to come — going to high school football games, getting a driver's license, wearing make-up, going shopping with your girlfriends, playing on a school team. But don't hurry them. Enjoy what you have right now — no money worries, time to play and daydream, permission to giggle your head off.

Be careful not to judge other people who have a lot of piercings or tattoos or disturbing jewelry. Now you know that many kids who go for that look have things they're trying to deal with. Pray that they'll let God help them, and in the meantime, don't just decide that they're "bad."

✳ Pray—a lot—for God to help you grow up just at the rate he wants you to.

✳ Remember that you can't rush God.

Notice that none of the suggestions above have anything to do with

✦ shocking people with your hairdo,

✦ grossing people out with your piercings,

✦ making a statement with your tattoo,

✦ going to extremes with your clothes so people will notice you, or

✦ showing zero respect for yourself because it feels like no-body else respects you.

Most of the suggestions we've made are positive things—do's, not don'ts. But it can be hard to do positive things when negative actions seem easier. That, of course, is why God is there for you.

But if you're angry or frustrated and think a tattoo or a nose ring will make you feel better, some of God's other words are much more helpful. They describe a Father who totally gets it and will guide you *through* your feelings and help you *solve* your problems in ways that are much healthier for you, and that actually work.

"Do you not know that your body is a temple of the Holy Spirit, who is in you, whom you have received from God?... Therefore honor God with your body."
—1 CORINTHIANS 6:19-20

Step One — Find a private place and vent to God — out loud or in a journal — about what you're feeling.

"Trust in him at all times, O people;
    pour out your hearts to him,
for God is our refuge." — PSALM 62:8

Step Two — Ask God for what you need: help sorting it out, courage to talk to your parents, strength to be yourself . . .

"In the morning, O LORD, you hear my voice;
    in the morning I lay my requests before you."
                                        — PSALM 5:3

Step Three — Wait and listen for God's answer. Keep talking to God and you'll know what to do.

> "Wait for the LORD;
>   be strong and take heart
> and wait for the LORD." — PSALM 27:14

Step Four — Do what God tells you, whether his instructions come to you through the Bible; a wise grown-up; or a still, small voice inside.

> "Give me understanding, and I will keep your law
>   and obey it with all my heart." — PSALM 119:34

Step Five — Repeat Steps One through Four, every day. The things that make you think you want The Bad Girl Look will be healed, and you will be more beautiful than ever.

> "God is our refuge and strength,
>   an ever-present help in trouble." — PSALM 46:1

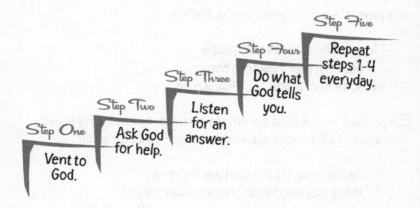

Step One — Vent to God.

Step Two — Ask God for help.

Step Three — Listen for an answer.

Step Four — Do what God tells you.

Step Five — Repeat steps 1-4 everyday.

Whether you have big issues or just occasionally get annoyed about a particular thing, it's healing to express how you feel in ways that don't hurt you or anyone else.

Start by writing down one thing that makes you feel angry, frustrated, resentful, hurt, or just plain cranky. Then choose one of these healthy ways to get your feelings out there where you can see them.

 Write fast and furiously in a private journal until you think you've said it all about that issue. Go back to it whenever you get those feelings and write some more.

 Paint a picture that shouts what you're feeling. Nobody else has to be able to tell what it is—just you. Finger painting is the most satisfying, but brush painting works too.

 Make a clay figure that's just like what's going on inside you. Feel free to turn it back into a ball and make a new figure whenever you want to.

You'll be amazed at how much better you'll feel and at the things that come into your head while you're writing, sculpting, or painting. Being creative with your hands frees your mind up so you can solve your problems. That's totally better than trying to look like The Bad Girl.

When I Did My "You're Good to Go" Project I Felt...

Inside
OUT

Although all the other kids were crowded around the classroom bulletin board, Betsy didn't want to see the list her teacher, Mrs. Post, was putting up. She hadn't liked the idea of voting for "class favorites" from the start, and then when the class had decided on the categories, she'd liked it even less.

Cutest Girl, Cutest Boy

Smartest Girl, Smartest Boy

Most Talented Girl, Most Talented Boy

Best Dressed Girl, Best Dressed Boy

Most Athletic Girl, Most Athletic Boy

Most Popular Girl, Most Popular Boy

Funniest Girl, Funniest Boy

When Mrs. Post had asked if there were any more suggestions, Betsy raised her hand. She was getting better about that. "How about Most Honest?" Betsy said.

One of the girls — who was sure to be voted Most Popular — snorted. "That's lame," she said.

"No negative responses," Mrs. Post said. "All suggestions will be considered."

Jason grunted. "What about Most Ridiculous, then?"

What about Most Rude? Betsy thought.

Mrs. Post considered Jason's suggestion for about three seconds, but she wrote Betsy's on the board. Then Madison raised her hand.

"Friendliest," she said.

"Isn't that the same as Most Popular?" somebody said.

"It *should* be," Mrs. Post said. She frowned. "But it isn't always. Let's make that a separate category."

There was a lot of eye rolling.

But everyone had voted. And now as Mrs. Post parted the crowd to step away from the bulletin board, they all rushed the list, pushing and elbowing to be the first to know who the favorites were.

Everyone but Betsy. She sat in her desk, and she thought.

She had filled her beauty chart with stickers every day for months. She'd cleaned out her closet, and gone shopping with her mom, and felt real (and cute!) in her clothes. She had a new haircut and the most fun glasses ever, and only one person had teased her about them. She was praying for Jason every night.

Just when I was feeling like I might be beautiful just being me, Betsy thought, *they have to go and have a contest. I know who's going to get Cutest Girl and Best Dressed, and then everybody's going to think they have to totally look like them.*

Why did we have to choose "favorites"?

"Hey, Betsy!" Madison called from the bulletin board. "Guess which one you got!"

"Me?" Betsy said.

Now what?

Let's leave Betsy in suspense while we look at one more beauty ingredient — the most important one. After you've read this chapter, you'll have a chance to write the ending for Betsy, in *"That's What I'm Talkin' About."* Yours will be the final vote!

In this book, we've talked about

- ❖ you being your unique self;
- ❖ hair care;
- ❖ face facts;
- ❖ mani's and pedi's;
- ❖ getting smooth;
- ❖ fashion fun;
- ❖ The Bad Girl Look; and
- ❖ beauty bummers.

At the same time, we've hinted that who you are inside—your true, genuine, authentic self—is really what makes you a good lookin' gal. Now let's put the spotlight on that. If you don't remember another thing from this book (although hopefully that's not the case), remember this:

No matter how great a girl's hair, skin, nails, and clothes are—no matter how free she is of physical "flaws"—she will not be truly beautiful unless she shines from within.

She may win beauty contests or get a modeling contract or have boys flocking all around her. That means she's cute, or pretty, or practically perfect from head to toe. That doesn't mean she's beautiful.

A beautiful girl can have bad hair days, pimples, and hairy legs. She may not be able to sit still long enough to have a manicure or tweeze her eyebrows or worry that she towers over the whole rest of her class. She is beautiful because she focuses on these beauty secrets:

- ✦ confidence in her God-given gifts and talents that smoothes her brow
- ✦ joy that makes her eyes sparkle; honesty that makes them clear

- a sense of fun that gives her a dazzling smile
- energy in helping, sharing, and doing her best that makes her skin glow; kindness that softens it
- positive, encouraging words that make her lips lovely
- love for God, others, and herself that makes her attractive in a way no one can explain

That Is SO Me

Try an experiment so you'll see exactly what we mean.

Pick out a few girls you know who are considered cute or pretty. Watch them whenever you can. If you see one being rude to someone or using bad language, watch even more closely. Is she still pretty? What if someone caught her on camera at that moment? Would a magazine put it on the cover? (Don't point this out to the girl. Go back to chapter eight and review what to do.)

Go through a magazine you can tear pages out of. Collect all the pictures of what you think are pretty girls. Then put them in two piles: (1) girls who you'd like to be friends with, and (2) girls you might steer clear of. What's the difference? Which pile shows truly beautiful girls (from what you can tell)?

Make a list of the people you love. Next to each one, write in a few words why you love that person so much. Then picture each one in your mind or look at the person for real if you can. Do you see any of those people as ugly? If you want to watch someone become even more beautiful, tell the person why you love him or her. You'll be more beautiful too.

Wouldn't it be cool if you could just say, "From now on, I am going to be confident, joyful, fun-loving, energized, kind, encouraging, and loving"? It would be like an instant beauty treatment.

Developing those qualities takes time—and it takes God. We can't do it by reading books or following rules or copying women we admire—although those things help. We can only do it by turning our whole selves to God, every day, so he can remind us, heal us, forgive us, and lead us. Now that *is* a great beauty treatment, and there's enough to last a whole lifetime.

> "'Love the Lord your God with all your heart and with all your soul and with all you mind.' This is the first and greatest commandment. And the second is like it: 'Love your neighbor as yourself.'"
> — MATTHEW 22:37–39

> "Whatever is true, whatever is noble, whatever is right, whatever is pure, whatever if lovely, whatever is admirable — if anything is excellent or praiseworthy—think about such things.... put it into practice. And the God of peace will be with you."
> — PHILIPPIANS 4:8–9

> "Live in harmony with one another; be sympathetic, love as brothers, be compassionate and humble. Do not repay evil with evil or insult with insult, but with blessing."
> — 1 PETER 3:8–9

These are the inner beauty basics God gives us. Do these things every day, just the way you do the things on your beauty chart. This is your beauty manual.

You're Good to Go

Learn these verses if you want to, but definitely live by them. If you do, you will be one gorgeous little woman. We usually think of being sympathetic and compassionate and humble as things we do for other people. But it's just as important to apply them to ourselves. Jesus said, "Love your neighbor *as yourself.*" If we don't know how to treat ourselves lovingly, how will we be able to care about other people that way?

So let's start the inner-beauty treatment with you. Next to each beautiful quality God wants you to have, write down one thing you could do for yourself to show yourself that lovely trait. The prompts are there to help you, but you can also come up with your own if you like.

Be sympathetic with yourself.
(For example: Let yourself cry about _____.
Rock yourself to sleep.)

Be compassionate to yourself.
(For example: Stop beating yourself up about _____.
Hug yourself.)

Be humble about yourself.
(For example: Give God the credit for _____.
Write God a thank you note.)

Repay yourself for a mistake with blessing.
(For example: Forgive yourself for _____.
Take a cleansing bath.)

Be honest with yourself.
(For example: Admit that you _____.
Apologize to yourself.)

Stand up for yourself.
(For example: Go to _____ (person who has
hurt you) and explain (lovingly) how he/she has hurt you.
Share a cookie.)

That's What I'm Talkin' About

Go back to the beginning of this chapter and read about Betsy again.

Decide which "favorite" Betsy was chosen as. Think about how she'll react and how she'll feel. Imagine what she'll see next time she looks in the mirror.

Now, the next page, write the story ending, just the way you see it.

Betsy has come a long way, hasn't she? She isn't the only one.
Right now, you are as beautiful as . . .

You!

Betsy's Story Ending...

Read this excerpt from another book in the *Faithgirlz!* series!

faiThGirLz!
the beauty of believing

Everybody Tells Me to
BE MYSELF
but I Don't Know Who I Am

Nancy Rue

chapter one

Who, ME?

Molly Ann McPherson trailed her fingers over the contents of her brand-new suitcase:

A stack of neatly folded — and very cool — shorts.

Another pile of matching tops, the cutest ever.

A pink zipper bag with her own bottles of everything from shampoo to orange-flavored mouthwash.

And the perfect stationery — shaped like flip-flops — so she could write home every day.

Her summer dream was packed in that suitcase. But suddenly Molly shivered in a blast of cold fear.

"I don't think I want to go to camp, Mom," she said.

Molly's mother looked up at her over the swimsuit from which she was removing the tags. "What?" she said. "All I've heard from you for the last month is how much camp is going to rock."

"But I won't know anybody there," Molly said. "What if everybody thinks I'm a loser? What if I don't make any friends? What if I get left out of everything?"

Molly's mom shook her head. "Don't be silly, Molly," she said. "Just be yourself and you'll be fine."

When her mom left to find the sunscreen, Molly stared miserably at the suitcase full of coolness she'd been so excited about.

Be myself? she thought. *Who's Myself?*

Was she the Molly who was careful to do only what the really popular kids did?

Was she the Molly who always agreed with her friends about every little thing?

Was she the girl who secretly dreamed of being a famous lawyer, or the one who took piano lessons because her mom did when she was a kid, or the one who refused to cry in front of anybody, no matter how sad she was?

Molly slumped on her elbows onto her perfect stacks of camp clothes.

"How am I supposed to be myself," she wailed, "when I don't even know who I am?"

now what?

Poor Molly is having a major case of homesickness, and she hasn't even left her house yet. But there's something else going on too, something that can strike any of us, whether we're thousands of miles from our family or sitting in our own bedroom. It's an attack of the "Who Am I's?" and it can be pretty scary.

The good news is that this book is here to help you

✳ figure out who you really-deep-down-inside are, and

✳ be that person no matter who you're with.

It's like a vaccine against future attacks.

Right now we have our Molly, suffering the worst case of the "Who Am I's?" ever. If you were there in the room with Molly and her suitcase, what would you say to her? Would you give her advice? Or would you be absolutely clueless what to say because you feel that same way . . . a lot?

Whatever you want to tell Molly, write it in the space below. There are no right or wrong answers, so be honest. If, as you read the rest of this book, you discover something that makes you change your mind about how to encourage Molly, you'll have a chance to "talk" to her again in the very last chapter.

Dear Molly...

Here's the Deal

How many times have *you* heard grown-ups say, "Just be yourself"? Like that's supposed to prepare you for a situation where you don't know anybody, or you don't know what you're supposed to do, or you have that feeling that you are *not* going to fit in at *all*.

In the first place, what do they mean by "be yourself"? They're talking about a thing called *authenticity*. When you're *authentic*,

- ❀ you're completely honest;
- ❀ you don't pretend to be rich, or way smart about something, or totally into horses (or whatever everybody else is into) when you're not;
- ❀ you don't copy the way other kids dress or talk or laugh if it doesn't feel natural to you;
- ❀ you go after the things you're interested in even if nobody else does; and
- ❀ you make up your own mind when it comes to decisions, according to what you know is right and wrong.

That sounds pretty easy, doesn't it? You just do all that stuff and you're authentic.

Yeah, well, if it were that simple, there wouldn't be this book about it, right? Maybe right this very minute you're thinking of one of these problems:

- ❀ What if I'm so honest I hurt people's feelings?
- ❀ What if I just do my thing and everybody thinks I'm weird?
- ❀ What if I always do what's right, and nobody wants to be with me because I'm too "good"?
- ❀ What if I don't even know what I like, and what I'm interested in, and how I want to dress? What about *that*?

Take a big ol' sigh of relief, because this book is here to help you turn every one of those "What Ifs" into a "What Is." You'll learn how to

- ✿ be honest and encouraging at the same time;
- ✿ know what your own "unique thing" is and go for it without caring if other kids think you're weird;
- ✿ show people that "good" is cool; and
- ✿ discover more and more the special, one-of-a-kind person you are . . . and love you!

Wait . . . did we just say you're going to love yourself? Isn't that conceited?

Selfish?

Stuck up?

Let's see what God has to say about that.

GOT GOD?

Even if you've only just started thinking about God on your own, you probably know that God-loving people believe God the Creator thought each one of us up, made us, and put us here for a reason. The Bible, where God talks to us, says that over and over. One of the coolest verses is this one:

[God] has shaped each person in turn; now he watches everything we do.
—Psalm 33:15
(The Message)

faiThGirLz!
the beauty of believing

Nonfiction

Everybody Tells Me to Be Myself but I Don't Know Who I Am
ISBN 978-0-310-71295-4

This addition to the Faithgirlz! line helps girls face the challenges of being their true selves with fun activities, interactive text, and insightful tips.

Girl Politics
ISBN 978-0-310-71296-1

Parents and kids alike may think that getting teased or arguing with friends is just part of growing up, but where is the line between normal kid stuff and harmful behavior? This book is a guide for girls on how to deal with girl politics, God-style.

The Skin You're In: Discovering True Beauty
ISBN 978-0-310-71999-1

Beauty tips and the secret of true inner beauty are revealed in this interactive, inspirational, fun addition to the Faithgirlz! line.

Body Talk
ISBN 978-0-310-71275-6

In a world where bodies are commodities, girls are under more pressure at younger ages. This book is a fun and God-centered way to give girls the facts and self-confidence they need as they mature into young women.

Sophie Series
Written by Nancy Rue

Meet Sophie LaCroix, a creative soul who's destined to become a great film director someday. But many times her overactive imagination gets her in trouble!

Check out the other books in the series!

Devotions

No Boys Allowed: Devotions for Girls

This short, ninety-day devotional for girls ages 10 and up is written in an upbeat, lively, funny, and tween-friendly way, incorporating the graphic, fast-moving feel of a teen magazine.

Girlz Rock: Devotions for Girls

In this ninety-day devotional, devotions like "Who Am I?" help pave the spiritual walk of life, and the "Girl Talk" feature poses questions that really bring each message home. No matter how bad things get, you can always count on God.

Chick Chat: Devotions for Girls

This ninety-day devotional brings the Bible right into your world and offers lots to learn and think about.

Shine On, Girl!: Devotions for Girls

This ninety-day devotional will "totally" help teen girls connect with God, as well as learn his will for their lives.

Bibles

Every girl wants to know she's totally unique and special. This Bible says that with Faithgirlz! sparkle! Now girls can grow closer to God as they discover the journey of a lifetime, in their language, for their world.

The NIV Faithgirlz! Bible

The NIV Faithgirlz! Bible

The NIV Faithgirlz! Backpack Bible

Introduce your mom to Nancy Rue!

Today's mom is raising her 8-to-12-year-old daughter in a society that compels her little girl to grow up too fast. *Moms' Ultimate Guide to the Tween Girl World* gives mothe practical advice and spiritual inspiration to guide their mini women into adolescence as strong, confident, authentic, ar God-centered young women; even in a morally challenged society and without losing the childhoods before they're read